VIXEN'S TEMPTATION

Danielle knew Adam was affected by her nearness, also knew that she must make him admit to it while he was vulnerable. With her arms clinging tightly around his waist, she placed a soft kiss on his neck.

"Stop that," he growled, his smoothly muscled chest rising and falling with his quickened breathing.

"Why?" she asked, throwing him an innocent look before stringing kisses across his bare chest.

"Danny," he choked. "You don't know what you're doing."

"I know," she said, looking up at him with misty eyes. "I know, outlander. I'm a doin' it on purpose. Don't you like it?" She laughed huskily and flicked her tongue out as she pressed her body closer to his.

With a strangled cry, he lifted her in his arms and carried her to the bed. . . .

BETTY BROOKS
HEART OF THE MOUNTAINS

ZEBRA BOOKS
KENSINGTON PUBLISHING CORP.

This book is dedicated to Billie. Although she's a woman now, she's never aged a day in my memory. She's still the little dark-haired sister with laughing eyes and dimpled cheeks, and she's never lost the ability to make the world a little brighter for those around her.

ZEBRA BOOKS

are published by

Kensington Publishing Corp.
475 Park Avenue South
New York, NY 10016

First printing: September, 1991

Printed in the United States of America

Chapter One

"Whoa," Danny called to stop the mule. Then she bent over the plow and wiped the sweat from her brow. Fatigue dragged at her.

The air in the field was hot and heavy, perfumed with the scent of dogwood and flowering plum trees. But the breeze that lifted her honey-colored hair and licked at her neck brought little relief. And the damned mule kept balking, intent on doing everything he could to hinder her progress.

At the rate she was going, she wouldn't be through plowing for weeks. To top it all off, all day she'd had this nagging sense of foreboding. No matter how hard she tried to shake it, it hung over her like a thunderstorm about to break.

But enough of that nonsense. She still had the damned field to plow.

"Giddy-up there, you ornery, lop-eared jackass,"

she hollered. "Quit foolin' around and pull this damn plow."

The mule slowly swiveled his head, stared blankly at Danny, twitched his fool ears, then shuffled a few more feet down the row.

Suddenly, metal clapped against rock.

Swearing, Danny hurried to drag the obstruction aside. Then, as she straightened up, all her forebodings swept back in a rush.

Danny was no longer alone.

For a moment, she wondered if the man who seemed to materialize from nowhere was a dream or a nightmare. She suspected the latter.

He was over six feet tall, a good foot taller than she was. Despite the noonday brightness of the field, an aura of darkness surrounded him, with his black hair, black breeches and black shirt. His face was lean, somber, and dangerous-looking, and the dark eyes that fastened on her added to the dark image.

Maybe the devil had sent him to punish Danny for her evil thoughts about the mule.

The scar that slashed the man's temple from his hairline to his ear might have been responsible for her wariness, but she felt an overwhelming certainty that he was either the devil's disciple . . . *or soon would be.*

Her hands tightened on the plow, and the feel of the wood handles against her flesh restored a sense of reality. The man before her was just that: a man. And he was trespassing on *her* property. "What do you want here?" she asked bluntly.

"This Tucker's Ridge?"

She nodded, relieved to find he was just a stranger asking directions.

"Storekeeper down in Possum Hollow said I would find Danny Tucker up here. Could you tell me where he lives?"

"Could." Danny leaned against the plow. "Won't help you none."

His expression hardened. "Why?"

"Danny ain't there."

"Nevertheless, I'd appreciate it if you'd tell me. I found a cabin back in the woods. That the Tucker homestead?"

"Might be. Then again might not." She pulled a handkerchief from her back pocket and swiped it across her forehead. "What do you want with Danny?"

"I have a message for him."

A message? Fear prickled across Danny's skin. *Pa! He didn't come home last night. Had something happened to him?* "Whoever gave you the message shoulda told you Danny Tucker ain't no he."

The stranger strode closer, crossing the plowed furrow with an unbelievable grace, stopping about six feet away from the back edge of the plow. Her anxiety increased. The man seemed aggressive, and he appeared even bigger, when seen at such close range. "What do you mean by that?" he growled.

"I'm Danny Tucker."

Whatever she'd expected, it wasn't his anger when he discovered her identity. If possible, his countenance darkened. "You can't be him!"

"And here I thought you might be slow. You're

right. I'm not 'him.' I'm a her!" She eyed him warily. "Did you come about my Pa? Did something happen to him?"

"I don't know anything about your pa." His dark brows were pulled into a frown as he returned her gaze coldly. "That's a damned peculiar name for a girl."

"Name's Danielle." She straightened the plow, digging the metal into the earth. As far as she was concerned, the discussion ended when he admitted he hadn't come about her father. She had a field to work, had no time to waste on outlanders.

"You got a brother?"

"Nope." She whipped the reins, snapping them loudly behind the mule. "Giddy-up, mule!"

The man was next to her before she could move, snatching the reins from her. "There must be another Danny Tucker."

She glared at him. "Don't rightly know all the folks in the world, not even in these here mountains. But if you're lookin' to find another one in Calhoun county, you can forget it. I'm the only one here."

Even as she made the statement, she inwardly cursed herself. Her loose tongue was going to get her in trouble one of these days. Here she was, alone on Tucker's ridge, faced with the devil's disciple and she was makin' damn sure he knew she was the one he was looking for.

She plucked the reins from his hand and snapped them again. "Get along there, Caesar. We ain't got all day."

"Wait." The smile that cracked across his face was like a break across a frozen pond—and just as

8

dangerous. "I've come a long way to find you, Miss Tucker. The least you could do is hear me out."

She faced him with squared shoulders. "Mister, this day ain't gonna last forever. I gotta get the plowing done and I ain't got nothing to do it with but an ornery mule that's about seen his last days. Now if you got something to say, say it and let me get on with my work."

He seemed momentarily taken aback by her outburst but he was quick to recover. "This won't take long," he said. "My name is Adam Hollister." She sidestepped impatiently. "Last week I met an old mountain man called Buck. He sent me to find you. He's laid up and couldn't come himself."

"That it?"

He frowned. "I'm supposed to take you to him."

She nodded, then yelled, "Giddy-up, mule."

He tightened his hand on the plow, stopped her a third time. "Miss Tucker, the old man is bad off. He said it was important that he see you."

The man must think her a fool if he believed she would just go off like that. She didn't know any old mountain man named Buck. "Are you expectin' a 'thankee kindly' for deliverin' the message?" she asked sarcastically. "I got too much on my plate already to go afeelin' sorry for somebody I ain't never met. There's plenty of folks right here in Calhoun County that needs my help, and they'll get it before this friend of yours. So take your hand offa my plow and get out of my way so's I can finish my work before dark."

His lips had tightened into a thin line while she spoke but he remained silent throughout her tirade.

9

"I promised I'd bring you," he said, his voice as hard as tempered steel, "and bring you, I will." A barely restrained fury seemed to burn through his powerful body.

"Well, that's just too damn bad," Danny retorted, letting her anger win out over the chill his words sent through her. "A body shouldn't go makin' promises they can't keep."

"This one I'll keep." He grabbed her wrist and yanked her toward him.

"Leave me be!" She kicked out at him, but he didn't even flinch when she connected. He simply enfolded her in arms that seemed forged of iron. "You ain't got no call to take me nowhere," she screeched as he dragged her along behind him.

Panic washed over Danny as she tried to free herself. The stranger was obviously bent on taking her with him and she knew they were totally alone here on the ridge. Danny had only herself to rely on.

Only she could stop this man.

She dug her heels into the ground, but the earth was too soft and gave her no purchase. Ignoring her efforts, the stranger dragged her on, across the freshly plowed furrows and out of the field.

Desperately, she scrambled for the pistol in his right holster. He swore, knocked her hand away and yanked her hard against him, binding her arms to her sides with his hands.

"If you don't want to be tied up like a stuck hog, then you'd better behave yourself," he snapped.

She kicked his shin as hard as she could.

This time he seemed to feel it. Swearing profusely, he picked her up and slung her across his shoulder.

"Put me down! You—you—polecat!" She wriggled her legs and buttocks against his restrictive grasp and beat her fists against his back.

"Settle down!" He whacked her . . . smack dab on the softness of her rear end.

"Aa-ah! I'll kill you for this! Just you wait and see if I don't!" She bucked and kicked, her long honey-colored hair flying about her face as she struggled wildly, pounding her fists against the small of his back.

For all the good it did her.

"What about my mule?" she asked, when he refused to even acknowledge her struggle. "I can't leave Caesar strapped to that plow."

Hollister stopped; she supposed to think since she couldn't see his face. Then he retraced his steps to the plow and bent, burden and all, to unhook Caesar's traces. But the hook on one chain stuck, just as Danny had known it would. She had been meaning to fix the damn thing, but never had the time to spare. While Hollister struggled to free the hook, she began to wiggle, squirming until her feet touched the ground.

Hollister cursed and tightened his grip. "Make up your mind, lady," he gritted between his teeth. "Either you stay still or your damn mule rots under these traces."

Her freedom or Caesar's? There was no choice involved; she didn't even *like* the blasted mule. Besides, if she was free, so was he. She redoubled her efforts.

The hook pulled free, and Hollister turned his full attention to Danny. Standing, he shook her once, threw her over his shoulder, then slapped Caesar on the rump.

The mule brayed, rolled his eyes at Danny, then cantered off, displaying more spirit now than he had all day long.

Danny pushed her hair out of her eyes and gazed upside down at the ground. Her stomach jolted against his shoulder with each long stride that carried them forward.

Swallowing back a rising sob, she raised her fists again, then stopped, her eyes caught on the pistols resting in their holsters. Could she possibly reach one of them? She'd have to try because anything was better than being carted like a sackful of grain on the shoulder of this brute of a man.

She twisted and squirmed, trying to work herself lower, stretching her hands to their fullest extent. Her middle finger brushed the Colt in his right holster. She twisted again, lower, lower. . . .

He delivered a hard blow. Smack! Again on her rear. Who in blazes did he think he was! "Stop it, damn you!" she shrieked. "Watch where you're hittin' me!" She twisted, grabbed a handful of hair and yanked.

"Turn it loose!" he commanded, reaching back with his free hand to pry her fingers loose.

When pigs fly! Danny told herself, tightening her grip. The more he pried at her fingers, the harder she pulled.

Swearing profusely, he smacked her harder, hard enough to really hurt. Tears of pain filled her eyes and she blinked hard to dry them. Maybe she ought to rethink her options since she had little chance of

12

winning any battles of strength with him.

But she wouldn't let him see her cry.

She drooped back over his shoulder, assuring herself that it was merely a battle lost, not the war.

When he reached the horse he'd left near the edge of the woods, he plunked her in his saddle. Before she could recover her breath, he swung onto the horse behind her and wrapped an arm around her waist.

A curious feeling swept through her; an exhilarating mixture of fear and excitement. His touch seemed to burn through her clothing, searing the flesh beneath. "You can't get away with this!" she said in a strangely breathy voice.

Ignoring her words, he urged his mount into the woods. "We'll stop by your cabin and get a change of clothes for you," he said, his voice quietly controlled. "And you can leave a note so your father won't worry. I'm not sure just how long we'll be gone."

Danny quickly considered her options, devising and discarding several plans for escaping.

Although the stranger was undoubtedly crazy, he was right about there being no one to stop him. No one but herself, and so far she'd had no luck at all. Nor would Pa be much help, but at least the man who called himself Adam Hollister was allowing her to leave a note for her father.

Not that Pa'd be able to read it, she silently told herself, *but at least when he sobers up enough to worry about me, he can find someone to read it to him.*

Adam Hollister pulled his horse up before the cabin. It was a ramshackle affair, built by her mother's father from logs. Although Danny had hoped her father would be home, the cabin was empty. *He's more'n likely still over at Abner Johnson's shack, guzzling down a jug of corn liquor.*

Against the doctor's advice, her father had made drinking corn liquor a daily habit in the last two years. Danny placed the beginning of her father's habit along about the time his brother had fled the Ozarks with his family. Danny believed guilt drove her pa Silas Tucker; guilt because he'd not spoken out against the hill folk. Instead, Silas had remained silent, as fearful as those who branded her cousin Angellee a witch.

Remembering the loaded rifle hanging on the wall, Danny slid from the horse and hurried into the cabin, but Hollister stayed right on her heels. Lowering her lashes, she peeped through the fringe at him, saw him sweeping the cabin with his searching gaze and then paused on the rifle before moving on.

"We have no time to waste," he said, taking the rifle from the wall and breaking it open. "Bring a change of clothes. We'll get whatever else is needed in town." Even as he spoke he unloaded the rifle. "Just don't forget to leave a note for your father." He looked sharply at her. "You can write, can't you?"

"Of course I can write!" she snapped. Grimly, she crammed a change of clothes into a pillowcase, then she took pencil and paper and began to compose a note.

Pa, she wrote. *A stranger came and made me leave with him. His name is Adam Hollister.*

Dammit! Why hadn't she found out where he was

14

taking her? Was it too late? She turned to him. "Where are we going? Thought it'd make Pa feel better to know."

Frowning, he leaned over her shoulder and read her note. His lips thinned and he snatched up the paper and wadded it in his hands. "Just write that you're going away for a few days and tell him not to worry because you'll be safe."

She set her jaw stubbornly. "How can I be sure of that?"

"You can't. But if you write anything, it will be what I tell you."

"Then I won't write nothing," she said, doubling her hands into fists.

His face was calm and expressionless. "That's fine by me," he said. "If you're not worried about your father's health there's no reason why I should be either."

The color left her face and she went still. "What do you mean?"

"Simply that finding you gone without a word of explanation might put too big a strain on his heart."

Her hands clenched into fists. "Damn you!" she gritted. "Who told you about Pa's heart trouble?"

"The storekeeper in Possum Hollow just happened to mention it." He studied her intensely. "We have to be leaving, so make up your mind. Are you leaving a note for him or not?"

Danny's fingers trembled with anger as she wrote the note. Keeping in mind her father's heart condition, she simply said that she needed some time alone. She was going to visit Callie and would be

15

back in a few days.

"Who's Callie?" Adam Hollister asked when he'd read her note.

"I went to school with her," she said curtly.

"Will your father check out your story?"

"He could if he's a mind to. Callie lives in the next county."

But he won't, she silently told herself. Not after the harsh words they'd exchanged the other night. She'd told him then that she was leaving. He would probably think she'd carried out the threat. But she wouldn't tell Hollister that. She wouldn't tell him he was right about the strain on her father's heart. It wasn't necessary.

"Let's hope he doesn't have a mind to," Hollister said. "I wouldn't want to be responsible for doing the old man an injury."

She felt an hysterical giggle begin and stifled it. He'd said he wanted to do no harm. *What the hell did he think he was doing now?*

"How about supplies?" he asked, looking around the sparsely furnished cabin again. "Do you have any food to spare?"

"There ain't much here. Nothin' but a couple dozen jars of honey. I was going to take 'em to Possum Hollow and swap for flour and such."

Hollister seemed to have learned quite a bit about them from the storekeeper. Had he also been told that she had been working the farm alone for the past year? She hoped not, hoped no one in the county even realized, because she wanted neither pity . . . nor charity from anyone. Especially not from the likes of him.

16

After all, she need offer no explanations to the man who was abducting her. And she'd be damned if she'd apologize because she was low on groceries!

"Bring along a jar of that honey and we'll make do tonight. I've got hard tack in my pack. Tomorrow we'll pick up supplies." He pulled out two twenty dollar gold pieces from his pocket and tossed them on top of the note. "That should be enough to see your pa through until I'm done with you."

What the devil kind of man was he, anyway? He showed no qualms in kidnaping her, yet worried about her father's health. It didn't make a whole lot of sense.

But she had no time to worry about it, because Hollister snatched up the pillow case with her extra clothing, slung it across his shoulders, gripped her upper arm and pushed her out the cabin door.

Then, he tossed her into the saddle and mounted behind her. Danny had time for one last look at the cabin and for a moment, she wished she had her cousin's gift of sight. Never before had Danny's future appeared so uncertain, so bleak.

She was jerked forward as Hollister urged his mount into the woods, away from her home and everything she held dear to her heart.

Chapter Two

The horse rocked like a bouncing cradle beneath Adam and the girl. And with each step, Danny's soft rounded bottom moved against him. To make matters worse, the wench refused to keep still. *Had she no idea what she was doing to him?*

"Dammit!" he growled. "Keep still." Did the little chit know nothing about men, about their bodies and what stirred them? Obviously not, from the appearance of her. She looked like an innocent child, in spite of her strength.

The last thing he'd expected when he'd set out on this journey was to have to kidnap a girl who was little more than a child.

But knowing would have changed nothing. He owed the mountain man.

First, Buck had saved him from the noose. If not for the old man, Adam would be buzzard meat now. Then, when his temper had flared over his unjust near-hanging, he'd lashed out indiscriminately. As a result, Buck had become careless, putting himself in the path of an angry rattlesnake.

What else could Adam do then but grant Buck's request to fetch one Danny Tucker?

The girl twitched again in front of him. "For gawd's sake," he swore. "You act like crickets raised you. Can't you stay still?"

She glared at him across her left shoulder. "How long we gonna have to ride this way?"

"Until we get to Lizard Lick. I'll buy you a horse there."

"Why're we goin' there? Possum Hollow ain't near as far. We could be there in a coupla hours."

"We're going to Lizard Lick," he said sternly. He had no intention of telling her that he'd chosen Lizard Lick because she was less likely to run into anyone she knew there. He didn't want to fight his way out of town.

"You better be tellin' it true about gettin' me a horse, mister. I ain't ridin' far like this."

"You think it's easy for me to ride behind the saddle?" he snapped.

"Don't reckon it is at that." He heard the smile in her voice. "Not the way you're built."

He felt a flush creep up his neck. Had he been totally wrong about the girl's innocence? But one look at her guileless face before she turned around again, told him she was totally unaware of having said anything unusual.

Adam felt himself growing hard and curbed the urge to spur his mount forward, to cover the distance between them and the town as soon as possible. He cared too much for the welfare of his horse to risk injuring him on this rough, uneven ground.

19

But that was the source of his problem. Because the animal's gait was uneven, Adam had to keep his arm around the waist of the girl in front of him to keep her seated. And, with each step his horse took, the lower swell of her breasts came in contact with his hand. When he tried moving his hand downward, placing it across her stomach, she drew in a sharp breath and snatched it away, rounding on him with blazing eyes.

"Don't do that!" she snapped.

"Where the hell do you suggest I put it then?" he asked.

"Just don't put it there."

"There," he wanted to tell her, would be considered the lesser of two evils. Instead, he let his hand swing free. He rode in this uneasy state for five minutes or so, then his horse stepped into a depression and lurched foward. Instantly he reached for Danny, finding the roundness of her hips.

With a muttered oath, he slid his hand against her midriff and heaved a long-suffering sigh. Tomorrow he'd get another horse, come hell or high water. He had no intention of riding double with her again.

Night had cast purpling shadows across the forest when they stopped for the night. Although Danny felt uncomfortable about spending the night alone with her abductor, she was tired enough to welcome the chance to rest her weary body.

Adam built a fire, but they ate a cold meal out of necessity. Even so, Danny found it satisfied her hunger. Her fear of the stranger had begun to recede and her curiosity about him had come to the foreground.

She wanted some answers.

Adding another stick of wood to the blazing fire, Danny lifted her gaze to the man who sat across from her. She tried to examine his face, but all she saw was a dark profile and a jaw set in harsh, almost cruel lines. She wanted to know more about him, but lacked the courage to ask.

There was something almost overpowering about him; a quality of dominance—of superiority—that made her feel insignificant.

"Stop looking at me like that," he growled. "I'm not going to hurt you."

Danny felt heated blood rush to her face. She had been told before that her cheekbones reddened when she was embarrassed; she felt them burn now and scrubbed at them with the back of her hands.

Hollister moved into the firelight and she saw his lips twitch. He seemed to read her thoughts. "It's never been my desire to bed a child." His eyes swept down her body to her feet, then back up to the hair falling across her shoulders.

She stirred uncomfortably, acutely aware of her shabby clothing.

He shrugged with unconcealed impatience. "I hope you're not going to stay awake all night waiting for me to attack you. We've got a long distance to cover tomorrow and you'd best get some rest."

"Rest your mind easy, outlander." She forced a steadiness into her voice as she lied through her teeth. "You ain't gonna cause me to lose no sleep."

"Good," he grunted. "You can take one of those blankets over there, but leave me the other one."

Obviously he intended the words as dismissal.

Danny found herself a place beneath a flowering bush and spread out the blanket, pulling half of it up for protection from the cool night air.

When she heard him moving around, she tensed. Then silence fell and she knew he must have sought his blanket as well. Willing her tense body to relax, Danny closed her eyes and tried to sleep.

When she heard the cry, Danny thought it was a figment of her imagination.

Then she heard it again.

Her heart gave a frightening lurch and she jerked to a sitting position, searching the shadows for the source of the sound.

"What's wrong?" asked Adam.

Danny ignored the man across the campfire. Her body was rigid, her head cocked into a listening position, waiting for the cry to be repeated. The forest around her was dark, almost secretive, the pine trees were still, as though they watched her. The wind soughed through the trees, the leaves rustled on the branches.

"What did you hear?"

"A cry," she said. "Didn't you hear it?"

"Your imagination is working overtime." He lay back down and pulled the blanket over him. "Go to sleep. We'll be breaking camp at first light."

He might, she silently told herself. But long before then she intended to be gone; she would leave as soon as he fell asleep. Meanwhile, she'd grab a few winks while she waited, for she felt incredibly tired. Danny stretched out again and forced her tense body to relax.

This time it crept up on her. She heard it first as a sigh and thought it was Adam Hollister. But it didn't stop. The sigh became a sound—just a short, thin cry, heard for only an instant before it was gone, but it was enough to snap her eyes open and bring her to her knees. She peered into the dark; the shadows seemed to beckon her, inviting her to learn their secrets. Despite Adam's presence, she felt vulnerable and alone. Fear wrapped itself around her, washing over her like a dark wave from a distant shore. But she refused to allow herself to succumb to it.

"Something is out there!" she snapped. "And it's something I ain't never heard the likes of before."

He sat up abruptly and glared at her. "Dammit, girl! Are you determined to keep me awake all night?"

She stared hard at him. "Why're you pretendin' you can't hear it?"

"I'm not pretending," he said. "I heard nothing. At least not until you started making so much noise."

Danny shivered, wondering if her sanity had finally taken flight. Why would he lie to her? But then, why not? She didn't know a thing about him.

"I can't sleep," she said. "Not with a wild animal roamin' around in the woods. Could even be a mountain lion. There's plenty of 'em around these parts. If you want to be et by one, then go ahead. . . . Sleep! But me . . . I'm gonna stay awake an' keep watch. Hand me your rifle."

"Forget it," he said grimly. "Nobody handles my weapon but me. If you're afraid to sleep over there by yourself, then bring your bedroll over here and spread it next to mine."

"Go to hell!" Danny tossed him a heated glance. "How do I know you ain't put somebody up to making that noise just so's I would come over there."

He gave a harsh laugh that ended abruptly. "I don't need to pull cheap tricks like that to get a woman in my bed if I wanted her," he added pointedly. "Which I don't. The only thing that interests me right now is sleep."

"One of us needs to keep watch," she insisted stubbornly.

"Then watch," he growled. "But see if you can keep quiet while you're doing it. We've got a long ride ahead of us tomorrow and I'm looking to catch a little shut-eye tonight."

Gritting her teeth, Danny leaned back against the thick trunk of the pine, and pulled the blanket over her to ward off the chill. She stared into the darkness, knowing there was no way she could bring herself to sleep now. Not with some kind of creature lurking in the woods. Some *dangerous* creature . . . possibly even more dangerous than that damn man across from her. *But why did he insist he couldn't hear anything?*

Suddenly the sound came again and Danny's heart gave a fearful lurch. Because the cry hadn't come from the forest as she'd thought. Instead, it came from the air directly above . . . hanging over her still form, motionless, insubstantial . . . a thin, undulating . . . almost ghostly cry that slowly built in volume until it became a wail.

It was more than she could take.

Jerking to her feet, Danny snatched up her bedroll, sped around the campfire and hurried toward the man who was still rolled up in his blanket.

When Danny tossed her blanket down beside Hollister, he opened his right eye a bare slit and peered up at her.

"Don't you go gettin' no funny ideas," she snapped. "It just makes more sense for us to stick close together. Safer that way."

He remained silently watchful as she spread her blanket and stretched out on half of it. Then she pulled the other half of the cover over her head, hoping to hide from whatever . . . or whoever was producing the God-awful sound.

Danny held her breath for a long moment, waiting for the cry to be repeated, but all she heard was the sounds of the night. The frogs *hurruummphing* near the creek where they croaked and splashed and the crickets giving off their steady chirruping sound.

But there was something here! Danny knew it. She was positive of it. They were not alone in this clearing.

Danny's teeth began to chatter and she clamped her jaws tightly together, knowing it was fear rather than the cold that shuddered through her. *What's happening?* she silently questioned. *Can it be true what the hillfolks say about haunts?* Danny knew every kind of animal that dwelled in this forest, and yet, even though she had told the outlander she'd heard a mountain lion, she couldn't really identify the sound she'd heard.

Danny. The voice came softly in her mind, almost feathery.

Danny reacted instantly, yanking the covers off her head and staring into the purple shadows of the night. She knew that voice. Knew it well.

"Angel?" she whispered unsteadily. "Is that you, Angel?"

"What?" Hollister shoved his blanket aside and stared down at her.

Her gaze jerked to his. "Did you hear that?" Her voice was low, barely above a whisper.

Hollister gave a long suffering sigh. "What in hell is wrong with you?" he growled. "There's nobody here but us. Now go to sleep." Stretching out again, he mumbled something about delivering him from females with too much imagination before falling silent again.

Confused, Danny lay silently beside him. She had never been accused of having too much imagination before. Old Granny Bess used to say Danny had no imagination. It was her other granddaughter, Angellee, who had the gift . . . the reason her family had been driven from the Ozarks by the superstitious mountain folk.

Angellee. . . .

The voice Danny had heard . . . and she had heard it. . . . sounded like Angellee's. But how could that be possible? If Angellee were around, she would have no reason to keep hidden from Danny.

A sudden thought struck Danny. Could Angellee be dead? Danny remembered the stories Granny Tucker used to tell them. Stories about spirits, roaming the world, unable to rest until someone helped them find peace. Could that be what was happening now? Was Angellee dead, her soul tormented? Had she come back seeking help from her cousin?

The thought sent another shiver of fear through her. Even though Danny had loved her cousin, the thought of facing her in spirit form was terrifying.

Don't think about it, an inner voice warned. *Put it out of your mind.*

But try as she might, Danny couldn't stop thinking about Angelle's restless spirit wandering the earth, searching for release. Danny shivered and the fine hairs on her neck lifted. Goosebumps popped out on her arms and Danny wiggled a tad closer to Hollister.

Heaving a long-suffering sigh, he wrapped an arm around her and pulled her close.

"What—what're you doin'?" she asked, staring up at him with fear.

"Keep still and go to sleep," he commanded. "There's nothing here that's going to hurt you."

Danny's heartbeat thundered loudly in her ears and her breath hissed as she released it. Perhaps she shouldn't trust this stranger. But, somehow, she took comfort from his closeness. At least he was something real . . . something substantial. And, she silently told herself, he was strong.

Oughta be able to whip near anythin' that went up against him, she silently told herself.

Finding solace in that thought, Danny closed her eyes . . . and her mind . . . against all thoughts of ghostly spirits and allowed her thoughts to drift.

The minutes ticked slowly by and Danny's clenched hands slowly uncurled. The tension drained away, loosening Danny's tight muscles, and she felt sleep approaching. Just before she entered the netherworld of dreams, she had a premonition that she would never see her mountain home again.

Chapter Three

In the half-light before dawn, Danny drifted awake. Snuggling into the cozy warmth against her body, she arched against it sensuously, nestling closer against the delicious heat.

Still half-asleep, Danny poked at her pillow. Why was it so hard? Her jabs didn't even dent it, not at all like her feather pillow.

She opened one eye to a bare slit . . . and saw a broad expanse of chest.

Jerking her other eye open, Danny stared in horror at the arm resting across her breasts—the arm that held her firmly clamped to Adam Hollister's body!

Reality flooded over her and Danny's eyelids closed over her panic-stricken eyes.

God! What did I go and do? she wondered wildly. Despite her intention to stay awake, to escape from her captor, she had slept through the entire night. She'd lost what might be her only chance.

Her eyes narrowed. Then again, maybe she hadn't. Hollister hadn't moved a muscle yet. He must still be asleep. If she could just sneak out from under his arm, then maybe . . .

Suiting thought to action, she wrapped her fingers around his forearm and tried to lift it away. She felt it tighten around her instead.

"Good morning, Danny."

The deep voice, coming from directly above her head, yanked her gaze upward to dark eyes that glittered with something like amusement. His scar seemed more prominent, viewed from only inches away. And the black hair falling across his forehead made the whitened, puckered skin even more visible.

"Um . . . good morning," she said, watching him warily. *What did you say to a man you'd slept with?* she silently wondered. Never having been in this situation before, she didn't know.

Propping himself up on one elbow, he studied her face with an intensity that disconcerted her. A shiver of apprehension, and something she couldn't put a name to, crept over her.

"Did you sleep well?" he asked, his voice curiously gruff.

Danny licked lips that had suddenly gone dry and said hoarsely, "Y-yes."

He pushed a strand of hair out of her eyes and tucked it behind her ear.

Sucking in a sharp breath, Danny knocked his hand away. "Stop that!"

His gaze narrowed on her face. "Stop what?" he asked.

Giving a delicate shiver, she whispered, "Don't mess with my hair. I don't like folks touchin' me."

His eyes darkened and his expression became grim.

29

"I had no intention of forcing my attentions on you," he said harshly. "But if I had gotten the wrong idea, it's no wonder. After all, you chose to come to my bed."

Heat flushed Danny's cheeks as fury surged over her. She kicked his shin sharply and felt a great deal of satisfaction when he groaned.

"It ain't polite to remind me! You know why I came over here," she snapped. "They was somethin' in them woods last night. But you lied about hearin' it just so's I'd be afeared. Well, I got more sense than you give me credit for, outlander. Maybe I was afeared last night . . . just a little. But it was pitch dark then. Now it ain't. The sun's a shinin' down an' they ain't nobody gonna make me think my cousin's spirit is lookin' to haunt me."

"Is that what you thought?" His right boot slid over his foot. "I wondered what brought you over here in such a hurry." He picked up his left boot and looked up at her. "Roll up those blankets and get out the tin of hardtack and some of that honey."

"You ain't tellin' me what to do," she muttered, turning away from him.

"Don't be stubborn, Danny. We've got a long way to go yet. We'll get there faster if you cooperate with me."

Danny set her jaw stubbornly. Why should she make it easier on him? She was being dragged along against her will and she'd fight him every step of the way.

Go ahead! an inner voice chided. *Be your own stubborn self. Fight him hard. If you try hard enough, he might even oblige by tying you up and make it even harder for you to escape.*

She might be better off if Hollister thought she was resigned to going with him. But she shouldn't give in too easily. He might become suspicious.

"How far we gotta go?" she asked.

"Texas."

"Texas! That's a far distance from here," she said. "Gonna take us a spell to get there, ain't it?"

He reached for his gunbelt and pulled it around his lean hips. "Several days," he said, fastening the belt buckle. "Maybe longer. Depends on how many problems we encounter. Are you going to get the food out?"

"I'm gonna do it." She lifted her chin and did her best to stare down her nose at him; an impossible task since he topped her by a good twelve inches. "But just 'cause I want to. Not 'cause you told me to."

"That fact is duly noted," he said, his cheek dimpling near his mouth.

Danny was so startled, that she couldn't look away from the dimple. Hollister really wasn't bad looking, she decided. When he smiled like that, a body didn't half-notice the scar. She lifted her gaze to the puckered edges. *How did he get it?* she wondered.

"Compliments of a woman," he said grimly as though guessing her thoughts.

Flustered at being caught staring, Danny covered her confusion by taking refuge in sarcasm. "You was likely tryin' to make her do somethin' she wasn't ahankerin' to do," she said acidly.

Even as she uttered the words, a feeling of shame swept over her. If the truth be known, Adam Hollister had done her no real injury. Although she

31

had been forced to go with him, he had offered her no harm. Instead, when she had been scared out of her wits, he'd offered her comfort. A man like that couldn't be as bad as he looked.

Silently, feeling his eyes on her, Danny crossed to the pack and extracted the ingredients for their breakfast. She took the coffee, coffeepot, honey, and hardtack out of the pack and knelt to build a fire, trying to keep her thoughts away from the man in whose arms she had wakened this morning.

Adam was still chafing beneath Danny's words as he drank his second cup of coffee and ate the last of his honey-covered hardtack. She was right. He *had* deserved the wound. But not for the reason she'd implied.

He fingered the scar, as memories of the man who'd put it there filled his thoughts. Big, red-headed, freckle-faced Nicholas. Nicky had been little more than a boy when Adam had killed him.

Carlotta had a lot to answer for.

His eyes dwelt on the girl who sat across from him. It made no difference to Adam what she thought about him. They would only be together for a short time, just until they reached the Circle J Ranch in Texas. Danny's gaze flicked toward him, then quickly away again, but not before he'd seen the unrest glittering in her eyes.

Adam knew the scar he bore was responsible for the fear he raised in women and children. But sometimes, in cases such as this, it worked for the best. If Danny feared him, then perhaps he would have less trouble from her.

He tried to put all thoughts of how she'd felt in

his arms out of his mind. She was obviously an innocent, and he made a habit of leaving women like her strictly alone.

She sat across from him now, her expression pensive. She had remained silent throughout their meal, making him wonder what she was thinking about.

Lifting her cup to her mouth, Danny swallowed the last of her coffee, tossed the dregs on the ground and lifted her eyes to meet his.

"Was you telling it true?" she asked suddenly. "'Bout some old mountain man bein' the reason you stole me away from Tucker's Ridge?"

Adam frowned at her choice of words. "I didn't exactly steal you away, Danny."

"What kinda name would you put on it then?" she muttered crossly. "I was plowin' in the field when you slung me 'cross your shoulder and carried me outta there."

Adam ground his teeth with frustration. Dammit! Although she'd complained, he had thought she'd resigned herself to going with him. How in hell could he go into town—any town—to buy a horse for her when she believed she'd been abducted? The last thing he needed right now was trouble with the law.

"I know you didn't agree to come," he said, trying to make his voice agreeable. "But surely you've had time to consider how important it is."

"Outlander, you ain't given me no reason to change my mind."

"Suppose we strike a bargain," he said. "Would you consider hiring out to me?" When a flush crept up her cheeks and her eyes grew stormy, he hastened to add, "You've got it all wrong. You don't have to do anything for me. Just come along with me to see Buck and you'll earn a hundred dollars."

Her eyes narrowed suspiciously. "You ain't said how long you'd want me for. Could be I might never get back to Tucker's Ridge."

"You'll get back," he reassured her. "Within a week you'll be back home. You have my word on it."

She reached for the coffee pot and poured herself another cup. He felt she was considering his proposition until she looked up at him and met his gaze. There was not an ounce of trust reflected there.

"Once a tinker man, a stranger like you, come to our cabin."

Her voice seemed to lift at the end of sentences, as if she were always asking questions.

"Well, that tinker man, he told me 'bout a miracle cure that was goin' to keep Pa from guzzling moonshine. Said all Pa had to do was drink five bottles of that miracle cure. Said he'd be more'n happy to trade the cure for some of my honey. You know what, outlander? I didn't have no trouble gettin' my pa to drink down that miracle cure. He guzzled down all five bottles and tore up the cabin a lookin' for more. Now the way I see it, a body's gotta be addlepated to take the word of a stranger. And nobody ever accused me of bein' addlepated."

Adam felt amused and frazzled at the same time. "How could I convince you my word is good?"

"It'd take time that you ain't got," she said.

"Then we have a problem," he said quietly. "Because I'm taking you with me."

She nodded her head. "Know that. You said you'd

34

give me a hundred dollars. You could give it now."

His eyes narrowed. "Trust works two ways," he said. "How do I know you won't take my money and run off anyway?"

"You don't."

"How about me giving you half of it? With the other half to be paid when we reach our destination."

"First I gotta know where we're goin'."

"We're headed for a ranch a few miles west of Mineral Wells, Texas. I left Buck, the old-timer I told you about, there to recuperate."

She studied him thoughtfully for a long moment. "I guess maybe you can give me the fifty dollars. I reckon I can wait 'til we get there for the rest."

He noticed she hadn't said she trusted him, but at least she'd agreed to accompany him. Digging in his pocket, he extracted a roll of greenbacks. After counting out the correct amount, he handed it across to her.

Danny studied the money for a moment, then a wide smile broke out on her face. "Seems like we got us a deal, outlander."

Chapter Four

The western sun went down in a blaze of glory as the horse carrying its double load clip-clopped down the main street of Lizard Lick.

The town, only fifty-some odd miles northeast of Tucker's Ridge, lay crouched in the foothills of the Ozarks. It waited like some huge, monstrous reptile, ready to surprise the unwary traveler.

It was a small town, boasting one general store, one mercantile, one grocery, one hotel and the usual livery and saloon. It was a town that had nothing to make it stand out above others except the name above each establishment: Keller. Adam knew it wasn't the name of the town, so it must be the name of the man who *owned* the town.

He urged his mount toward the hotel—the sign above it proclaimed it The Keller Star—located at the other end of the town's main street. He spared a brief glance for the saloon—Keller's Red Garter Saloon—as they rode past, promising himself he'd have a drink there later, then stopped in front of The Keller Star.

Removing his saddle bag, Adam hooked it over his left arm, then led the way into the spacious lobby. The hotel clerk was a small, dapper man, and he was deep in conversation with another man who had the look of a cowboy.

"Be back in a minute, Earl," the clerk said to his companion. Forming his lips into a polite smile, he moved down the counter toward Adam and Danny. "Evenin', folks. Need a room?"

"Two," Adam replied.

The clerk flicked a quick look at Danny, then returned his attention to Adam. "It's a pure waste of money," he said, smoothing down his black, pomaded hair with his palm.

Adam arched a dark brow. "First time I ever had anyone try to talk me out of spending money."

The clerk gave a short laugh. "I'm not exactly doing that," he said. "Just makin' sure you have a good time in our town. We want folks to come back and visit again." Leaning his elbows on the desk, he continued, "Now, the beds in our hotel are extra roomy . . . big enough for you and the kid both. You could save a bit here and spend what you saved over at the saloon. Always a game of poker goin' on there." He gave a sly wink. "An' plenty of fancy girls if you've a mind for one."

"We want two rooms," Danny said shortly. "They ain't no way in hell I'm sharin' my bed with nobody."

At the sound of her voice, the clerk's eyes had

37

widened, and the cowboy's head had jerked up, his mouth dropping open in surprise.

"Well, I'll be damned!" the clerk exclaimed. "You're a female." His gaze dropped down the length of her, running over her shirt and breeches as though trying to find evidence of her gender.

"If I was you, Mister," Danny said, ignoring the clerk and eyeing the cowboy, "I'd close my mouth before a fly gets in." She laughed at his stunned expression. "Ain't you never seen a female before?"

"Don't think I have seen one like you," he said, his gaze running over her boyish form, seeming to stop overlong on her slender hips and the slight bulge of her small breasts.

She felt irritation flow over her, and her lips tightened. Even though he wasn't bad to look at, and some might even call him handsome, she didn't trust the glint in his eyes.

Lifting her chin slightly, she turned away, intent on ignoring his presence. The clerk had quit staring and was speaking to Adam.

"Just sign the register," he said, pushing a book toward Adam. "Number twenty three is vacant. And next door is . . ."

"You're wrong, Clyde," interrupted the cowboy. "I rented twenty three a little while ago. Traveling salesman was passin' through town and decided to stay overnight. He's over in the saloon right now, wettin' his whistle."

The desk clerk flicked the cowboy a surprised look that quickly gave way to something like comprehension. A grin lifted his lips as he turned back to Adam. "Sorry about the mistake, Mister. Didn't know about that travelin' salesman feller. I was . . . out for awhile. Earl musta rented the room while I was gone." He pointed his thumb at his companion. "This here's Earl Keller. His family owns the hotel and he helps out here sometimes." The clerk looked at the keys on the backboard and seemed to consider them for a long moment. "Uh . . . Earl . . . what rooms are still empty?"

"Twenty and twenty nine are open," Earl answered, reaching for the keys on the board and passing them along to the hotel clerk. Although Earl's eyes were on Adam, Danny had a peculiar notion that the cowboy's attention had never left her. "Couldn't help but notice the two of you was ridin' double when you rode into town," he said. "You wouldn't be aimin' to buy a horse would you?"

"That's the second thing on my list," Adam said. "First one is a visit to the saloon. A man can get mighty thirsty out on the trail."

Earl gave a wide smile that didn't quite reach his eyes. "The saloon is across the street. And the livery's at the other end of town."

"I saw that when I rode in," Adam said. "Noticed the Keller name above both. Looks like your family owns the whole town."

"We surely do. My grandpap was the first man here. He shoulda named the town Keller, but he was a superstitious old coot. He hadn't no more than decided on the spot for his town then he saw a lizard settin' on a rock. That lizard stuck out his tongue and licked that rock and Grandpap decided right then and there it was meant to be a sign. I suppose if the lizard hadn't of done nothin' but set there, then the town woulda been named Lizard Rock. Or Lizard Settin' on a Rock."

Danny laughed. "I always wondered how the town come by its name. Even up on Tucker's Ridge we heard about this place." *And the Kellers*, she silently added. And what she'd heard didn't instill confidence in her about their stay here.

Earl Keller turned the register around and looked at it. "Well, Mister Hollister," he said. "I hope you have a nice stay in our town. When you get to the saloon, tell Joe, the bartender, that I said the first drink is on me."

"Mighty nice of you," Adam said.

Danny listened to the quiet flow of conversation between the men while she studied her surroundings. She'd never been in such a fancy place before. Never in all her life had she seen so many pretty things. Pictures with ornate frames hung on the walls, and couches covered with gold-colored material that shone so brightly they would put the sun to shame were placed at intervals around the room. It was hard to believe people actually had the nerve to sit down on one of them, like the nattily dressed man who was bent over his newspaper.

Crossing the room, she ran her palm across a marble table top. Its smooth, cool surface even felt expensive, she decided. She'd seen one in a magazine the tinker man had shown her only a few months before.

When Danny felt her arm taken in a hard grip, she looked around to find Adam standing behind her. "Come on," he said. "Our rooms are on the second floor."

Frowning, she went along with him. She felt tired, almost as though she'd been plowing the fields behind that ornery mule all day. She guessed it was the strain of her watchfulness, for no matter how much Adam said he meant her no harm, she really didn't know whether to believe him or not.

The door marked twenty was at the head of the stairs. Adam hesitated before it, glanced at the two men watching from below and passed it by, continuing on down the hallway to the other end. "This is twenty nine," he said, grasping the knob and pushing the door open. "You'd better take it."

Danny looked curiously around the room. It was sparsely furnished, the four-poster bed dominated the room. Against the far wall was a wardrobe and beside it stood a washstand holding a chipped washbowl and matching pitcher. "Now ain't that nice?" she said. "They fixed it so's I can wash up in here."

He tossed the saddle bag across the bed. "Have you never been in a hotel before?"

"Weren't no reason to. Never been away from home all night before." She moved to the rocking chair that was placed near the window and gave it a little push, watching it rock back and forth, then she turned back to him. "My, my," she said. "Ain't this grand?"

Adam shrugged his shoulders. "It's no different than most hotel rooms," he said.

"You mean they're all this grand?"

He laughed. "I wouldn't exactly call this grand."

"Would'cha look at that!" she exclaimed, hurrying to one of the walls. "Somebody's gone an' put

41

paper on the walls an' colored purty little pink flowers all over it." She caressed the wall paper. "Must be kinda nice when winter's coverin' the land," she said wistfully. "When they ain't nothin' but snow all around it must feel real good to be settin' in that rockin' chair just looking at the wallpaper." She turned to him. "Don't you reckon?"

His lips twitched slightly and he raked a hand through his dark hair. "I hadn't thought about it much."

She moved to the bed, turned her back to it and gave a little jump, landing on the mattress with her buttocks. "Now ain't that nice," she said, patting the mattress with her hands. "Them feathers is real soft—like. Musta took a lotta ducks to fill that mattress." She jumped up and down several times, feeling the softness of the mattress. "That's the test of a real mattress," she said. "If you jump on it and it springs back? Well, that means you're gonna be able to sleep real good." She patted the mattress again. "Wish I had duck feathers in my mattress, instead of the feathers outta them old chickens."

A grin tugged at his lips, then disappeared as he pulled a derringer from his pocket and handed it to her. "Keep this with you while I go see about a horse for you. And Danny, stay in your room until I get back."

Surprised that he'd given her the weapon, Danny stuck it beneath a pillow, then promptly forgot about it as she continued to explore. Not more than five minutes had passed when there was a knock at her door. Thinking it was Adam returning, she opened it and found herself staring at Earl Keller.

The confident grin on his face lifted the hairs on the base of her neck. "What do you want?" she asked.

"I figured you'd be wanting a bath," he said.

Danny's gaze flicked to the wooden washtub he was carrying, then to the two girls coming down the hall with buckets of steaming water. Immediately, she felt mean. She must have misjudged Earl.

"That's right neighborly of you," she said. "We been on the trail for two days now an' a bath would feel mighty good." She stepped back to allow him to enter the room.

Adam strode into the saloon and bellied up to the bar. "Whiskey," he told the bartender.

The bartender shoved a glass in front of Adam and filled it to the brim. "You're a stranger here," he said.

Adam nodded. "Just rode in a few minutes ago," he said, lifting the glass to his lips and draining it in one long swallow. "Hit me again," he said.

The bartender obliged. "I seen you ridin' in with another man," he said. "You stayin' in town long?"

Adam drained the glass again then set it back on the counter. He looked up at the bartender. "You this curious about every stranger that rides in?"

"No offense," the bartender said, holding his palm forward in the universal sign of peace. "Just passin' the time by makin' small talk. Gents over there got a card game goin'." He nodded toward the table where four men were bent over their cards. "They won't mind another hand," he added. "But if that ain't to your likin', they's plenty of female company to be found in here." He winked at Adam. "If you know what I mean."

Adam followed the bartender's gaze to where several painted ladies in gaudy-colored dresses were laughing with a man who, judging by his drunken state, had obviously been in the saloon for awhile. A dark haired woman in a flame red dress that displayed an enormous amount of bosom looked up and saw Adam. Detaching herself from the group, she started toward him.

Adam quickly slapped a coin down on the counter and left the saloon. Although he was usually willing to partake in a little self-indulgence, he was in no mood for it tonight. He had an errand to run, he told himself, even while his mind conjured up a picture of a slim, boyish form clad in masculine clothing.

Feeling irritated for some reason, he made his way to the livery.

Danny sighed with sheer pleasure as she relaxed in the steaming tub. She'd forgotten how wonderful a hot bath could feel. More often than not she was too tired at the end of the day to heat water and just stripped off beside the creek and bathed there.

Reaching for the bar of scented soap the maid had brought, Danny soaped herself down, savoring the silky feeling of the lather, then reached for the washcloth. "This is hog heaven," she muttered aloud. "Some day I'm gonna do this again."

After she'd washed and rinsed her hair, she stood up in the tub and reached for the last pitcher of water, intending to have one last rinse. A click at the door caught her attention and she turned around.

Standing in the doorway was Earl Keller!

"Get out of here!" she gasped, bounding out of the tub and snatching the bedcover up to cover her nakedness.

Instead of obeying her, the man entered the room and shut the door behind him. "No call to get heated up," he said. "I was just bringing you a little refreshment."

"I didn't ask for none," Danny snapped.

"Don't have to ask in this hotel," Earl said, placing the bottle and two glasses on the washstand. "And there's no extra charge either. The bottle comes with the hotel's compliments."

Danny frowned. She didn't know about such places as this. Maybe it was usual to bring a bottle. Even so, he could have knocked. Her fingers trembled as she tried to secure the ends of the bedsheet and pretended to exhibit a composure that she didn't feel. "Thankee kindly for the bottle," she muttered.

When he didn't leave, she frowned at him. "It ain't fittin' for you to be here. I ain't dressed decent."

His lips lifted in a smile and he started toward her. "You look decent enough to me. And womanly. A sight different than when I first saw you."

She backed away from him. "You better leave now," she said coldly, realizing that she should have trusted her instincts. "If you don't, I'm gonna scream this place down."

He laughed. "Won't do you no good," he said. "The hotel's empty except for us. Fact is, not many people want to spend the night in Lizard Lick. Most

45

of the ones that do stay in town spend the night with the whores at the saloon."

Earl reached for her, but she backed away, her thoughts whirling frantically. If only she had a weapon. . . .

The gun! Adam had given her a gun.

Danny's gaze sought the bed. Despite its rumpled state, the pillow where she'd hidden the gun had remained in place. If she could reach it . . .

Changing her direction, Danny moved closer to the bed. "Adam's going to be back any minute now," she said. "An' he ain't nobody to be messed with."

"Hollister won't be back tonight," he said.

"How do you know that?"

"Joe, the bartender, knows what to do when he gets that message about a free drink. He'll get Hollister so drunk the girls will have a hard time getting him to a room upstairs."

Danny's stomach knotted at the thought of Adam in a room above the saloon with one of those painted ladies she'd heard about. She shuddered to imagine what went on in those saloons. It was something so gosh-darned bad that the womenfolk avoided talking about it. "Why'd you go an' do that to him?" she whispered.

"I guess its because I'm tired of those sows over at Joe's," he said, reaching out for her.

Danny eluded his grasp, sliding sideways and out of his grip. "Lemme alone," she snapped, her mind returning to the hidden gun.

She was brought up short when the back of her knees struck the frame of the four-poster bed. Keeping her eyes on Earl, she spread her hand, searching for the pillow where she'd hidden the gun.

"Dammit, come here!" He lunged toward her, gripping her arm with a hurtful grasp as he ripped the wrap from her body and flung it aside.

"Leave me go!" she yelled, clawing at him. Her curled fingers sliced into his face, giving her immense satisfaction as beads of blood seeped from the wound.

The explosion of the door slamming open jarred the walls.

"What'n hell is going on here?"

Chapter Five

Danny snapped her head around, and relief flowed through her as she recognized Adam.

"Get outta here!" Earl snapped, his grip tightening on Danny. "This ain't none of your business."

"The hell it's not!" Adam's lean jaw tightened ominously. With the swiftness of a cougar, he bounded into the room, and wrenched Danny away from the other man.

Earl reached for the knife sheathed in his belt, pulled it free and turned the blade toward Danny. "If you want her to keep on livin' then get outta here!" he growled, his eyes slitted and glared.

Before the threat was finished, Adam flung his forearm up and blocked the knife, flinging Danny aside at the same instant.

Caught off balance, she stumbled backwards until the back of her knees struck the edge of the bed. Losing her balance, she landed with a hard thump on the mattress.

Danny could hardly take in the action that followed. She watched breathlessly as Adam brought his strength to bear against the other man, holding Earl's knife hand immobile while he struck him a hard blow to the chin with his right fist.

Earl swayed beneath the impact but remained on his feet. He kicked out at Adam; his boot connected against Adam's leg hard enough to cause the leg to buckle beneath his weight. Adam, grimacing with pain, stumbled. His grip on Earl's knife hand loosened as he fell to his knees against the hardwood floor.

Quick to take advantage, Earl raised his knife and leapt for the fallen man.

Danny's breath hissed between her teeth. "Adam!" she cried. "Look out!"

But she needn't have bothered. Adam had apparently seen the danger. Even as she called the warning, he was rolling away, moving with sinuosity and lightning speed worthy of a striking snake.

The knife sliced down, a bare fraction away from Adam's chest.

His failure to kill Adam left Earl momentarily unbalanced. And before he could steady himself, Adam again curled his fingers around his opponent's wrist and squeezed.

Muttering curses, Earl dropped the knife with a clatter. Then, Adam sent the knife spinning across the floor with a well-aimed kick.

Bellowing with rage, Earl chased the knife. But Adam reached it first, bringing his knee up between Earl's unprotected crotch. Earl screamed, dropped

49

the knife and fell to his knees.

Adam grabbed for the fallen knife.

So did Earl.

"Adam! Look out!" Danny screamed.

Both men stared at her dumbfounded, as though they'd forgotten her presence during the heated battle. Earl recovered first and scuttled toward the knife. Adam met him halfway and kicked the man's crotch again, showing no mercy. Earl squealed out and covered his privates with his hands.

"Get out of here," Adam said harshly. "And if you know what's good for you, you'll stay out of sight until we leave town. If I ever catch you near Danny again, I'll make you wish you were dead."

Earl's gaze found Danny's and never, in all her years, had she seen such hatred directed toward her.

"Bitch!" he spat. "This is all your fault." His rage seemed to infuse strength into him, because suddenly the knife was in his hand and he made a leap toward her.

Adam yanked her behind him and met Earl's attack with one of his own. Adam's foot lifted, his boot connected with Earl's knee. Earl's leg buckled and he fell toward his knife.

Danny watched in horror as Earl thudded to the floor . . . watched as a bright red stain began to spread around the fallen man.

"Where's all the blood comin' from?" Danny didn't even try to squelch the accusing note in her voice. "Have you gone an' killed him?"

"He's not dead," Adam growled, turning Earl over to expose the long gash that started at the bridge of his nose and continued down across the fleshy part of his cheek to just below his ear. "He's just marked a little. Looks like he fell on the knife."

Even as Adam spoke, Earl's lashes fluttered and he groaned loudly. When Earl's eyes opened to a mere slit, Adam opened the door to the hallway, grabbed him by one arm and dragged him out into the corridor, leaving a trail of blood.

Danny stared at the blood on the floor, then the man who was barely conscious. "Hadn't we oughta get him a doctor?" she whispered.

"He's not so bad off that he can't get himself to a doctor," Adam growled. He stepped back into the room and slammed the door behind him, shutting the fallen man out and the two of them in . . . alone.

When Adam turned his gaze on her, a shiver ran over Danny. Her teeth began to chatter as she took in the danger he exuded. Suddenly, realizing how exposed she was, Danny wrapped the spread around her body to conceal her nakedness. Adam reached her in one long stride and stood over her, breathing heavily.

"How the hell did he get in here?" he growled.

She swallowed hard. "He—he just o-opened the door and walked in while I was takin' a bath," she stuttered.

A loud commotion in the hallway told her others had discovered the wounded man. A moment later a loud knock sounded at the door.

"Get over against that wall," Adam ordered sternly. "The open door will hide you from whoever's out there."

He waited until she obeyed before he pulled open the door.

Danny peered through the crack left by the open door. The desk clerk and a heavyset man in a gray suit were leaning over Earl's motionless body.

Gray suit looked up and frowned at Adam. "I'm Elias Jones, the hotel manager," he said shortly. "What in hell's going on here?"

"I'm afraid Earl and I had a little disagreement," Adam said calmly.

"I can see that," the man said, straightening himself upright. Like Adam, he was a big man, and he looked formidable. "Maybe you don't realize who that man is," he said shortly. "Earl Keller's pa owns this town."

"So I've been informed," Adam said harshly. The scar stood out on his face as he held the manager's gaze with icy contempt, ignoring the man on the floor and the desk clerk who knelt beside him. "But I don't give a damn who he is or what his name is. There's no excuse for mauling innocent girls."

The hotel manager threw an uneasy look at Earl. "Earl might get a bit rambunctious when he's had a little too much to drink," he said. "But he really doesn't mean any harm. I can see no reason whatsoever for him to have been treated so severely." He glanced at Earl again, then his eyes returned to Adam. "He's going to carry a scar for the rest of his life and he won't like it one little bit. Not Earl. Not when he's always fancied himself a lady's man."

The clerk spoke up. "When Earl comes to, he's going to have blood in his eye." Earl groaned loudly and his eyelids flickered. Apparently he was coming around. The desk clerk looked up at Adam. "You're a dead man, Hollister. Dead and don't even know it."

"It'll take more than the likes of Earl Keller to kill me," Adam said.

"There'll be more than the likes of him. He's got a passel of kin to back him up. Not to mention his old man's gunslingers," Clyde said.

"Shut your mouth and take care of Earl," Elias reprimanded. "Put him in one of the empty rooms and fetch the doctor for him. It looks like he's going to need some stitches in his face." He frowned at Adam. "You had better get out of town, mister. Earl puts a lot of stock in his appearance. He's not going to be happy about being scarred up like that."

"Just for the record," Adam said. "I didn't scar him. He did it himself by falling on his own knife."

"That won't make any difference to him," Elias said. "Earl doesn't always see things the way other folks do. If there hadn't been a fight between the two of you, then his face wouldn't be sliced all to pieces. I know the man, know the way he looks at things. And it's the same way with his daddy. The old man won't take kindly to—"

Adam shut the door in the man's face and turned to Danny. "Put some clothes on," he ordered. "We've got a man to see about a horse." He strode across the room to the window and looked down into the street where shadows were swiftly gathering.

Danny hurried to put on her clothing while his back was turned. Not only had he instilled fear in the hotel manager, but in her as well. And she didn't like

53

the feeling. A few minutes later they were hurrying down the stairs and out the front door.

Night had fallen and darkness clutched at them as they made their way toward the livery stables. The only light came from the lanterns, hung at intervals on nails beside the doorway of each business, spilling a soft yellow light into the shadows.

"Looks like rain," Danny said, casting a quick glance at the clouds that covered the moon.

Adam grunted, apparently feeling no need to comment on the obvious. Pushing open the big doors of the barn-like structure, he motioned her inside.

Instantly, the pungent smell of hay assailed Danny's nostrils. The lantern hanging from a nail on one of the rafters did little to dispel the shadowy interior, and Danny thought they were alone in the building until Adam spoke.

"Let me see that filly again."

"She's in the corral." The voice belonged to a white-haired old man who stepped from the shadows. "If'n you're aimin' to see her good, then you're gonna need the lantern."

"Okay if I take this one?" Adam asked.

"Reckon so," the old man replied. "So long's you put it back when you're done."

Adam lifted the lantern off the nail and followed the old-timer out the back door.

Danny, unwilling to remain alone, hurried after the two men.

The curious filly sniffed at the hand Adam held out to her, then flung her head back and shied away.

Her coat glistened red in the amber light shed by the lantern. Danny fell in love with the animal immediately. "You really thinkin' on buyin' her?" she asked, holding out a hand toward the horse. She was surprised when the filly came close and allowed herself to be stroked.

"If the hostler will sell her to us," he answered. He pointed at the sign over the livery that read Keller's Stable.

Apparently the stabler hadn't heard of the fight, for he grinned at Danny. "Seems like you an' that filly was made for each other. Guess I could let her go for a hundred dollars. If you was wantin' the bridle too, you can have the whole kit and caboodle for a hundred and fifty."

"Dollars?" Danny asked, her eyes widening with disappointment. She gave a long sigh and patted the horse's nose again. "Sorry, girl. I know you're worth it, but . . ."

"We'll take her," Adam said, pulling some greenbacks from his pocket and counting them out to the hostler. "We'll leave her here overnight, but we'll need her first thing in the morning."

The clip-clop of a shod horse swiveled the old man's head around. Adam followed the stabler's gaze to the passing horse and rider.

"Better think again, mister," the oldster said. "You might find it healthier to leave right now."

Something about the old man's tone caused Danny's heart to give a jerk of fear. She narrowed her eyes on the horse and rider, but saw nothing to cause her alarm. The man was the typical cowboy, nothing

55

out of the ordinary.

"You got some reason for saying that?" Adam asked quietly.

The old man nodded toward the rider. "That's Charlie Goodall. Nice enough feller most of the time. But he's right handy with a gun. That's why old man Keller hired him."

"He's one of Keller's bunch?" Adam asked.

"Yep. One of more'n fifteen hands Keller owns. An' don't never suspect he don't own 'em. Some men would do most anythin' for the kind of money Keller pays. Charlie don't have a whole lot to do. His biggest job is keepin' Earl out of trouble, seein' he don't get hurt none." He worked up a spit and let it fly at the ground, then fixed Adam with a hard stare. "Word gets around fast in this town, mister. I done heard what happened over at the hotel. Now, the way I figger it, Charlie's gonna go in the saloon lookin' for Earl. Won't take him long to find out what happened. When he does, the two of you better not be around these parts."

"We can't be blamed for what happened," Adam said. "Earl attacked Danny. He deserved what he got. There's no reason for us to run."

"Guess you don't hear so good," the old man said. "The reason to leave just rode down that street. You got maybe an hour at most to get a head start . . . could be a whole lot less than that. It's a damn cinch that it ain't safe in this town for you, nor the girl. Even if you could hide from Charlie tonight, come morning every one of old man Keller's hands will be lookin' for you."

56

Danny clutched at Adam's arm with shaky fingers. "We better listen to him," she muttered. "I heard about Keller's bunch afore. They ain't nobody to be messin' around with."

"My saddle bag is still at the hotel," Adam said.

"Better forget it," the old man said. "Unless you got somethin' in it that's worth dyin' for."

Adam nodded his head. "Thanks for the advice," he said. "But I'm wonderin' why you gave it, since you work for Keller yourself."

"Cause Earl's just like his old man about women. And I got a daughter that old Josh Keller makes use of whenever he's of a mind." His mouth twisted bitterly. "Josh Keller ruined my girl so's no decent man would have her. Now she works over in the saloon."

"Why do you stay here?"

"One day them Kellers is goin' to bite off more than they can chew. I want to see that day happen." His eyes rested on the filly. "If'n you need supplies, then I reckon you'd better see to 'em while I get the filly saddled. Word's gonna spread fast about that fight betwixt you and Earl. Charlie's gonna come lookin' with blood in his eyes. When he don't find you at the hotel, he's sure to come here."

"Will there be trouble for you?" Adam asked.

The old man grinned, showing tobacco-stained teeth. "Nothing I can't handle," he said. "That filly belongs to me. Bought her today from a travelin' salesman. Keller don't known nothin' about her. I was thinkin' on givin' her to my girl." His lips twisted into a semblance of a smile. "Maybe in a way, you can say that's what I'm doin'. In a way I'm gettin' a little revenge on that bunch for what they done to Thelma." He stared at Danny with cold, gray eyes. "Yeah. That's what I'm doin'. I'm gettin' revenge for my girl." Turning back to Adam he added, "Better hurry, mister. Take this girl and get her outta town afore Charlie comes looking for you. Take her somewhere far enough away so's they can't find you."

Danny wondered if they could ever go far enough to escape the Kellers' wrath. From what she'd heard, they were a tough bunch. And no matter how tough Adam was, even he could not stand up against fifteen men of the type Keller hired to do his bidding.

Chapter Six

Adam led the saddled horses outside the building and found the night had grown darker. Flicking a quick look at the sky, he realized a storm was brewing. Dark clouds had gathered overhead, completely obliterating the moon and the stars.

When Danny gripped the saddlehorn, preparing to mount, Adam bent to give her a boost. At that moment the sound of loud voices swiveled his head around.

Adam sucked in a sharp breath as he saw two men exit from the saloon.

One of the men was Charlie Goodall!

He was unmistakable in the glow of the yellow light spilling from the lantern that hung beside the saloon door.

Adam's reaction was instant. Wrapping his hard fingers around Danny's upper arm, he dragged her ruthlessly into the shadows of the livery stable.

"What're you doin'?" she snapped, fixing him with a baleful glare.

"Quiet!" he grated, his brows drawn into a heavy frown. "That's Keller's man!"

Immediately, Danny leaned around Adam's bulky form, obviously intent on seeing Charlie for herself. But Adam moved, deliberately blocking her body with his own.

"Lemme see!" she snapped, attempting to step around him. "He ain't had time to find out about Earl yet!"

But Adam knew she was wrong. If the old man could find out so fast, then so could Charlie. "He knew," he grated, jerking his thumb toward the stabler.

"Charlie knows all right," the old-timer said. "But I 'spect he won't come looking for the two of you until he talks to Earl."

"Which won't be long, from the looks of it. He's headed for the hotel now," Adam muttered.

"Then you ain't got no time to spare," the other man said. "Another five minutes and Charlie'll be rounding up every one of the Keller hands that're in town. Then I wouldn't give a snowball's chance in hell for the two of you gettin' outta this alive. Wait here until I bring the filly inside. Then ya'll can leave by the back way. It's pure luck they's a storm brewin'. Them clouds is hidin' the moon tonight, and they ain't nary a lantern out back to give you away. The dark out there will make the leavin' that much easier."

Adam watched the old man leave the building, wondering if he should leave or stay. There would have been no question in his mind if he had been alone. Not once, in all his years, had he ever run from

60

a fight. But there was Danny to consider, and if the old man was right, then Adam was greatly outnumbered. What would happen to Danny if he should be killed?

"Maybe we better listen to him," Danny said. "An' it ain't like we got any real reason to stay in town."

Indecision weighed heavily on Adam's shoulders. "We have plenty of reason," he said. "I'm tired and hungry. And I expected to get a good night's sleep here. I think we should lay it all in the sheriff's lap."

"Sheriff won't help you none," the old-timer said from beside Adam. His gnarled fingers clutched the filly's reins. "Keller's got the law in his hip pocket. You ain't got no time to lose," he growled. "I just seen Charlie comin' outta the hotel and he's headed for the saloon on the run. Prob'ly figgerin' on rounding up the two of you before old man Keller finds out what happened."

"I don't like running from trouble," Adam said, grudgingly realizing that he had no choice. He was responsible for Danny's welfare. And if he couldn't rely on the sheriff to keep her safe, then there was nothing left to do except run.

"They's times to fight and they's times to run," the white-haired gent beside him said. "If you're aimin' on takin' on the whole Keller bunch, then it'd be better for you to choose your own ground."

Adam could see the fear in Danny's eyes as she waited for his decision. "I ain't got no hankerin' to die for the likes of Earl Keller," she in an unsteady voice.

"Then we'd better mount up," he said, bending to give her a leg up.

61

They left town a few minutes later, hidden by the shadowy darkness.

Keeping in mind they'd probably be followed, they rode hard and fast. The slight breeze had turned into wind. It whipped Danny's hair, making it fly wildly around her face, but she scarcely noticed.

Soon, jagged streaks of lightning stretched toward the ground in the distance and the heavy rumble of thunder told Danny that rain wasn't far behind. She welcomed the sound, knowing that rain would make it impossible for their pursuers to track them.

But fate was against them. Even though the elements raged around them, the gusting wind threatened to rip them from their mounts, the rain held off until near midnight. By then, they had put over thirty miles between them and the town of Lizard Lick.

The numbing effects of the long day had taken its toll on Danny. Weariness weighted her shoulders. Total exhaustion made it hard to keep her body upright and the hard riding had caused the saddle to chafe her inner thighs.

Danny heaved a sigh of relief when Adam pulled up beside a narrow stream where the banks were lined with cottonwood and sycamore trees.

"It should be safe enough to rest here," he said. "Keller's men won't be able to track us in the dark. We'll make camp beneath that cliff overhang across the stream." He nodded at the ledge jutting out from a sheer rock cliff. "It'll shelter us from the storm that's brewing."

Danny felt the first drops of rain as the horses splashed through the stream and stopped beneath the cliff. Grasping the saddle horn with one hand, she slid to the ground. Her legs seemed to be made of rubber and threatened to buckle beneath her.

"I'll take care of the horses," Adam said. "You go ahead and fix our beds." He dismounted and tossed the bedrolls on the ground near her feet.

After unsaddling the horses, Adam led them away, keeping beneath the cliff overhang to avoid the falling rain.

Heaving a tired sigh, Danny turned her attention to the bedrolls. She felt confident that Adam would make certain the horses were secured where they could graze when the rain let up.

The sound of rain falling against sycamore leaves was like music to Danny's ears. She spread Adam's bedroll out, then moved a few feet away and tossed hers on the ground. It took only a minute to remove her moccasins and slide into the bedroll.

It was only moments before Danny was fast asleep.

But Danny's sleep afforded her little rest. Instead she tossed beneath the covers and dreamed . . . dark dreams that were full of thunder and blasted by jagged streaks of lightning that barely penetrated the shadows of a landscape without form. Even so, she knew the strange world was inhabited by the unseen . . . fearful creatures that waited only a breath away . . .

Or was it a dream?

How could it be a dream when her eyes were wide open?

And they were open.

They had to be.

How else could she see the dark shape that was hovering near her bedroll? A menacing something that had no form . . . hovering in the darkened shadows. As she watched, portions of the darkness seemed to move, to shift and form itself into something . . . not exactly a shape but a solid mass of coalescing doom. It was a pulsating darkness that embodied all evil. While she looked on, it moved forward, a great lump of throbbing blackness. Then it stopped, hovering around a vague, slender shadow that she hadn't seen before. Something about the shadow seemed familiar. It had a delicate fragility about it, an insubstantial something that made her ache.

God, let me be dreaming.

A shivery feeling tingled across her body and she waited, dreading what was to follow. The threatening mass settled over the misty shadow, then moved forward toward Danny . . . something icy touched her flesh . . . a hissing sigh of incredible sadness flooded over her. . . . Was it her own sigh? Or did the sigh come from the misty shadow? She had no way of knowing.

Danny.

Her name seemed to be an echo, reverberating through her head. In her dream, she raised her hands, and pushed out at the encroaching darkness. "No," she muttered. "Go away. Leave me be."

Danny.

She whimpered, frightened of the unknown, wanting the dream to end and for the cold feeling to go away. She tried desperately to wake, didn't want to hear that whispery, frightening voice again.

Suddenly, Danny heard a shriek . . . a loud wail that went on and on, rising and falling, and she sat bolt upright, staring into the surrounding darkness . . . the wet darkness where rain was still falling.

Danny's knuckles gripped the blanket as though she were a drowning swimmer and the blanket was the lifeline she'd been thrown. She was completely awake, uttering bird-thin cries, full of dread, shuddering against the rigid form of the man beside her.

Adam knelt beside her. His arms surrounded her. His warm tender touch dispelled the cold and lonely dream.

"What happened?" His voice seemed to come from a great distance and she turned desperately in his arms, burrowing her head against his shoulder.

Danny's heart thumped rhythmically, like the steady beat of hooves, thundering across the plains. "Help me," she whispered raggedly.

Instantly, she felt his arms tighten around her. "Did you have another nightmare?"

"Yes," she said, her voice sounding smothered. "It *was* a nightmare. It musta been. But I thought I was awake." She *had* felt that way, but knew it couldn't be so. But when had she wakened? At what moment did she leave that terrifying dream world and enter the real world? She couldn't even begin to guess.

Adam lifted a hand and smoothed the hair back from her face. "Stop trembling so," he muttered. "You're awake now. It was only a dream, and it's all over."

"It seemed so real," she said. "How can it seem so real?"

"That's the way of nightmares." Adam ran a soothing hand across her shoulder and down her back. "Haven't you ever had nightmares before?"

"No." She shivered. "Not ever."

"Then you've been lucky," he said. "There was a time when I had more than my share." He gave her shoulder a comforting squeeze. "We're both tired and we've got a long day tomorrow, Danny. Would you rest easier if you lay closer to me?"

Chiding herself for being a coward, she gave a silent nod and watched while he spread her bedroll beside his. Danny made no protest when he pulled her into his arms. As though sensing her tension, he began to speak soothingly, telling her about trail rides he'd been on. What he said was of no consequence, just the mere sound of his voice was enough to make her relax.

Danny's fear began to evaporate and a warm glow caused by Adam's continual stroking of her back flowed over her.

A strange excitement coursed through her baffling yet delighting her. Danny knew she should tell Adam she was all right now and he could go to sleep. However, she delayed, wanting to enjoy the feeling he was creating, the aching sweetness in her body . . . if only for just a few moments longer.

Chapter Seven

"Danny?" Adam's voice was husky. "Do you feel better now?"

She considered lying, wanting him to keep up his stroking movements, but her innate sense of honesty got the better of her. "Yes," she replied. "I ain't afeared no more." For some reason, her voice sounded sleepy. But she wasn't sleepy.

In fact, Danny had never felt more alive than she did at this very moment. "I ain't sleepy neither," she added. "You can keep on arubbin' my back if you've a mind to."

His laugh was soft, deep, and came just inches away from her right ear. "Would you like that?"

"Yes," she said. "I purely would. It's makin' me feel all tingly-like. An' I got goosebumps broke out all over me."

His lips brushed her ear in a soft caress, and she shivered with pleasure. A funny feeling, like a butterfly turning over, traveled through her stomach and she looked up at him. "Do that again," she said.

"What?"

"What you done to my ear."

"Like this?" He demonstrated by caressing her ear again.

Her bones turned to jelly. "Yes," she said shakily. "I never felt nothin' like that before." Danny brushed her lips across his left ear. "You feelin' it too?" she whispered softly.

"Feeling what?" His voice sounded breathless, as though he'd been running.

"That butterfly feelin'? Like a big yellow butterfly turned over in your stomach? Did you feel it?"

"Yes," he said, tightening his embrace. "I felt it too. But I wasn't sure of the color."

"Had to be yellow. On account of the sunshiny feelin' that followed the flutter. Will you do it to me again?" she whispered softly.

"Danny . . ." His voice seemed reluctant. "Danny, we shouldn't—" He broke off as she circled his ear with the tip of one finger. "Danny," he said again, pulling slightly away from her.

Then, with a loud groan, he captured her lips beneath his in a long, passionate kiss that sent her senses soaring and her pulses leaping. She wanted to return his kiss, but knew her inexperience would show, so she remained passive beneath him, feeling a pleasure so intense that she thought she might explode with it.

When Adam's lips left hers, Danny's followed his mouth like a babe followed its mother's nipple. Then he found the sensitive cord at the nape of her neck and buried his lips there.

Danny gasped as her lower belly tightened. What in the world was happening to her? Was this the man-woman thing she'd heard about? Why did everyone whisper about it? Why didn't they shout it from the hills so the whole world would know about the feeling of pure pleasure it brought?

The answer escaped her . . . and really she had no time to think on it further, because his lips had traveled down her neck to the swell of her breast. She felt she should stop him . . . but she couldn't.

God! She didn't have the strength it took, wanted more of the feeling, and squirmed her hips to get closer to him—closer to his pulsing body.

"Danny," he whispered, raising his head and looking down at her. "Stop moving around. I'm trying to control myself but you're not making it easy."

She looked up at him with wide eyes. "Are you goin' to stop kissin' me now?" she asked.

"I think it would be best," he said gently. "Otherwise, there's no telling what might happen."

"You mean the man-woman thing might happen?"

"God, Danny!" he groaned, releasing her and turning over onto his back. "I almost forgot how young you are."

"I'm a woman fully grown," she said.

"Perhaps," he said. "But you're as innocent as a babe."

"I learn fast," she stated firmly, rolling on her belly and leaning on her elbows to look at him. "An' I'm thinkin' as how maybe I shouldn't've been pushing Jimmy Carson down whenever he was after puttin'

69

his hands on me. I didn't know touchin' could be so pleasurable. Pa always said I was to let no man touch me that way."

"Your father is right too," Adam said firmly. "You shouldn't let anyone touch you that way. Not until you're married. Or at least," he amended, "until you've met the man you're going to marry and have an understanding with him."

"Does that mean you're gonna stop?" Danny asked, feeling decidedly unsettled at the thought. Although she knew Adam was right, she wanted his kisses; wanted to feel his touch again; wanted the fluttery butterfly feeling in her stomach again.

"Yes, Danny," he said. "Bad as I hate to, I *am* going to stop."

Her breath hissed between her teeth, making her aware that she'd been holding it. Although she was disappointed, she knew Adam was right. The feeling he'd aroused between them was so intimate that it had to be a husband and wife thing. She only suspected this; she had no proof. If only her mother had lived, or if her aunt had been around or her cousin. But after they left, she had no women relatives. Only her father. And a girl couldn't talk about things like this with her father.

"Go to sleep, Danny," Adam said. "We have to get up early in the morning."

"I know," she said. "But I feel wide awake. Can I come next to you again?"

"You are next to me," he said.

"Well . . . against you," she said. She pretended to shiver. "I guess I ain't got over . . . I mean, it's kinda cold out here under the stars."

"Pull your blanket up," he said. "It will keep you warm."

Dammit! she didn't want her blanket. She wanted his arms around her.

Sighing heavily, she lay down on her pallet but sleep was long in coming.

Someone called her name distantly, obviously from a long way off . . . insistent, piercing the sleeping folds of exhaustion she had drawn around herself. "Danny, wake up."

A hard shake accompanied the words and Danny groaned, trying to push the hands away. She was unwilling to relinquish sleep, but her consciousness was aroused. She opened one eye and saw Adam's face above her, its edges blurred by her sleepiness. "Go away," she muttered. "Leave me be. It ain't even daybreak yet."

"Get up, Danny," he commanded. "There's no time to waste."

The urgency in Adam Hollister's voice quickly dismissed the remaining fogginess surrounding her. She blinked her eyes several times until his face finally focused. Then, it was obvious, even in her sleep-dazed condition that something was amiss.

Propping herself on one elbow, she peered into the moon-washed shadows. Raindrops sparkled on the leaves, and the air smelled fresh and clean as it always did after the rain, but she found nothing amiss. Her gaze swept to Adam and she watched him buckle his gunbelt around his lean hips. "What's the matter?" she asked.

"Somebody ridin' fast. Coming from our back trail. Figured we'd better not count on the riders being friendly."

Cocking her head in a listening position, she said, "I don't hear 'em."

"You'll have to take my word for it. They're coming all right. And not more than a couple of miles away."

Sudden fear sliced through her, perhaps merely a vague impression left from the nightmare she'd been plagued with only hours before. Could the ominous darkness from her dream be revealing itself in this way? Coming after her in the shape of horses or gunmen? "You think we're in danger?" she asked, her voice wobbling slightly.

His gaze narrowed on her pale face. "I don't want to frighten you, but it could be Keller's gang of cutthroats. No sense in taking chances. Get those bedrolls rolled up while I fetch the horses."

Although Danny still heard nothing except for the crickets, frogs and an occasional nightbird, she flung back the blanket and leapt to her feet. Adam Hollister was obviously an experienced man . . . experienced enough to know when they were facing a dangerous situation. And he was right—she would have to take his word for it.

But if it was the Keller bunch, she was puzzled as to how they could have followed so quickly. The rain should have wiped out any tracks Danny's and Adam's mounts had made.

Adam returned with the horses and quickly saddled them. It was when he was tightening the cinch belt on her saddle that she heard the hoofbeats.

Adam had been right!

"Over here," he said, tugging the horses toward the rocks to their left. "There's a gash in the rock back this way. It looked wide enough to hide the horses."

It was, but just barely. When they had the horses inside, Adam pulled brush in front of the entrance to better hide their place of concealment.

Barely in time, for she heard the riders drawing closer. The horses did not even break their stride as they drew abreast of the crevice. But even so, Danny recognized the lead rider.

Charlie Goodall's face was grim and dangerous looking. Danny knew Adam had been right to trust his instinct. Close behind him rode Earl Keller, and the expression on his face said he was all set to cause somebody a heap of trouble. And it was a fact that the *somebodies* they were after were Adam and herself.

Danny swallowed back her fear. They were well-hidden, and had escaped Earl's immediate rage.

But suppose Earl found out who she was? And where she had come from. . . . *God! He could cause a heap of trouble if he tracked me back to Tucker's Ridge.*

Her thoughts whirled furiously as her mind tried to come to terms with the consequences of their short stay at Lizard Lick. The stay might have been short, but there'd been time enough to get on the bad side of the Keller bunch.

She squeezed her eyes shut tight. She didn't even want to think about the trouble they would cause.

But try as she would, she couldn't put it out of her mind.

Chapter Eight

The riders doubled back until they found the place where their quarry had spent the night.

"Looks like they got away," Charlie Goodall said.

Earl Keller's face was gray with fury. Pain throbbed through his temples, pulsing beneath the stitches holding the puffy edges of his flesh together. His fingers found the wound and his anger grew, becoming more intent until the sweat popped out on his forehead. And with the sweat his fury increased and it focused on one person. "Danny," he muttered, curling his hands into fists. "That's the bitch's name. I'll get the both of them. I want the man killed first. But leave the bitch alone. I've got something special planned for her. . . . She's the cause of it all, and she ain't gonna get off so easy."

When they reached Little Rock, Arkansas, Adam urged his mount toward the nearest hotel. After he rented their rooms, he turned to Danny. "Do you want to freshen up before we eat?"

"I reckon not," she said. "I'm near hungry enough to eat a bear."

His lips twitched. "I'd say that's hungry."

An hour later she pushed back her chair and stared down at her empty plate. "I can't believe I ate all that," she said.

"Neither can I," he laughed. "You put away as many beans and biscuits as two lumberjacks would have. Where in the world did you find room for all of it?"

His eyes lazily examined her body and Danny felt a flush creep up her neck and stain her cheeks. She wondered why her insides jangled like a church bell on Sunday morning every time the outlander looked at her.

"Must be comin' down with somethin'," she muttered.

"What did you say?"

"I said I must be comin' down with somethin'. My innards feel all quivery-like."

His expression became concerned. "You're getting sick to your stomach? When did it start?"

Just since you been lookin' at me. Aloud, she said, "Just since we finished eating."

He frowned across at her. "I hope the beans weren't tainted. You go on up to bed. Maybe you'll feel better after you get some rest." He laid a key on the table in front of her.

"What're you gonna do?"

"I'm going out for supplies. I'll be up later. Make certain you lock your door. We don't want a repeat of what happened in Lizard Lick."

75

After Adam paid for their meals, they went their separate ways.

Danny slept little that night. She was plagued by dark dreams as she had been every night since she'd been with Adam.

She woke alone in the hotel room, shaking with fright, staring wide-eyed into the shadowy corners of the dimly lit room. Making herself stay in bed, she was unwilling to wake Adam yet another time.

Sweat beaded her forehead as she forced herself to hold her silence and waited for the dreaded blackness to come. When it didn't, she felt a great relief slide over her. Was it over now? Could it be the dreams were sent only to warn her about something?

The thought had only materialized when Danny put a lid on it, as though it were an evil spirit to be corked in a jug of corn liquor. She knew she couldn't afford to allow such thoughts to reach full bloom, for surely madness lay that way.

Danny knew she was not like Granny Bess! Nor was she like her cousin, Angellee!

Unlike the two of them, Danny knew nothing of premonitions, forebodings and warning signs. In fact, she didn't really believe in them. She would not *allow* herself to believe in such doings.

No!

There had to be another explanation, she silently told herself. Had to be another reason she was being plagued by the bad dreams . . . dreams that began after she had met Adam.

Adam.

He had come because the old man had sent him. But why? What could the old mountain man possibly want from her? The time was long overdue for her to learn more about that old man.

Flinging back the covers, Danny slid from the bed and donned her britches and shirt. Then she padded barefoot across the hall to Adam's room.

Knock, knock, knock. Her knuckles rapped sharply on the door.

She listened to the silence for a long moment, then rapped again.

Knock, knock, knock.

"What is it?"

"Open the door," she called.

"Danny?" His voice, muffled through the heavy wood, was followed by the squeaking of bed springs. Then a thump sounded against the floor and footsteps followed.

Suddenly the door was flung open and Adam stood before her. "What is it?" he asked again, raking a hand through his tousled hair.

"Wanta talk to you," she said, putting a hand on his bare chest and pushing him back into his room.

"What about?" He peered behind her as though expecting to find the answer there.

Danny opened her mouth to answer, but no sound came out. Instead, she found herself staring dumbly up at him, totally aware of the curly matte of hair beneath her fingertips. The reason for her actions had completely slipped her mind.

"Danny?" He frowned down at her. "Is it the nightmare again?"

Nightmare? Danny's breathing seemed constricted and she swallowed hard. This was no nightmare. It was a dream. Adam wore only breeches and the top

77

button was opened, exposing the indentation of his navel, the way the crisp dark hair angled down to it . . . and below.

"Danny!" he said sharply, gripping her shoulders and giving her a hard shake. "Answer me! Did you have another nightmare?"

She jerked her eyes back to his face. "Yes," she muttered, trying to marshall her thoughts. *Yes, certainly,* she silently told herself. What must he think of her, standing there ogling him like that?

"Are you all right now?"

"I . . . uh . . ." Suddenly she remembered why she'd come. "The old man . . . that mountain man feller . . . how did he know about me?"

He studied her flushed cheeks. "Buck? He didn't say. Just said he had to find you." He studied her features with intent dark eyes. "If you're worrying about him, then don't. I'd swear on my life that Buck means you no harm."

"It don't make no sense," she said. "Some old man I never heard of. Can't figger out why he'd want me, unless my cousin sent him."

"Don't worry about it," he said, smoothing the hair back from her face. "We'll be there in a couple of days. Then you'll have your answer. Buck will explain everything."

Danny shifted impatiently. She didn't want to wait. She wanted answers now. A sudden thought struck her. "You said he was bad sick when you left him. He might even be dead by now."

"He could be," Adam admitted.

"If he is you won't need me no more," she said

78

quietly. "I figger you'll be takin' me home afore long."

"You'll be going back soon," he said gruffly. "But I won't be. I'll see you on a train with enough money to pay your expenses back home."

Her lips tightened. "You ain't gonna see I get back to Tucker's Ridge safe? What about that Keller bunch?"

"I'm sure you won't be bothered by them." His voice sounded odd to Danny's ears.

Suddenly he reached up and crushed her hand in his. "Don't do that," he said sharply.

"What?" she asked, unaware that she'd done anything.

"You shouldn't be touching me like that," he said. "Things like that . . . well . . . they tend to put ideas into a man's head."

Her mouth dropped open. She hadn't really been aware she'd been stroking the curly matte on his chest, not until he spoke. "Are you gettin' ideas?" she asked, feeling intrigued by the idea.

"Certainly not!" he snapped. "You're only half my age. Just a child."

"I ain't no child," she flared. "I been a woman growed for nigh on to two years now."

"Hardly," he gritted.

"I—"

"Danny," he snarled. "I refuse to stand here in the middle of the night discussing your age. It's late and I'm tired." He gave her a shove toward the door. "And what's more, the door is standing wide open. Anyone passing by could see us and—"

79

"We could always close the door," she suggested.

"Go," he said, sounding like a demented man, pushing her across the hall and into her own room.

Grasping the door knob, he stepped into the hall and slammed the door behind him, leaving her alone in the room.

She stared at the door for a long moment, then gave an exultant laugh. Half his age indeed! The fool man. He wasn't near as hard as he pretended. And he certainly wasn't repulsed by her. She'd felt the way his heart had raced under her hand, felt the sudden clamminess of his skin.

So . . . he thought all he had to do was snatch her up from Tucker's Ridge and cart her off to Texas, easy as pumpkin pie. Well, he certainly had a surprise waiting for him. She'd given him her word she'd go with him, and she would. But she hadn't promised him it would be *easy*. Nope, she hadn't said a word about that.

Adam lay on the bed and stared up at the ceiling. Sleep was proving to be elusive. He couldn't get Danny out of his mind, nor could he forget how it had felt to hold her against him.

His jaw tightened. He was committed to accompanying her to the Circle J where he'd left the mountain man. He didn't know why the old man wanted to see her. He only knew that it was important to Buck, so he had promised to bring her.

He owed the old man. And whatever else Adam had become, he'd not yet sunk so low that he would go back on his word.

Besides, idleness didn't appeal to him and he'd had nothing better to do. So it had been no hardship for him to fetch Danny to the old man.

There was a time when he'd had plenty to do. An only child, he'd been raised as the heir to the vast Hollister holdings in northern Montana. He had been denied nothing as a child or as a young man, had been given the best education money could buy, attended the best university. It was there he met Judd . . . and Nicholas . . . and Carlotta.

Adam could even now hear Carlotta's mocking laughter, and as if it were yesterday, he relived his own anguish over his friend's death.

But even as he hated Carlotta, the guilt they both shared would always bind him to her.

Though the law had refused to blame him, Adam had pronounced his own sentence for his crime. Renouncing his wealth, he'd left the university and begun wandering. He'd virtually cut himself off from his parents, believing himself unworthy of their unquestioning love. When they died within weeks of each other, he'd been locked up in Arizona, arrested after he'd forced the hand of a crooked gambler . . . with the aid of his six-gun.

He hadn't learned of his parents' deaths until six months later, another pound of guilt added to the load he already carried.

During this past year with Judd and Michelle, his friends had nagged him about his self-punishment. Time and time again, they had insisted he wasn't to blame.

He knew better.

He'd searched for years but so far had found no way

81

to expiate his guilt. If he could think of even one, no matter how difficult it might be, he'd have paid the price a hundred times over.

No, some people had no right to the beauty the world had to offer. Some people deserved living in hell, both in this life and in the next.

He scrunched his pillow beneath his head and rolled over.

Life held no more illusions for him. Love and marriage were for other—more worthy men. For him, happiness would always be a fairy tale, the product of writers' and poets' imaginations.

For that reason, though he was tempted by the girl across the hall, he had to leave her strictly alone. She was as innocent as a newborn fawn, tottering on trembling legs.

The last thing a girl like Danny needed was a man like him.

Chapter Nine

The western sky was ablaze with the glow of the setting sun when three days later they rode into the town of Mineral Wells, Texas.

"It's not far now," Adam said. "Judd McCord's place is west of town. Just beyond the Brazos River."

"That's where we're headed?"

"Yeah."

The town was a surprise to Danny. Bustling, busy ladies and gents in lightweight fabrics strolled down the street as though they had nothing better to do. Danny noticed that a good many of the ladies were carrying bottles.

When Adam pulled his mount up beside a water trough, Danny did the same. While the horses drank their fill, she turned to Adam with a puzzled frown. "They sure is a lot of fancy women totin' bottles around. Don't the ladies around here object to it?"

"Why should they?" he asked.

"Back home they wouldn't dare show their faces out of the saloons carrying them bottles. They'd be tarred and feathered afore the sun was set."

The frown on Adam's face was replaced by a grin. "Those aren't saloon women, Danny. They're tourists."

"Tourists? What's that?"

"Those are people who come here to tour the area. Most of them are on vacation."

Since Danny had never heard of vacations, that was also explained to her. While she was trying to take it in, she was distracted by the sight of a wagon rolling down the street spraying water on the hard ground. "Somebody oughtta tell that feller he's losin' water outta his wagon," she said.

He laughed. "The driver already knows. He's laying water down to settle the dust."

"Well, imagine that!" she exclaimed. "Is they some kind of celebration goin' on here?"

"No. Mineral Wells is named for the wells located here," Adam explained. "See that building over there? It's a drinking pavilion. For a dollar a week you can have all the mineral water you can drink. That's what the tourists were carrying. The water is healthy. Tourists flock here by the thousands to drink and bathe in it."

"Glory be," she said. "I heard about such places from the tinker man. They's one in Hot Springs, Arkansas. Do you reckon we could try some of it?"

He nodded absentmindedly. "Possibly later," he said. "Right now I'm anxious to get on to the ranch."

Danny was sorry to leave the town behind. She would like to have stayed to see the sights, but she knew Adam was anxious to reach the Circle J Ranch. They followed the road through green shaded cedar

84

woods, until they reached the river. The wagon ruts they'd been following continued on, dipping down the bank, then disappeared into the water. Danny's gaze traveled farther, saw the wagon ruts emerge on the far side of the river.

"Are we gonna go right through it?" Danny asked. She measured the distance with her eyes. "Looks fair deep along here."

"River's up," Adam said. "It's more'n likely been raining up north, but the horses can make it. There's plenty of gravel on the river bed."

Shortly after they left the river, the road stopped before a wooden gate fastened between two tall poles. A sign high above the gate carried the words, Circle J.

"This is it," Adam said, leaning over to unlatch the gate.

The days of traveling were catching up to Danny and she arched her back, stretching tired muscles. She was relieved the journey was finally over. As soon as she talked to the old man, she would have earned the rest of her money. Fifty whole dollars. Added to the fifty she had tucked deep in her pocket, that made one hundred. Although it seemed like an incredible amount of money, she had earned every penny of it. If she'd known how long the trip was going to be, she would have held out for more.

The ranchhouse was a two-story log cabin built as two separate buildings connected by an open dogtrot. Danny saw a porch had been built across the front of the structure. The door to the bunkhouse, located near the barn and corrals, stood open to catch the evening breeze. The place seemed deserted, but Danny knew enough about cattle ranches to know that calving would be in full swing. And the men would be putting in long hours with very little sleep. She guessed they were out riding herd.

Adam reined his mount up beside the porch as a woman stepped into the dogrun. Spying the two of them, she came forward, put her hands on her hips, and looked accusingly up at Adam.

"It's about time you got back," she said. "Took your own good time, didn't you?"

"Don't fuss, Sarah," he said, sliding down from his mount. "I got back as soon as I could. How's the old man doing?"

"He's alive," she said. "But we came nigh on to losing him more'n once." She turned her attention to Danny. "Adam ain't much on manners." She stuck out her work-roughened hand. "Name's Sarah. I'm the housekeeper around here."

"I'm Danny. I mean Danielle Tucker," Danny said, shaking the other woman's hand. "I'm right glad to meet you."

"Danny, huh?" Sarah looked surprised. "You ain't quite what we was expecting." A grin tugged at her lips. "Buck's gonna be right surprised to see you." She shook her head. "You ain't more'n a child, and you look plum tuckered out." Her gaze swept back to Adam. "Did you drag her here without feedin' her?"

"Of course I didn't," he said. "But you know yourself I had no time to waste."

"Well, now she's here, she's gonna get fed before you take her to that old man."

"I can wait," Danny said. Although she was hungry, she wanted to see the old man and find out

86

why he'd sent for her.

"Where is Buck?" Adam asked.

"He's in the bunkhouse," Sarah said. "Michelle tried to get him to stay in the house, but soon's he come to hisself, he moved in with the men. Said he felt more at home there."

Adam gripped Danny's forearm. "Let's go find out what this is all about."

They found Buck in the cookshack, whittling on a chunk of wood. He was slightly stooped and gave the appearance of age. It was obvious he'd been ill from the pasty color of his skin. His wrinkled face was weathered the same color as the buckskin that clothed him. Deep lines ran from the flare of his nose, disappearing into the snow white walrus mustache. His chin was covered with a beard the same color and fullness of his mustache.

Adam stepped into the room and Danny followed, aware of the old-timer's faded blue gaze on the two of them.

Buck studied Danny for a long, silent moment, working a chaw of tobacco around in his mouth. Suddenly he spat a long stream toward the spittoon. It landed with a plop, square on target.

He offered Adam no greeting. Instead, he pointed the tip of his knife toward Danny. "What's this?" he growled.

"*This* is a girl," Adam said grimly. "Her name is Danny Tucker. Miss Danielle Tucker." He gave emphasis to the first name.

The old man lifted a beetled brow, and studied her as he worked at his tobacco some more. Danny was beginning to feel like a bug he was inspecting and she didn't like the feeling one bit.

"You don't say," the old man finally said.

"I do say," Adam replied. "You should have told me I was going after a woman."

A woman.

Even though Danny was uncomfortable beneath the old man's gaze, she was aware of Adam's words. Before, he had called her a child. She wondered when he had changed his mind about her.

"Didn't know you was," the old man said.

Danny shifted impatiently. She was tired. And she didn't like being kept standing like this. She opened her mouth and told them so, finishing with ". . . it ain't polite not to tell me who you are an' why you had *him* come all the way to Tucker's Ridge to haul me off down here."

His face broke into a grin. "Guess it ain't at that," he said. "Was just kinda surprised to see you was a girl is all." His attention turned to Adam. "Get 'er a chair, Adam. Them friends of yours ain't here to make the girl welcome so it's up to us."

"Where is everyone?" Adam asked, swiveling his head around to scan his surroundings as though expecting someone to materialize from somewhere nearby. "I haven't seen a soul except for you and Sarah. This place looks deserted."

"It's calving time, boy," Buck said. "Michelle went to town after supplies and Judd's out with the men. Even took the bunkhouse cook. Sarah, that old warhorse, brings me my meals."

"You better not let Sarah hear you calling her a

warhorse," Adam laughed.

Since they seemed to have forgotten Danny's presence, she found herself a chair and waited.

Finally, Adam remembered her. "It's past time for explanations," he said. "All along I've been wondering what you wanted with Danny. It would be nice to know why I went to so much trouble."

"You had some trouble?" Buck asked.

"We had a bit," Adam admitted.

"The bunch who was bent on stretchin' your neck?"

"No," Adam replied. "We ran into a man that took a shine to the girl. He's been following us."

Buck turned his attention to Danny and nodded his head. "Yeah. She would attract men," he said, studying her with shrewd eyes. "They prob'ly buzz around her like bees to honey. She's got *her* look. But I ain't surprised at that. Kinda figgered she would have."

Danny realized there was a compliment in the old man's words but his reference to an unknown *her* was puzzling. "Whose look?" she asked impatiently.

"The look of the angel."

Danny stiffened and her gaze flew to his. *Angel.* The old-timer couldn't mean her cousin. *Could he?*

"Yes," he said, nodding his white head. "If'n you had the red hair, you could durn near pass for her."

He *was* talking about Angellee. Danny's cousin, Angellee Tucker.

"She could pass for who?" Adam inquired, studying Danny's face intently as though to read the answer there.

89

Danny's eyes remained fixed on the old man. "What do you know about Angel?" she asked. "Have you seen her?"

"Not recent-like," he said. "But I know her. It's been nigh on to two years since I seen her. But they was a time when we was mighty close to each other."

"Is she all right?" Danny asked. "And my aunt and uncle. Do you know about them too?"

"They's both dead," he said grimly. "Killed whilst on the way to California. It near broke the young'un's heart too. She was on the trail of them what kilt 'em, ridin' to revenge 'em when she met Jake Logan. He's her husband now and the attorney general. The angel did herself proud when she picked that man."

The whole thing was hard for Danny to take in all at once. Her aunt and uncle were dead, and Angellee was married. "I didn't know," she muttered. "I didn't even have time to bid goodbye afore they was gone from the hills. Pa told me what'd happened the day after."

And gave me a warning, she silently added. *A warning that must be heeded.*

Her knuckles whitened and she was almost certain her face had gone pale too. She looked at Buck grimly. "I never believed what they said about her. It wasn't true. Them folks just made it up 'cause they wanted somebody to blame."

"There's no need to get upset, Danny," Adam said. He sat beside her and took her hand in a steadying grip. "What's this all about, Buck? I can see there's more than what you're telling."

"You keep shut," Danny snapped. "My family's

doin's ain't got nothin' to do with you." She didn't want Adam to know the secret—he might believe it.

"Calm down," Adam said. "I know the news of your aunt's and uncle's deaths must have come as a shock to you." He looked hard at Buck. "Was that all you wanted with her? To tell her that her folks were dead?"

"No," the old-timer said. "Wish it was all I had to say." He studied Danny with shrewd eyes. Finally, after what seemed an eternity, he spoke again. "Angel's missin'."

Danny froze and her heart skipped a beat. "What do you mean?" she asked.

"Nobody seems to know where she's at."

"Her husband . . ."

"Ain't seed hide nor hair of her nigh on to four months now. He's mighty worried about her."

"But how? Why?"

"Hold on and I'll tell you. Angel and Jake live in Pittsburgh. She was on her way to visit some friends in New Mexico. Silver City, it was. But she didn't get there. Just plumb disappeared off the train she was ridin' on."

Fear trailed icy fingers down Danny's spine as a dark foreboding crept over her. As she listened to Adam and Buck talk, their voices seemed to come from a great distance.

"Maybe she just got off somewhere else," Adam suggested.

"Maybe," Buck conceded. "But Jake don't think so. He's plumb convinced she was took off that train,

91

but ain't no way of knowin' where she was took off at."

"Why would anyone kidnap her?" Adam asked.

"Now that's somethin' I don't rightly know. I ain't talked to Jake myself. It was Robert Shaw who contacted me. Knew I'd want to help find the angel."

"Who is Shaw?" asked Adam.

"It was the Shaws, Robert and Heather, that the young'un was goin' to visit. They's mighty worried about the angel, but they couldn't find a lead in Silver City. Nor nowhere else in New Mexico. Only thing we was able to find out was she wasn't on that train when it got to El Paso. The conductor said they was only one woman on the train there. And she was too old to be the young'un. Besides, she didn't look nothin' like Angel."

"Angel's all right," Danny insisted. "Ain't nobody more able to take care of theirselves then her. Her Pa taught her the ways of the forest. She can throw that knife of hers into a squirrel's eye at . . ."

"Fifty yards," Buck said with a grin. "An' you're right about her bein' able. I had me a rifle when we met, but it looked like a standoff for awhile there. She was threatenin' me with her knife, said she could put it through my heart afore I could level my rifle and pull the trigger." He guffawed at the memory, then his eyes took on a faraway look. "Whatever happened musta took a bunch of 'em to carry it off. 'Cause she could take care of herself all right. Yep, she purely could."

The old-timer's words brought back memories of her cousin and Danny swallowed hard. She and

Angel had been close once. "I wish there was something I could do to help find her." She searched his face. "Why did you send for me? Did you think I had seen her?"

He studied her for a long moment. "I was hopin' you could tell me where she was," he admitted.

"How could I do that?" she asked.

"I was hopin' that, like the young'un, you had the gift."

Chapter Ten

The Gift? Sheer black fright swept over Danny as she stared at the old man in horror. *God! How could he know about the Gift? Had Angellee told him?* Danny knew that must be the answer.

"No!" she gasped, shaking her head in denial. "I ain't got it. If somebody told you different, then they was dead wrong."

"What's this?" Adam asked, a frown pulling his dark brows together, making the scar seem even more prominent as he looked from one to the other. "What gift are you talking about?"

Danny's stomach muscles clenched tight as she flicked Adam an apprehensive glance, then returned to meet Buck's shrewd gaze.

Don't tell Adam! she silently pleaded.

"We're just talkin' about an' old thing my granny give my cousin," Danny muttered, lowering her thick lashes to hide her expressive eyes.

God! Why did Buck go an' mention Angellee's gift of second sight? Didn't the old feller know how afeared it made folks? Danny didn't think she could bear it if Adam looked at her in the same manner the mountain folk had looked at Angellee.

Danny shifted restlessly beneath Buck's probing gaze, then lifted her eyes to meet his. He frowned at her, scratching his beard with a gnarled finger as though wondering how to proceed. Finally, he spoke. "You ain't heered nothing from or about your cousin at all?"

"No," Danny said, shaking her head, but even as she did, something dug at her memory.

"That's odd," Adam said.

"What?" Buck swiveled his head to look at the other man. "You remembered somethin'?"

Adam nodded thoughtfully. "Yes. While we were on the trail Danny dreamed about her cousin." His gaze turned to Danny. "Remember?"

The moment he'd spoken up, she *had* remembered. And the memory drained the color from her face.

"You *dreamed* about her?" Buck asked gruffly. "You sure it was a dream?"

"That's the odd part," Adam replied. "At the time she thought it was real." He turned to her. "Didn't you, Danny?"

She nodded her head. "Yeah," she muttered. "But it wasn't real. It was a dream."

"Uh huh. S'pose it musta been." Buck worked his chaw around in his mouth, moving it from one side to the other, then back again. Finally, he turned and spat a long stream of tobacco toward the spittoon. His eyes followed it, watching it land neatly in the center of the jar, then he turned back to Danny and studied her thoughtfully. "You gonna tell me what

95

that dream was about?" he finally asked.

"I d-don't r-remember," she stuttered, swallowing convulsively. She looked pleadingly at him. She couldn't help him. Dammit! She would if she could. But she couldn't.

"Remembering her nightmare isn't going to help you find her cousin," Adam said. "It looks like you've come to a dead end in this direction." He took Danny's arm. "Sarah was right. You look worn out."

"Wait." Buck's voice stopped him. "We ain't done yet. I got to know about the nightmare, girl. It might be important."

Danny swallowed convulsively. He wasn't going to leave her alone. For some reason, he suspected her of lying about the gift. But she wasn't! She wasn't lying! Again, her eyes pleaded with him to stop badgering her, but his expression was relentless. Her breath hissed out between her teeth, and only then did she realize she had been holding it.

"I dreamed she was a haunt," she said. "She was acallin' out to me."

"What else?"

"They wasn't nothin' else!" She glared at him. "I told you everything. She was just acallin' out to me. It made me afeared." Danny shivered at the memory.

"You was afeared of the angel?" Buck asked.

"No-o-o-o." She drew the word out thoughtfully. Then, she shook her head firmly. "It wasn't Angel that was makin' me afeared. It was the other thing."

"What other thing?"

"The big black one. It was—"

Suddenly she stopped and jerked her head toward

96

the open door. She could hear the sound of a carriage approaching.

"That's prob'ly Michelle comin' back home," Buck said. "And about time too. I was beginnin' to worry about her."

Danny took the opportunity to escape from Buck's questions. She moved to the door to stand beside Adam, and when the wagon came into view, Danny saw a dark haired woman sitting on the high seat.

The three in the bunk house were silent as they waited for the carriage to arrive. The woman pulled up beside the house and leapt lightly to the ground, then turned toward the bunkhouse, and the man in the doorway.

"Adam," she called, crossing the distance between them. "I'm glad to see you finally made it back."

"What do you mean by finally?" Adam replied. "I made the trip in record time. Figured this old coot would die before I made it back if I didn't." He introduced Michelle to Danny.

"I'm pleased to meet you," Michelle said. "Adam, would you unload the supplies for me?"

Adam winked at Buck. "Isn't that just like a woman," he grouched. "Not even a proper greeting before she starts ordering me around."

"Oh, you!" Michelle struck him playfully on the chest. Then, standing on tiptoe, she placed a light kiss on his lips. "Is that better?" she asked.

"Hmmm." He studied her face. "Some," he said. "Since Judd's not here to object, you could have done better."

Danny had felt a surge of jealousy at the kiss. The

97

woman was married and had no business kissing Adam. Not to her way of thinking, anyway. But then, what they did was really none of her business.

Michelle turned her attention to Danny. "You look completely worn out," she said. Although her eyes were curious, she asked no questions. "Come on up to the house with me."

Danny had no intention of declining the invitation, for the need to escape from Buck's questions had become all-consuming.

"Go on with her," Buck said, as though giving his permission. "We'll finish our talk later." His shoulders drooped as though weighted down with weariness, reminding her that the old-timer was far from well.

She followed Michelle to the house, and the housekeeper met them at the door.

"Is the baby asleep?" Michelle asked.

"He was a few minutes ago," the woman answered.

Excusing herself, Michelle hurried up the stairs. Sarah shook her head, pretending exasperation. "She can't be away from that young'un no more'n a few minutes without worryin' about him." Then, to Danny she said, "You look plumb tuckered out, child. Come on into the kitchen and I'll get you some coffee."

Danny felt tired and irritable as she followed Sarah across the breezeway to the other cabin. Buck had hit her with surprising news. She would have declined the coffee if she had been given a choice. Since she hadn't, she watched Sarah pour the coffee, then took the steaming cup from her.

"Set yourself down and drink that," the house-keeper said.

"I'd be right proud to help you," Danny offered, waiting until Sarah declined before seating herself.

Danny's mind was in turmoil over what she'd learned from Buck, and what he'd almost revealed to Adam. She would have to go out later and talk to him alone, beg him not to tell Adam about the gift, because just the thought of him finding out sent her into a panic. *But why?* Danny silently wondered. It really shouldn't matter to her what Adam thought about her.

But it did. Somehow, it *did* matter. It mattered a *whole* lot.

Her thoughts came to a jolting halt as Michelle joined them. "The baby is sound asleep," she said.

"Told you he was," the housekeeper said.

"You know I had to see for myself." Michelle poured herself a cup of coffee and joined Danny at the table. "Sarah does a great job of looking after us," she said. "She practically rules this household."

"No such thing," Sarah denied.

Michelle laughed. "Now, Sarah. You know you do. But you know we love it." She turned back to Danny. "Every household should have a Sarah in it. Not only does she keep the house, but she looks after the baby for me. And the meals she cooks are just out of this world."

"Are you tryin' to butter me up for some reason?" Sarah asked suspiciously. "If it's on account of that cobbler you wanted, then you're wasting your time."

"Sarah! You promised!"

Sarah grinned and her eyes twinkled. "I know I did. And I ain't never broke a promise in my life. The cobbler's done made. Made it before you left for town, an' it took the whole pail of blackberries Michael picked."

Michelle screwed up her nose. "You made it this morning, Sarah? Why didn't you tell me? I would have had some earlier."

"That's the reason I didn't say anything. I don't like my good berry cobbler cut into before a meal."

"Tyrant," Michelle accused.

Danny liked the way they teased back and forth. Even though it was obvious Michelle was from moneyed folk, she didn't put on airs with her help like Danny knew some people did.

As though to prove Danny's reflections, Michelle leaned over and kissed the older woman on her pink cheek. "Thank you, Sarah. Michael and Judd will be so pleased about the cobbler."

"Michael is so besotted with Flo that he don't even know what he's eating these days," Sarah said. "Can't imagine what's gonna become of that boy. He might even take a notion to marry her."

Michelle looked worried. "Do you really think she'd marry him? Poppa would probably disinherit him if he did." Suddenly, she turned to Danny. "We're being rude," she said. "Michael's my twin brother. You'll be meeting him at dinner."

"If he makes it to the house," Sarah said. "He spends most of his time at the bunk house now. When he's not off to town," she amended.

Michelle winked at Danny. "Michael likes to spend his time with Buck," she said. "He really took

100

a shine to him."

"Don't know why anyone would like that ornery ol' coot," Sarah grumbled. "He was sent here to make my life miserable."

Michelle's lips twitched. "You can't fool me, Sarah. I've seen you give Buck extra helpings of dessert."

"No such thing," Sarah said. "And if I did, it was only right. Man don't look like he's been fed proper for years. He could use a little extra feed while he's here." She took another cup from the cupboard and filled it with coffee. "Reckon I got time to set down with the two of you," she said. Pulling out a chair, she joined them at the table. "Was you able to help Buck?" she asked Danny.

"I don't think so," Danny said. The housekeeper's words caused her fear to spread anew. "Did he tell you why he sent for me?"

"He told us he needed your help. Didn't say how." She studied Danny curiously. "Sometimes he's windy as the old North wind. Other times seems like you couldn't drag the words outta him with a twenty mule team."

"Has Buck been very sick?" Danny asked although she knew Sarah was waiting for an answer to her unspoken question.

"We didn't think he had much of a chance when we first saw him," Sarah replied. "The poison from the rattler had already spread when they got here. His leg was swole up tight as a drum and he was plumb outta his head with the fever. Kept on sayin' he had to find you."

"Adam did everything he could to help Buck,"

101

Michelle inserted. "He cut the bite with his knife and tried to suck out the poison, but you never can get all of it. Anyway, the old man wouldn't stay put. Insisted he had to find you. Adam took over the job." She smiled at Danny. "It was good of you to come here to see him."

Suddenly, Danny felt guilty about Adam having to make her come. She would return his money the first chance she had. After all, he'd not brought her for his own good. He'd been trying to help the old man and, ultimately, her cousin.

It was late when they heard the sound of hoofbeats. Michelle had brought the baby downstairs and Danny was watching him play with a set of wooden blocks.

"It's Judd," Michelle cried happily, setting aside her embroidery and rushing to the door.

Danny heard male voices greeting Michelle, then boots sounded on the porch. A moment later, Michelle returned with two men.

Curious, Danny's gaze moved between the two men. The older man, obviously Michelle's husband Judd McCord, was around Adam's age, while the younger man appeared to be in his early twenties.

Danny would have guessed the younger man's relation to Michelle even if she hadn't been told. Although Michael was taller and his features masculine, they were as alike as two tits on a sow's belly. Both had the same jet black hair, the same blue eyes fringed with dark lashes, and they both had the same straight nose.

Her gaze shifted to the older man. Judd McCord's expression was severe as though he were a man who

102

rarely smiled, but his love for his wife was apparent in every look he gave her. After introductions were made, Judd scooped the babe off the floor and cradled him in his arms.

"How's daddy's boy?" he growled.

The child gurgled happily and slapped at Judd's face.

"Little Adam has been waiting impatiently for his daddy to come home," Michelle told Judd.

"I suppose he told you so," he said, tossing a teasing look at his wife.

"Of course he did," she said. "Didn't you, sweetheart?"

Danny watched the byplay with a catch in her throat. Judd was obviously a loving husband and doting father. She couldn't help but envy Michelle's happiness. Danny silently wondered if she was to be deprived of such feelings.

Her gaze slid to Adam, and she sucked in a sharp breath. He was watching her in a most peculiar way. Her stomach began to roll and tumble as though it were a tumbleweed being blown by a gusting wind. When his eyes dropped to her mouth, her lips tingled as they had when he had kissed her so thoroughly.

"I hope you're going to stay with us awhile this time, Adam." Judd's voice intruded on Danny's thoughts.

"I never did make it to Montana," Adam said. "And there's been some trouble back there that the foreman says he can't handle. I figure I better leave tomorrow."

Leave! Danny tensed. "What about me?" she asked shortly.

"Judd will see you get back home," he replied.

Just like that! Damn him! He thought he'd bring her here, then dump her on somebody else! Well, he had another think coming. She swallowed down her anger, unwilling to bring the others into her quarrel with him.

Realizing she was too angry to swallow another bite of food, she pushed away from the table and made her apologies to Michelle. "Can't remember when I ever ate better tastin' food," she said. "But I'm filled plumb to the gizzard. If you folks don't mind, I'm goin' out to talk some more with Buck."

"What about my cobbler?" Sarah asked. "Don't you want some of it?"

Danny was aware of Adam's gaze as she declined Sarah's offer. "I gotta work off some of what I already ate, before I can put any more in my stomach."

"I know how you feel," Michelle laughed. "But you have more willpower than I have. I'll eat some of that blackberry cobbler if I have to stuff it in."

Danny left the kitchen while the others were laughing and accusing Michelle of gluttony.

Buck was in the bunk house. He sat at the table, his leg stretched out on a chair; the empty dishes on the table told her he'd managed to finish the huge meal Sarah had sent him.

"How's your leg?" she inquired, seating herself at the table.

"Fair to middlin'," he said.

"I wanted to come eat with you," she said. "But Adam said you was tired and better left alone for awhile."

He nodded his grizzled head. "He was right," he

104

said. "That poison took a lot out of me." He looked at her sharply. "But it ain't because I'm old," he said. "That rattler was big and filled with poison. It was enough to lay a young man down."

"I know," she said. "Adam told me so."

"Just wanted you to know I ain't some helpless old fool," he said gruffly.

"Would you like me to go away so you can go to bed?"

"No," he said. "I'd like company for awhile."

"Would you tell me about my cousin?" she asked.

He grinned. "Nobody I like talkin' about better," he said. "She's some kinda gal, that little angel. Got a mighty lot of strength packed in a small package. Jake Logan would be a dead man if'n she hadn't got him away from them Injuns. She had to dig a bullet out of his shoulder an' he was laid up with fever when I got there." He gave a loud guffaw. "Didn't have the foggiest idea she was a gal. But it was easy for me to see that she had a hankerin' for that man."

"It's hard to believe Angel is married," she mused. "I hope he's a good man."

"He is that," Buck said, digging into his pocket and extracting a chaw of tobacco. "The angel purely loved that man."

"He didn't mind her bein' unlearned. Nor that she knew more about bein' a hunter than bein' a woman?"

"Well, as to that, it did cause a few problems," he admitted. "Not the schoolin' part, but the part about bein' a woman. Now, she was woman enough, but she hadn't learnt to let her man be the strength betwixt 'em. She figgered because she knew more

105

about guns and such that it was up to her to keep ol' Jake safe. That's where the problem lay. Ain't no man wants his girl always ridin' to the rescue when he's in trouble. Makes him feel like he's not so much a man."

"Your cousin sounds like quite a woman to me," came a deep voice from the shadows.

Danny spun around and saw Adam standing there. Instantly, her anger flared anew.

Placing her hands on her hips, she glared at him. "You didn't say nothin' about bringin' me here an' dumpin' me like an unwanted parcel," she said tightly.

For a moment he looked taken aback. "Am I doing that?"

"Looks that way to me, outlander," she said through gritted teeth. "I heard you tell them folks in yonder that you was aleavin' tomorrow."

"Yes," he agreed. "I did say that."

"Well, you ain't goin' nowheres, outlander. Not 'til you pay me the rest of my money."

A slow flush crept up Adam's face, making the puckered edges of the scar stand out in sharp relief. "I had no intention of leaving before we'd settled up," he said stiffly. "Excuse us for a minute, Buck."

Without another word, he stepped outside, and Danny followed him with her heart beating fast with trepidation.

Chapter Eleven

Adam's face was thunderous when she faced him. "I see no reason to tell the world about our financial arrangement," he said, his eyes black and dazzling with fury.

She bristled with indignation. "I ain't got cause to feel shame about it," she said, shooting him a cold look. "It was you that hauled me away from the ridge when I wasn't hankerin' to go nowheres. It was you that—"

He interrupted her vehemently. "I'm getting a little tired of you harping on that. We reached an agreement and—"

"Which you ain't willin' to keep!" Her accusing voice stabbed the air between them.

"Dammit! You mercenary little devil! I never once said I wasn't going to—" He broke off, dug in his pockets and threw some coins at her. "There!" he grated. "There's your damn money."

Her heart hammered wildly in her chest as she regarded the coins he'd flung on the ground.

"Does that satisfy you?" he asked harshly. "Go on! Count them! Make sure I haven't cheated you."

His obvious contempt choked her voice, made it impossible for her to speak. Unexpected tears stung her eyes when he spun on his heels and strode away, disappearing into the night.

Her hurt could no longer be controlled. Silent tears trickled down her cheeks and she wiped them away with the back of her hand.

Damn him! He owed her the money. Why had he been so angry when she asked for it?

She stared at the coins on the ground. She didn't want them. Not now. For some reason, she felt like a Judas, felt that she'd betrayed a trust.

But I didn't! He owed it . . . he owed it. . . .

Wiping the back of her cheeks again, she knelt on the ground and began to pick up the coins.

Adam's mind was in turmoil as he sat beside the river and thought about the scene he'd left only a short time ago. His anger had been way out of proportion. But when Danny had implied he was trying to cheat her, a scalding fury had enveloped him and he'd let it erupt. Perhaps, he reasoned, it was because he'd felt incredibly hurt by her accusation. He'd thought their relationship had become one of mutual trust, but it seemed he'd been mistaken.

The accusations he'd leveled at her were groundless. Danny was no more mercenary than he was. He owed her an apology, and she'd certainly get it before he left in the morning.

Adam felt a heaviness in his chest as he thought of leaving her. If things had been different . . . if he'd met her years ago . . . before Carlotta and Nicholas, then perhaps . . .

His lips curled, but his smile was without humor. Danny was only a child when he'd met Carlotta. The thirteen years that separated them might as well have been thirty.

Uttering a long sigh, Adam rose to his feet and turned his steps toward the ranch. "Might as well get some rest," he muttered. "It's a long way to Montana."

The dream started slowly.

At first it was only a feeling of foreboding that invaded Danny's sleep, making her curl inward, imitating the fetal position. She tried to push away the dark uneasiness that curtained her slumber, but it was useless. Dread crept over her in numbing, icy waves.

No! she silently cried through the invading terror. Go Away! Leave me alone!

She told herself it was only a dream . . . all she had to do was open her eyes. . . . But they refused to open, and someone was nearby, whispering in her ear. She knew it was going to happen . . . tried to stop it, but . . .

The cry woke Danny.

She sat bolt upright on the bed and stared, wide-eyed, into the darkness. Her heart pounded with fear as she waited . . . listening to the silence, trying to see the room's furnishings. She needed desperately to see something real . . . something tangible.

Danny.

There was someone in the room, whispering in her ear like the rushing wind.

Her body froze. She could not move. "Who's there?" she whispered, probing the shadows with her gaze, but there was no one in the room except herself.

Danny.

The voice came again, disembodied, seeming to hang in the air above her.

"Angel?" Danny didn't know why she asked the question. The voice had to be her imagination, didn't it? Unless someone was playing cruel tricks on her.

"Who are you?" she asked sharply, flinging the cover back and climbing from the bed. The hem of the too long nightgown Michelle had lent Danny whirled around her feet, making it difficult to move about. "Where are you?" she demanded, intent on finding the person responsible for the voice. "Why are you doing this to me?"

Danny heard a sound. It sounded like the squeak of door hinges. Swiveling her head toward the noise, she searched for the source. Her narrowed gaze found the bedroom door. She was certain she'd heard something there, but it remained closed.

Leave me alone.

Danny started and jerked around. The voice was behind her . . . there! It had come from the shadows. But there was nothing there. At least, nothing distinct. Instead, she had the impression of a vague shadow . . . an outline or something . . . moving in a rocking motion.

Get out! The voice was angry and sharp. Yet, there

110

was something else in it that was undefinable. Danny was so disturbed by the voice that she could not think rationally. She could not put a name to the feeling she was receiving from the indistinct form. She only knew that it was undecidedly feminine.

Danny backed away from the blackness. Her leg struck a straight back chair and sent it skidding across the floor until it struck the wall, but she paid it little mind. The incredible blackness was spreading, drawing nearer to her. "Get away from me," Danny shouted, throwing up her forearm to protect herself from the unknown. "You get away and leave me be!"

"What in hell is happening?" came a harsh voice from behind her.

Jerking around, Danny saw Adam standing in the doorway, barefoot, bare-chested, and disheveled. Behind him stood the lean tall figure of Michael.

"I . . . I . . ." Danny stole a quick look behind her, but the darkness or apparition was gone. She opened her mouth to tell Adam about the spreading darkness, then clamped her lips shut tight. What could she say to him? "Nothing's happening," she said.

"Then who were you talking to?" Adam growled, raking a hand through his tousled hair as he strode into the room. "Are you having nightmares again, Danny? You're not walking in your sleep now, are you?"

"Course I ain't," Danny said quickly.

"Who were you talking to?"

"Nobody," she said quickly, flicking a quick look around the room, feeling as though someone or

111

something was going to suddenly appear to dispute her words. "They ain't nobody here, is they? I was just . . . just dreamin' again."

"Those must be some dreams you're having," Michael said, bending over to pick up the fallen chair.

Danny avoided Adam's eyes. He was staring at her so fiercely that it made her nervous. Taking refuge in anger, she lifted her chin, set her jaw, and faced him down.

"You ain't got no call to come in here," she said. "This room was give to me for sleepin', an' it ain't decent for menfolk to come in whilst I'm doin' it." Gathering up the hem of her nighgown, she moved back to the bed, keeping her eyes away from the corner where the shadows had teased her. But it had only been her imagination. That was all it could have been.

"Nightmares are nothing to be ashamed of, Danny," Adam said.

"I ain't ashamed . . . I . . ."

"What's going on?" came a voice from the doorway.

They all looked around. Judd and Michelle stared at them. Danny felt stricken. Now she had the whole household up.

"Leave me be," she said, pulling the covers up around her neck. "I want to go to sleep."

"Come away and leave her alone," Michelle said. She pushed the men from the room and shut the door behind them. Then she came and sat down on the edge of Danny's bed. "Would you like to talk about

112

what happened?" she asked gently.

"No," Danny said. "I just want to sleep now," How could she confide in the girl? She didn't know her. And she was positive that if she confided in Michelle, the woman would be certain to think she was crazy.

No. She could confide in no one.

Except, perhaps, the old man who believed in visions.

Michelle patted her hand and stood up. "I won't press you," she said. "If you want to talk later, then I'll be glad to listen."

"Thank you," Danny said.

She watched the other girl leave the room.

Adam had waited outside in the hallway hoping Michelle had discovered what was wrong with Danny, but she had nothing to tell him. When he started toward Danny's room again, Michelle took his arm and stopped him.

"Leave her alone," she said. "She doesn't want to talk now. Maybe later she will."

Against his will, Adam let himself be persuaded to go back to his own bed. But it was a long time before he was able to go to sleep.

Danny woke to the clatter of dishes and found Michelle leaning over her with a tray. "I brought you some coffee," Michelle said. "Thought you might like to join us for breakfast, but if you'd rather, I could bring it on a tray."

"No!" Danny gasped, feeling completely horrified

113

at the idea. "You ain't got no call to be waiting on me." The idea of a lady such as Michelle doing menial work was more than her mind could deal with.

Michelle laughed lightly. "Very well. I can see you're not one to enjoy breakfast in bed. Sarah will have it on the table in fifteen minutes. Just time for you to drink your coffee down and dress."

"You hadn't oughta be bringin' me coffee," Danny muttered, her cheeks pink with embarrassment.

Michelle moved gracefully across the room and pulled the heavy drapes back, allowing the sun to shine through. "It's my pleasure," she said. "Now hurry up and dress." She left the room with a smile.

It didn't take Danny long to dress and brush her hair. She left it loose around her shoulders and then she joined the others at the table.

After breakfast, she sought out the old man and told him what had happened. Her voice was strained as she spoke.

"I didn't see Angel," she said. "I swear I didn't. It was . . . somethin' else."

"What?" he demanded gruffly.

"I-I ain't rightly sure," she said. "It was just somethin' kinda dark . . . like a bunch of shadows. . . ." She swallowed hard around her fear. "It mighta had some kinda shape to it . . . maybe coulda been a haunt . . . musta been one 'cause there ain't nothin' here now."

He sighed deeply. "They ain't no reason to be scared. Maybe that's why you didn't know her, 'cause you was afeared."

114

"Her?" Although she questioned him, she knew he was referring to her cousin.

"The angel. It musta been her you seen."

"No." She shook her head. "It wasn't Angel. The thing was bigger . . . a whole lot bigger than her."

"You got the gift," Buck growled. "You got it all right. You just don't know how to use it. And you gotta learn, gal. You gonna have to learn. For the sake of the young'un."

"Buck." She hesitated. "There's two kinds of dark shapes I'm seein'. One of 'em's big . . . and evil. The other'n could be a lady. An' she calls me by name. But they's somethin' about 'er. I don't know what. But I been hearin' a cry. All along, I been hearin' somethin' . . . maybe a hurt animal. And it's sufferin' somethin' fierce . . . cryin' out . . . a thin, sorta high-pitched cry that sends a shivery feelin' all through me. I think the lady is lookin' for the thing that's makin' that noise."

"What makes you think that?" Buck asked.

"I don't rightly know," she said. "But the lady . . . the thing—" She didn't want to call the shape a ghost. "She's a hurtin' mighty bad when she comes to me." Danny barely noticed that she was finally admitting that something *or* someone had been there. Perhaps only a figment of her imagination, nothing tangible, but her subconscious had latched on to it and made it real.

"It has to be the angel," Buck said gruffly. "It must be her. She's tryin' to tell you somethin'. And you've got to open your mind, girl. You've got to help us find her."

Danny had never felt more helpless in her life, nor more terrified. She would help her cousin if she knew how. But she didn't. "Tell me how," she said. "Tell me what to do an' I'll do it."

"I don't rightly know what to do," Buck admitted. "But maybe Jake will. He's a mighty smart man and if anybody can figger this thing out, it'll surely be him."

He gave Danny's shoulder a reassuring squeeze. "But you go see him, young'un," he said. "We'll get tickets to Pittsburgh tomorrow."

She met his eyes. "You ain't well enough to travel," she said.

"Wouldn't be right for me to leave you to go alone," he said.

"She won't be alone," Adam said from behind them.

Danny whirled around, her eyes widening. "How long you been standing there?" she gasped.

"Long enough to know you haven't been honest with me," he said. "I don't put much stock in visions, but if you think you can be of some help to your cousin, I have no objection to acompanying you to Pittsburgh."

Buck sighed. "That would take a load off my mind, son. But wasn't you needin' to go to Montana?"

"It can wait," Adam said abruptly. "At least until you're done with Danny. We can take the train from Millsap."

"That'd be better than ridin' horseback all the way," Buck agreed. "Faster too."

Danny's stomach felt as though it were filled with

butterflies. Things were going too fast for her. She'd been prepared to say goodbye to Adam today. Instead, he would be traveling north with her.

How long would the trip last? she wondered. Long enough to break down the fence that she'd erected between them last night with her accusations?

She certainly hoped so.

Chapter Twelve

Danny strode toward the ranch house, intent on offering her help to Michelle, when she met Michael, who was obviously headed for the corrals.

"I was hoping to see you, Danielle," he said. "I hope you aren't thinking of leaving anytime soon. I would like a chance to get better acquainted with you."

Danny smiled up at him. She liked this intense young man who was only a few years older than herself. "We're gonna leave on Wednesday," she said.

"Wednesday?" He frowned down at her. "That's the day after tomorrow. And tomorrow Judd and Adam are expecting me to go to Graham with them." He studied her intently. "That doesn't give us much time. Maybe you would consider . . . no. I couldn't ask that of you. Not after all the days you've spent in the saddle to get here."

"What?" she inquired curiously, feeling intrigued by this young man.

"Well, I thought perhaps . . ." His voice trailed away and a flush stained his cheeks.

"Yes?" she prompted.

He shuffled his feet, obviously embarrassed. "I thought maybe you would like to go out on the range with me today. But I guess not. It will be hot and dusty and . . ."

"To the calving?" she asked excitedly. "Would you really let me go with you?"

"You'd like to come?" he asked.

"I darn sure would. I ain't never been around cattle much. 'Course, we got Bess, but she don't count for much."

"Bess?"

"Bess is our milk cow," Danny explained. "An' she's nearly as ornery as Caesar. A body can't depend on neither one of 'em. She's nearly as bad as Caesar with them hind legs of hers."

"Whoa! Who—or what—is Caesar?" Michael tilted his hat back and stared bemusedly at her.

"Why, Caesar is our mule. An' he's the most cussed critter they ever was. They ain't another mule within a hundred miles of Tucker's Ridge that's as stubborn as Caesar when he takes a notion to quit pullin' the plow."

Michael laughed heartily. And that's how Adam found them. He took Danny's arm in a proprietary grip and gave Michael a cordial nod. "Didn't expect to see you still around," he said. "Thought you'd already be out on the roundup."

Michael's smile was goodnatured. "I would have been except Judd left me here to move some furniture

119

about for Michelle. I was just on my way out when I ran across Danielle. She told me you're not leaving until Wednesday."

"That's right," Adam said.

"I'm goin' with Michael today!" Danny exclaimed.

Adam's lips thinned and his eyes glinted. "That's not a good idea," he said gruffly. "We rode hard to get here. Danny had very little rest last night and . . ."

"I ain't the least bit tired," Danny protested. "An' I might never get another chance to see how a real ranch is run."

Adam dropped her arm as though it were a live coal. "I hardly think you'll find out today," he said stiffly. "But if you're set on going, then take one of Judd's horses. The filly needs to rest, even if you don't."

While she was still mulling his words over in her mind, he turned on his heels and strode away.

"Whew!" Michael exclaimed, eyeing Adam's departing figure. "What was that all about?"

Danny's lips twisted wryly. "He's gettin' a mite ornery these days."

Michael's lips twitched. "That's putting it mildly." Turning his attention back to her, he said, "You go tell Michelle our plans while I see to the horses."

Nodding, Danny turned her steps toward the ranch house. But the sound of hoofbeats jerked her head around and she stopped to watch Adam ride by. He spared her only a brief look as he passed her, then his eyes were fixed firmly ahead as though he'd already forgotten she even existed.

After reaching town, Adam went directly to the telegraph office, intent on letting Danny's father know she was all right and would be returning home in a few weeks. Since Possum Hollow was the nearest town, he sent a cable to the general store there, feeling certain the owner of the establishment would see that Silas Tucker received the message.

After he had composed the message and paid the man at the counter, Adam felt a measure of relief.

The clerk read the message, then looked up at Adam. "You wanta wait around in case there's an answer?" he asked.

"I don't expect there will be," Adam replied. "But I have some things to buy, then I'll be stopping at Murphy's for awhile." A grin tugged at his lips. "Flo still work over there?"

"She's still there," the man said. "Sounds as though you ain't no stranger to these parts." He studied Adam's face, then looked down at the signature of the message he held. "Adam Hollister. The name sounds familiar, but I don't recognize the face. You staying at one of the hotels in town?"

"No. I'm staying out at the Circle J Ranch. Judd McCord's an old friend of mine."

"Sure," the man said, extending his hand across the counter. "I've heard Judd talk about you. You was at the university together, wasn't you? I'm Amos

121

Crown. Guess Judd's real busy out at the ranch right now."

They shook hands and Adam agreed that Judd was indeed busy with the calving season on them. Disinclined to talk more, Adam took his leave of the telegraph office and turned his steps toward the saloon.

He was still there an hour later when the messenger from the Western Union found him. "Telegram for you," the boy said. "Amos said I might be lucky enough to find you still here. Sure am glad you was. It's a mighty long ride out to the Circle J Ranch."

Adam frowned down at the envelope. There was no question in his mind that it was from Possum Hollow. But why had the storekeeper there felt it necessary to reply to his message? Could Danny's father have been in the store when the message arrived?

"Only way to know what's in there is to open it," Flo said from beside him.

Realizing she was right, Adam tore the envelope open and read the contents. SILAS TUCKER DEAD OF HEART ATTACK STOP BURIED TODAY. It was signed by Elias Whitney, the sheriff of Possum Hollow.

Dammit! Adam swore inwardly. He must have caused Tucker's heart attack by making off with his daughter. God! How much guilt could one man carry?

Adam crushed the paper in his hands. How the hell was he going to tell Danny that her father was dead and buried?

*   *   *

Danny and Michael had been riding the range for long hours when Judd sent Michael to help with the birth of a calf. It was then that Danny decided to do some exploring on her own.

She was glad to leave the dust of a hundred cattle behind her, felt as though she'd been breathing it for days.

Before long she found a sun-drenched glade and decided to rest for awhile. She reined the bay up before she saw the two mule deer standing motionless a few yards away.

They stared at her for a long moment. Then suddenly, with a flick of a white tail, the deer bounded away, leaping through the field of tall bluebonnets in their flight.

As Danny watched, a squirrel peeped warily around a tree while high above, on the branch of a postoak tree, a blue jay scolded her for disturbing the peace.

A quick glance at the sun told Danny she had been away from the others for over an hour. She emerged from the cedar brake and spied a ribbon of green bordering a small creek that glinted silver in the sun. Michael had told her that the cottonwood and willow trees that grew along the creek's banks offered concealment for stray cows, so she urged the bay in that direction, thinking to save Michael the need of checking there.

Finding no sign of a living thing beside the narrow creek, she guided the bay downstream.

Soon the gravel beds gave way to a muddier surface

123

and Danny decided it was time to retrace her path. But even as she reined the bay around, she heard the bawling of a cow in the distance. And the animal sounded as though it were in distress.

Urging the bay around the bend, she stared in dismay. A heifer, obviously about to calve, was in the middle of the creek, up to its knees in the mud, bawling piteously.

"Dang fool critter," Danny muttered. "You shoulda had better sense than to get in the creek in the first place."

The cow bawled loudly, rolling its eyes at Danny, who could only stare at the heifer in consternation.

The animal obviously needed help immediately and the others were too far away. Danny was going to have to help the cow out herself.

Untying the rope from the saddle, she made a loop and tossed it toward the heifer. The loop fell short by several feet. Danny reeled the rope in and repeated the procedure, only to fail again.

Grimacing ruefully, she removed her boots and socks, determined to get the heifer out even if she had to go in after her.

She rolled up the legs on her jeans and with a grimace of distaste, squished through the mud. When she was close enough, she threw the loop over the heifer's head and returned to the bay where she tied the rope to the saddle. Then she urged the horse backwards with a steady hand.

Immediately, she heard a strangling noise accompanied by the heifer's bawling and she grabbed the bay's bridle and pulled him forward to ease the strain on the cow's neck.

"Won't do to strangle you," Danny muttered. "That'd be a sure way to lose the calf." Putting her hands on her hips, she glared at the cow in disgust. "Stupid critter. Couldn't you see the creek was muddy? You ain't got no more sense than old Bess."

The cow bawled loudly again. "All right," Danny said, trying to make her voice sound reassuring. "I ain't gonna leave you alone. I'll figger somethin' out." Her chin lifted and she scratched the end of her nose thoughtfully as she studied the situation. The cow was only buried up to her knees. If Danny got behind and pushed, then perhaps she could encourage the cow to try harder to help herself.

She squished through the mud until she was behind the cow. Hesitantly, she put her hands on the animal's rump and said, "When I push, you try to lift your legs. We'll soon have you out of here."

Danny pushed, but nothing happened. She might just as well have been trying to push a boulder over a mountain. Spreading her legs wide, she put everything she had into her shove, but the cow remained stuck.

Breathing hard from exertion, Danny wiped droplets of sweat from her brow and eyed the cow balefully. It just wasn't going to work. The doggone critter was too heavy and it wasn't even trying to help.

The heifer bawled, increasing Danny's ire.

"I'm doin' everthing I can, you mangy critter," Danny snarled, striking the animal across the rump with the palm of her hand. The loud smack that sounded relieved her feelings slightly but did nothing to help the situation.

The cow mooed and swung her tail, lashing Danny across the face with enough force to make her flesh sting.

Enraged, Danny grabbed the cow's tail, giving a hard yank, and instantly, the animal lunged. Danny's gaze widened, and she grinned smugly. *Okay,* she thought, *all right.*

She jerked the tail again, causing the cow to lurch once more.

Then, suddenly, with a loud sucking noise, the heifer's front legs were free, then with another thrust, the hind legs came loose and Danny's face registered astonished satisfaction that quickly changed to chagrin as she helplessly felt her feet begin to slide in the mire.

Grabbing out in a futile gesture, Danny's fingers closed over . . . only water, extremely insubstantial water. And then she was sitting on her rump . . . right in the middle of the mud with the cold stream flowing gently past her.

The creaking of saddle leather alerted Danny and her whole body tensed. *God! Don't let anyone see me here,* she silently prayed. Her breath hung in her throat as she listened to the rustle of denim against leather. She heard the gravel crunching beneath a pair of boots and slowly, reluctantly, she turned toward the sound.

"Having problems?" Adam asked.

"What does it look like?" she asked, huffily.

"Looks like you're wallowing in the mud," he said with a grin, tipping his hat to one side as he stared down at her in amusement. "Couldn't you find a better place to swim?"

126

"If I'd wanted to swim," she said, smiling in spite of herself. "But I didn't. The doggone cow was about to give birth right here in the dadburned creek. I was just tryin' to help her out."

He looked at the cow in question. "She's in labor, all right." His gaze came back to her. "Are you going to come out of there?"

She gazed innocently up at him and extended her hand. "How about givin' me a hand?"

He gave a short burst of laughter. "I'm not coming near you until you get cleaned up."

The water swirled around Danny's legs as she waded to the bank. She looked down at her wet and muddy clothing and wrinkled her nose in disgust. "I reckon I am a mess," she conceded. "I need to wash this stuff off me."

"I'll watch the cow while you bathe," Adam said, untying a slicker from his saddle and tossing it to her. "Put that on while your clothes dry. There's a deep hole of water down there." He pointed the way. "Past those willow trees."

Danny hurried to the seclusion of the willows and stripped off her muddy garments. Although the mud was cloying, she didn't take long to wash herself. Then she rinsed her clothes in the creek and hung them out to dry on the bushes.

After donning the slicker, Danny joined Adam and found he was already helping the cow deliver her calf.

"It's a heifer," he said.

"Is it all right?" Danny asked.

"Right as rain."

After washing himself in the creek, Adam joined

Danny beneath the shade of an old oak tree.

Danny's senses tingled at his nearness and she was aware of her naked skin beneath the slicker. She kept her eyes lowered, wondering if she should take the opportunity to clear the air between them. She snuck a look at him from between her lashes. He seemed unusually solemn.

"Adam," she began. "I—"

"Let's don't talk right now," he said quickly. "Let's just take the time to relax for a minute."

Danny subsided, relaxing against the cottonwood tree. Sighing, she closed her eyes and listened to the sounds of the woods, to the birds chirruping as they hopped from limb to limb and the drone of bees as they went about the chore of gathering nectar from the wild flowers nearby.

Suddenly, Adam sighed and she opened one eye and peeked at him. "What's wrong?" she asked.

"Everything," he said, studying her with a serious expression. "Something's happened Danny." He picked up her hand and stroked it lightly.

He ain't goin' with me to Pittsburgh, she silently told herself. He changed his mind. He's goin' on to Montana an' I ain't never gonna see him no more. "Don't think I wanta hear it right now," she said. "Look up yonder." She pointed to a cluster of clouds in the sky. "See that bunch of clouds?"

"That bunch?" he asked, leaning closer and squinting down her forefinger. "The ones that look like a flying duck?"

"That's the ones!" she said, her husky voice revealing how disturbing she found his nearness. Her gaze roamed farther. "Can you see ones that look

128

like a witch riding a broomstick?"

He searched for a while then admitted he couldn't find them. "Show me where they are," he said.

"I don't see them neither," she said, laughing at his confusion. "Guess there ain't none up there."

His laugh was husky as he drew her to her feet. "Your clothes should be dry enough to put back on now. Judd will be wondering what happened to us."

The sound of pounding hooves swiveled her around. "Looks like they're already wonderin'," she said. "That's Michael comin' now."

His lips thinned and his expression darkened. "You're not interested in him, are you, Danny?"

She glanced at him from beneath lowered lashes. Did it matter to him? "Why're you askin'?"

"I wouldn't want to see you get hurt," he said gruffly. "And mixing the two of you would be like trying to mix oil and water. It wouldn't work."

Hurt warred with anger as Danny fixed Adam with a baleful look. "You think I ain't good enough for him, don't you?"

"I didn't say that."

"You didn't have to, outlander. I'm readin' you like a book. An' I ain't likin' what I'm readin' neither."

Before he could reply, Michael pulled his mount up beside them. "Wondered where you'd got to," he said, looking curiously at Danny.

Realizing she was still wearing only the slicker, she said, "We been birthin' one of your calves for you." She looked ruefully down at herself. "Got my clothes all muddy doin' it too. Had to wash 'em in the creek."

"Is the calf all right?" Michael asked.

"Right as rain," she said. "Adam can tell you all about it while I get my clothes back on." She left them there without a backward glance.

Danny wondered at Adam's mood. He had been silent throughout the meal, but no one seemed to have noticed except herself. Her appetite, which had been so good only a few moments before, had suddenly left her, but she was determined not to let anyone know and continued to eat her food.

After the meal was over and the others had retired to the living room, Danny sought the privacy of her room. More tired than she'd like to admit, she suddenly felt as though she would be intruding by following. It was only moments later that a knock sounded on her door.

When she opened it, she found Adam standing outside with a package in his hand.

His expression was a study in seriousness as he shifted the parcel from one hand to the other. "This is for you," he said, handing her the package. "A present."

Danny's throat clogged up. "A present? For me?" Her words whooshed out breathlessly. She felt a warm flush stain her cheeks. "Thank you, Adam," she said softly. "Thank you."

He surprised her by entering the room and shutting the door behind him. "Aren't you going to open it?" he asked.

"I don't think so," she said huskily. "I just want to look at it for awhile. Nobody ever gave me a present before."

Something glinted in his eyes. *Concern? Pain?*

"Danny." His voice was harsh, grating, like sand against steel. "It's not much. Only a . . ."

"I don't care what's inside," she said fiercely. "It don't matter. What matters is you cared enough to buy it for me."

"Poor little thing," he said quietly. There was such deep tenderness in his voice that her eyes closed at his tone.

Unexpectedly, he pulled her against his bare chest and rested his chin on the top of her head. "Don't get too fond of me, Danny," he muttered. "I don't have anything to give you."

She pulled away from his embrace. "You act so hard," she said. "But that ain't the way you are. Deep down inside you're as soft as mush. If you wasn't, then you wouldn't have bought me this present."

"Danny . . . Danny. . . ." He sighed. "You've had a hard life, little one."

"I ain't complainin'," she said shortly. "'Sides, lots of folks lived hard lives."

"You're right, they have. But they aren't you." He shook his head wonderingly. "I'm amazed at how you take your hard knocks as if they were what you deserved."

What was he saying? "Life is made up of hard knocks," she said. "Ain't nothing you can do but take 'em when they're dished out."

There was a sudden understanding in his eyes that quickly shifted and disappeared. "Some man is going to be mighty lucky one of these days," he said, stroking her hair. "You're going to make some fella a real good wife, Danny. In a few years."

131

Immediately she huffed up. "You keep talkin' about how young I am."

"Compared to me, you're still a baby."

"The life in the hills makes babies grow up real fast," she said. "I been doin' the work of a man since I lost my ma. I had to—my pa quit doin' it. Then when Angellee and her folks left the ridge, Pa's drinking got real bad so I had to take care of us both."

"You don't have to convince me your life has been hard, Danny. I already know it." He smiled almost tenderly. "Maybe I'll even help you find a husband."

Abruptly she turned away from him. "Thankee kindly, outlander, but I'll be doin' any findin' of husbands all by myself." She lay her package on the bed, moving closer against him, spreading her hand out across his chest, and moving it gently against the fabric of his shirt.

Sucking in a sharp breath, he caught her fingers in a hard grip and held them fast. "Don't do that, Danny. Things like that tends to give a man the wrong ideas."

"What if them ideas he was gettin' weren't the wrong ones," she said, moving her other hand upward and groping at his shirt buttons. She kept her eyes on his as she worked at the top button of his shirt. His eyes darkened as she loosed the button and placed her lips against the warm flesh of his throat.

"Stop that," he groaned, loosening her fingers and pulling her tight against him.

Delighted, she popped the other buttons free until her cheek rested against the matte of curly hair. Then she opened her mouth and traced an oval across his shoulder with the tip of her tongue.

He reacted as though a bolt of lightning had struck him, sucking in a sharp breath and stiffening. She could feel something happening to his lower body, a hardening that definitely told her she had been more than successful in stirring him up. But her body was doing strange things as well. Her innards felt as though they were thrashing around inside, trying to find a place to get out.

Her knees felt as though they were made of rubber, and threatened to buckle beneath her. But she didn't care. With an exultant laugh, she traced a wider oval with her tongue. When she encountered the roughness of his flat male nipple, she dragged her teeth across it.

A loud groan told her she'd discovered his weakness. She latched on to the nipple and he sounded like he'd been strangled.

"Danny!" he choked. "Stop it!"

He tried backing away, but she clamped her teeth down and went with him. When he reached the edge of the bed, she pushed. Instantly, they fell against the mattress with a loud crash. The sound was enough to make her turn loose and stare at him with consternation.

The thudding of feet in the hallway alerted her that someone was coming. "Quick!" she said frantically. "Scrunch down behind the bed."

Muttering curses beneath his breath, Adam rolled across the bed and dropped behind it just as a knock sounded on Danny's door.

"Danny?" Michelle's voice sounded through the thickness of the door. "What's happening? Are you all right in there? Can I come in?"

"Yes," she said, raising her voice to be heard. As the door began to open, she shrieked, "I mean, no! No! You can't come in. I'm not—" She ripped her blouse off and tossed it on the bed. "—not decent." A hand went to her skirt, tore it away. "Give me a minute to get something on," she called, yanking at the bedspread to pull it around her, but the spread was resisting her efforts. Her eyes darted back and forth, the door was opening wider. "No, Michelle!" She yanked at the bedspread again, wound it around her shoulders but the darn thing seemed to be stuck and wouldn't come any farther.

Scooting into the middle of the bed, she managed to cover herself.

A quick glance told her Adam was hidden properly and she called. "All right, Michelle. You can come in now."

She opened the door and looked at Danny. "What happened?"

"I just . . ." Danny's eyes moved frantically around the room, searching for an answer. Her gaze fell on the hairbrush on the dresser. "The . . . the hairbrush," she stammered. "I just dropped the hairbrush, Michelle. That's all. I was brushing my hair and dropped the hairbrush."

Silence followed the statement, a silence that lasted for a long minute. Then, "If you're sure you're all right, then I'll say goodnight."

"I'm sure," Danny said. "Good night."

Michelle's expression was puzzled as she left the room. Danny listened to the footsteps receding down the hallway, then she crawled to the other side of the bed and pulled the spread off of Adam.

He glared at her, rose stiffly to his feet and began to button his shirt.

"Do you think Michelle believed me?" Danny whispered.

"I don't give a damn whether she did or did not!" he said in an icy voice. "I am not accustomed to hiding beneath beds. Furthermore, I fail to see the reason why you thought it was necessary."

Tucking his shirt in his breeches, he left her alone without a backward glance.

Chapter Thirteen

The next morning, Michelle awakened Danny with a knock on the door and a quick greeting. "Breakfast in ten minutes," she called.

"I'll be right down." Danny flung back the covers and slid from the bed. Five minutes later, her face washed, hair combed, teeth brushed and fully dressed, she began to tug the linens straight on her bed. As she circled the huge four-poster, her toe collided with an obstacle beneath one edge of the bed. The obstacle shifted, scooting farther across the floor.

What in blazes is that? She squatted next to the bed, reached under it and withdrew . . . the package Adam had left last night.

Her present! How could she have forgotten it?

With fumbling fingers, she ripped off the wrappings, opened the box and stared down at the contents breathlessly.

A dress.

Tears stung her eyes as she fingered the soft, blue

mohair dress that was heavily piped with braid. "Oh, Adam," she muttered. "Why'd you go and do that?"

Danny buried her face in the soft fabric, feeling almost overwhelmed with gratitude. She'd never in her life owned a store-bought dress. Never even dreamed of owning anything so pretty.

Her heart was overflowing with gratitude for Adam's thoughtfulness . . . and something else that she wasn't quite ready to acknowledge.

Joy sang in Danny's heart as she smoothed the gown free of wrinkles and hung it in the wardrobe.

Her steps were eager as she hurried downstairs to find Adam, bent on thanking him for his present.

Danny found the others already seated around the breakfast table. After greeting the room in general, she seated herself at the empty place beside Adam and smiled at him.

"Adam, I ain't never had nothin' so pretty in all my born days. You shouldn't oughtta done it. I—"

Adam, obviously not wanting the others to know about the gift, kicked Danny beneath the table. "We were discussing the trip to Graham," he said.

"What are your plans for today, Danny?" Michael asked.

"I don't have any," she replied, accepting a platter of biscuits from Adam.

"How about coming to Graham with us?" Michael asked.

"That'd be plumb grand," she said exuberantly. After selecting a biscuit for herself, she passed the platter on to Michelle, then turned to Adam. "Are you goin' to Graham with 'em?"

"Yes. But I don't think it's a good idea for you to

go. You could stay here and use the time to get better acquainted with Michelle."

Something about his voice told her he was far from pleased with her. Danny's eyes met Adam's and held. No. She *hadn't* been mistaken. He *was* angry with her. But why? Surely it wasn't because of what had happened between them last night.

Michelle seemed to sense the tension between them, because suddenly she spoke up. "I'm going into Mineral Wells today, Danny, and I would love to have your company. You could see what our town has to offer."

Danny grabbed at the offer. "That'd suit me just fine," she said. "I was wantin' to stop when we come through there, just to see what all the hoopla was about."

"Then it's all settled," Michelle said. "It will be good to have company. I usually have to go alone."

Danny's rumbling stomach reminded her that she was hungry and she settled down to the business of eating her breakfast. Although she was disappointed that Adam didn't want her company, she managed to hide it. As soon as the men finished eating, they left, intent on reaching Graham before the auction barn opened.

The mid-morning sun felt hot against Danny's skin as they rode into Mineral Wells.

"We'll leave the buggy at the wagon yard," Michelle said. "That way we won't have to bother about it until we're ready to leave."

"They's so many folks here," Danny said wonderingly. "It puts me in mind of the county fair."

Michelle laughed. "The town does have a festive

138

air," she said. "It's because of all the tourists. There's not a day goes by without another group arriving."

"An' it's all because of them waters?" Danny asked.

"Um hum." Michelle guided the horses past a group of laughing women who had just stepped into the street. They seemed indifferent to the horses and buggies already using the road.

A few minutes later they reached the yard and Michelle and Danny went about the business of unhitching the horses, putting them in the corral, and making certain the horses had water and hay.

After they'd finished, Michelle turned to Danny. "I'm looking forward to this," she said, her lips curling in a smile. "It will be like seeing the town again for the first time. Where do you want to go first?"

"I saw a little building with colored glass all over it whilst we was comin' here," Danny said. "Maybe we could go there first so I can see it up close. Then I wanta try some of them waters so's I can see what all the hollerin' is about."

Michelle laughed. "We can kill two birds with one stone, then. That building happens to be a drinking pavilion. It's the Carlsbad Well."

"Sure is gussied up to be a water place," Danny said, following Michelle down the street.

They passed a building with a sign that read The Famous. A sign in the window advertised fur and wool hats at fifty cents on the dollar.

They turned a corner and Danny found herself facing the Carlsbad Well. The figure of a man was engraved in the stained glass. "Why's he dressed so funny?" she asked Michelle.

"Because people dressed differently when he was alive. That's supposed to be Ponce de León and his famous Fountain of Youth," Michelle explained.

Danny pointed to the sign above the door. "Is that the reason the sign says Carlsbad Water Fountain of Youth?"

"I suppose so," Michelle said, leading the way into the building.

They approached the man behind the counter. "Good morning, Dennis," Michelle said. "Would you get us two glasses of mineral water? My companion has never tried it before."

"Coming right up," he said, turning to fill two glasses with water. Glancing over his shoulder at Danny, he said, "You're about to sample a miracle, young lady. This water can perform wonders. It'll cure cancer, neuralgia, nervousness, rheumatism and just about any other ill the human flesh falls heir to." He plunked the glasses down on the counter and stood waiting.

Feeling self-conscious at being watched so closely, Danny took a tentative sip, then screwed up her nose. "It tastes kinda funny," she said. "But I don't feel no different."

"You gotta swallow it all down," said the man behind the counter.

Michelle laughed. "You don't have to drink it if you don't want to, Danny."

Danny set the glass down. "Since I ain't got none of the ailments you mentioned, I don't believe I'm gonna drink it. But it might be good for my pa. Guess it wouldn't hurt to take him a bottle. How much does this stuff cost?"

After paying for a bottle, Danny took it in hand and followed Michelle from the drinking pavilion. The rest of the morning was spent tending to Michelle's shopping. Noon saw them seated in a small restaurant enjoying huge plates of chicken and dumplings, biscuits and iced tea.

Finally, replete, Danny pushed her plate away and smiled across at Michelle. "Thank you for bringin' me with you," she said.

"Don't thank me, Danny. I've enjoyed your company."

The smile left Danny's face. "Adam don't." At Michelle's puzzled look, she explained. "He don't enjoy my company."

"I'm sure you are wrong," Michelle said.

"No," Danny sighed. "I ain't wrong. He didn't want me to go to Graham with 'em."

"Perhaps he had a reason."

"You know him 'bout as good as anybody does, don't you?" Danny asked.

"Except for Judd," Michelle said. "They've been friends for years. They were at the same university. That's where they met. At the University of Pittsburgh."

"Pittsburgh?" Danny looked at her thoughtfully. "He didn't tell me he went there. Do you reckon he knows my cousin's husband? Do you reckon he knows Jake Logan?"

"I don't think so," Michelle said. "Otherwise, he would have mentioned it."

"How'd Adam come by the scar on his face?"

Michelle flicked a quick look at Danny, then studied her glass of iced tea. "Umm . . . Danny.

141

Adam is terribly sensitive about the circumstances surrounding that scar. I don't think he'd want me to discuss it."

Hurt flooded through Danny. She felt as though she had been slapped in the face. Adam was too sensitive for her to be told. But he obviously didn't mind Michelle knowing.

"Does Adam's scar bother you, Danny?"

"No." Danny's voice was stiff.

Michelle was silent for a moment. Then, "Have I said something to make you angry?"

"No. It's just that . . ." Danny's voice trailed away, as she realized she was on the point of baring her soul to the other woman . . . something she had no intention of doing.

"You care about Adam, don't you?"

Danny felt a flush stain her cheeks. She raised her eyes to Michelle, saw the certainty in them.

"Don't be embarrassed," Michelle said. "Love is as natural as breathing. But you'll have to go carefully with Adam. He's scarred not only on his face, but deep inside as well. Despite that, he's a gentle man at heart . . . a good man to have on your side."

"I know," Danny muttered. "But I ain't so sure about the gentle part." Absentmindedly, she played with her fork. "How would a person . . . a girl . . . go about making him . . ." Her voice trailed away as she realized she couldn't ask Michelle how to make Adam love her.

"Care for her?" Michelle finished softly.

Danny nodded her head. "I done tried everything I know to let him know I ain't opposed to him, but so far, it ain't done no good."

"Maybe that's the problem, Danny. Maybe you are trying too hard. Most men like to do the chasing themselves."

"But, suppose they don't do it?"

Michelle smiled across the table at her. "I think you don't know much about being a woman, Danny."

"Wasn't nobody to learn from," Danny told her. "My time was took up with plowin' and such. Besides, they wasn't no men on Tucker's Ridge except my pa and his old cronies. And I didn't have to work at making them take notice of me."

"Perhaps—"

"Michelle!" came a voice from behind them. "I didn't recognize you for a minute there."

Danny looked up at the dark-haired woman who had spoken.

"Hello, Florence," Michelle said. "I didn't see you come in. Would you like to sit with us?"

Apparently she would, because she slid into the nearest chair and yelled, "Maisie! Bring me some iced tea!"

"Right away, Flo," the waitress called.

The woman Michelle had called Florence turned her attention to Danny. "Who's this?" she asked.

Michelle's lips twitched. "Danielle Tucker, meet Florence Bailey."

"Morning," the woman said, shoving a hand at Danny. "You a visitor here?"

"Yes," Danny said, shaking the woman's hand. Danny was glad of the interruption, because she'd been on the point of revealing her innermost secrets to Michelle. "Mighty proud to meet you." A moment

143

later, Danny wished the words unsaid.

"What's Adam doing today?" Florence asked Michelle. "He hasn't left town yet, has he?"

Danny's gaze narrowed on Florence. What did she have to do with Adam?

"No," Michelle replied. "He went to Graham with Michael and Judd today. Judd's hoping to buy another bull for breeding."

Florence's lips twitched. "If you didn't have the baby to prove different, then I'd swear Judd never thought about nothing but them darn cows of his," she said. Suddenly, her face became serious. "I hope the telegram Adam got yesterday wasn't bad news."

"Telegram?" Michelle said. "He didn't mention a telegram. I suppose it had something to do with his Montana holdings. I know there's been some trouble up there."

"Well, you tell him he better not leave without coming to see me first." When the waitress set a glass in front of Florence, she gave the girl a smile. "Thanks, Maisie."

After refilling Danny's and Michelle's glasses, Maisie took herself off to wait on another customer. The conversation flowed around Danny as she thought about Florence's words. Adam had obviously been to see the girl when he'd come to town. What was their relationship? The question continued to nag at her as they took their leave of Florence Bailey and began the journey back to the ranch.

The next day, Earl and Charlie rode into town.

Earl reined his mount up beside the saloon where a man was busy sweeping off the sidewalk.

"I'm lookin' for a man and woman," Earl said gruffly. "They prob'ly come through here a coupla days ago. You seen any strangers in town?"

The man on the sidewalk spat a long stream of tobacco on the ground, then looked up at Earl. "We got lots of strangers here," he said. "Get 'em all the time."

Earl shifted in the saddle. "The man I'm looking for is easy to spot. He carries a scar on his face."

"Something like yours?" the man with the broom asked.

Earl's lips thinned. "That's right."

"An' you say there's a woman with him?"

"Yeah. But she might be mistook for a boy. She was wearing britches when I last saw her. You got any idea where they are?"

"Reckon not," was the answer. "Don't recollect seein' nobody like that."

"His name's Adam Hollister. She goes by Danny."

Suddenly, the saloon doors swung open and a dark-haired woman joined the man on the sidewalk. "Heard you askin' about Hollister," she said. "What do you want with him?"

"You seen him?" he asked, turning his attention to her.

She shook her head, but Earl was almost positive she wasn't being truthful. Well, two could play that game. "Could be to Hollister's advantage was I to find him," Earl lied.

"I'd ask the sheriff about him if I was you," she said. "Maybe he's seen Hollister. Sheriff's office is

145

down that way." She pointed the direction.

Realizing he would get nothing else from her, he urged his horse forward. But he had no intention of going to see the sheriff. He had been foolish to ask for Hollister. If he was known around here, then he would likely have friends.

"What are we going to do now?" Charlie asked.

"We're going to find another saloon," Earl said. "Then we're going to keep our eyes open and listen to the good folks in town talk to each other. Could be somebody will mention Adam Hollister. And when they do, we'll be there to hear it."

Danny paced uneasily on the platform. Why was she so nervous? Was it just the train trip?

She didn't think so. Granted, she'd never ridden on such a contraption before, but how different could it be from a mule-drawn wagon? Not much, she decided, aside from the fact that it was a hundred times bigger and traveled at least that much faster!

But still, that wasn't what seemed to be bothering her. No, it was more worrisome than that. All morning, thoughts of Earl Keller had been plaguing her, buzzing around in her head like flies on an open sore.

They weren't done with him yet; somehow she was sure of it, though she didn't know where her certainty came from. He'd followed them, yes, but they'd lost him a long time back. Surely he wouldn't come this far after them.

From around the bend came the scream of a steam whistle. *Thank God. The train was finally coming.*

146

When it shuddered to a stop next to the platform, Adam picked up his valise and the one Michelle had lent Danny, then helped Danny aboard.

Rows of seats lined the sides of the long, narrow car. Adam led Danny down the passageway until he located an empty row, stood beside while Danny scooted into the window seat, then threw their valises onto the shelf above, and sat down next to her.

The train jerked, then snorted out of the station and chugged down the line.

Still bedeviled by her nagging, biting feelings of fate closing in, Danny pressed her nose against the sooty window as the train gathered speed.

In the distance, in a cloaking cloud of dust, two riders raced toward the Millsap station.

Suddenly Danny's feelings coalesced and she realized it hadn't been fate she'd felt closing in on them . . . but evil, pure and simple.

Chapter Fourteen

Rage, pure and unadulterated, flowed through Earl when they reached Millsap and found the train had already left town. Immediately, he headed for the ticket office. A few moments later, the terrified clerk had given him the information he sought.

His quarry was bound for St. Louis, Missouri where they would switch trains for Pittsburgh, their final destination.

"Looks like this is the end of the line," Charlie growled from beside him.

Earl's head snapped around. "That's where you're wrong," he said. Turning back to the clerk, he asked, "When does the next train leave?"

"You don't mean we're going there?" Charlie inquired sharply. "You gotta be crazy, Earl. The old man won't like it."

"The old man is the one that taught me not to let anybody get the best of me," Earl said. His fists clenched and unclenched again. "That bitch is going to pay for what she done to me."

* * *

The train was hot and close, the red plush seats prickly and grimy with cinders. Outside, the early morning sun shone hotly, promising a trying day. And the traveling dress of blue mohair, heavily piped with braid, did little to allay Danny's discomfort. It served, instead, to increase it.

The next two days proved to be the longest, most tiring journey she had ever encountered. Its novelty and excitement were countered by the dirt in which Danny felt as if she had been mortared. The heat plastered her clothes to her body, and made her dress itch and sting under the arms and across the shoulders where it fit snugly. Her face, which she could not manage to wipe often enough, burned scarlet. Her usually crisp hair hung limply about her forehead.

As though that weren't enough, a rockslide just outside of Little Rock, Arkansas, covered the tracks and took hours to clear. As a result, they arrived in St. Louis too late to make their train connections and had to lay over for the night.

"You can wait at the depot if you're of a mind," the conductor said. "But since your train won't be leaving until seven in the morning, you'd do better to find a hotel and get some rest."

"That sounds like a good idea since I'm not partial to sleeping on benches," Adam said. "Could you recommend a hotel?"

The conductor could and did. But the hotel, located only a block away, proved to be full.

"Try the Silver Dollar Hotel on State Street," the

man behind the counter told them.

After asking directions, they went on their way, but the Silver Dollar Hotel was booked up too, and so were the next two they tried. Danny's spirits were at a low ebb when they entered the fifth hotel. She stood just inside the door while Adam inquired after a room.

"You're in luck," the desk clerk told him. "One of our guests just checked out."

Adam frowned. "One?"

"Yes, sir! Has a nice big double bed."

Adam turned to Danny, a frown on his face. "Do we take it, or keep looking?" he asked.

"Wouldn't do no good to look elsewhere," the clerk said. "We got races in town this weekend. The whole town is full of people come to see them."

Adam reached for the register. "Do you have a dining room?" he asked, scribbling his name on the appropriate line.

"We got one but it's done closed up. There's a cafe down the street that's open late." He looked pointedly at Adam's hips. "Better lose that gunbelt. Town Marshall's orders. Keeps trouble down."

After paying the man in advance, Adam led the way upstairs to the room marked 224. After tossing the bags on the bed, he turned to her. "I'm hungry enough to eat a horse. Do you want to wash up before we go?"

Heaving a tired sigh, Danny sank onto the mattress. "You go ahead. I'm too tired. I just want to sleep."

"I could bring something back for you."

She shook her head. "I'll be asleep when you get back."

"All right," he said. "I'll take the key with me. That way I won't have to wake you up when I get back." He unbuckled his gunbelt and hung it over the bedpost, then he turned to study her face. "Don't let anyone in the room while I'm gone."

She gave a short laugh. "Don't worry. I won't open the door to nobody. I learned my lesson back in Lizard Lick."

Adam reached for the doorknob, then paused and turned back to her again. "I'll sleep in the chair, Danny. Just leave one of the blankets over it."

When the door closed behind him, Danny stripped off her clothes and slipped into the nightgown Michelle had given her. After spreading the blanket across the chair, she crawled into bed. Moments later she was fast asleep.

Earl leaned back in his seat and closed his eyes. The motion of the train, the hypnotic clatter of the iron wheels against the rails, lulled him into a trancelike state. Thoughts eddied lazily through his mind. At times his thoughts were light and pleasant, dwelling on the last time he'd been on a train; the time he'd accompanied his father to Kansas City.

His lips twitched, as though a smile threatened to stretch his lips . . . to lighten his features. He'd left the hotel one night when his father was sleeping . . . and he'd met Katie.

Katie. . . . She was his first whore.

151

Although she'd probably been twice his age—he'd only been fifteen—Katie had been taken with him, and before the night was over, he'd been initiated into the ways of a woman.

Earl's thoughts turned to other women he'd bedded in the past, on the sweet body curves and skin textures, the way he'd felt buried in the softness of their bodies. But then his thoughts turned dark and frightening as he recalled the last woman he had been intent on bedding . . . *Danny*. . . .

An icy rage, almost reptilian in nature, popped his eyes open and he traced his index finger along the edges of the bandage that covered his wound.

The flesh was sore to his touch, and if he wasn't mistaken, the wound was seeping.

Had it become infected?

His jaw tightened and he clenched his teeth to keep from bellowing out his rage. The need to find Danny had become all-consuming. The whole thing was all her fault. And she would pay . . . and pay . . . and pay. . . .

She would learn that no woman could scar Earl Keller like that and get away with it.

He would get her . . . and when he did, he would make her wish she had never been born!

When Adam reached it, the cafe was locked up tight.

Slowly, he retraced his steps.

Dammit! He was tired and hungry and he didn't want to return to the hotel where Danny waited. He recalled, too vividly, the place in Arkansas where

152

they had spent the night. He recalled, even more vividly, how much he had wanted her there. And his feelings hadn't changed. Nor had his intentions. He would not take her.

But he knew himself well, knew he was vulnerable where she was concerned. It would be much better for the both of them if she was asleep when he returned.

The rinky-dink sound of a piano reached him from a saloon across the street. A moment later he pushed through the swinging doors and crossed to the bar.

"Whiskey," he told the bartender.

The liquor the man served him slid warmly down his throat and struck his empty stomach with a jolt. Motioning for another, Adam eyed the room. At a table nearby a card game was in progress. Carrying his filled glass with him, he joined the men at the table.

The train wheels ground to a screeching halt and came to a stop at the St. Louis depot. People poured off. Among them were two men, obviously strangers, because they seemed disoriented for a moment.

The man with the bandage on his face flicked his gaze searchingly until he found the exit door. Then, a sense of purpose seemed to take hold of him. He turned his feet in that direction, unmindful of the travelers hurrying toward the trains.

But he had no need to mind them. One look at his face . . . at the barely restrained rage emanating from him . . . sent them scurrying aside.

*   *   *

Adam pocketed his winnings and left the saloon. As he passed the train station, he saw two men leaving the depot and recognized them immediately: Earl Keller and Charlie Goodall.

What in hell were they doing in St. Louis?

Adam slid into the shadows of a nearby alley, hoping to remain unseen, but the hope was in vain. A shout alerted him of discovery.

And he had left his weapon at the hotel.

Silently cursing his foolishness, Adam raced down the alley, making for the opposite end. Almost instantly, he heard a crash in the darkness behind him.

Dammit! He was in a fix. He could hardly go to the law since the men had committed no crime. But neither could he return to the hotel where he had left Danny.

Adam heard the scream of a train whistle, then the screeching clatter of wheels against steel rails and realized he was nearing the train yards. Could he escape them there?

Instantly, he changed direction.

But his pursuers were too close. He heard a shot, then a bullet pinged against the nearest railroad car, barely missing his right ear. Adam dodged behind the train as another shot sounded. He heard curses, then running footsteps, footsteps that came closer with every second.

Leaping over the railroad tracks, he dodged into the caboose.

"Where'd he go?" The voice belonged to Earl Keller.

"Couldn't see," said another male voice that had to

154

be Charlie Goodall's. "It's too dark."

Adam tried to control his breathing as he crouched beneath the window. Having to hide galled him, but he'd be worse than galled if he showed himself now.

Bang!

Adam jerked when he heard the sound of metal against metal only a few feet away.

Had he been discovered?

Bang!

"What'n hell are you doin' Charlie?" Earl's voice came from just outside the window where Adam was crouched.

"Thought I could scare him into showing himself." Charlie's whispered words came faintly to Adam's ears.

"You keep bangin' around with that gun and you're gonna shoot yourself with it," Earl growled.

Seconds ticked by, turning into minutes as Adam listened to the sound of their breath whooshing in and out from their exertion. Only a thin layer of metal separated him from his pursuers.

Adam's heart thumped loudly, sounding like a runaway locomotive in his ears as he sought to control his breathing. His right leg was cramped, tingling, and he knew it was on the point of going to sleep.

Moving cautiously, Adam flexed the muscles in his leg . . . his foot struck something hard, sent it rolling across the floor of the car.

Suddenly, Earl's face appeared at the window. "He's in here!" he cried.

When Charlie appeared in the doorway, Adam leapt to his feet and aimed a kick at the man's head.

The blow sent him reeling back and his weapon clattered against the floor.

Immediately, Earl joined the fray, swinging his gun toward Adam, who made a dive for Charlie's weapon. Just in time. The bullet would have killed Adam; had he not moved. Instead it only grazed his right cheek. With blood flowing down his face, Adam raced through the caboose with Charlie following close behind him.

Danny woke with a start, her heart thumping with fear, sweat beading her forehead. Something was wrong . . . dreadfully wrong.

"Adam?" Her questioning voice broke the silence in the room, but there was no other sound. Even so, she couldn't shake the feeling that he was in danger.

Throwing back the covers, she padded barefoot to the window and stared down into the darkness.

Across the street, two men stumbled along, singing a ribald song. Her eyes traveled farther, stopped on a lone man stepping into a saloon.

Can that be Adam? The man had Adam's build. *Dammit! Why's he still gone?*

Unable to stand the suspense any longer, she donned her clothing and went to look for him.

She was nearing the saloon when a man came sailing through the saloon doors to land in a heap in the dust at her feet. The dust had hardly settled when a half dozen men poured through the doors and circled around the fallen man.

Wondering if the fallen man was Adam, she tried to elbow her way through, but the men ignored her, yelling and calling insults at the man on the ground.

"Git up from there," one man roared. "You ain't gonna get off so easy. I got a week's pay bet on you!"

"Let me through," she said, shoving against the nearest man. "Let me pass."

He ignored her. "Come on!" he yelled. "Put them fists up and clobber the hell out of Jobe. You can't give up so easy."

God! Had Adam got himself in a fight with someone? You couldn't tell what men would do when they'd had too much corn liquor.

She kicked the nearest man's shin and he let out a yelp and swung on her. Dodging, she sent another kick his way, this one aimed at his ankle. Cursing a blue streak, he stumbled and fell and Danny got a quick glimpse of the man on the ground. It was all she needed to know that it wasn't Adam.

The man she'd kicked grabbed her arm and yanked it viciously, pulling her down on top of him. She eyed him balefully.

"Let go of me!" she snapped, grabbing a handful of hair and giving it a hard jerk.

Yelping with pain, he released her . . . just as a woman appeared, running out of the saloon door, holding her skirts halfway up to her knees as she pushed her way through the crowd.

"Ed, baby," she cried. "What're you doing down—" Suddenly she stopped and her eyes narrowed suspiciously on Danny. "Who's she?"

"How the hell would I know?" Ed asked. "She just appeared out of nowhere and kicked my leg."

"What're you doin' holding her for?" she asked, her eyes flashing angrily as she turned on Danny.

"The whole thing was a mistake," Danny said hastily. "I thought it was somebody else on the ground."

When the woman turned her attention to the man on the ground, Danny beat a hasty retreat. She hadn't accomplished much in her efforts to find Adam, but she'd found out it was dangerous to be out on the street alone. She had no choice except to go back to the hotel and wait for him.

To Adam, time had become a runaway train. So far, he'd raced the length of every car, barely eluding the bullets flying around him. Now he was in the caboose and he could hear Earl and Charlie approaching fast; too fast for Adam to reach the cover of the buildings over three hundred yards away.

The train whistle sounded.

The caboose groaned, then gave a lurch forward.

Adam knew it was time to make his stand, knew as well he couldn't make it on the train.

The caboose lurched again. Charlie appeared at the other end of the caboose. Adam sent a shot winging toward Charlie. The man flung himself aside and his gun roared. Adam felt the sting of the bullet as it plowed a path through the fleshy part of his cheek.

Dammit! he swore, sending another shot toward Charlie. Adam's shot went wild, striking the metal frame of the door.

"Dammit, Charlie!" Earl's voice came from somewhere behind Charlie. "Get outta the way! I can't get a shot off at him."

Sending off another shot, Adam leapt to the ground. His boot twisted beneath him and he sprawled forward. His finger squeezed the trigger and he felt the wind displaced as the bullet narrowly missed his ear.

Pushing himself to his elbows, he twisted his head . . . Charlie was standing on the platform of the caboose, taking careful aim with his gun.

Adam rolled quickly aside as the weapon roared. Dust and gunpowder filled his nostrils as he rolled again. Then he was on his feet and running in a zigzag fashion toward the buildings, intent on escaping the two men.

"Stop him!" Earl yelled.

A gun roared and Adam waited for the bullet to strike him. But it never came. Instead, he heard Earl shout. "Charlie!"

Adam flicked a quick look behind him. Earl was kneeling over a man who lay crumpled on the ground. *Charlie?*

His question was answered when Earl jerked to his feet. "Damn you, Hollister!" he shouted. "You caused me to kill Charlie."

Adam stopped where he was. The time had come for a showdown between himself and Earl. Adam watched Earl stand up. "Now it's just you and me," Adam called. "Just you and me, Earl."

"I can take you any day," Earl said harshly. "I don't need Charlie's help to kill you."

Adam waited until Earl holstered his gun, then Adam did the same.

"On the count of three," Earl said. "One . . ."

The trail whistle sounded and Adam flicked his

gaze toward the caboose. He sucked in a sharp breath. The caboose was moving backwards . . . and Earl stood in its path.

"Earl!" he called. "Watch out for the train!"

"Two . . ." Earl counted, adding in a sneering voice, "Tryin' to back out on me?"

"The train's going backwards," Adam warned.

But Earl paid no attention. His body was tensed, his gunhand hovering above his pistol. "I'm gonna kill you, Hollister," he said. "Nothin' you say is gonna save you." Suddenly he frowned as though becoming aware all was not as it should be.

Adam remained unmoving. Earl's head turned . . . his gaze fastened on the train. Crying out, he stepped forward . . . his boot caught on the rail and he fell.

Realizing he couldn't be cold-blooded enough to watch the train run over Earl, Adam started toward the fallen man. But Adam knew he'd never reach Earl in time for the caboose had picked up speed.

Earl screamed.

Danny's head jerked around as she heard the key in the lock.

Adam! Adam was at the door! He'd finally come back!

She hurried across the room, intent on opening the door when a thought stopped her.

Suppose it wasn't Adam!

The memory of the night in Lizard Lick surfaced in her mind and her heart began to beat with dread as she tiptoed across the room and pressed her ear against the door.

"Who's there?" she demanded harshly.

"It's me." Adam's voice came faintly through the thickness of the door.

Relief swept through her as the knob turned and the door opened, allowing light from the hallway to stream around the figure of a man. "I was trying not to wake you," Adam said.

Relief washed over Danny as she peered through the darkness. Adam closed the door, shutting them away from prying eyes.

"How come you was gone so long?" she asked, crossing the room to the bed. Now that he was back, she could get some rest.

Pulling back the covers, she crawled onto the bed, intent on getting some sleep. Then, she stilled, aware of his silence. "Adam? Why'd it take so long?"

"Decided to take a walk," he said gruffly.

Her eyes narrowed. There was something about his voice, a peculiar breathlessness that alerted her there was something wrong.

"Did somethin' happen while you was gone?" she asked, sliding from the bed and approaching him.

He didn't answer. Instead, he backed away from her. But, in doing so, he moved closer to the window. Moonlight fell across his face, and she sucked in a sharp breath. One side of his face had a dark, purple-colored bruise.

"You been in a fight?" she asked, unable to keep from touching the bruise, meaning only to comfort the hurt flesh. But her fingers had no more than

161

touched him when Adam jerked away as though she had struck him. "Adam?" She stared at the sticky wetness on her fingers, smelled the coppery scent of it. "Adam? Is this blood? Are you bleeding?"

"It's just a little scratch," he muttered. "Nothing to worry about."

"They's somethin' you ain't telling me, Adam."

He sighed heavily. "I'm dog-tired, Danny. I don't want to talk about it. Not right now."

She swallowed thickly, feeling curiously hurt that he wouldn't confide in her. "Will you let me clean the wound?" she asked.

"I guess you'd better."

Adam removed his bloodstained shirt and straddled the chair beside the washstand while Danny lit the kerosene lamp and placed it on the bureau nearby. When she bent to examine the wound, she sucked in a sharp breath. It looked as though a bullet had furrowed his cheek. A few more inches to the right and he wouldn't have returned.

With shaking fingers, she cleansed the wound, then washed the blood from his shirt. Although she appeared calm, inside she was a quivering mass of nerves. He could so easily have been killed, and she'd never have known it until she woke in the morning and found him missing.

Unbidden tears welled up and she turned away from him, blinking rapidly, willing them not to fall. But they overflowed and trickled down her cheeks.

"Danny?" The voice was ever so gentle. "You aren't crying, are you?"

"No!"

He captured her chin in one hand, brushing the

162

other across her cheek. "Then what is this?"

She looked at the wetness on his fingertips, swallowed hard and backed away. Instantly, he was on his feet, gripping her shoulders, pulling her into his embrace.

"Don't cry," he said gently, smoothing his hand across her tousled hair. "You don't need to be frightened. It's all over now."

She began to sob and he groaned, tightening his embrace. "Danny. Stop it." His voice sounded shaky.

"I'll c-cry if I w-want to," she stammered.

"Why do you want to?"

"B-because you might have been killed." She burrowed her head against his chest and clutched tightly at him.

He threaded his fingers through her hair and cupped her neck. "I wasn't killed," he said. "Now stop it."

Slowly her sobs died away, but she stayed where she was, with her body pressed hard against him, wanting to feel the warmness of him, proof that he was still breathing. Suddenly, a tingle began deep inside her, turning into an incredible heat that became even hotter, spreading outward until she felt every inch of her was burning up.

She lifted her face to his, wondering if he felt it too. His eyes were dark, unreadable, but his lower body was hardening against hers, making her ache in a curious manner.

Adam, she silently cried. What are you doing to me?

As though he sensed her feelings, his breathing quickened and he pushed roughly at her shoulders,

163

trying to put her from him.

But even though his actions denied it, Danny knew he was affected by her nearness, also knew that she must make him admit to it while he was vulnerable. With her arms clinging tightly around his waist and still holding his gaze, Danny placed a soft kiss on his neck.

"Stop that," he growled, his smooth muscled chest rising and falling with his quickened breathing. Tightening his grip on her shoulders, he made a half-hearted attempt to peel her away from him.

"Why?" she asked, throwing him an innocent look before stringing kisses across his bare chest.

"Danny," he choked. "You don't know what you're doing."

"I know," she said, looking up at him with misty eyes. "I know, outlander. I'm a doin' it on purpose. Don't you like it?"

"That doesn't matter. You're an innocent. Not for the likes of me."

"I don't want to be innocent," she said. "I'm a woman, an' it's past time you treated me like one. I want you to teach me the way it is betwixt a woman and her man."

"One day you'll know," he said. "When the time is right, some man will—"

"I don't want just any man to teach me," she said, tracing his ear with the tip of her tongue. "It's you I need outlander. Nobody but you."

"God, Danny!" He gave a shudder. "You don't know what you're doing to me."

She laughed huskily and flicked her tongue out again. At the same time she pressed her lower body against the swelling in his breeches. "I told you, outlander, I'm a doin' it on purpose."

With a strangled cry, he lifted her in his arms and carried her to the bed. His movements were jerky as he stripped the nightgown from her slender body. Fumbling with the fastenings on his breeches, he slid them down his hips and kicked them aside.

When he covered her body with his own, she knew she had found her destiny. No matter what came in the future, even if he left her when their mission was over, there would never be another man for her.

Chapter Fifteen

Danny woke before dawn and turned to stare up at the man who slept beside her. She felt incredibly fit, but he slept like one who had exhausted every last ounce of energy he possessed.

A smile twitched at her lips. Perhaps he had used up all his strength. He had been insatiable, waking her several times with his caresses, bringing her to heights of pleasure she had never before even dreamed about.

Her love-filled eyes found the ragged furrow the bullet had made across his cheek and she silently thanked God for sparing him.

It pained her to think how close she had come to losing him! Just the thought sent an icy chill creeping down her spine.

Suddenly, a train whistle intruded on her thoughts, reminding her of the journey ahead of them. But Danny was reluctant to wake Adam. Perhaps it wouldn't hurt to let him sleep just a little bit longer.

Then, her rumbling stomach reminded her that she hadn't eaten the night before, and that she was incredibly hungry now. She slid from the bed. Hadn't the hotel clerk said there was a restaurant downstairs?

Danny donned fresh clothing, then slipped from the room. A cup of hot coffee ought to wake Adam beautifully.

Although the hour was early, the restaurant was already crowded and it took longer than she had intended. When she pushed open the door to their room, Adam had dressed and was fastening the buttons on his shirt.

His movements stilled. "Where have you been?" he demanded harshly.

"Downstairs fetching breakfast." She kicked the door shut behind her. "What're you so steamed up about?"

"You should have let me know you were leaving," he said tightly. His eyes seemed almost accusing as they held hers for a long moment.

Danny frowned. What was wrong with him? He seemed so angry. Whatever she had expected from him this morning, it certainly hadn't been anger. Last night he had been so different, so loving, so passionate. Now she felt as though he had deliberately erected an invisible wall between them.

Remembering her boldness of the night before, she felt a blush staining her cheeks. Was he regretting what had happened between them? Was he telling her it would never happen again?

Well, he needn't! The whole thing had obviously

167

been a mistake. She had thought he was attracted to her, thought he might even love her a little. But it seemed she had been wrong.

Determined to keep him from knowing how badly she was hurting, she cleared her throat and spoke in a carefully controlled voice. "I brung us some coffee and donuts. Knew you was tired after the trouble you had with Earl and Charlie." *And the lovemaking afterwards,* she silently added. "Thought I'd save us some time this way."

Adam walked jerkily to the window, looking down on the street. "Danny." His voice sounded strange with his back turned to her. "About what happened last night . . ."

"Last night?" She interrupted quickly. "You mean when you showed me what happens betwixt a man and a woman? Well, I thankee kindly for the lesson, outlander. It was greatly appreciated. At least now I know what goes on. And I know they ain't really all that much to whoop and holler about. Guess if I never do it again, it won't bother me none."

Adam swung around to face her, his brows drawn together in a frown. "Why?" He was obviously piqued by her words. "Don't pretend you didn't enjoy it, Danny. I know better."

"Guess it was okay." She sent him a tight little smile. "Not that I'd be wantin' to do it very much. But I suppose if I was to get hitched up with a man, then I wouldn't have no trouble doin' my duty by him."

"Doing your duty?" His mouth tightened into a

thin line and he glared at her with fury-darkened eyes.

"Come drink your coffee, outlander," she said. "We got us a train to catch." She poured the cups full of the steaming liquid, then selected one of the hot donuts for herself, convinced she had managed to salvage her pride.

But the donut that had seemed so mouthwatering at the restaurant tasted like sawdust when she bit into it. And when she tried to swallow, she had to force the food past the lump that swelled her throat.

When Adam moved suddenly, Danny's breath quickened, her fingers trembled and she spilled coffee into her saucer. Even so, she forced herself to appear calm, at least on the surface. She continued to sip at the hot brew as though she hadn't a care in the world while her heart cried silently at the loss of her barely-formed love.

After the train left St. Louis, Danny and Adam traveled in silence, each alone with their own thoughts. Danny's shoulders felt weighted by a deep and abiding hurt at Adam's rejection, and her stomach felt as though her innards were twisted into knots.

But Danny wasn't one to bemoan her fate, and as the day wore on, she closed the door against what had gone before and turned her thoughts toward the future. She was going places she'd never been before, seeing sights that she might never see again. She had questions about the countryside they were traveling through and there was no one to answer them except Adam.

At first, his answers were stiff, almost resentful, but finally, he loosened up and began to point out places of interest to her.

Two days later they reached their destination.

Pittsburgh was not the least bit as Danny had expected. It was located in a narrow valley where the Allegheny and the Monongahela rivers joined and the Ohio began. It was surrounded by hills rising to the height of four or five hundred feet. Although once picturesque, these mountains had been uselessly mutilated by man's eternal search for coal.

Danny had the window seat. As the train neared the city, she could see great buildings outlining the landscape. Their tall chimneys spewing forth columns of inky blackness that rolled and whirled in fantastic shapes until it finally merged with the general murkiness above.

"What are them buildings?" she asked, turning to Adam. "The ones that's puttin' out all that god-awful smoke?"

"Those are factories," he replied. "They manufacture steel."

"Ain't so sure I'm gonna like the city none," she said. "The air seems a mite dirty here. Can't be too healthy for a body to breathe. Beats me why somebody like Angellee, born and bred in the mountain air, would want to live here."

Her gaze was suddenly caught by the mountain-side they were passing and the railroad tracks that gridironed the ground everywhere. The smoke-blackened mountains were bare of vegetation, nothing but yellow mud and piles of black coal. There were piles of debris scattered all around and it seemed every available spot was taken up by huts and hovels.

"This place is ugly," she said, turning to Adam again. "What's all them little bitty railroad cars goin' into that hole in the mountain for?"

"The cars carry the coal out," Adam explained, then directed her attention out the window again. "We're going to cross over the Monongahela now. Look at all the barges and tugboats on the water. Those barges are from the south, and over there on the Allegheny, those barges are carrying freights of crude petroleum."

Although Danny found it all interesting, she knew nothing in the world could have induced her to live in such a place. It was crude and ugly, with its dirt and soot. A woman would have to constantly struggle to keep things clean.

"It ain't nothin' at all like the Ozarks," she said. "An' it beats me why Angellee would ever want to live in a place like this."

"From what Buck told me, your cousin would've gone anywhere her man wanted to live," Adam said, breaking his silence. "Which is the way things were meant to be."

I'd go anywhere you wanted me to, Adam.

But Danny didn't utter the words aloud. She couldn't. Michelle had told her a lady kept her feelings to herself and used other ways to tell a man his attentions were welcome.

Perhaps that was why Adam had been so angry with her. It was a fact that her boldness instigated their lovemaking. Hurt swelled her breast and she

171

forced her thoughts away from that night, turning them instead to her cousin, where they belonged. Was it possible Angellee had already been found? she wondered. *God! Let it be so!*

The screech of metal against metal told her the brakes were being applied. She looked out the window, saw they were pulling into the station and gave a sigh of relief.

The change of air as they descended from the cars was delicious, even though it was the rank, smoky air of the terminal.

Adam ordered her to stay close by him and led the way. An inquiry at the nearest counter proved more then helpful.

"If you're looking for Jake Logan, there's no need to hire a carriage," said the man behind the counter. "That's Logan over there." He gestured toward two well-dressed gentlemen on the other side of the station.

One was tall, dark-haired and well-built, the other slender, blond and elegant. They appeared to be deep in conversation.

"Logan's the dark-haired gent," the clerk advised.

But he needn't have, because suddenly Danny knew . . . and a peculiar thing was happening. Danny felt a chill; goosebumps broke out on her arms. Her heart hammered and there was a roaring in her ears.

While she wondered what was happening, her surroundings began to fade as though they were not real, but merely fragments of a dream that were slowly dissolving. Danny's knees felt like rubber, threatening to fold beneath her as she saw a misty fog slowly rising from the floor. She didn't feel the least surprised when she saw the figure of a woman forming in the mist.

Angellee?

While Danny tried to gather her courage around her, the phantom figure floated toward Danny, her arms outstretched.

God! It *was* Angellee. It *was* her!

Danny flicked a quick look at Adam, but he seemed not to notice anything out of the ordinary. "Are you tryin' to tell me somethin'?" Danny muttered.

"What did you say, Danny?" Adam's voice seemed to come from a great distance . . . from the far end of a tunnel. Danny spared one quick look at his puzzled face, then turned her eyes toward the phantom again. But she was no longer there.

Angellee had simply disappeared . . . quickly as though she'd never been there. And just as suddenly, Danny was tumbled back to reality.

"Are you all right?" Adam asked, studying her pale face.

Finding herself unable to speak, Danny simply nodded her head. After all, what could she say? How could she tell Adam what she'd seen, when she didn't really know herself?

Although Adam studied her a moment longer, he seemed satisfied with her answer.

"I suppose Buck wired Logan we were coming," Adam mused as he and Danny weaved their way across the station to the pair the clerk had indicated.

But the look Logan turned on them when they arrived held no measure of recognition. Instead Logan seemed to register annoyance at their interruption, Danny would be willing to bet.

Adam ignored Logan's annoyance—did he even recognize it, Danny wondered.

"Jake Logan?" he said. "I'm Adam Hollister. I'm glad to find you here. Did Buck wire you that we were coming?"

Now Logan appeared confused. "Buck? I'm afraid I don't know anyone called . . . Do you mean Buck Winters?" At Adam's nod, he added, "No, I didn't hear from him. Did Buck send you?"

"He did," Adam acknowledged. "He hoped Danny might help in your search." His hand on Danny's elbow urged her forward, "This is Danielle Tucker, your wife's cousin."

Logan's face lit up, but before he could respond, his companion said, "Jake, I'm afraid I have to take my leave now. My train should be departing momentarily."

With a staying hand on Danny's wrist and a small squeeze of acknowledgement, Logan turned to the blond man. "Of course, Mark." Then he released Danny to shake his friend's hand. "Have a good trip."

"And you, Jake, keep your chin up. And I pray to God that Angel will be home soon."

"As I do," Logan muttered as Mark left. "Now." He turned the full force of his attention on Danny. "God bless you for coming Danny. I've been in such a strain since Angel disappeared I haven't even thought of notifying any of her relatives back in the Ozarks. She would have been glad to see you. She kept talking about having you here." Then to Adam, he said, "I did receive a wire from Robert Shaw saying Buck was helping search for Angel. Has he

174

found anything? Any clues?"

Adam shook his head. "I suppose that means you still haven't heard from her," he said.

Jake shook his head sadly. "It's as though she dropped off the face of the earth."

Jake's shoulders were bowed as though he carried an incredible weight on them. He gave a long sigh. "Pardon me for keeping you standing here like this. I know you must be exhausted from the long trip. I have a carriage waiting outside. It won't take us long to get home."

As he'd said, it didn't take long. As the Hansom cab made its way down the street, Danny was haunted by the idea that a terrific thunderstorm hung over the place. In the sky an ominous darkness lingered, the kind that usually meant a storm was approaching and every street seemed to end in a huge black cloud. Jake explained that it was only the smoke hanging low over the blackened hills that surrounded them.

Soon, the carriage pulled up beside the wrought-iron gatepost of a large brick house. While Jake paid the cabby, Adam unloaded the bags. Danny looked up the gravel path to the wide front steps of the house. Obviously her cousin had married a very wealthy man.

Danny saw an overalled gardener raking freshly mowed grass. The wizened man bent over, picked up a bunch of clippings and piled them into a wheelbarrow. Then he seemed to realize she was watching. He tipped his hat and nodded deferentially toward her.

With a dip of her head, she acknowledged him. Then she took in the rest of her surroundings; the large oak and elm trees that shaded the wide grounds. Danny felt amazed at the immaculate neatness of their store-bought freshness. The square flower beds boasted an abundance of stiff cannas, lilies and red sage.

Jake pushed open the gate and led the way up the gravel path past an ornamental urn on a filigree pedestal filled with striped and mottled leaves of trailing English ivy.

They climbed the wide front steps, then Jake opened the door and motioned Danny to enter. In the foyer, she had an overwhelming sense of Angellee's presence. Before she could examine the feeling properly, a stout little woman with her hair skewered on top of her head hurried toward them. She wore a large checked apron and a striped pink calico dress the same color of her cheeks.

"Who be you bringin' home with you, Jake?" she asked, putting her reddened hands on her heavy hips and eyeing Danny sternly.

Jake introduced Adam and explained how they'd met at the train station. Then, putting his hands on Danny's shoulders, he pushed her forward slightly. "Adam was kind enough to escort this young lady here. Her name is Danielle Tucker. And she's Angellee's cousin."

The woman took her time studying Danny, then gave a quick nod of her head. "She looks somewhat like Miz Angel," she said. "'Tis sad, it is, that the missus is not here to meet you. She'd be happy to see you."

"Would you put fresh linens in the guest rooms, Mrs. Gruber?" Jake requested. "They'll both be staying here with us."

Adam protested immediately. "Don't bother on my account," he said. "I've only brought Danny here. As soon as we've talked, I'll find a hotel for the night."

"Don't be daft," Mrs. Gruber said, holding up a staying hand. "Wouldn't be right was you to stay elsewhere. Not when we got plenty of room in this big house."

"I think tea would be in order right now, Mrs. Gruber," Jake said. "I know they must be hungry after the trip."

But food was the last thing Danny wanted. She felt bombarded by memories of Angellee's presence in the house. Was it just because she had lived here? She didn't know, but she wanted time alone, time to think about it. "I ain't wantin' nothin' to eat," she said. "But I thankee kindly for the offer."

"Then I'll be after showing you to a room," the woman said kindly. "You must have come a far piece."

"Yes," Danny admitted. "But I don't mind helpin' you fix the menfolks somethin' to eat first."

"That's nice of you, lovey," the woman said, leading the way through the stone passage into the kitchen. Danny studied the room curiously, her gaze resting on a towering copper boiler glowing red. She wondered at its purpose, but before she could ask, the housekeeper lifted a short piece of hose from the wall, and to Danny's astonishment, shouted into it.

"Bridget!" she cried. "Bridget, come down here!"

Danny heard a rattle in the hose, coming from far away, then the housekeeper turned to her. "Bridget

177

will show you upstairs."

Bridget proved to be a pleasant faced Irish girl dressed in a striped uniform of blue and white calico with a big starched collar, a white apron and a ruffled cap that did little to conceal the crisp, curly red hair that sprang strongly from her white forehead.

After she'd been introduced, Bridget bobbed a curtsy and smiled at Danny. "'Tis sorry I am the mistress ain't here to greet you her ownself," she said. "But never you mind, Miss. Mister Jake will be after finding her soon. And when he does, she'll be happy to see you."

Finding herself unable to reply, Danny merely nodded her head. She followed the girl up the stairs and along a hallway.

Suddenly, Danny heard a familiar laugh. She stopped and looked at the closed door.

Angellee?

Twisting the door knob, Danny pushed the door open and stepped inside. Her gaze traveled over the sheet-shrouded room, obviously unused . . . stopped on a shadowy figure sitting near the dressing table with a hairbrush in her hand.

Then, a gasp escaped from her lips. Just as suddenly as the figure appeared, it was gone. But not before she had recognized the woman. It had been Angellee. Or the memory of Angellee?

"This was the mistress's room," Bridget said from beside her. "The master had it closed up when she disappeared. He couldn't bear to come in here, wondering if she'd ever return."

Danny backed out of the room and closed the door. What was happening to her? she wondered. But she could find no answer.

She followed Bridget along the corridor to the big squared room she'd been allotted.

There were four windows on two sides of the room, each one boasting freshly starched curtains. A flowered carpet covered the floor, and paper with bunches of pale roses and pink lilacs covered the walls. The woodwork had a light varnish, easy to keep clean; and the furniture was ample—a large mahogany bureau, a wardrobe, a center table with a coal-oil lamp on it and a chair on either side. A four-poster bed was located on one side of the room, near a washstand fitted with a white china bowl and ewer. Danny had never had so much space and privacy before.

"Should I unpack for you, Miss?" Bridget asked.

Danny's gaze fell on her valise. She shook her head. "I ain't got much to unpack," she said.

"Then I'll be after leaving you, but if you be needing anything, Miss, you just let me know," Bridget said. "There's a bell cord by the window. If you'll pull it, a bell will ring in the servants' quarters." Curtsying lightly, she left Danny alone with her thoughts.

Adam followed his host into a large, airy room that seemed to be designed solely for comfort with overstuffed leather furniture. A deep piled Turkish carpet covered the floor. Bookshelves filled with books lined three walls from floor to ceiling.

At Jake's bidding, Adam sank down on the nearest chair. He was worried about Danny. Something was

179

wrong with her. Something he couldn't put his finger on. He felt anxious to be alone with her, to find out what was happening.

But he must wait.

He listened quietly while Jake told him all he knew about his wife's disappearance, finishing with, "I don't quite understand why Buck thought you could be of help, but I certainly do appreciate your concern. At this stage, I'm ready to grasp at straws. I've hired the Pinkerton Agency to look for her, but so far, they haven't come up with much. We do know that she never reached Missouri." He raked a hand through his dark hair. "God! I don't know what to do, but I have to do something soon. I feel as though time is running out. The baby will be born soon."

Adam frowned. "Baby?" This was a new development.

"Angel is expecting my child."

"Damn!" Adam muttered. "That is bad news. How long has she got before the baby is due?"

"I'm not sure," Jake said in a ragged voice. "I think a couple of months. I didn't want her to go out west, but she insisted. She said she wanted to visit with Heather while she could still travel. But I couldn't leave yet. I had to stay here for Mosley's trial. God! Why didn't I make her wait for me?"

"If she's anything at all like Danny, you'd probably have a hard time making her do anything she didn't want to," Adam replied. "Danny's the most hard-headed woman I've ever met."

"You haven't met Angellee. She can bend with the wind, unless she gets her dander up. Or if she thinks someone is being mistreated. Then she comes on like

180

a thunderstorm. That's what this whole thing is about. When she found out the miners were working under such unsafe conditions, she started asking questions. We uncovered things that the mine owners didn't want uncovered." His hands tightened into fists. "Dammit! I can't stand much more of this . . . the not knowing what happened to her . . . the knowing that Mosley knows where she is. And the realization that the whole thing is my fault. If I hadn't brought charges against Mosley, then Angellee would be safe at home."

"You're being too hard on yourself," Adam said.

"No. It's my fault, all right. It wasn't long after I brought charges of deadly harassment against Mosley's mining company that Angellee disappeared. He's the one responsible for taking her off the train, and he knows where she is. He's keeping her somewhere, trying to force me into dropping the charges."

"He's made demands?" Adam asked.

"Not demands that I could use against him. But I received an anonymous letter stating if I tried to find Angel she would be killed. That's the reason I can't leave the state. Also the reason the detective agency is having such a hard time conducting a search. They have to remain undercover while they are conducting the investigation."

"If Mosley is the one that took her, why doesn't he make demands?"

"The way I see it, he's waiting for me to drop the charges against him." Jake looked agonized. "But how can I do that? Lives have been threatened and I have a duty to the people of the state. And Angel wouldn't want me to give in to him." He pounded the chair arm with his fist. "I feel so helpless. So inadequate."

"We'll help in every way we can," Adam said.

"I hope Danny doesn't have to go back before my wife is found," Jake said. "It would mean so much to Angellee to come home and find her here."

"Danny has no reason to go back to the Ozark mountains," Adam said.

Then he told Jake about the telegram.

Chapter Sixteen

Sweat trickled down the back of Danny's neck as she flung back the covers and slid to the floor. She knew the hour was around midnight, but she'd been wakened again by the cry that seemed to have become her nightly companion.

After crossing to the window, she pulled aside the curtains and stared out into the night.

When the phantom voice came again, there was something different about it. . . .

Although it was still beyond Danny's understanding, she was no longer afraid of it.

"Angel?" she whispered. "Is it you that's hauntin' my dreams? Are you tryin' to tell me where you are? If it is, you gotta try harder."

God! Where was she?

Danny.

Danny spun around, looking for the source of the voice that had seemed to come from all around her. But, as she'd suspected, the room was empty. Had the voice been imagined? How could it have been otherwise, when she was alone?

Uttering a long sigh, Danny crossed to the window and peered into the darkness outside. The city below her gleamed with a thousand points of light that were reflected off the river. She didn't know which river. There were too blasted many around here anyway.

By day, the view had been different, cluttered and ugly with the eternal pall of smoke, the great black cloud that Jake had said always hung over the city. Now it was almost pretty.

But not pretty enough to turn Danny's mind from all she'd been hit with today. Now her nightmares were ever with her, the phantom voice constantly tormenting her. She tried hard to fathom what she'd heard, as she awakened, but it eluded her.

The phantom voice was only a memory when Danny woke the next morning. Since the only dresses she possessed—the one Adam had bought her and her Sunday-go-to-meetin' dress—were soiled, she donned breeches and shirt and was combing her hair when a knock sounded on her door. At her call, Bridget entered.

The girl took in Danny's attire, then exclaimed. "You'll not be wearing that, will you, Miss?"

Danny frowned down at her clothing, then met Bridget's concerned gaze. "They ain't nothing showin' that shouldn't be," she said.

"But, Miss. It's not proper for a lady to wear gentlemen's clothing."

Danny laughed. "Then I guess I ain't a proper lady, 'cause I sure been awearin' pants for a long

184

time. Besides, I ain't got no other clean clothes."

"Oh, Miss, I'm sorry. I had no idea your clothes needed laundering," the girl said. "Please let me take care of them for you."

"Only got two dresses," Danny admitted. "An' Adam bought me one of 'em. The other was give to me by a lady I met back in Texas. Wasn't much occasion to wear dresses up on Tucker's Ridge."

"That's quite all right, Miss," the girl said briskly. "Miz Angel has many elegant gowns. I'm sure Mr. Jake would want you to have the use of them until Miz Angel returns."

"You sure he won't mind?"

"Of course. In fact, Miz Angel has so many gowns, Mr. Jake probably won't even recognize them. Not that he'd begrudge you if he did."

"I don't mind wearin' my own clothes," Danny said doubtfully. "But I wouldn't want Angel's husband to be ashamed of me, either."

"Pshaw! Master Jake would never be ashamed of you! But he wouldn't want the ladies of Pittsburgh snubbing you either."

Danny was amazed by the array of gowns in Angellee's closet. How could her cousin possibly wear them all? After selecting one of the plainest, she allowed Bridget to help her dress. She was certain she could never manage all the tiny buttons that fastened down the back. Then, very properly clothed, she went downstairs to join the others for breakfast.

Later, she approached Adam about her desire to see more of Pittsburgh.

"You can't go out alone," he said.

185

"I ain't never needed nobody to take me no-wheres," Danny said, her brows drawing into a scowl.

"You're not in the mountains now, Danny," Adam said. "You'll find things are different in the city. A woman alone in the streets of Pittsburgh is an open invitation."

"We're not really so uncivilized here," Jake protested. "The suffragettes have a lot of support in Pittsburgh. Before Angel was abducted she often went about alone."

"And now she's missing," Adam reminded them grimly.

Jake looked sharply at him. "You aren't suggesting she was abducted here? That's impossible. I went to the train station with her. I saw her seated and I even gave the conductor her ticket."

"Then, by your own account, you got off the train and left her."

"Yes . . ." Jake put down his fork and stared hard at Adam. "I did get off the train. I had an appointment with . . ." His voice trailed off, his eyes widened with comprehension.

"Asa Mosley." Adam supplied the name. "An appointment made at that time, because he had no other time available. Which means he knew when your wife would be most vulnerable."

The two men exchanged long looks and fell quiet.

Realizing she was not going to get any more information about their suspicions, Danny persisted in her original argument. "I ain't gonna stay in the house all the time I'm here, Adam. If they's a chance my cousin was stole away from this town, then it

186

makes more sense for me to search the streets. Maybe I can feel somethin' out there. Somethin' that might help us."

"Feel something?" Jake looked puzzled.

Danny looked down at her plate, wishing the words had remained unsaid. Her careless tongue could easily lead her astray.

Before arriving in Pittsburgh, Danny and Adam had agreed that it would be best if Jake wasn't told about the voices she'd been hearing. After all, she wasn't sure what they meant herself. She had no proof her cousin was trying to contact her. The whole thing could be her imagination working over time.

"Your appointment with the detective agency is at three o'clock, isn't it, Jake?" Adam asked, diverting Jake's attention from Danny's slip of the tongue.

Jake nodded his head.

"Then I guess there will be time for me to show Danny around. We passed a park this morning. It was only a few blocks away." He turned his attention to Danny. "How about it?" he asked with a forced cheerfulness. "Would you like to go through the park, Danny?"

Although Danny felt as though she were a dog being thrown a bone, she agreed. At least it would give her the opportunity to talk to Adam alone. She didn't want to start an argument in front of Jake. But she refused to allow Adam to treat her like a child.

Besides, her trip to Pittsburgh would be useless if she were not permitted to aid in the search for her cousin.

She told Adam so an hour later while they were

187

strolling together down the graveled walkway circling the park.

"Getting yourself abducted wouldn't help your cousin," Adam said. "Jake has enough on his plate without that too."

His words stopped her cold. She turned to glare at him. "Can't you get it through your thick head that I can take care of myself?"

"You're attracting attention," he growled, taking her arm and pulling her along with him. "As for taking care of yourself . . . well, you didn't put up much of a fight at Tucker's Ridge when I dragged you out of that field."

She stopped again, yanking her arm free. "That ain't so! I reckon I put up a good fight! It was just— just—"

He chuckled. "That I was able to best you without too much trouble," he finished for her.

She scowled fiercely at him. "I just wasn't expectin' no stranger to come up an' haul me off like that!" she said through gritted teeth. "You didn't give me fair warnin', outlander."

"Do you think the crooks here will give you fair warning? If you do, then you're certainly an innocent."

"I ain't innocent," she mumbled. "Not no more." She threw him a swift glance, but he appeared not to notice her words.

"Come along and stop being so argumentative," he said, wrapping his fingers around her wrist and tugging her along with him. "Just keep quiet and see if you can enjoy all this fresh air."

Despite her best efforts to control it, a smile tugged

at her lips. The fresh air he spoke of was hot and heavy, quite unlike the sweet smelling air to be found in the Ozark mountains. Even so, she found herself enjoying the walk through the colorful array of flowers that seemed to bloom everywhere. The multitude of flowerbeds were filled with bright red and orange and magenta blooms.

Danny's anger fled as quickly as it had appeared and she took pleasure from the peaceful surroundings; and in just being with Adam, knowing their time together would soon come to an end.

A burst of high-pitched laughter sounded in the distance and Danny realized they were nearing the children's playground.

When Danny stopped to enjoy a flowerbed filled with daisies, a woman passed them pushing a baby carriage while a toddler dawdled along behind. Stopping beside Danny, the boy plucked one of the daisies.

"Don't pick the flowers, Thomas," the woman said sternly. "Hurry along now and don't fall behind me."

The child, perhaps three years old, smiled a wide-eyed smile and hurried to reach the buggy. He shoved the yellow daisy into the buggy and a moment later a wail filled the air around them.

"No, no! Thomas!" his mother cried. "Baby Amos doesn't want to smell the flower. Take the pretty daisy out of the baby's buggy."

Although Danny was vaguely aware that Adam was speaking to her, she paid no attention to his words. At the first sound from the baby carriage, her head had jerked up and fear, dark and terrible, sent

189

icy fingers trailing over her flesh.

All this from a baby's wail? But why? she wondered. She'd heard infants cry before . . . many times over. Yet, this time, there was something different about it . . . this time it tugged a response so elusive that she couldn't quite put a name to it.

"Danny?" Adam's voice was accompanied by a hard shake. She looked up and found him studying her intently. "Is something wrong, Danny? You look funny."

She shook her head. "Guess I'm just tired," she said, wiping the perspiration away from her forehead. "Could we go back to the house now?"

"If you'd like," he said, frowning heavily at her. "But I thought you were anxious to get some fresh air."

She knew he was puzzled, but she couldn't explain her feelings. What she needed was time alone, time to think, to work out her dilemma without interruption.

Chapter Seventeen

Adam followed Jake into the large, brownstone building that housed several offices. They went up the stairs to the third floor and stopped outside a door marked Smith Import Export. At Adam's look of inquiry, Jake explained, "Since we're certain I'm being watched, the agency suggested we meet at different places each time. And the operative is always a different man. One of Pinkerton's undercover agents." He knocked at the door and a muffled voice bid them enter.

The Pinkerton man, John Brown, proved to be as colorless as his name. He was a pale-faced individual, anemic-looking, and Adam guessed he spent most of his time in the drab surroundings of his office.

The man had no new leads, merely explained what the agency had accomplished . . . or rather, not accomplished in the last few days.

"We've had a man watching Asa Mosley ever since you contacted us," the little man said, tugging at his vest as though he found it uncomfortable. "So far Mosley's done nothing to cause suspicion."

Jake clenched his fingers. "I know damn well he's responsible. You people have the letter that came the day my wife disappeared."

"We have the letter," the Pinkerton man said. "But we learned nothing from it. Our handwriting expert insists Mosley didn't write the letter." His voice sounded almost defensive.

"That proves nothing," Jake said. "Mosley has plenty of hirelings to do his bidding."

"Do you have the letter with you?" Adam asked.

Brown flicked a glance at Jake, waited for his approval before opening the file in front of him. Brown extracted a paper and handed it to Adam.

The handwriting was dark and slashing, the words dug so harshly into the paper that at times Adam could see the light of the room shine through. It read, "We have your wife. Unless you want her back in bloody chunks, drop the charges against the mining company."

Although Adam studied the note, there was nothing to be learned from it. A tapping noise jerked his eyes around. Brown was nervously tapping the end of a pencil against his desk.

"As you see," Brown said. "There's nothing in the letter to give us the slightest clue to the writer."

"They don't name the mining company," Adam remarked.

"They didn't have to," Jake growled. "I only had charges pending against one: Monongahela Amalgamated." He glared at the Pinkerton man. "Will you stop that damn tapping?"

John Brown dropped the pencil as though it were a live coal. He cleared his throat and said, "I'm not saying Mosley's not involved. Just that he's done nothing suspicious since we've been watching him. He's been in contact with no one that could give us the slightest lead on your wife's whereabouts."

Jake slammed his fist into his palm and the resulting sound made Brown flinch. "Dammit! We've got to find her. We've just got to." He walked to the window and stared outside, the picture of a man in torment.

Brown fidgeted at his desk. "You can't blame our agency," he said. "We're doing everything humanly possible to find her. The abduction was obviously carried out by professionals. This doesn't appear to be the work of unskilled thugs."

"Such men would demand plenty for the job," Adam speculated. "Only a wealthy man could afford their services."

"Asa Mosley has plenty of money at his disposal," Jake said grimly, swinging around to face them. "But there's no way to prove he had anything to do with Angel's disappearance. And having him followed hasn't accomplished a damn thing."

"Well," John Brown said. "Your assumptions are purely circumstantial. No lawman would even consider pressing charges based on your allegations."

"Dammit!" Jake said. "Don't you think I know that? That's why I came to your agency instead of going to the police. That, and the fact that I'm afraid to because of the threat implied by the message. But I know with a certainty that Mosley has Angellee. I've had this feeling inside—everytime I come in contact with him—that he's recently been near my wife."

"Perhaps you'd do better to do as he asked . . . to drop the charges against the mining company," Brown said.

Jake glared at Brown, and the man looked as though he wished he hadn't spoken. "That is not an option," Jake replied. "I have a moral duty to the people of this state to carry through. That company has been responsible for the loss of too many lives. It's time they answered for it."

"What about your wife?" Adam asked.

"She wouldn't want me to give in to Mosley," Jake said, clenching his hands into fists. "She urged me to bring the charges against the mining company in the first place." He swallowed hard. "I'd do anything on earth to get her back, but Angel would never forgive me if I dropped the charges. She was personally acquainted with families of the dead miners . . . men who lost their lives in cave-ins that could have been prevented had safety measures been taken. Angellee worked hard to get evidence against the mining company. Too hard for it all to have been for nothing." He raked a hand through his dark hair and when he spoke again, his voice broke slightly. "But I must find her soon. If she hasn't already miscarried, she and our unborn child are in grave danger."

Danny stood at her bedroom window staring out over the garden below. In spite of the soot from the mills down by the river, the wide lawns were green and beautiful from constant watering and mowing. On the highest part of the Logan land, before it sloped away to the river precipice, the octagonal summerhouse with its cupola and ornamental iron screening was a charming spot. Clematis, trumpet vine, and Virginia creeper were trained to form a thick curtain about it. Inside were rustic chairs and settees and a bark-covered table. Jake had told them it was Angellee's favorite spot and she often served tea there.

"Company's come, Miss Tucker," the housekeeper said from the doorway. As though recognizing her confusion, the housekeeper explained. "Since the master's not home, you'll be expected to entertain the company."

"Are you sure Jake would be wantin' me to?"

Mrs. Gruber nodded her head. "He would. And so would the mistress. The lady downstairs is her friend. Both hers and Mister Jake's. Since you be the mistress's next of kin, it's expected that you'll receive her company."

Next of kin.

Danny straightened her shoulders. No other words could have done so much to make her aware of her duty. She *was* Angellee's next of kin. And, although Danny didn't particularly want to meet anyone, she was bound to do so. . . . As Angellee's kin, Danny knew she must take her cousin's place in the household until Angel returned.

Bridget entered the room, carrying a heavy fold of brown fabric across her arm. "I brought you a gown from the mistress's closet," she said. "It wouldn't be right for you to entertain without the proper dress."

Bowing to the other women's greater knowledge of what was proper in the city, Danny allowed herself to be helped into the heavy gown and buttoned up. Then she went down to greet the woman who waited for her.

The visitor stood in the parlor, gazing out the window with a faraway look on her face. Even with her back turned, Danny could see the woman's skin was lightly tanned and went well with her auburn hair.

For a moment Danny stood on the threshold, feeling as though she were an intruder. As though sensing her presence, the woman turned around and met her eyes.

"Hello," she said huskily, gliding gracefully toward Danny with an extended hand. "Please forgive me for intruding, but I just had to come and welcome you to Pittsburgh."

"I wasn't doin' nothin' except . . . except . . ." Danny's voice trailed away and she stared at the other woman. She had never seen such an elegant woman before. The green of her gown exactly matched her eyes and her hair was coiled on the top of her head, giving her an appearance of fragility that Danny felt was entirely deceptive, going by the strength of her grip.

"My name is Rebecca Mallory," the woman said. "Jake and I have been friends since we were children and Angellee is very dear to me. It is my understanding that you are her cousin."

Danny felt herself beginning to sweat and her hands twisted in her skirt. She was so unused to women like Rebecca Mallory. What would be her reaction if Danny messed up . . . showed her ignorance of city ways. "I—I—Angel's pa and mine was brothers."

Rebecca Mallory dipped her head gracefully, her gaze lingering on Danny's face. "I'm afraid Angel didn't talk much about her family," she said. "But the few times she did, it was obvious how much you meant to her. They call you Danny, don't they?"

Danny nodded her head, finding the tension almost unbearable. "My name's really Danielle," she explained. "But nobody calls me that."

"It's a lovely name," Rebecca said. "I'm just sorry we had to meet under such circumstances. Has there been no word at all from Angel?"

"We ain't heard nothing yet." Remembering her duty as hostess, Danny gestured toward a chair. "Kindly set yourself down and rest your feet. The housekeeper is gonna bring some tea."

After they had seated themselves, Rebecca turned to her. "I know you must be worried to death about Angel. It's bad enough to be abducted . . . but with her condition and all . . ." Her voice trailed off and she studied her hands for a long moment. "Poor Jake," she said softly. "He must be going out of his mind."

Danny nodded, trying to take in the other woman's words. What did she mean about Angellee's condition? Had she been sick?

Before she could voice the question, Bridget

entered carrying a big flowered black tray. Ruth, another housemaid, followed with a tiered muffin stand. On it were two openwork china plates, one of bread and butter, one of seed and ginger cookies, and one of chocolate layer cake.

Taking a deep breath of courage, Danny reached for the teapot with trembling hands. Would she be able to pour the tea without spilling it.

As though sensing her nervous state, Bridget spoke up. "Would you like me to pour, Miss?" she asked.

Danny nodded quickly, feeling relieved at the offer. She watched the steady stream of hot tea fill the delicate cups. She tried to concentrate on the job before her, unwilling to make a fool of herself in front of her guest.

As Bridget filled each cup, Ruth handed them around and placed the muffin stand within easy reach. Then, after asking if there was anything else she wanted, the two maids left them alone.

"Dig in," Danny said, helping herself to a slice of chocolate cake.

"Thank you," Rebecca said, reaching for a plate. "You remind me of Angellee. The way she was when she first arrived in Pittsburgh. She managed to set Pittsburgh on its ears." Her eyes misted. "God! I hope she's all right. I don't know how Jake will survive if he loses both her and the little one—" She broke off at the sound of voices, accompanied by boots striking against the hardwood floor.

"That must be the men," Danny muttered, jerking to her feet. "Scuse me!" Hurrying to the doorway, she called out. "Jake! We got company." Just in case, she

198

thought, he might be about to say something he didn't want others to know.

Danny's gaze went to Adam who entered just behind Jake. But Adam seemed not to see her, instead, his eyes were focused on Rebecca, who had risen to her feet at their entrance.

"Becky!" Jake exclaimed, crossing to her side and taking her in his arms. "I didn't realize you were back in town! God, but it's good to see you. And how nice of you to call."

Danny frowned. It wasn't seemly for Jake to be hugging another woman when he was married to Angellee. Maybe it was a good thing Danny had come when she had. Maybe, she silently told herself, Rebecca Mallory would bear watching.

"You don't look very well, Jake," Rebecca said, studying his face intently. "But I'm not the least bit surprised. Are you having trouble sleeping?"

"A little," he admitted, giving her shoulders an extra squeeze before turning her to meet Adam. After introductions were made, he turned back to her. "Apparently you've already heard about Angel's disappearance."

"Aunt Bess told me this morning. I'm sure you know how sorry I was to hear it."

Although Danny didn't want to miss a word of what they were saying, she was aware of her duty in the household and hurried to get some more cups from the kitchen. By the time she returned, the conversation had shifted from Angellee and turned to people that she had never heard of.

Disappointed, she seated herself near Rebecca and

Jake, determined at least to keep an eye on her cousin's man. He seemed awfully familiar with the visitor. Perhaps a shade too familiar to her way of thinking.

That night, the dream came again. But this time, the moment Danny woke, she sat bolt upright in bed. She recognized the cry now, the wail that had so confused her, but had made no sense.

There was no doubt in her mind now. The cry she was hearing was that of a newborn babe. But why should she be hearing such a cry?

Chapter Eighteen

The next evening before dinner, Danny sat in the parlor conversing with Jake, when Adam entered the room, followed closely by Mrs. Gruber.

"A messenger brought this, sir," the housekeeper said, extending the white envelope toward her employer.

"Just put it on my desk," Jake said. "Would you like a brandy, Adam?" At Adam's nod, Jake filled a glass and handed it to him. "Another sherry, Danny?"

"Thankee kindly," Danny said, her eyes flicking to Adam. Where had he been all afternoon? she wondered.

Suddenly, she became aware that Mrs. Gruber hadn't left the room. Instead, the housekeeper remained in the room, her hands clasped together, watching Jake with a peculiar intentness. Danny sensed a quiet waiting in the woman, and wondered why.

After Jake handed the drinks around, he met the

housekeeper's eyes. "Something else?" he inquired.

"I think you better open the message, sir," Mrs. Gruber said. "The messenger that brought it was from the Mosley mansion."

With an in-drawn breath, Jake snatched up the envelope, extracted a small white card and frowned down at it. Suddenly his expression darkened, became thunderous. "Damn him!" he gritted, crumpling the card in his hand and hurling it across the room. "How dare he taunt me in such a way!"

"What is it, Mister Jake?" Mrs. Gruber asked, bending to pick up the card.

"An invitation!" Jake snarled. "The damn cur had the nerve to send me an invitation!"

"An invitation to what?" Adam asked.

Mrs. Gruber handed the invitation to Adam who scanned the contents quickly.

"To a party!" Jake spat out the words. "He's having a celebration and he's inviting me to it."

"He included Danny in the invitation," Adam said.

"He's obviously heard she's here," Jake said. "There's not a damn thing happening in this city that Mosley doesn't know about." His hands clenched and unclenched at his sides as though he would like to have them around Asa Mosley's throat. "He's taunting me," he ground out. "Mosley is telling me there is nothing I can do to him." He stalked to the window and glared outside. "I won't even give him the courtesy of a reply."

The wheels in Danny's head had been turning. She wasn't sure how much stock could be put in her gift . . . if she even had one. But perhaps it ought to be put to a test. Maybe if she met Asa Mosley, she could find out something. She didn't know how or what, but at this point, they needed to try whatever they could.

"Jake," she said. "Maybe that ain't such a good idea. Where is the party going to be?"

Adam looked at the invitation. "It's at Mosley's place," he said, meeting Danny's eyes. As though sensing her intention, he added, "Danny's right, Jake. It might be a good idea to attend."

"If you're thinking he has Angel in his house, then you are on the wrong track," Jake said. "When all our efforts to discover where Angellee had left the train turned up nothing, I waited until there was no one there except a few servants, and went through that house with a fine-toothed comb." He reached for the crumpled invitation and glared down at it as though the card itself was responsible for his wife's disappearance.

Suddenly, his expression became thoughtful. "Angellee is definitely not there, Adam. But you may be right." He smiled grimly. "Asa Mosley certainly won't be expecting it. Yes . . . perhaps we *should* accept the invitation." His eyes glittered with cold amusement. "Maybe we'll just surprise Asa Mosley." His lips pressed into a thin line. "But since I'm not so sure I can keep from killing Mosley if I get that close to him, you can take my place, Adam."

The night of the ball, Danny stood before her bedroom mirror and stared in amazement at her reflection. Excitement glittered in her eyes. What

203

would Adam think about her? Danny imagined she must look like a fairytale princess in the ruffled dimity gown Jake had provided. Would Adam be pleased she was his partner?

In all her wildest dreams, Danny had never even imagined that she would be going to a party with Adam. No matter that it was held in the enemy's camp. Tonight was sure to be a night she would never forget. The delicate fabric of the gown she wore was a color that exactly matched her eyes and Bridget had dressed her hair in a froth of curls high on her head.

It was hard to believe the image reflected in the mirror was Danny Tucker. Would Adam find her appearance pleasing? Lord, she hoped so.

Danny could hardly contain her excitement when she joined him in the parlor. Her heart beat fast with anticipation while she stood in the doorway, waiting for him to notice her. When he did, his gaze slid over her and his eyes narrowed. Something intense flared in his eyes and she had to fight the overwhelming need to throw herself into his arms.

There was a tingling in the pit of her stomach and her heart jolted, her pulse pounded. His steady gaze bored into her as he rose to his feet and crossed to her.

"You're lovely," he said, taking her hand in his.

"You ain't so bad yourself," she said huskily, her flesh tingling where it touched his.

The grandfather clock in the hall sounded the hour, reminding them it was time to go.

In the carriage, Adam, like Danny, seemed content to remain silent. And, instead of going straight to the Mosley mansion, he had the driver detour up a hill,

204

telling her there was a sight that she shouldn't miss.

The street ran along the edge of a bluff, and when the driver stopped the carriage, Danny could look directly down on all the low areas of the city that neared the level of the rivers.

Self-consciously, she allowed Adam to help her down from the carriage amid a swish of skirts. Then she followed him to the edge of the abyss.

And stared in awe.

Looking over the iron railing, Danny gazed upon the most striking spectacle she had ever beheld. The entire space lying between the hills was filled with the blackest smoke she'd ever seen. It burst forth in tongues of flame from the chimneys that were hidden from her sight. Her ear drums assailed by the noise of hundreds of steam hammers.

Danny shuddered and moved closer to Adam, feeling as though she were gazing into the depths of hell . . . with the lid taken off.

"I used to come up here when I was at the university," Adam said softly. "Awesome, isn't it?"

She nodded and shivered again, finding herself unable to speak.

Adam seemed to understand her feelings, perhaps even shared them. Without a word, he helped her back into the carriage and they continued on their way.

The lights were bright in the Mosley mansion and the party was in full swing. Whatever the occasion, their host apparently felt it warranted the utmost festivity. Strings of Japanese lanterns were festooned from tree to tree across the wide lawn and music came from somewhere in the big house.

They were greeted by a butler who frowned at the crumpled invitation Adam offered him.

"Logan couldn't come so he asked me to escort Miss Tucker," Adam said.

"Your name, sir?"

"Adam Hollister."

"Please follow me." The butler led them through double doors that had been thrown wide to make a continuous sweep of the spacious rooms.

Music from a three piece orchestra situated in the front parlor echoed through the ground floor. Young men in lightweight flannel and girls in ruffled mulles and dimities waltzed and polkaed and laughed as Danny and Adam followed the butler through a wide center hall and into the large ball room.

Danny felt almost overwhelmed by all the glitter and glamour. Never in her life had she ever seen anything so fancy.

"Miss Danielle Tucker and Master Adam Hollister," the butler droned.

A man and woman separated from a knot of people near the door. Danny guessed it was their host and hostess coming forward to greet them.

The portly man sent a cold prickling sensation up Danny's neck. When he took her hand in his, a vision of a house on a hill flickered against the back of her eyelids which were shut against her sudden fear. It was gone as quickly as it appeared, but Danny had to fight to let the smooth-appearing gray haired gent kiss her hand.

"So you are Miss Tucker," he murmured. "It's

delightful to meet you, my dear. I've heard so much about you."

"From who?" she asked bluntly. "Didn't think nobody knew I was around." Had Rebecca Mallory been talking about her? Danny wouldn't put a thing past a woman who would go around hugging a married man.

Instead of answering her question, Mosley's gaze touched on Adam, then returned to Danny. "I'm afraid your escort is unknown to me."

"Adam Hollister," Adam said with a cold smile. "Jake asked me to come in his place. Hope you don't mind."

"Of course not," Mosley replied, studying Adam intently. "Certainly the lady needed an escort." He pulled the tall, slender woman beside him forward. "Let me present my wife, Victoria."

Danny took an instant dislike to the woman. Victoria Mosley's ash-blonde hair was drawn back from a youthful looking face. Her blue eyes were singularly bright as they gazed at Adam.

"Mrs. Mosley," Adam's smile was real this time as he took the blonde woman's hand and lifted it to his lips.

Danny's lips tightened. She didn't think she liked the city folks' ways of kissing hands. Especially when Adam was doing the kissing and Victoria was doing the receiving. What was he trying to do anyway? Match manners with Asa Mosley?

"Please call me Victoria," the woman murmured, her eyes never leaving Adam. "All my friends do. And I'm certain we will become friends."

"Victoria," Adam murmured huskily. "It's a name fit for a queen."

Danny shot Adam a cold look, but he seemed bent on ignoring her. And Asa Mosley seemed ignorant of the byplay between his wife and Adam.

"Come with me, Miss Tucker," Mosley said. "Let me introduce you around." Taking Danny's arm in a firm grip, he pulled her away from the two who were still mouthing pleasantries to each other.

Furious at Adam, Danny allowed herself to be led toward a group of business men. They looked up as Danny and Mosley joined them. After introducing Danny, Mosley singled out one of the gentlemen. "Gaylord is what is known as a steel magnate, Miss Tucker."

Although Mosley seemed to be waiting for her to question him, Danny had no need of doing so. She'd already learned what a steel magnate was from Jake.

"Have you installed a Bessemer converter yet, Gaylord?" Again, he looked at Danny. "Remind me to explain the conversion process to you later, my dear."

It was obvious to Danny that he was talking down to her. "No need," she said bluntly. "Jake's already done the explainin' and I don't have to be told nothin' twice."

A smile pulled at Gaylord's lips. His eyes twinkled at her for a moment. Then, as though suddenly remembering the question directed at him, he spoke. "I haven't installed a Bessemer yet, Asa. I'm still giving it my consideration though. But it's a big undertaking."

"While you consider it, Scott and Chapman are

208

turning out Bessemer rails on such a scale you'll never be able to compete."

Although Danny felt bored with the men's conversation, she remained with them, hoping to learn something that would help in the search for Angellee.

"I'm thinking about not making rails at all," Gaylord said.

"Not making rails? Good lord man! Why would you do that? The railroad is going places. That is where the money is. You need to get rid of that old Henrietta blast furnace and get one of those seventy-five foot Lucys that Chapman has."

"My Henrietta blast furnace is no banker's pawn," Gaylord said. "She was built to last and every foot of her is paid for."

He closed his lips firmly as if to indicate that he had said all he cared to on the subject, but his host wasn't to be deterred. Mosley kept his sharp blue eyes fixed on Gaylord's face.

"That may be true," Mosley said, "but the iron business is in a state of flux. Every single day there are new inventions and processes. A man's got to keep up with them to stay in business today."

"The same way you've kept up with safety regulations in those mines you run," came a caustic voice from his elbow.

Danny looked toward the speaker. A stocky gentleman with a mustache stood there with a glass in his hand, his eyes were like thunderclouds as they bored into Mosley's.

"What about the Widow Maker?" The gentleman who spoke was a stern-looking, bearded-faced man.

209

"The mine is called the Widdemer," Mosley corrected stiffly. "George Widdemer owns the property where the mine is located."

"Have you done anything to make it safe?" the bearded-faced man asked. "Are the charges against the company being dropped?"

"I'm confident they will be," Mosley said. "Contrary to our Attorney General's beliefs, I'm well aware of my responsibilities."

"I heard there was another cave-in at the Widow Maker yesterday," the mustached gentleman said.

The tension knit the group of men together, even as it divided them. They had become so absorbed in their controversy that Danny thought they had forgotten her—until Asa Mosley cupped her elbow with his long, elegant hand.

"We must be boring you, my dear," he said. "I'll have my housekeeper see that you are introduced to our young people." Looking out over the room, he snapped his fingers. Moments later a woman appeared next to him as if by magic. "See that Miss Tucker is introduced," he ordered.

Danny had no option but to follow the woman. Her gaze scoured the room, stopping on Adam and Victoria, still talking together, bent on ignoring everyone around them.

Damn him! Danny wondered if it had been Adam's intention all along to abandon her as soon as they arrived. She seethed with anger as the borrowed skirt swished around her feet. The fabric was so confining, and she suddenly felt nauseous. Was it really so hot, or was the heat that was slowly covering her due to her rising emotions?

Danny wanted to toss the lady Victoria on the floor and wring her fish-belly white neck . . . and she wanted to shake Adam until his teeth rattled. Had he so easily forgotten they came here to snoop? Not for him to make cow-eyes at Mosley's wife.

Danny was still trying to control her emotions when the housekeeper stopped near a group of people. After introducing Danny around, the housekeeper left Danny to fend for herself.

Chapter Nineteen

Although several of the young men expressed interest in Danny, the young ladies with them kept proprietary hands on their arms. Two by two they drifted away, leaving Danny alone with an elderly woman in a purple satin dress.

"Are you enjoying yourself, my dear?" the woman asked.

Danny, realizing it would be rude to admit she wasn't, merely nodded her head.

"That young man you came with seems to find Victoria captivating," purple dress remarked. "But then, most men do." She sipped from the glass in her hand and turned back to Danny. "I understand you are new to the city."

"Yessum," Danny replied, her eyes traveling to Adam and Victoria again. "Don't reckon I know anybody around here."

"You're not missing much," the woman replied. "I wouldn't give the stable boy's jackass for a soul in this room. Present company excluded, of course."

Danny barely stopped her mouth from dropping open. She couldn't believe the woman before her had spoken in such a manner.

"Surprised you, did I?" the woman said. "Well, sometimes I even surprise myself."

"Did that housekeeper tell me your name?" Danny asked. "If she did, I plumb forgot it."

The woman stuck out a hand. "The name's Bridie May Scott. I'm Victoria's mother."

"Oh." Danny turned away. Victoria's mother was the last person she needed to be talking to.

Bridie looked at her with keen eyes. "Don't tar me with the same brush as my daughter," she said. "Even though I'm her mother, I don't have to hold her views. Nor those of the man she's married to." Her lips tightened. "I raised her to know right from wrong. But she was smitten by Asa's wealth from the first day they met. I heard them talking earlier . . . Asa and Victoria. They didn't really expect you to show up, you know. The invitation was sent to make Jake Logan mad . . . to taunt him."

"Why'd they want to go an' do that?" Danny asked, turning her full attention on the woman. Maybe she could learn something here after all.

"I'm not sure," Bridie said. "They keep things from me. Probably because they know I don't approve of some of the things they do." She chuckled softly. "Most of the things, I might add."

"Since you don't approve, you might tell me where Mosley is keeping my cousin," Danny said bluntly.

"I wish I could, my dear," Bridie said. "But I

213

haven't heard her name mentioned in this house at all. That, in itself, is most curious."

"But you do know they got her?"

"No. I don't even know that." She studied Danny intently. "They don't even talk about the mines around me anymore. What they are talking about is sending me off to a little cottage he bought . . . probably for the sole purpose of getting me out of the way." She took a sip from her glass. "Not that I'll mind it. The cottage is near the ocean. I'm sure I'll love it there." Her eyes twinkled at Danny. "Wouldn't tell them that, though. They think I hate the notion."

"Sounds like you don't like neither of 'em much," Danny commented.

"You're absolutely right," Bridie said angrily. "Victoria's getting too prissy for her own good. She wasn't too happy about me attending this shindig tonight. Thinks I'm going to disgrace her by showing my face." Her eyes glittered as she stared at her daughter across the room. "She doesn't want anyone to know she came from farming people."

"I never saw no farmer's daughter that looks like she does," Danny said. "Guess money is what makes the difference."

"That it does," Bridie said. "It's a sin the time her maid spends cold-creaming and massaging her skin so it will stay young-looking. And her hair. Her maid spends an hour each night brushing it so it will shine like that. And she's that particular with it. Nobody is allowed to touch it except that maid of hers. The girl was trained in France by Dominique."

214

"Who's Dominique?" Danny asked.

"He's one of the most prestigious hairdressers in France. That's where the girls who work at Pierre's were trained." At Danny's puzzled look, Bridie added, "Pierre's is a beauty salon downtown. Nearly every woman in the city goes there to have her hair done. But not my daughter. Not Victoria."

Danny realized the woman was letting off steam and let her voice wash over her as she turned her attention back to the crowded ballroom. Although Adam and Victoria had moved, it took her only moments to spot Adam's tall graceful figure.

Dammit! He was still with Mosley's wife!

Danny's lips tightened into a thin line. Had he completely forgotten the reason they had come? How could he gather information if he didn't mingle with the crowd?

She looked away, determined to forget about him, forget about the pain that was curled tight in her breast, but her eyes kept returning to the whirling couple. In spite of his height and weight, he danced beautifully, wonderfully . . . she could hardly take her eyes off him. Neither could most of the other women in the room.

"Are you not dancing, Miss?"

The voice at her elbow surprised Danny. She whirled around to face a young man only a few years her senior.

She liked him immediately. His wide forehead and his large brown eyes beneath broadly arched brows gave him a look of childish innocence. His chin was square, slightly cleft, and his dark hair was parted in the center and smoothly brushed down.

"Would you honor me with this schottische?" he asked, bowing low over her hand.

A flush swept up Danny's neck and stained her cheeks. She was taken off guard, hadn't expected this. She had never danced, except sometimes at hoedowns. She'd certainly never done anything approaching what she'd encountered here. And yet, she hated to admit to her ignorance. Instead, she shook her head.

For a moment he looked stricken, then his expression brightened.

"But of course," he said, standing stiffly erect. "It would not be proper until we have been introduced." He turned to Bridie. "Would you do the honors?" he asked.

"Of course." Bridie's eyes twinkled at Danny. "Miss Danielle Tucker, may I present Roderic Fortunato."

"Charmed to meet you." He took her hand and brought it to his lips at the same time, making a polite bow. "I am at your service." He smiled widely at her, displaying even, white teeth. "Now that you know my name, would you honor me with this dance?"

"No."

He looked as though she'd struck him. "Please forgive my intrusion," he said, backing away from her. "My deepest apologies for disturbing you."

He turned to go and she found she couldn't allow him to believe she didn't like him. "No!" she said. "You ain't botherin' me. It's just—" She took a deep

216

breath of courage and admitted her fault. "The truth of the matter is that I don't know how to dance."

"Ahhh." Understanding gleamed in his eyes. "But that is nothing," he said. "Poof. I will show you how."

She shook her head again. She wasn't about to get out on the dance floor and make a fool of herself.

His expression saddened. His face grew long. "Then perhaps you would consider strolling through the garden with me?" he asked diffidently.

Danny didn't have the heart to refuse him again. Anyway, she told herself, what was she supposed to do left by her lonesome? Not that Adam seemed to care a whit for her solitary state. He was too busy cozying up to the lady of the house to notice.

"I guess I wouldn't mind seeing that garden," she said firmly. "I 'spect it's got a lotta pretty flowers in it."

A grin spread across his face and he extended an elbow toward her. "Indeed it has," he said, leading her across the floor to the patio door. "But I have something else in mind besides Victoria's prize roses."

Something else? His words nearly stopped her in her tracks . . . until she met his eyes and saw the smile in them. Whatever this young man had planned, he meant her no harm.

Adam, whirling Victoria around in time with the music, felt extreme disappointment that he'd learned nothing from her that would help them to locate

217

Angellee. When the music stopped, he said, "It's been delightful, Victoria. But I'm afraid I'll have to leave you now. I've left Danny alone much too long."

"Must you go?" she asked. "I'm sure Asa is looking after her nicely."

"I don't think so," he said with a frown. "I saw him a few minutes ago, and Danny wasn't with him."

Adam felt relieved when a dark-haired man claimed her attention. Without another word, he left them and wound his way through the crowded ballroom. Where could Danny be? Adam hoped to God she hadn't gotten herself into trouble.

"Adam!" a feminine voice exclaimed. "I didn't expect to see you here!"

Adam spun on his heels and found himself facing the woman he'd hoped never to see again. *Carlotta!* Beautiful, vibrant, Carlotta.

"Neither did I expect to see you," he said grimly.

"How long has it been?" she asked huskily, sliding closer to him.

"Not long enough," he said abruptly.

"Now don't be that way," she purred, brushing against him. "Surely you aren't still angry with me over what happened in the past."

"I've never forgotten what happened, Carlotta," Adam said harshly. "And I never will."

"You can't really hold me responsible for Nicky's death. It wasn't me who killed him."

"No," he agreed. "It was me. But we both know who was responsible, don't we?" He turned away from her, but she clutched his arm.

218

"Don't be this way," she cajoled. "There is so much for us to talk about. Aren't you the least bit curious about my life. About what happened to me since we parted?"

"Not in the least," he said, prying her fingers loose from his arm. "Now, if you'll excuse me. . . ."

"Suppose I don't!"

Her voice was raised slightly and Adam noticed they were attracting attention. Dammit! He didn't want that! He had come here to search for answers. He didn't need people watching him. And there was still Danny to find.

"Let's go into the garden," he said, taking her arm and leading her towards the door.

She smiled at him as though she felt she'd won a point. It shouldn't take long for him to convince her differently.

As the night cloaked them in darkness, the sound of laughter told Adam that the garden was already occupied. But that obviously didn't bother Carlotta. When the closing door shut them away from the crowd, she slid her arms around his neck and melted against him.

"It's been so long," she whispered. "But I've never forgotten you. Not for one minute." Before he could shove her away, she pressed her lips against his.

Danny laughed as she whirled around the garden in Roderic's arms. She was dancing! Actually dancing! And it was easier than she'd ever imagined it could be.

The night air was cool against her skin and the sky above was a vast black arc, sprinkled with starlight

219

that was occasionally obliterated by the flames gushing from some distant furnace.

"I never seen anything like them furnaces at night," she said softly, her ears attuned to the delicate strains of the waltz that drifted through the open doors.

"I have traveled through many countries," he said, "but never have I encountered a more beautiful city than Pittsburgh by night."

"Nor uglier than Pittsburgh by day," she said, thinking of her beloved Ozark mountains. But would the mountains hold as much pull for her now that she had given her heart to Adam? Her mind skittered away from the thought. "I guess there ain't no other way to get the coal out of the mountain without making such a mess."

"Still, it is unfortunate that the mines must spoil the land," he said.

They fell silent again. Danny felt the night was magical with the sweet fragrance of flowers teasing her nostrils as they swayed in time with the music. Gladiolus, lilies, phlox, and roses grew in abundance along the paths. And Danny was actually dancing among them. Not just doing a jig, but really dancing.

Danny's laughter mingled with the music as they dipped and swayed to the waltz. A quick turn brought her facing the house . . . and the couple who stood embracing. When they moved apart, Danny stopped short and stared.

It was Adam! Dammit! That was Adam kissing Victoria Mosley!

"What is wrong?" Roderic asked.

Before Danny could answer, the library doors were flung open, sending a stream of light flooding through the courtyard. The light showed the figure of a man who had just stepped outside. Asa Mosley. But it wasn't Mosley who captured her attention. It was the dark cloud that seemed to hover around him.

Danny stared in horror at the darkness . . . the pulsing, throbbing darkness that was so dense it blocked the light that should have been above the man's head.

She felt the color draining from her face . . . her skin was icy and her mouth was dry. How could this be? she silently asked herself. Danny knew she wasn't asleep now . . . knew she was wide awake, but still the spirit had come to haunt her.

"What is the matter?" Roderic asked in a concerned voice.

But Danny was unable to answer him. Her mouth was dry, her throat constricted. She felt as though she were unable to breathe. Her knees, feeling like weak rubber, seemed bent on buckling beneath her. Danny swayed and clutched at Roderic's arm.

God! Don't let me faint!

Suddenly Danny was wrenched away from Roderic. She stared up into a cold, hard, unsmiling face that she recognized immediately.

It was Adam.

"What have you been doing to her?" he demanded harshly, staring at the other man.

"He ain't done nothing," Danny said, finding her voice. "Just . . ." She looked around. The threatening darkness had disappeared from around Asa Mosley!

"I want to go home, Adam," she whispered shakily. "Take me away from this place."

Adam was breathing harshly, his body tense, threatening. With an oath, he put an arm around her waist to support her and hurried her out of the garden toward their carriage.

Moments later they left the brightly lit mansion behind.

Chapter Twenty

A sunbeam playing across her eyes woke Danny. Her gaze automatically scanned the room for an unseen presence, but except for herself, the room was empty.

The distant sound of voices reached her, then a door slammed and she heard boots thudding across the front porch. With her curiosity piqued, Danny flung back the covers, slid to the floor and padded barefoot to the window.

Pulling the curtains aside, she watched a man enter a hansom cab that had been parked near the drive.

Dammit! It was Adam. And he was obviously on the point of leaving.

Thoughts of last night filled her head, the way he'd cozied up to Victoria Mosley instead of tending to the job they'd been sent to do. Could that woman have something to do with his early departure? Just the possibility sent a surge of anger through Danny.

Adam was a fool if he allowed himself to be taken

in by Victoria's beauty; as he obviously had. Hadn't Danny seen him kissing Victoria with her own two eyes?

Dammit, Adam! Why'd you go an' do a thing like that? she silently questioned.

Tears filled her eyes, spilled over and slid down Danny's cheeks. She turned away from the window, swiping angrily at the moistness.

No use in cryin' over what's already done! That just wasn't her way. But she'd be damned if that prissy hussy was going to get Adam. Danny had first claim on him, and she wasn't going to give him up.

Blowing her nose, she dried her tears and turned her thoughts to Angellee . . . and to Asa Mosley, the man who'd had her abducted. He *was* responsible. Danny was positive of it now, had been positive ever since she'd seen him standing in the doorway surrounded by evil.

Danny flushed with embarrassment as she remembered her reaction to him. What must Adam think of her? She'd acted like a scared rabbit, nearly passing dead away from fright.

Mosley is just a man, she silently chided herself, *nothing else.*

But it wasn't Mosley you was afeared of, a silent voice said.

She had sensed evil there and had run from it when she would have accomplished more if she had stayed and faced it down.

Perhaps some way, some how, she could have gained some clue to her cousin's whereabouts from the man.

Suddenly, Danny frowned. There had been some-

MORE PASSION AND ADVENTURE AWAIT... YOUR TRIP TO A BIG ADVENTUROUS WORLD BEGINS WHEN YOU ACCEPT YOUR FIRST 4 NOVELS ABSOLUTELY *FREE* (AN $18.00 VALUE)

Accept your Free gift and start to experience more of the passion and adventure you like in a historical romance novel. Each Zebra novel is filled with proud men, spirited women and tempestuous love that you'll remember long after you turn the last page.

Zebra Historical Romances are the finest novels of their kind. They are written by authors who really know how to weave tales of romance and adventure in the historical settings you love. You'll feel like you've actually gone back in time with the thrilling stories that each Zebra novel offers.

GET YOUR FREE GIFT WITH THE START OF YOUR HOME SUBSCRIPTION

Our readers tell us that these books sell out very fast in book stores and often they miss the newest titles. So Zebra has made arrangements for you to receive the four newest novels published each month.

You'll be guaranteed that you'll never miss a title, and home delivery is so convenient. And to show you just how easy it is to get Zebra Historical Romances, we'll send you your first 4 books absolutely FREE! Our gift to you just for trying our home subscription service.

BIG SAVINGS AND FREE HOME DELIVERY

Each month, you'll receive the four newest titles as soon as they are published. You'll probably receive them even before the bookstores do. What's more, you may preview these exciting novels free for 10 days. If you like them as much as we think you will, just pay the low preferred subscriber's price of just $3.75 each. *You'll save $3.00 each month off the publisher's price.* AND, your savings are even greater because there are never any shipping, handling or other hidden charges—FREE Home Delivery. Of course you can return any shipment within 10 days for full credit, no questions asked. There is no minimum number of books you must buy.

4 FREE BOOKS

TO GET YOUR 4 FREE BOOKS WORTH $18.00 — MAIL IN THE FREE BOOK CERTIFICATE T O D A Y

Fill in the Free Book Certificate below, and we'll send your FREE BOOKS to you as soon as we receive it.

If the certificate is missing below, write to: Zebra Home Subscription Service, Inc., P.O. Box 5214, 120 Brighton Road, Clifton, New Jersey 07015-5214.

FREE BOOK CERTIFICATE

4 FREE BOOKS

ZEBRA HOME SUBSCRIPTION SERVICE, INC.

YES! Please start my subscription to Zebra Historical Romances and send me my first 4 books absolutely FREE. I understand that each month I may preview four new Zebra Historical Romances free for 10 days. If I'm not satisfied with them, I may return the four books within 10 days and owe nothing. Otherwise, I will pay the low preferred subscriber's price of just $3.75 each; a total of $15.00, *a savings off the publisher's price of $3.00.* I may return any shipment and I may cancel this subscription at any time. There is no obligation to buy any shipment and there are no shipping, handling or other hidden charges. Regardless of what I decide, the four free books are mine to keep.

NAME

ADDRESS _____ APT

CITY _____ STATE ___ ZIP

TELEPHONE ( )

SIGNATURE _____ (if under 18, parent or guardian must sign)

Terms, offer and prices subject to change without notice. Subscription subject to acceptance by Zebra Books. Zebra Books reserves the right to reject any order or cancel any subscription.　079102

thing strange about the pulsating darkness . . . the evil that clouded Mosley's image. It had—suddenly, Danny's eyes widened and her brow smoothed as the frown disappeared. *God! She knew why!* The pulsating evil that had surrounded Mosley strongly resembled the image she'd seen in her very first vision. The black evil that had overshadowed the wispy gray figure.

But this time, when she saw the apparition she had been standing on her feet . . . as wide awake as she could be!

Excitement coursed through her.

That was the clincher as far as Danny was concerned. Now she felt positive that her cousin was somewhere nearby. Angellee might even be in the city. And if she was, then it might be possible for Danny to contact her cousin.

With that thought in mind, Danny squeezed her eyes shut and concentrated on reaching Angellee.

Angel . . . Angel . . . Danny sent the thought out . . . *Are you there, Angel?*

Almost immediately Danny felt a cold tingling at the base of her neck, and her stomach muscles twisted into a knot. She waited for an answer.

Waited.

And waited.

But long seconds ticked by and there was nothing.

Only the waiting silence.

Why?

"Angel, where are you?" Danny muttered. "I can't help less'n you tell me. You gotta say where you're at."

Still there was no answer. But Danny felt she was

no longer alone. There was something there . . . some waiting *presence.* But it seemed distant, somehow, just beyond her reach.

Then, as suddenly as it came, the presence was gone. As though it had been a tenuous strand on a spider's web—a strand that had suddenly snapped.

Tears of frustration filled Danny's eyes. The presence she'd felt had been Angellee. Danny was certain of it . . . but why had she gone? It was as though she were too weak to remain.

Oh, God! Was Angellee dying?

They must find her! They just had to!

Danny's brow wrinkled, her face tightened as she concentrated on sending out thought waves. *Angel! Come back!* But it did no good. Whatever it had been . . . whether it had been a presence or a ghostly spirit . . . the wispy, half-formed presence had completely disappeared.

But even as that thought left her mind, Danny knew she was wrong. It *was* there . . . hovering slightly beyond her reach, perhaps on another plane of existence. . . .

But it was there!

Danny knew it for certain now. Her cousin, Angellee, was out there . . . in this city. And despite Adam's admonitions to remain at the Logan mansion, Danny intended to search the city until she could feel her cousin's presence again.

Her chance came an hour later when she saw Mrs. Gruber give Bridget a list of supplies to buy at the market. The girl complained it would take her all day and she'd have to go all over town to purchase

226

the items. Immediately, Danny offered to accompany the maid.

Bridget's intense gray eyes widened. "Oh, no, Miss. You wouldn't be wantin' to do that. I'm only going for a wee bit of shopping. No place a lady should be bothering herself with."

Danny smiled wryly and lifted the skirt of the freshly laundered white cambric dress she was wearing. "These fine duds don't make me no different than you, Bridget," she said.

Bridget's lips twitched. "I won't be calling the mistress's housedress fine duds," she said. "She would be sad if she knew you wouldn't wear the other gowns in her wardrobe."

"This dress was the only one I found in that standing-up box that would hold up to wear," Danny stated firmly. "All the other ones were either slicky-shiny or they was made of that velvety soft stuff that puts me in mind of the moss growin' down by the creek. I'd be afraid to move in 'em for fear I'd get 'em all dirty. An' it's a fact, them dresses wasn't made for dirt."

"But, Miss . . ." Bridget protested. "You can't possibly go with me to the market wearing such rags."

"Danny's right, Bridget. She couldn't go with you to the market wearing anything else," Mrs. Gruber said soberly. "She'd be sure to attract attention in one of Miz Angel's satin or velvet gowns."

An hour later, while Bridget shopped, Danny concentrated on keeping an open mind, periodically sending her thoughts out in search of her cousin, but

227

she had no answer . . . felt no sense of Angellee's presence. They had only one more stop to make when Danny saw Victoria Mosley entering a small business establishment across the street. The sign above the door simply read Pierre's.

Danny frowned. "What's that place?" she asked, pointing to the building.

"Pierre's?" the girl asked. "It's a beauty salon. They opened up only a few months ago. Most of the ladies of quality go there to have their hair fixed. It's become all the rage."

Danny's curiosity was piqued. Why was Victoria entering the beauty salon? According to her own mother, no one but Victoria's maid was allowed to beautify her hair.

"Miss? Is something wrong?"

Bridget's question brought Danny back to the present. "You go ahead, Bridget," she said abruptly. "Finish your shopping. I'll meet you here in a few minutes."

"But, Miss—"

Danny paid no attention to Bridget. She was already hurrying across the street, intent on reaching the salon. But when she entered the establishment, she saw no sign of Victoria Mosley.

"Can I help you?" asked a female voice at her elbow.

She swung toward the clerk who had addressed her. "I was thinkin' on getting my hair fixed," she said.

Although the woman did her best to look down her long nose at Danny, as though she suspected her of being inferior to herself, the clerk turned her attention to Danny's wind-tousled curls. "What exactly did you have in mind?" she asked.

"I don't know," Danny said, her gaze sweeping the room again, dwelling for a moment on each of the room's three customers, then moving on to search for hidden corners. But there was no need. Although the room was large, there seemed to be no place where a woman of Victoria's stature could hide.

She seemed to have completely vanished.

But Danny knew that was impossible. No one could physically disappear. Not a real live person. So Victoria Mosley must have left by way of a back door.

Realizing the woman clerk was still waiting for instructions, Danny said, "Maybe I'll come back after I decide what I want."

As she joined Bridget again, Danny continued to puzzle over Victoria's disappearance. Why would the woman have gone out the back door if she wasn't hiding something? Danny felt certain now that Victoria Mosley's actions had something to do with Angellee.

Danny was still puzzling the matter over in her mind when they reached home and were told there would be company for dinner.

That evening, Danny felt intimidated by her surroundings—sitting in the dark, paneled dining room, wearing one of Angellee's gowns, a blue satin affair. In the kitchen was a bewildering variety of food, all in handsome silver dishes and platters, just waiting to be served. At the other end of the table, Bridget and another maid were busy passing out steaming plates of mock turtle soup while Rebecca Mallory, wearing a green velvet gown, tried to

229

engage Danny in conversation.

Although Rebecca's manner was pleasant, Danny couldn't help feeling intimidated by her. She was a beautiful woman, obviously used to such surroundings. Her husband Grant, a dark-haired, austere man, sat to Danny's right.

Danny felt she didn't belong here surrounded with such luxury—the rich, heavy linen, the massive silver, and the Waterford tumblers that were as heavy as rocks. Danny listened with half an ear to the woman who sat across the table from her . . . the other half was tuned to the men's conversation.

Jake wore a scowl on his face as he told the Mallorys about the report he'd received from the Pinkerton Agency.

"Dammit!" he swore. "There has to be something they are missing. I don't understand how Mosley can afford not to keep in contact with the men who have Angel."

"Jake," Rebecca admonished sternly. "I know how worried you are about Angel. We all are. But the dinner table is not the place to discuss Mosley. You'll give us all indigestion."

"Of course you're right," he said, picking up his spoon. "Please accept my apologies. It's just that I've become obsessed with finding Angellee . . ." His voice trailed away and he stared down at his plate.

"You'll find her," Rebecca said quietly. "Now, what culinary delight has Gruber prepared for us tonight?"

"Looks like mock turtle soup," Adam said. "It's been awhile since I've had such fare."

When Adam picked up his spoon, Danny reached

for hers. Scooping up some of the thin broth, she carried it to her mouth. At home she would have carried the bowl to her mouth, but apparently that wasn't the way with monied folk.

She was halfway through the soup, when Danny felt a sensation of being watched. Lifting her eyes, she met Bridget's intense gaze. The girl's eyes dropped to Danny's spoon, flicked to Adam, who was seated on Danny's left, then returned to Danny's spoon again. Realizing Bridget was trying to tell her something, Danny frowned. She looked down at her spoon, then at Adam's. Adam's spoon was larger than her own. Danny's gaze traveled around the table, touching on each spoon in turn. Everyone but Danny was using the larger spoon.

Danny felt a flush rising to her cheeks. Why hadn't Adam told her? She kicked him beneath the table, but he seemed not to notice. She kicked him again, harder this time.

Now she had his attention.

"Why didn't you tell me I was usin' the wrong spoon?" she whispered fiercely.

"I don't give a damn which spoon you use," he muttered. "It's really not that important. You've been functioning quite well with that one."

"Dammit! You just wanted me to make a fool of—"

"Something wrong, Danny?" Jake asked. "Is the soup not to your liking? Bridget can bring you something else if you'd like."

"The soup's just fine," she said, laying down the spoon she was holding and picking up the right one.

After the incident, she watched Adam closely to see

which eating utensil to use, unwilling to make herself look a fool in front of Rebecca Mallory.

Everything was strange to her. She had never seen a fine family at dinner before. Mealtimes in her experience were a business of filling the stomach with food. At home, they had rarely talked at meals, applying themselves strictly to eating. But apparently it was different with society folk.

Rebecca kept up a running conversation as Jake carved the roast, a huge leg of mutton resting in a wreath of parsley. Adam was thoughtful throughout the meal and his gaze rested often on Danny.

She was relieved when the blanc-mange with raspberry jam sauce and angel food cake had been served and she knew dinner was almost over. Finally the moment came to withdraw.

Jake had given the order for the gentlemen's coffee to be served in the study, where the men could smoke the cigars they never lit elsewhere in the house.

"Jake," Rebecca said softly. "I think Danny would like to be in on the discussion. I know I would."

Danny shot her a grateful look.

Moments later they were seated in the study and Jake was wondering how Mosley kept in touch with his men.

"Could be Mosley is not physically in contact with them," Adam said. "Perhaps they send messages back and forth."

"That angle has already been covered," Jake replied. "Pinkerton has two men on Mosley at all times. Anyone who comes in contact with him is followed. So far it's done no good."

"What about his wife?" Danny asked. "Could be

she's passing information on."

"Impossible," Jake said. "Her every movement is followed. In fact, I was given an updated report on Victoria's activities today. The report reads exactly like the last one did."

Danny sat up straighter. "It hasn't changed at all? How could that be?"

Jake shrugged. "She's obviously a woman of habits."

Victoria Mosley—a woman of habit? Danny didn't believe it for one instant. And what about the beauty parlor? Did she go there and disappear every single day? Something was fishy somewhere.

"Could I see the report?" she asked.

Jake took a file folder from a nearby table and handed it across to Danny. She scanned the sheet of paper. It was obvious Victoria Mosley had an active life. But like Jake had said, each day read like the one before. She made several stops every day, but the same ones she'd made the day before . . . and the day after. The dressmaker's, several friends . . . each of whom had been dutifully followed afterwards . . . and the beauty salon.

Danny's gaze narrowed on one line. Victoria visited the beauty salon each day? When her maid fixed her hair? And when Danny went in, the woman was nowhere in sight. The whole thing was becoming more and more curious.

"Something wrong, Danny?" Adam asked.

"Just wonderin' why Mosley's wife goes to the beauty parlor every day," she said.

"Victoria is a very meticulous woman, Danny," Adam said. "She's very careful of her appearance. I

233

see nothing unusual about her going to have her hair done."

"Her maid does her hair," Danny said sourly.

"How could you know that?" Adam asked.

"Heard her say so."

Adam shrugged. "Pierre's is a place of prestige. I can't see Victoria letting her maid do her hair when there are trained people to do it."

"Her maid is trained."

"This isn't the Ozarks, Danny," Adam said in a preoccupied voice. "Women of quality have different ways than what you're used to."

Danny gritted her teeth. Adam's attitude was completely maddening. He acted as though he thought she was some ignorant backwoods jack-ass, and she was getting just a little bit tired of it.

As though sensing Danny's feelings and trying to avoid an outburst from her, Rebecca changed the subject. "Have you seen William Rafferty lately, Jake?"

"Not since last week," Jake said. "I've been meaning to get back over there and make sure he's all right. I tried to get some protection for him, but Mosley hasn't made a move in his direction yet. The law won't do anything towards protecting him until he's been harmed."

"It would be too late then, wouldn't it?"

"Yes," Jake agreed. "It would. And right now, Rafferty is our only witness against Mosley. Without him, I'm afraid we would have no proof."

Danny leaned back in her chair and let the conversation flow around her. She knew they were discussing the case that was pending against Mos-

234

ley . . . the case that was responsible for Angellee's abduction, but she really knew little about it. She did know that Victoria Mosley was involved in it somehow . . . that the woman knew where Angellee was being held captive. But there was no use discussing Victoria further at the moment. Adam didn't seem to be prepared to listen to her.

But he would!

Danny would make sure of that.

Chapter Twenty-One

It was late when Adam bid Jake good night and went upstairs. He paused beside Danny's room, controlling an urge to go in, then passed on by. When he opened the door to his room, he was startled to find Danny curled up on his bed, sound asleep. Her skin appeared almost golden in the lamplight and the lighter wisps of hair curling around her eyes heightened the effect.

God! She looked so young . . . so incredibly vulnerable.

Like water bursting from a damn, his feelings for her came rushing to the surface. He had tried so hard to suppress them, had tried to forget the feelings she had aroused in him that night in St. Louis.

But he couldn't.

He remembered, all too clearly, the sweetness of her lips against his, and the soft moaning sound she had made as she threshed beneath his searching hands.

Even now, the memory had his lower body stirring

to life. God! He wanted it all again. Wanted to take her in his arms and crush her against him.

But he could not! He *must* not!

Because, no matter how much he wanted her, Danny deserved more. She deserved a man without a past, a man still virtually untouched by life . . . a man like Michael DeLeroy.

Dammit! He should have left her in her mountains . . . should never have taken her away.

Even as the thought surfaced, his mind rejected it. How could he wish never to have met her? Even though they were fated to part, he would have the memory of her locked inside his heart. And although he would never know the joy of having her again, Adam knew there was something . . . some tangible bond that would always bind him to her.

Suddenly, footsteps sounded somewhere down the corridor, and Adam realized that someone was coming.

He couldn't let Danny be found in his room. Her reputation would be torn to shreds. He closed the door firmly behind him.

Crossing to the bed, he bent over her sleeping form. "Danny," he whispered. "Wake up, Danny."

Her lashes fluttered, lifted, and she gazed up at him with sleep-dazed eyes. "Hello, Adam." His heart turned over as her lips curled into a peculiar half-smile. "What are you doing in my room?" she asked.

Adam tried to throttle the dizzying current racing through him as he smoothed her hair from her eyes with a trembling hand. "I'm not in your room," he said softly. "You're in mine."

"Oh." She rubbed at her eyes with her knuckles.

237

"Why'd you bring me here?"

Adam's gaze fell to the creamy expanse of her neck. He fought the urge to crush her against him. Instead, he spoke in a lightly teasing voice. "I didn't bring you, sleepyhead. You were already here when I came in, so you must have brought yourself."

"Oh," she said again, staring bemusedly up at him.

Gripping her below the elbows, he pulled her to a sitting position. "You know you shouldn't be here. Your reputation won't be worth two bits if anyone knew."

"Why?"

He laughed shortly. "Never mind," he said. "I'll see you to your room."

"No! Wait," she said, twisting her wrist away from him. "I remember now. I came to see you about that woman."

"What woman?"

"Mosley's wife."

"Victoria?" His gaze sharpened. "What about her?"

"She's up to something, Adam. There's something she's tryin' to hide. I followed her in that place, but she wasn't there."

"You're not making sense, Danny. What place wasn't she in?"

"That beauty place."

"Pierre's? What do you mean she wasn't there? If she went in the door, then she must have been there."

"If she'd'a been there, then I'd've seen her," Danny retorted.

"Your imagination is working overtime, Danny. You don't like Victoria. That's why you're trying to make her out to be something she isn't."

Danny stiffened as though he had struck her. "You're the one that's tryin' to do that," she retorted angrily, sliding off the bed. "You got the eyes of a blind man when it comes to that hussy. But I know what's goin' on betwixt the two of you. I seen you kissin' her in the garden."

"Kissing Victoria? Don't be ridiculous! I never did any such thing!"

"I know what I seen," she said. "An' I seen you kissin' her."

He frowned at her, realizing she must have seen him with Carlotta. "That wasn't Victoria. You saw me with Carlotta."

"Who's Carlotta?"

"Never mind." He had no intention of explaining Carlotta to her.

"You're tellin' me to never mind, 'cause they ain't no such person. You just made her up to save Victoria's reputation."

"Danny, you're completely wrong about her." He cupped her face and made her look at him. "Listen to me. Pinkerton has two men following Victoria every time she leaves the house. They watched her go in Pierre's and waited for her to come out again. Which she did. I read the report. She went in there. An hour later, she came out. It's the same every day. They fix her hair for her."

"No they don't," she said stubbornly. "I already told you her maid does it."

239

"Stop it, Danny," he said, running his fingers through his dark, unruly hair. "It's been a busy day and I'm tired. I was looking forward to going right to bed. Instead, I find you here waiting for me."

The anger seemed to drain away from her as quickly as it had come. "It was the only way I could see you alone," she muttered. "Ever since we got here you been with Jake. We ain't had hardly a minute to ourselves."

Reaching up, she smoothed the hair back from his face and rubbed at the frown on his forehead. His flesh prickled at her touch and he pushed irritably at her hands.

"Don't do that," he growled, giving her a dark look. *Dammit!* Didn't she know how it affected him to be touched by her? Why did she have to look so feminine? So totally, utterly, desirable?

A shadow darkened her eyes and she lowered them. But not before he had seen the glitter of tears. "Go on, Danny," he said gruffly. "Go back to your room. And for heaven's sake don't let anyone see you leave mine."

Instead of leaving, Danny held his gaze. "What happened?" she asked. "What did I do? You been treatin' me like I was poison ivy since that night in St. Louis." Her gaze softened. "Don't you remember how it was then, Adam? Don't you know it could be that good between us now?"

He swallowed hard. "That was a mistake," he said gruffly. "I never meant it to happen. It *shouldn't* have happened. I shouldn't have allowed it to."

Her lips twisted bitterly. "No. I guess you

240

shouldn't have. Not since you're feelin' the way you are about it. I thought we had something kinda special goin' betwixt us. But looks like I was dead wrong about it."

Adam felt lower than a snake's belly in a wagon rut. He knew he had hurt her and it pained him deeply. He hadn't meant it to happen. "Danny—"

"Just forget it, outlander!" she snapped, her voice wobbling slightly. "Forget I even mentioned anything about that night."

Her eyes sparkled with unshed tears as she pushed her way past him and left the room, slamming the door behind her.

Danny barely reached her room before the tears she had been holding back overflowed. Shutting herself into the privacy of her room, she ran to her bed and flung herself across it.

Then she allowed the tears to fall.

Damn him! Damn Adam Hollister! Why had he made love to her if he didn't mean it?

But even as she asked herself the question, Danny knew the answer. She was as much to blame as Adam. Even more so. He had tried to back away, but she had wanted him so badly. Even though she realized that, it didn't help ease her pain. Not in the slightest.

Spasms shook her slender frame as she continued to cry for the love she had so carelessly given away to a man who didn't even want it.

Muffling her sobs in the pillow, she gave release to her agony until her sobs finally ceased and she lay on her back staring at the ceiling with glassy eyes.

It was late when she finally fell asleep from

exhaustion. And when she was wakened next morning by Bridget, she felt as though she had been drugged.

"Time to wake up, Miss," Bridget said, setting the tray she was carrying down with a thump on the nearest table. Crossing to the windows, she pulled the curtains wide, allowing the midmorning sun to stream through.

After partaking of tea and crumpets, Danny splashed water on her face. She dressed herself in a gray and pink calico dress and left the room.

"Top o' the morning to you, Danny," came a voice from down the hall.

Danny's head jerked up and she saw the housekeeper on the point of entering a room. She returned the woman's greeting and continued on her way. But as she passed the open door, she stopped short. The room was obviously outfitted for a baby, judging by the crib and other furnishings.

Curious, Danny stepped inside.

"Was this Jake's room when he was a baby?" she asked the housekeeper.

"Land sakes, no!" the woman said. "Back then the nursery was on the top floor. Jake's ma and pa didn't believe in havin' the baby on the same floor as the grown-ups."

"It's a mighty pretty room," Danny said.

The woman nodded her head. "That it is, Miss. The missus fixed it up for the wee babe that's soon to be born."

"What wee babe?" Danny asked.

"Why, the one that the missus and the master is gonna be havin'," Mrs. Gruber said.

It took a moment for the housekeeper's words to sink in. When they did, Danny's eyes widened and her heart skipped a beat. "Angel is gonna have a baby?" she whispered.

"You didn't know? No. You couldn't have." Mrs. Gruber answered her own question. "Yes. It's a fact. And Miss Angel and Jake was that happy about it too." She gave a long sigh. "Poor things. She'll be nearin' her time now, an we're all worried about Miss Angel and the wee babe. I pray every night that the folks that have her will see she gets the care she needs when the babe is birthin'."

A cold chill settled over Danny . . . freezing in its impact, rooting her to the spot. "It's done happened," she whispered. "God! That's what Angel's been tryin' to say. She's done had the babe. But somethin is awful wrong."

The housekeeper's face blanched. "What do you mean?" she asked.

But Danny had no time to explain. Gripping the woman by her upper arms, she said, "Where's Adam?"

"In the study."

Whirling around, Danny raced out the door and down the steps, literally bursting into the study where she found Adam and Jake deep in conversation.

"Danny!" Adam said. "What in the world is wrong? Has something happened?"

She skidded to a halt in front of him, last night completely forgotten. Grasping him by the shoulders, she looked up at him. Her breasts heaved with exertion when she spoke. "Adam!" she cried. "Angel's . . . gonna have a babe. . . . I mean . . . she's got a babe. That's what it's been all this time. Back in the forest, and at the ranch house. It was the babe cryin'. It's been Angel's babe cryin' all along."

"What are you saying?" Jake demanded, his face draining of color. "How could you know she's had the baby?"

"I don't know . . ." She stared up into his angry face, moving closer against Adam who drew a protective arm around her.

"Take it easy," Adam told Jake. He bent his head to Danny. "Calm down," he said. "You're out of breath with all that running."

She sucked in huge gulps of air. "I can't calm down," she said. "I gotta say it."

He nodded. "I know."

"What in hell's going on?" Jake demanded.

Adam waved a hand at him. "Just a minute, Jake. Give Danny a chance to tell us. Take all the time you need, Danny. But catch your breath first."

"You know the cry . . . the one I thought was an animal? It wasn't no animal, Adam. It was the babe cryin. An' Angel was askin' me for help. I know she was, but it may be too late now."

"Somebody better explain what the hell is going on here," Jake snapped.

"Hold on!" Adam said. "We didn't tell you before because we were afraid it would do no good. That it would only raise your hopes uselessly."

"Dammit!" Jake gritted. "Tell me what?"

"Apparently, Danny has some kind of . . ." Adam frowned, "well, she calls it a gift. She can sense things and—"

244

Jake's reaction was immediate. He reached for Danny, gripped her forearms roughly. "You've got it too!" he said harshly. "Why didn't I think of that? What do you mean, it might be too late?"

She flinched away from him. "I-I don't know," she stuttered. "I ain't seen the wispy dark thing for awhile. Just the evil one. An' the other'n coulda been Angellee. I had a feelin' it was."

"Start from the beginning," Jake said. "And tell me everything about this . . . vision . . . you're having."

"I wouldn't exactly call it a vision," Adam said. "It's more like a nightmare."

"Whatever it is, I want to know everything," Jake said. He looked at Danny. "Tell me all of it. From the first time you were aware of anything unusual."

So she did.

Chapter Twenty-Two

Danny's words tumbled over one another as she hurried to tell Jake about the visions that had plagued her since she'd met Adam.

"Thought at first I was havin' nightmares," she muttered. "Then I thought Angel must be dead and her spirit had come to haunt me." Jake's face paled at her words, and she hastened to reassure him. "Now I know different. It ain't no haunt that keeps callin' to me. I know that now. It's Angel, right enough."

"Do you know where she is?" Jake asked.

"She's all aroun' us," Danny said. "Ever since I come to this city where she lived, I been seein' her. I been hearin' her laugh an' I been hearin' her cry, an—"

"But can you tell where she is, Danny?" Jake's voice was insistent. "Can you tell where she is being held?"

She shook her head. "No. But when we was at Mosley's the other night, I seen the evil dark circlin' around him, just a hoverin' there like some ol' buzzard awaitin' for the last speck of life to drain outta his body so's it could set in eatin' away at his body. An' I felt all cold-like when I touched him, an'—"

"But did you see anything at all that would help us find Angel," Jake interrupted.

"No. But he's got 'er all right. I'm certain of that."

Jake's shoulders slumped and he looked as though he were a man who was near the breaking point. "I was already positive of that, Danny. For a moment there I thought we were closer to finding her." He jammed his hands in his pockets and strode to the window and Danny felt as though she had let him down. "She's already had the baby." He swung back to her. "Can you tell . . . are they all right? Are Angel and the baby well?"

She shook her head. "I don't know, Jake. I purely don't."

"I've got to find them," he said desperately. "I've just got to."

"We will," Adam assured him.

"I was thinkin' maybe if I was to hunt through the city . . . well, maybe I could get one of them feelings about her . . . maybe I could tell when she was close by."

Jake studied her grimly. "I really don't think Mosley is keeping her in the city. It would be too risky. And Mosley is not a man who would take such a risk. If I find Angellee, then he has no hold over me. No. I'm certain she's not here. We need to look farther afield." Pulling his watch from his vest

247

pocket, he checked the time. "I have an appointment in an hour. But it shouldn't take long. When I return we'll take a drive in the country. I know it's a long shot, we don't have anything else to go on."

"Let me go now," she said eagerly.

He shook his head. "I want to be with you. Just in case we get lucky."

Danny felt frustrated as she watched Adam and Jake leave. Minutes ticked by and Danny began to pace the room. Each minute that passed seemed like an eternity. She stopped beside the parlor window and stared out at the gray, overcast skies.

How could she be expected to stay inside after discovering the source of the cry she'd been hearing for so long? Jake and Adam were being unreasonable to ask it of her. Didn't they know she needed to do something, needed to find a way to help Angellee and her babe?

She turned with a start when someone touched her arm.

"Company's come," Mrs. Gruber said.

"Tell whoever it is that Jake ain't here," Danny said. She didn't feel like entertaining anyone, be it Jake's friends or Angellee's.

"He's come to see you," the housekeeper said.

"Me? Who is it?"

"Come and see," the woman said mysteriously. "You can't help but be pleased."

With her curiosity piqued, Danny followed the housekeeper to the foyer where Roderic Fortunato waited. Danny stared blankly at him.

"I realize this is an intrusion," he said, striding

248

forward with his hand outstretched. "I only meant to inquire after your health."

"Reckon I'm healthy enough," she said, not certain she wanted to waste the time entertaining him. But it seemed she really had no choice. Mrs. Gruber was already showing the young man into the parlor.

"I'll bring some tea and cakes," she said, leaving them alone.

"Obviously I have called at an inconvenient time," Roderic said, running a hand across his already smooth hair.

"As a matter of fact," Danny said, "It is kinda inconvenient. Maybe you should just—" She broke off suddenly, staring at his tall, thin frame. Adam had told her not to go out alone. If Roderic was with her, then she wouldn't be alone.

"Is something wrong?" Roderic asked. "You seem distracted."

"I reckon as how I am," Danny said, her gaze resting thoughtfully on the young man. "I was just thinking on something. Maybe you could help me with it." She continued to look at him, barely noting that he was fidgeting beneath her inspection. "Yes. You could help me with it," she went on. "'Cause I just decided that I ain't gonna do it, Roderic. No matter what they said, I ain't gonna just sit here and do nothin' about it."

"Pardon me?"

"Adam and Jake shouldn't expect me to," Danny muttered. "They's gotta be something I can do. But whatever it is, I ain't gonna find out if I stay cooped

249

up in this house the way both of them is sayin' I should."

"You set yourself down and have your tea, Danielle," Mrs. Gruber said from behind Danny. "Mr. Fortunato don't know nothing about this. And Adam knows what he's doing. He's that worried about you, afraid Asa Mosley will hear about this . . . about your . . . gift. Or whatever it is. And if Mosley sees you as a threat, he's likely to have you abducted and stashed away where he's got your cousin."

Danny could see by the frown on Roderic's face that he was totally confused by their conversation. "Maybe it wouldn't be so bad if he did," she said. "Maybe that's the way to find Angellee and her babe. It's a sure bet that I ain't gonna stay stuck in this house . . . doin' nothing until Adam gives me the go ahead to start looking for her."

"Just be patient," Mrs. Gruber said. "The men will be back this afternoon. Then you can ask them to take you about so you can look for the missus and her babe."

"I ain't gonna wait until then!" Danny snapped. "I done told you. I got me a feeling about that highfalutin' woman. That Victoria Mosley! They ain't no way she's going to that beauty parlor to get her hair fixed. She's up to no good. An' since she's bein' so sneaky about it, then I'm wantin' to know why. Today, when she goes through the door of that beauty parlor, I aim to be right behind her."

"You're not going nowhere by your lonesome," the housekeeper said sharply.

250

"No!" Danny agreed. "I guess I ain't at that. Roderic's going with me." She turned to him. "Ain't you, Roderic?"

"I would be happy to escort you anywhere," he said gallantly. "But I must confess that I am confused by all this."

"That's all right," Danny said kindly. "You don't need to understand. All you need to do is go with me."

She reached the door in a few long strides. Moments later she was hurrying up the street with Roderic keeping pace beside her.

"Where are we going?" he asked.

"Pierre's."

"The beauty salon?"

He stopped in his tracks, but she was having none of that. "Come on," she said. "We have to hurry."

Reluctantly, he followed along behind her, looking as though he wished he were anywhere but there.

They barely made it.

They reached the bench located in the small park across the street from Pierre's as Victoria Mosley's carriage pulled up in front of the salon.

"I'm goin' in there too," Danny said. "You comin'?"

"I will wait here for you," Roderic said.

"Fine."

Danny had already put Roderic out of her mind. Her attention was focused entirely on the carriage across the street. She watched the liveried driver leap to the ground and help his passenger alight. Victoria was so intent on her destination that she paid little attention to her surroundings. A fact that Danny was grateful for since she was only a few paces behind the other woman.

Immediately, a woman stepped from behind the counter and blocked Danny's way. "Good afternoon," she said. "Could I help you?"

"No!" Danny snapped, stepping around the clerk, intent on following Victoria, who had headed straight for the door set in a back wall. It had barely closed behind the other woman when Danny swung it open a mere crack and peered through the narrow opening. She saw an alley . . . an empty alley, but there was no sign of Victoria Mosley.

Fearing she had lost the woman, Danny slid through the door . . . and stopped abruptly.

The faint sound of voices told her the woman was just around the corner.

Moving closer, Danny listened to the conversation.

"There must be no delay in delivering the message," Victoria was saying. "Asa was adamant about that. He wants them moved today."

Them? Danny's heart fluttered wildly. Who did Asa Mosley want moved so fast? The answer could only be Angellee and her babe!

"Shultzy ain't to home right now," an ancient voice whined.

"Then take it yourself!" Victoria snapped.

"Me?" The voice held injured surprise. "You expect me to go all the way out there? I ain't so young as I used to be. It's hard for me to get around anymore."

Danny peered cautiously around the corner and

saw Victoria with an old woman whose skin was wrinkled and gray, her breasts sagging, her fingernails ragged and dirty. Danny felt completely repulsed by her.

"I don't care how you do it," Victoria said. "Just do it."

After a long silence, the old woman spoke again. "I'll need more money. Have to hire me a horse to ride."

Victoria took several coins from her bag and gave it to the old hag. "Now hurry up and go," she said. "Else there'll be the devil to pay."

Danny retreated immediately, scuttling toward a stack of boxes nearby and scrunching down behind them. When she heard the door open and close, she crept out of her hiding place and hurried after the old woman. There wasn't time to find Roderic. He was in the other direction, and despite the old woman's claim to being unable to travel, she went at an unusually quick pace. Danny knew if she returned for Roderic, she would surely lose the old woman.

The old crone didn't hire a carriage, instead, she hurried to the west end of town, then continued traveling by foot. An hour later, they entered the forest and continued in a southwesterly direction.

Another hour had passed before Danny saw the house on the hill.

She sucked in a sharp breath and her heart gave a wild leap of joy. Angellee was there! Danny felt positive of it, because the house on the hill was identical to the one in her vision.

Danny knew, even before the old woman opened

the door, that the house was her destination.

God! Danny felt elated at her discovery. Mosley had lost. Jake would rescue Angellee as soon as Danny told him where she was being kept. *We'll have you out soon, Angel.* Although Danny pushed the thought outward as hard as she could, she felt no response to the message. Even so, she had no doubt that Angellee and her babe were nearby.

She turned to retrace her steps, then stopped abruptly. What about the message the old woman had brought? Suppose Mosley had sent instructions for Angellee and her babe to be moved elsewhere? Danny knew she couldn't take a chance. She would have to stay awhile and keep watch.

Danny waited, hidden in the thick shrubs, her ears attuned to the sounds of the forest.

Reeeee, reeeee, reeee . . . the crickets sounded their steam whistle cry. The air around her seemed to vibrate with the piercing noise, a sound like chalk scratching across slate, until her teeth seemed to pulsate with the sound.

Perhaps part of her reaction was the certain conviction that all was not well. Something evil was lurking, hiding in the nearby brush, waiting to take her unawares before leaping out on her.

Stop it! she silently ordered herself. *You're gonna scare yourself so bad, you ain't gonna be no good to Angel when the time comes.*

Danny wondered, and not for the first time, if she'd been wise to come alone on this escapade. But what choice had she? There had been no way to alert the others, and keep the old woman in sight. And somehow, she had been certain that the ancient crone was going to the place where Mosley had hidden Angel and the babe.

And it wasn't as though she'd come unarmed. The derringer Adam had given her in Lizard Lick fit snugly in the reticule she carried. It would only take a moment to retrieve it if she needed.

Danny moved north across the mountainside, keeping a watch on the house she could see in the distance.

Reeeeee, reeeee, reeeee came the ceaseless sound of the crickets. As if that were not enough, there was the noise of the wind, continuously rustling the leaves on the trees. There was no way she could hear an enemy approaching.

But the ever-present sound of the leaves rustling in the wind and the never-ending cry of the crickets would cover any noise she might be making and lessen her chances of being found.

Suddenly she heard a hollow, mournful sound and pressed herself against the trunk of a pine tree. Fumbling in her reticule, she extracted the pistol and held it ready. The rough bark prickled her skin, but she paid little attention. Frozen in place, she listened fearfully, peering warily around the brush, trying to penetrate the forest with her gaze.

She heard a clatter, as though feet had dislodged stones, and she gave a start. With fear widened eyes, she slid around the tree, taking refuge from the sound.

It seemed an eternity passed while she waited. Frozen with fear, her gaze darted from left to right in her search for the enemy.

A whisper of sound came to her . . . something moving through the brush . . . definitely not the wind.

Silence.

She waited, her grip tightening on the pistol in her hand . . . ten seconds . . . twenty . . . thirty. . . .

God! Had she been found out!

Her limbs were frozen. She dared hardly breathe. She listened.

The wind rustled.

A bird trilled.

What's out there?

Suddenly, the waiting was over.

Something darted toward her, bending low to the ground.

Her heart leaped wildly as Danny uttered a cry of terror. She willed her body to move . . . to escape from the . . .

The rabbit!

It *was* only a rabbit.

Danny laughed hysterically. She had managed to frighten herself with a rabbit. The whole thing had been nothing more than her imagination. Certainly nothing to be frightened of.

Nothing!

She stepped boldly forward.

Too soon.

A cracking sound behind Danny warned her, but not fast enough. Before she could react, the pistol was wrenched from her hand and flung aside.

"Oooof!" The sound was squeezed out of Danny as

muscular arms wrapped around her. *Thrum, thrum, thrum.* Danny's heart beat loudly in her ears, drowning out all other sound as she strained against her captor.

But it was useless. She was encircled by arms that seemed to have the strength of steel. She couldn't fight with her arms pressed so tightly against her sides. The man who held her captive seemed impervious to her kicking feet.

Sheer panic welled through Danny as she twisted to face her attacker.

Chapter Twenty-Three

Adam kept pace beside Jake, picking his way across the Flats through a rutted and littered yard. They skirted the rusty tracks where the ore cars lurched, groaning and screeching, up and down with their loads of material for the ironworks along the riverside.

They crossed the cindery patch in front of a shanty door and Jake raised a hand to knock.

The door opened abruptly and a woman looked out at them.

"I hope I haven't come at a bad time, Mary," Jake said. "But I need to talk to William again."

"Times all the same to us since William's legs was taken away from him. There's not an hour of the day when he's free from his pain."

"Is that Mister Logan?" came a gruff male voice from inside. "Don't keep him standin' out there, woman. Let him in."

"Come inside," the woman said dourly, stepping back to allow them entry.

Across the room, Adam saw a man in a crude wheelchair. It seemed to be fashioned from an old rocker and three iron wheels. The man's legs hung limp, resting on a wooden footpiece. According to Jake, William Rafferty had worked for the Monongahela Amalgamated before his legs had been crushed in a mine cave-in.

After greeting Jake, William nodded at Adam. "Is he a man to be trusted?" he asked Jake.

"I am sure he is or I wouldn't have brought him," Jake replied.

William stared hard at Adam, rubbing his long jaw, seeming to take Adam's measure with his eyes. As though he was satisfied, he gave a short nod of his head. "Guess a man couldn't ask for more." He turned to his wife. "Make us some tea, Mary."

"You're a blind old fool, William Rafferty," the woman said harshly, clenching her hands beneath her apron. "You'd serve the lot of us better if you'd keep your mouth shut about the doings amongst us."

"Mary, I know you've suffered along with William," Jake said. "But please believe me. I wouldn't do anything that would bring more pain for the two of you."

"You can say that easy enough," she said harshly. "But what good does it do? Is it gonna give my William's legs back to him? Is it gonna take away the pain he feels every day? What's done is already past. And they ain't no changing it neither. William's legs has been taken away from him by the Widow Maker. But God was merciful. Even though the doctor said he'll be in that chair until the day he dies, my William's life was spared. Now you come here,

259

wanting him to tell you things. Wantin' to put him in danger again."

Jake asked quietly. "Has someone threatened William with harm if he talks to me?"

"I ain't sayin' another word," she said grimly, her mouth compressing in a tight line. Her eyes found her husband's. "And neither should you, William. Neither should you." The last words were more like a sob.

"Quit your blatherin' and get on with your tea makin', Mary," William said gruffly. "Leave us menfolks to talk on menfolks' doings."

Mary Rafferty's chin lifted and the woman held her body stiffly as she left the room. They could hear her banging pots around in the kitchen, voicing her disapproval in a not-so-silent manner.

"Set yourself down," William told his company. When they had done so, he spoke again. "You'll have to overlook Mary. We had more than our share of company around here today. Not more'n a couple of hours have passed since the union man was here."

"The union man?" Jake questioned. "What on earth does the union want with you, William?"

"Now why wouldn't the union be wantin' the likes of me? Who better to come to? There ain't many can lay claim to surviving a cave-in at the Widow Maker." His lips stretched into a cold smile. "That's what's got Mary on her high horse. The union's wanting me to speak out against the Amalgamated."

"I see," Jake said. "What did you tell them?"

"Said I'd have to think on it. But that ain't the half of it. When the union man left, Mary saw another

260

man follow him. She said it was Patrick Donnahey. And he was actin' kinda sneaky-like. Keeping close against the buildings like he didn't want nobody to see him."

"Donnahey?" Jake's brow furrowed. "Why should he worry about being seen? Isn't he one of you?"

"Thought he was," William replied. "But now I'm thinking maybe he's not to be trusted. Could be he's working for the mine owners."

"That doesn't sound good," Jake said. "Not good at all."

For a long moment Danny stared in disbelief at the man who held her. How had she allowed herself to be captured? She had grown careless! Was he alone, or were there others with him?

Her eyes darted past him, but she saw no sign of anyone else. She was alone with the man, alone under skies that had become heavy with the threat of storm. Clouds so deeply gray they were almost purple hung pendulously in the sky.

Danny was conscious of the pines stirring in a fret of wind, of the leaves fluttering and rustling.

Her gaze returned to the man standing before her . . . tall, broad, and undoubtedly strong. The cast in his pale blue eyes told her she was in danger. And, even the smile on his face did nothing to reassure her.

"Who're you?" she asked.

"I'm the man who's gone and caught myself a little bird. Lucky by name and lucky by nature." His smile widened. "The old woman said she was sure she'd been followed. Looks like she was right. I reckon Mosley's gonna pay me plenty for catching you."

Although panic rioted within her, Danny swallowed around her fear. "Are you talking about Asa Mosley?" she asked sharply.

"Who else would I be talking about?" he asked with a malicious grin. "He's the only Mosley I know around these parts. Except for his wife, that is." His gaze was curious. "Why you following the old woman? And why're you so curious about that house up yonder on the hill?"

Instead of answering him, she posed a question of her own. "What business is it of yours?"

He favored her with another wide grin. "Maybe somebody's paying me to watch that place. To see who might be a little too interested in it. I ain't saying that's the way of it, just that it could be." He was obviously playing with her and thoroughly enjoying it.

Danny's thoughts whirled furiously. Why did this have to happen to her now? Now, when she was so close to finding Angellee. And she *was* close. She knew Angellee was in that house on the hill.

Even though Danny could not actually feel her cousin's presence there, she felt positive that she had found the place where Angellee and her newborn baby were being held prisoner. And there was no way she was going to let this weasel stand in the way of setting Angellee free.

"How much is Mosley paying you?" she asked coldly.

He favored her with a wide smile that served only to make him appear more menacing. "Why you wanting to know?"

"Because whatever it is, I'll pay you twice as much. And all you have to do is go away and leave me be."

He tapped his chin with a long finger and studied her thoughtfully as though actually considering her offer. "You don't look like somebody who's got that much money?" he said.

"Maybe not. But somebody I know does." She was certain Jake would pay this crook off, although it went against her grain to even consider it.

Lucky's eyes glittered. "Girlie, it would cost me my life to take you up on that offer. There ain't enough money in the world that'd be worth runnin' the risk I'd be taking. If I let Asa Mosley down, I couldn't never show my face anywhere in this state again. Mosley is a mean son-of-a-bitch when he gets riled. And if I did what you're suggesting, I reckon he'd be plenty damn riled."

"You don't have to stay in this state," she said angrily. "You could go somewhere else and start your life over."

Thunder rumbled in the distance, followed by a flash of lightning over Lucky's left shoulder as Danny waited for his answer.

He paid the heightening storm no attention as he ran the back of his fingers down her cheek. "You ain't half bad," he said, allowing his hand to stray beneath her chin, touching her neck, sliding across her breasts.

Sucking in a sharp breath, she recoiled from his

263

touch, hitting out with clenched fists.

"You're something. I gotta admit that. But I kinda like the life I already got. Back home there's a yeller-haired schoolteacher that took a shine to me. And they ain't no way somebody like you could measure up to her."

For some reason that hurt. She didn't care that he preferred some schoolteacher, but if a low-down jack-ass like this didn't want her, how could she expect someone like Adam to?

These thoughts flickered through her head as she waited for the right moment to make her escape. The moment came when a searing bolt of lightning crackled horizontally just above the tallest tree and a second later thunder shook the heavens, making them both flinch.

Lucky's grip relaxed and, quick to take advantage, Danny wrenched her arm away and took flight.

With a muttered oath, he took up chase.

Danny crashed through the forest, heedless of the noise she made as she tried to outdistance Lucky. Bushes reached for her, tangling in her clothes and ripping the fabric when she pulled free. She ran as fast as she could, her heart pounding, chased as much by the loud bursts of thunder and the streaks of jagged lightning as by Lucky himself.

A fallen log blocked the path ahead of her, but she leapt over it. Stumbling in her haste, she quickly righted herself, knowing she couldn't falter lest she be caught. Her heart pounded like a drumbeat; her head ached savagely, a crashing throb to the tides of her pulse.

Danny knew she must find cover, knew she must escape from the man who pursued her. . . .

She was almost past the crevice when she saw it, partially hidden by brush and the protruding ledge. It looked as though a giant hand had shoved two huge boulders almost together, leaving only enough space for Danny to enter.

Casting a quick look behind, she darted inside, and almost instantly, a rotten smell hit her, stopping her almost dead in her tracks. What in blazes had died in here?

Shuddering, she moved on, making her way down the shadowy length of the crevasse. At any moment she expected to hear the shout that would mean discovery. The ground was slippery, strewn with rotting, decaying leaves and other debris.

When Danny reached the opposite end, she stepped out into the sunlight and turned to look back. Her pulse leapt as she saw the figure blocking the light from the other end.

Her pursuer had obviously discovered the path she had taken.

With her heart beating like a trip-hammer, Danny ran until her breathing came in short, sharp pants; until every step she took felt like someone was jabbing her ribs with a sharp knife. She needed to rest, but if she stopped, she would surely be caught.

She drew up short near a sapling and clung to it for support. Casting her gaze around, she searched for shelter; her eyes lit upon a stand of thick bushes and she made a dash for them. At first she thought they were impenetrable . . . then her eyes found the small opening and she squirmed through and scrunched her body into the smallest possible position.

Lucky's voice, calling threats and uttering curses, followed her through the tangle of leaves and branches.

Holding her breath lest he hear, she listened to her pounding heart and the sound of his large body crashing over broken underbrush. He neared then passed her hiding place.

But even though he'd passed on by, Danny knew she wasn't safe. If Lucky had followed her all the way across country, he wouldn't give up so easily. He would keep searching until he found her.

She must find a better place of concealment!

Darting from her hiding place, she hurried along in the opposite direction, intent on putting as much distance as possible between herself and her pursuer. She was in a cluster of rocks when she heard him coming back.

Danny's stomach churned with anxiety and frustration, and a wave of dizziness swept over her.

God! She couldn't faint now!

Locking her knees in place, Danny put out a hand to steady herself, but instead of finding solid rock, her fingers found empty space. Her gaze narrowed on the opening in the rocks and hope flared strong in her heart.

Was the opening a cave?

Before the thought had even solidified, she began climbing.

A bolt of lightning split the sky and thunder shook the heavens, rolling downhill and grumbling like a runaway coal car on wobbling wheels as the first rain started. But Lucky ignored it, keeping his gaze fixed on the ground, intent on finding the girl who had eluded him so far.

Lucky knew he had to find her. He didn't dare show his face around Mosley until he did. Asa Mosley could be ruthless when it came to getting what he wanted. And he didn't suffer fools gladly.

Suddenly Lucky's gaze narrowed and he leaned closer to study the print of a small shoe. A lady's shoe. There was no doubt in his mind that it was hers. When he found her, she would suffer for putting him to so much trouble.

Nobody . . . nobody . . . especially some little ridge-runner bitch was goin' to make a fool of Lucky Ryan and get away with it.

The rain fell in huge, cold splatting drops that hit the ground with audible cracks and sent up spurts of fine dust as Adam and Jake made their way back to the Logan mansion. Although Adam tried to keep his mind on the search for Angellee, his mind was on her cousin.

Danny occupied too much of his thoughts these days. He would be glad when they found her cousin and he could leave here. Glad . . . and yet sorry. Leaving her would be hard, probably the hardest thing he would ever have to do.

When they entered the mansion the housekeeper hurried forward, her gaze sliding past them for a moment before coming to rest on her employer's face.

"Saints preserve us!" she muttered. "Something awful's happened, sure."

Jake stiffened. "Has there been word of Angel?" he asked harshly.

"No," Mrs. Gruber replied grimly. "But I'm afraid something's happened to the poor girl's cousin."

The words slammed into Adam, almost robbing him of breath. "What are you saying? Where is Danny?"

"There lays the problem," the woman said. "She's been missing this live-long day."

Jake frowned. "Missing? Did she leave the house alone?"

"No, I'm afraid I was with her."

Adam spun toward the man who had spoken. He stood in the doorway of the parlor.

"I am deeply sorry," Roderic Fortunato apologized. "But Danielle was so insistent that I accompany her, and I really saw no harm in it."

"He's not to be blamed," said the housekeeper stoutly. "I thought it would be all right. She was restless, kept pacing back and forth. And she was that determined to go, there was no stopping her."

"We aren't looking to place the blame," Jake said. "When did you see her last?"

"It was just before noon," Roderic said. "We left here and went straight to Pierre's. I waited at the park across the street while she went inside. And she didn't come back out." He looked at Adam. "I am sorry. When I finally went in to look for her, the woman who runs the place said Danielle had gone out the back door."

"I'm thinking that Asa Mosley has something to do with the poor girl's disappearing like that," the housekeeper said.

"I wouldn't put anything past him," Jake replied, his eyes cold and forbidding. He turned toward the front door. "I'm going to report her missing to the local authorities."

"Little good that'll do," the housekeeper said. "Miss Angel was reported missing a long time ago. She ain't turned up yet."

"You don't have to remind me, Mrs. Gruber," Jake said angrily. "Well I know it. After all, it is my *wife* that is missing."

"I know, Jake," the housekeeper said with the familiarity of a longtime acquaintance. "And I ain't saying you haven't done everything a body could possibly do to get her back. It's just that I'm worried about her, and Miss Danny too."

"We all are." Jake opened the door. "Are you coming, Adam?"

Adam shook his head. "You go on ahead," he said. "You won't need me."

"Is there nothing I can do?" Roderic asked.

"I think you've done quite enough!" Adam snapped, then immediately felt ashamed. The boy really couldn't be blamed. Adam knew how stubborn Danny could be and if blame was to be applied, then Adam knew he was the one who deserved it.

Roderic looked stricken. "If there is nothing I can do, then I will leave you," he said.

After the door had closed behind Roderic, Mrs. Gruber looked at Adam. "You oughtn't go blaming him," she said. "Danielle is willful. When she makes her mind up to something, there's just no stopping her."

Adam ignored her words. "What do you know

269

about Pierre's?" he asked.

"Not much," she admitted. "They ain't been open very long. The man who owns it is a Frenchman, name of Pierre Dupont, but he ain't local. Way I hear it, he just showed up in town one day. Before a month had passed he opened up that hair place. Really set the townsfolk on their ears . . . a man owning a place like that."

"A woman in your position must hear things," Adam said. "Not only about his place of business, but about his personal life."

"Guess I have," she said, her eyes twinkling with malicious amusement. "Folks do wonder why there's no sign of a woman friend. And folks do wonder where he gets all his money. More'n that place could ever bring him. It's rumored that maybe Asa Mosley's wife is more than a friend."

"Do you put much faith in such rumors?"

"I never put no faith in idle gossip," she answered. "But you did say you wanted to hear everything I been told about him."

"Yes," Adam replied, nodding thoughtfully. He knew he was grasping at straws, but he meant to get to the bottom of Danny's disappearance somehow. And he must do it quickly, for he had a gut feeling that Danny's life depended on her being found right away.

This very night.

Danny shivered in the gloom of the small cave, realizing how lucky she'd been to find it. The odor of damp decay wrapped around her. She could hear the plip-plop of dripping water from somewhere close by and knew it was still raining outside.

Adam! she silently cried. *Help me, Adam!*

Tears coursed down her cheeks and she wrapped her arms around her torso, trying to control her shivering. She had to remain where she was . . . couldn't leave her hiding place because Lucky was still searching somewhere nearby. She was almost positive of it.

Hugging her arms tightly around her upper body, Danny curled herself into a ball and slumped to the floor. Leaning her head against the rock wall, she willed her tense muscles to relax.

Chapter Twenty-Four

Thunder rumbled in the distance, followed by a jagged streak of lightning that split the sky. The wind blew and whipped Adam's hair, seeming bent on tearing it from his head, but he scarcely noticed. His dark eyes were focused on the ground in the alley behind the beauty salon. But, although he studied the area thoroughly for some sign of Danny's passing, the storm had wiped any prints she might have left away, as successfully as though the ground had been swept clean with a broom.

Adam's stomach twisted into knots and his heart was heavy with pain as he made his way to the nearest bar and ordered a drink.

Where could Danny be? he silently wondered.

He had been searching the streets for hours and he was close to despairing. He couldn't bear the thought of Danny alone somewhere out on the street . . . possibly hurt. But then, he found the thought of her not being alone even more unsettling.

God! What could have happened to her?

When the bartender set a drink in front of him, Adam downed it quickly, slapped some change on the counter and left the saloon.

Mosley is at the bottom of this, Adam silently told himself. He would go to Victoria and he would get some answers from her. One way or another.

A norther had blown in and the air outside had turned colder, penetrating the cave where Danny was hidden. Feeling chilled to the bone, she huddled against the farthest wall, with her arms wrapped around her torso.

"He musta give up by now," she muttered, taking comfort from the sound of her own voice.

Soon she would leave the cavern and find her way back to town.

A scrabbling noise at the entrance caused Danny's heart to leap with fright. Her eyes narrowed on the small opening. Had Lucky discovered her hiding place?

Danny scrabbled sideways, edging farther into the darkness, hoping to remain undiscovered by the intruder. Her gaze remained fixed on the opening. She hoped she'd been mistaken.

Suddenly she heard a harsh laugh that was almost a growl. "I know you're in there," Lucky called. Suddenly, his body blocked the entrance.

Although Danny's heart thumped madly, threatening to jump from her chest, she remained silent, outwardly calm, as she slipped farther back into the shadows.

If only she hadn't lost her weapon. Without it, she

273

had no defense against the man.

Realizing she could not go backwards, because her way was blocked by solid rock, Danny kept her eyes on the man and shuffled to her left, seeking to put more distance between herself and her pursuer.

Suddenly her foot found empty space, and her heart gave a wild leap of hope as Danny realized she'd found a gap in the rock.

Was it wide enough for her body to go through?

Her heart beat with trepidation as she pushed herself through the narrow crevice; a crevice that was merely a crack, hardly enough space to squeeze through.

"Might as well come on out, girlie," Lucky said. "They ain't no use in hidin' because I got you trapped in there. Only way out now is past me."

Danny smiled grimly, inching her way down the crevice, toward the narrow strip of light in the distance. Where there was light, there was an opening. God willing, she would escape that way.

Suddenly a light flared and she jerked, twisting her head around. Lucky's face was illuminated by the match he held in front of him.

"Come out, come out, wherever you are," he sang softly, mockingly.

She stood frozen, hardly daring to breathe . . . until she realized he couldn't reach her. He was too big to enter the narrow crack.

"I could shoot you if I was a mind," he taunted. "But then you'd be dead and useless to me." He grinned widely. "Reckon I'll just wait until—" Suddenly he broke off and swore. "Dammit!" Dropping the match, he sucked on his thumb, having obviously burned it.

They were abruptly plunged into darkness as the match flared, then went out.

Danny could hear Lucky fumbling in the darkness, and guessed he was reaching for another match. She heard a scraping noise, then saw a momentary flare of light before the flame went out.

"Dammit!" he muttered.

She thought he was cursing the darkness until she heard a light clatter and realized he had dropped something. Curious, she waited and watched his bulky shadow fumbling around in the crevice. She realized he had dropped the matches . . . dropped them into the crevice . . . *and he could not enter it!*

Without another thought, she scrabbled toward Lucky. If she could retrieve his matches while keeping out of his reach, she could remain safely hidden from him in the darkness.

"There you are," he muttered as she neared.

When he uttered the words, she thought he'd spotted her, but as her eyes became more accustomed to the dark, she could see that he was still kneeling. That meant he had found the matches, meant also that he hadn't seen her approach.

With his head bent low, he scraped a match against the rock wall. But she was ready for him. As soon as the light flared, she reached for the matches, snatched them out of his hand and stumbled backwards, all before he could recover enough to grab her.

"Bitch!" he shouted. "Them matches won't do you a bit of good, because there ain't no way you can get out of there without going past me first."

Refusing to acknowledge his taunting, Danny

continued to scrabble away from him, taking comfort in the knowledge that he couldn't follow her through the narrow crevice.

"I ain't going to go away," he chuckled. "I'll just wait out here until you get tired of playing hide and seek. I can stay as long as it takes. You'll have to come out some time. Unless you want to starve to death."

She heard the sound of crunching boots and realized Lucky had left the crevice. But she guessed he wouldn't go far. He would make good his threat to wait her out.

Time ticked by slowly as Danny tried to find a way out of the situation she was in. With the cessation of movement, she became aware of the cold again. Her teeth began to chatter and she clinched her jaws tight. If only she could use the matches she held clutched in her hand to start a fire. But even if she found fuel in her narrow prison, a fire would expose her, and Lucky might change his mind about killing her if he got cold enough.

Danny continued to wait. She waited . . . and held her silence . . . until her aching legs refused to hold her and she knew she couldn't stay there much longer.

And yet, what was the alternative? To go out and allow herself to be captured by Lucky?

God! If only there was another way out.

She studied her surroundings, her gaze fixing on the narrow shaft of light filtering into her place of confinement and hope flared instantly. How could she have forgotten about it? Since there was light, there must be another exit . . . and it had to be somewhere nearby.

276

Unhesitatingly, she moved farther into the crevice, searching for the source of light. About fifty feet further, the crevice gave way to another small chamber, about six feet in circumference and perhaps ten feet high. It was through the roof the light had filtered. Danny studied the hole in the roof. Small, but perhaps she could squeeze through if she was able to reach it.

A short time later, Danny slumped against the floor of the small chamber. Try as she would, she had been unable to climb the slick walls to reach the hole.

"Adam," she muttered, wiping at the tears coursing down her cheeks. "I shoulda listened to you. I shoulda waited until you come back."

Realizing she couldn't give in to despair, she pushed herself to her knees and started to rise. Suddenly she froze, her gaze fixing on the hole only a few feet away. How could she have missed it?

She fumbled for the matches, struck one against the rock wall, and held it to the opening. Although the way was narrow, it appeared to be a passageway that opened into a larger cavity farther back.

Danny counted the matches in the waterproof container.

Six.

Realizing she could not waste any of them, she searched for something to serve as the base of a torch. There was nothing in the cavern except for a few stones, and a bit of moss and leaves that had blown inside the cave.

Nothing that would serve her purpose. She raked idly at the leaves and struck something solid. Her heart leaped with hope and she dug through the pile until she uncovered a fallen log. Although it was too big to make a torch, it would keep her warm for awhile.

With that in mind, she raked the rest of the leaves away from it. Her spirits plummeted when she realized the log was too damp to burn. It would only fill the chamber full of smoke and suffocate her.

Sighing, she leaned back against the wall and something scraped her back. A moment later she pulled aside a thick stick of wood. Soon she was tearing a strip off the bottom of her shirt and wrapping it around the moss-covered stick.

When she finished fashioning her torch, she set it aflame and entered the passage. Almost instantly, the floor plunged away and she found herself descending sharply into darkness.

Danny struck bottom with a hard jolt, felt something solid strike her forehead and fought against the blackness that threatened her. She didn't know how long she lay there stunned, fighting to recover her breath.

Something warm trickled down her forehead and she wiped it away. Was it blood?

She was pushing herself upright when she realized she'd lost the torch in her fall. With her head spinning dizzily, she swept her hand through the darkness, searching for the torch.

Her hand struck something solid. The torch? The object clattered away and she scrabbled after it.

Ummmph!" She cried out in pain as she struck her forehead sharply against the rocks overhead. Tears of pain stung her eyes and she bent backwards to avoid the rocks, realizing at the same time that she was perched on a wide rock shelf.

But the torch was not there. Apparently it had continued its downward plunge to the bottom.

And she must retrieve it.

Cautiously, she inched forward, moving to the edge of the ledge, searching with her foot into the blackness beyond. The best she could determine, the rock slanted downward, resembling a slide. Would she be safe in descending? Should she retrace her steps, instead of going on?

It took only a moment to rule that out. She couldn't climb the slope that led to the chamber. She would have to stay where she was, or go on.

Since she really had no choice, she took a deep breath of courage, threw caution to the winds, and slid down the rock. She laughed when she reached the bottom. It had only been a matter of six feet or so before she reached the earthen floor where the soil had been packed hard by the centuries.

Danny found herself in total darkness . . . velvety, but cold, the kind of total eclipse that automatically generates panic.

She shivered, rubbed her hands together and blew warm air over her fingers. Kneeling, she searched the darkness with outspread hands. Elation swept through her as her fingers brushed something warm.

Her torch! Gripping it tightly, she was on the point of turning back when her foot struck something solid.

Curious, Danny struck a match, light flared suddenly, then flickered as though it would die. Quickly, she held it beneath her makeshift torch, holding her breath until it caught. Then, with the torch held before her, she surveyed her surroundings.

The rocky walls of her underground chamber were rough and looked as though they had been cut by man. Her gaze swept the floor, came to rest on a smooth length of wood near her foot.

The object, obviously man-made, was about six inches long. It was rounded at one end and broken at the other. Although she wasn't sure what it had been, it proved that someone had been in this darkness before her.

Danny found that reassuring, because it must mean there was another way out. And if there was, then she would find it.

A sense of strength came to her as she searched the chamber for another exit. She was near despair when she found it . . . a narrow tunnel was hidden by a rock protrusion. Danny's heartbeat quickened as she entered the passage and stumbled forward until suddenly, abruptly, she found her way blocked by solid rock.

Despair filled her until she realized it was only a bend in the tunnel.

Suddenly she became aware of a low, heavy rumbling, like distant thunder.

Elation flowed through Danny. She must be near the surface. She had to be. Otherwise, she wouldn't be able to her the thunder.

Her pace quickened.

A visit to the Mosley mansion proved useless. The butler informed Adam that both Asa Mosley and his wife Victoria were away from home.

Adam's hopes of discovering that Danny had returned to the Logan mansion while he was gone went unrewarded. He knew that the moment he stepped into the house. Even so, his eyes posed the question while Mrs. Gruber took his coat.

She shook her head. "Sorry, sir, there's been no word at all."

"Is Jake back?"

"He's in the parlor."

Adam joined the other man, shaking his head at Jake's silent inquiry. "I found no sign of her," he said. "The storm covered any tracks that might have been left there."

"It's Mosley's doing," Jake said. "He's got her hidden away somewhere." He raked a hand through his dark hair. "God! It's all my fault."

"We're not talking about fault here," Adam said. "I think it's time we paid Pierre a little visit."

Jake stayed where he was. And when he spoke, his voice was like a death knell. "I'm afraid we won't find out anything from him," he said. "I've just come from his house and it seems that Pierre has disappeared."

When she saw the light ahead, Danny could hardly believe her eyes. She was nearly there! She had to be close to the surface. Everything was going to be all right.

She turned another corner and stopped abruptly, staring at the carbide light hanging on a protrusion high on the rocky wall.

Except for herself, the tunnel was empty. So who

281

had left the carbide light? *And why leave it burning?* And where did the tunnel lead?

She stepped forward and her foot struck something hard. Her question was answered as she saw the rails beneath her foot. She was obviously in a coal mine.

Danny realized her prayers had been answered. All she had to do was follow the tracks and they would take her out of the mine.

She hadn't counted on the rats.

Chapter Twenty-Five

Adam's whole body seemed engulfed in tides of weariness and despair as he lay on the four-poster bed and stared up into the darkness. Although the hour was late, his thoughts would not allow him to rest. He couldn't stop thinking about Danny.

God! What had happened to her? Where could she be?

He had asked himself the questions over and over again, but he found no answer.

If only he had left her in her mountains!

He would not allow himself to even consider the possibility that Danny might be dead, because even the thought was too painful to bear.

Besides, he would know if she were dead. Wouldn't he?

During the short time he had known Danny, she had come to mean everything to him.

If she were dead, he wouldn't want to go on living. Even though he could never have her, the knowledge that Danny was alive, somewhere in the world, would bring a certain amount of comfort to him.

And she *was* alive! Adam knew he must hold on to that certainty. He *must* hold on to it, because it was the lifeline he needed to keep him going.

But, God! Where could she be?

Danny's forehead creased with anxiety as she held the carbide light before her and stumbled through the muddy tunnel. She knew she had been lucky to find the light, because her torch would have gone out long ago and with no means of lighting the tunnel, it would have been next to impossible to make her way through the darkness.

There was a steady stream of water on the floor of the passage that made the ground slick beneath her feet, forcing her to cling to the sides whenever she could. Already, she had slipped several times and her feet and skirt were soaked. And she was chilled to the bone.

Suddenly, Danny froze at a dry, rustling sound, like autumn leaves tumbling in the wind. She pressed herself close against the cavern wall, her ears throbbing with the sound of her own heartbeat.

Thump! Whoosh!

Something moved, barely visible at the edge of her peripheral vision. Goosebumps popped up on her arms and the hairs on the back of her neck rose.

Sucking in a sharp breath, Danny tried to pierce the shadows with her narrowed gaze.

Thump! Whoosh! There it was again. Danny shivered with panic, afraid to go on . . . and just as afraid to retreat.

"Who's there!" Her voice came out in a croak. Swallowing hard, she tried again. "Is anybody there?"

Silence.

"I-I k-know you're there!" she chattered. "I h-heard you!"

Silence.

An eternity seemed to pass while she stood there waiting for something to happen. Finally, unable to stand the strain, she took a tentative step forward, then paused and listened . . . to the silence.

They's nothing there! She silently chided herself. The sound was what it seemed, dry leaves rustling in the wind.

But they ain't no wind down here, she silently argued.

Nevertheless, she forced herself to go on. With her heart beating like a trip-hammer, she stumbled forward again, her eyes darting back and forth, trying to penetrate the veil of shadows. She could feel a presence, something dark, hiding in the shadows.

In the dimness, she could barely distinguish a black, stiff-furred body and two red, glaring eyes.

Relief washed over her.

"Only a rat," she muttered, giving an uneasy laugh as the creature came farther into the light. Since she had never been one to fear such creatures, she continued on her path, even when another rat joined the first . . . then another and another.

Suddenly, she stopped, puzzled and more than a little nervous. She held the light lower, and her hand trembled. Her gaze remained fixed on the rats staring at her with malevolent eyes.

Danny realized something was wrong. The rats should be running away from her. It wasn't natural for the creatures to face her like this. But natural or not, that was exactly what they were doing.

Go on, an inner voice chided. *They won't hurt you! Not while you're on your feet.*

But suppose I fall again? she silently questioned. *If I fall they'll be all over me!*

Memories of stories she'd heard about grown men who'd been eaten by rats during a heavy snow came back to her. She trembled and slumped wearily against the passage wall.

Adam, she silently cried. *Help me, Adam!*

Adam woke with a start, bathed in sweat. He had been having the most awful nightmare in which Danny had been menaced by monster rats. But it *was* only a nightmare, he consoled himself. Rats didn't grow to be that size. His anxiety over Danny had crossed the grounds of reality and entered his dreams.

He lay still, forcing himself to be calm, but he couldn't rid himself of the uneasy feeling. He knew, with a certainty, that Danny needed him.

Realizing she could not give in to her terror and weariness, Danny gathered her courage around her like a mantle and strode boldly toward the rats. For a long moment they faced her, then they scattered, like leaves scattering in a brisk wind. Danny's breath whooshed out in a sigh of relief, and she stumbled along the passage, keeping out of the muddy water as much as possible.

But even though the rats had fled, Danny knew they hadn't gone far. She sensed eyes on her, heard the scurrying of tiny clawed feet, and her heart quickened with fear.

Why were the rats following her?

Despite her exhaustion, Danny quickened her pace. Her footsteps echoed hollowly in the curved passage as she hurried toward the rumbling sound in the distance. She knew when she reached the source of the rumbling, she would find the coal miners, and they would surely take her out of this underground world. Her nerves were stretched almost to the breaking point as she rounded a curve . . . and stopped.

Something had moved in the darkness ahead. She was certain of it. Suddenly, above the thudding of her heart, she heard the all-too-familiar scurrying sound.

Another rat?

Danny swung the light back and forth. *There! Just ahead . . . where the light ended and the shadows began.*

Her gaze narrowed, she moved the lantern again. The light flashed across a bristle-haired humped back; the creature tensed, but held its ground.

She swallowed hard.

"S-shoo," she said, her voice sounding shaky. "Go on! Get out of here!"

The rat glared at her with wicked eyes, almost seeming to dare her to come any closer. Suddenly, without any warning, it darted forward and she screamed, kicking out at the rodent. Her kick landed, hurling the rat against the far wall. But another had taken its place.

Her eyes darted frantically as she searched desperately for something to throw. Her gaze lit upon a fist-sized black rock. Scooping it up, she threw it with all the force she could muster. It landed with a clatter that sent the creature fleeing into the darkness.

Gathering up the hem of her muddy skirt, Danny hurried on her way.

Dawn brought clear skies. It found Adam, who'd been unable to fall asleep again, searching out the corridors of the hospital for Danny. Each bed he passed brought mixed feelings. One of relief that she wasn't there and one of despair that he still had not found her. An hour later, he left the hospital, his despair like a steel weight around his heart.

Danny's carbide light was on the point of going out when she became aware of a dim glow down another corridor. Unhesitatingly, she stumbled that way, thinking perhaps she would find another exit to the outer world . . . and dreading that she would not.

The fear that she would be left alone in the darkness . . . alone with the rats . . . had become all consuming.

She rounded a corner and her eyes fixed on a point of light. She stumbled onward. She tripped and fell to her knees, pulled herself up and stumbled forward again.

Danny knew she must be going crazy because she thought she heard the murmur of voices mingled with the everpresent sound of the coal cars. Realizing it was probably her imagination, she staggered on toward the light. As she neared, her chin lifted, her gaze fixed unwaveringly. She had already reached for the light when she became aware there was a face beneath it.

A man's face. Dirty and grimy, from digging coal, but it was a man . . . another human being.

He was real! Not her imagination! God! Her prayers had been answered! She had beaten the darkness . . . had survived the rats . . . she was safe. Even as her mind registered the surprise on the stranger's face, a red haze formed around her vision, her knees buckled, and a blanket of darkness smothered her as her legs gave way beneath her.

Danny wavered in and out of consciousness. Voices came and went . . . always unfamiliar voices.

"Adam," she mumbled, wetting dry lips with her tongue. "Help me. The rats are coming . . . the rats . . ."

"What's this about rats?"

Danny heard the male voice coming from somewhere above her and tried to open her eyes. Her eyelids seemed too heavy to lift. She licked dry lips, forced words past her swollen throat. "Don't you see them?" she whispered. "They're all around me . . . waiting in the dark. . . ."

"There's no rats in here," the same masculine voice soothed. "There's nothing here to fear. Nothing at all. You're safe here with us."

Safe with them? With who? Danny didn't recognize the speaker's voice, so he must be a stranger . . . like Lucky . . . the man who . . .

Danny's eyes snapped open and she stared up at a white-coated figure. "Angel!" she muttered, struggling to push herself upright. "The babe . . . must tell . . . about Angel . . ."

"So you've finally decided to wake up," said the man who had assured her she was safe. "Are you up to telling us who you are?"

"Angel," she whispered, "The babe . . . must find Angel."

"You won't be joining the angels just yet," the man said. "We're going to make you well." He bent lower, pressing her eyelids open with his fingers and peering at her eyeball.

She struck at him, struggling to get up. "Angel . . . have to find."

"She is hallucinating!" snapped the doctor. "Nurse, hand me the sulphonal. A dose of that will help calm her down."

Hands pressed against Danny's shoulders, forcing her back down against the bed. "I am not so sure she is out of her head, doctor," a female voice said. "I think she is trying to tell us something."

"Are you questioning my judgment, nurse?"

"Of course not, doctor," the female voice said.

A moment later Danny felt hands on her head, lifting it up, and a foul liquid trickled in her mouth. "Come on, now," the woman's voice coaxed. "Drink it up for me like a good girl. It will help you to sleep."

Sleep! But she didn't need to sleep! She needed someone to listen to her. Twisting her head, Danny avoided the glass. "No!" she mumbled, pushing weakly at the glass. "Don't want it!" She couldn't take something that would put her to sleep. She must stay awake. Must tell them about the house on the hill.

But the hands holding her were stronger than her efforts to avoid them. Her nose was pinched together and she opened her mouth to breathe.

Instantly, the liquid was poured in; she coughed, her stomach retched, her throat gagged as she tried to reject the Sulphonal, but her captor maintained a grip and she had no alternative except to swallow.

When the glass was finally drained, Danny was laid back against the mattress and she felt something wet pressed against her forehead.

"Poor little thing," the woman's voice murmured. "You have been through an ordeal, haven't you?"

The sympathy in her voice stirred Danny. She reached up and gripped the woman's hands, opened her eyes and stared up at her. The woman's face was fuzzy . . . Danny squinted her eyes, trying to bring it into focus. "Please . . . help me," she whispered. "Must speak to . . . Adam."

A shudder racked her small frame and her teeth began to chatter.

"Relax, now," the woman's voice soothed. "Don't fight the medication. Let it take over and sleep. When you wake up you can tell me all about it."

"No," Danny protested. "Must talk now . . . tell him . . ." Her lips felt rubbery; she was having trouble making herself understood. She felt hot, then cold, became aware that people were asking her for a name.

"Adam," she whispered. Her throat was raw, her voice hoarse. "Adam."

"Adam who?" a voice inquired. "Who do you want me to get? What's your name?"

"Adam," she said, answering the first question.

291

"Your name is Adam?"

"Of course it's not," another voice said. "Any fool can see this is a female. She's been calling for Adam ever since she was brought in."

"Find out who she is," said the first voice.

"Danny," she whispered. Suddenly her body began to shake with tremors and she couldn't talk.

"Drink this, honey," a soft voice said. "You'll feel better after awhile."

"No," she said, shoving the hand away. "Must tell . . ." Another tremor shook her and her teeth began to chatter.

"Come on, now," the voice said. "Drink this. We'll find out who you are later."

A glass was held to her lips again and she discovered she'd have to swallow the liquid or choke on it.

She swallowed.

Chapter Twenty-Six

The cold was bleak and penetrating; the sky was dark gray, matching Adam's mood as he strode up the walk to the Logan Mansion. Fat snowflakes swirled around him, and already there was a light covering on the ground.

Adam stepped into the foyer and allowed Mrs. Gruber to take his coat. "We was wondering where you'd got off to," she said. "The mister is already at the table."

"I was checking the hospital." Adam followed her to the dining room, greeted Jake, then seated himself before the empty plate.

"The hospital!" Mrs. Gruber exclaimed. "Land sakes alive! I never even thought about that! She wasn't there?"

"No." When Bridget hurried to serve him, Adam waved the food away. "Just coffee," he said.

"You'll need food if you're going to keep looking for Danny," Jake said.

Realizing Jake was right, Adam allowed the girl to

serve him breakfast. When she'd finished, he picked up his steaming cup and sipped at the strong black coffee. His gaze went to the window and beyond, to the falling snow. "It's cold out there," he said. "Danny wasn't dressed for weather like this."

"Don't think that way," Jake said. "Danny's not out in this mess. If she was we'd have found her by now."

"We can't be sure of that," Adam said. "That's what makes it all so horrible. The uncertainty of the whole thing. And knowing that it's all my fault. If I'd left her alone, she'd be safe in her mountains."

"Don't go blaming yourself," Mrs. Gruber said. "It's that scoundrel, Asa Mosley, who's taken Miss Danielle."

"The important thing right now is to get her back," Jake said. "But her disappearance has told me something. Somehow, in some way, Pierre is connected to Mosley. And I'd bet anything I own that Victoria Mosley has been carrying messages for her husband."

Adam pushed back his chair. "Then Asa Mosley is the one I should see. I'm going to find him. And when I do, he'll tell me where Danny is if I have to beat the information out of him."

"You'll not be going after him, Sir?" Mrs. Gruber asked. "That man is surrounded by guards. You'll not be getting anywheres near him before they'd kill you sure. And, to my way of thinking, that's the last thing that child would be wantin'."

"Mrs. Gruber is right," Jake said. "If it would have helped, don't you think I'd have already done that? Mosley has Angel hidden away somewhere. And she means every bit as much to me as Danny does to you."

Adam shot Jake a dark look. "You're wrong if you think there's anything between Danny and me," he growled. "There isn't. But I brought her to the city and it's my duty to see her safely back to Tucker's Ridge. That's all there is to it. Plain and simple."

"Whatever your reason is," Jake said. "We both want to find her. Angel would never forgive me if anything happened to her cousin."

"The good Lord will protect the both of them," Mrs. Gruber said. "And the babe as well. The missus is a fighter. Wherever she is, whatever the circumstances, she's going to take care of herself and the wee one . . . and if Miss Danielle is there with her, she'll be took care of as well."

Adam sincerely hoped so.

Later that day, Adam accompanied Jake to the building where his office was located. Adam stopped short when he saw Mosley descending the steps with two of his henchmen.

Adam blocked his way.

"Where have you got Danny?" he asked bluntly.

"Danny? Do you mean Miss Tucker?" Asa Mosley's surprise seemed genuine, and if Adam hadn't known better, he would have thought the man's reaction *was* sincere. "Has she come up missing?"

"You know damn well she has," Adam said bitterly. "And you're not fooling me one bit, pretending you know nothing about it. You're the only one who would stand to gain from her disappearance."

"Gain?" Mosley raised his eyebrows mockingly. "How on earth did you come to such a conclusion?"

"Adam, be careful," Jake warned, putting a cautioning hand on his friend's forearm.

But Jake's warning went unheeded. Adam's anger was a scalding fury and he made a lunge for Mosley. Mosley dodged sideways and his men caught Adam between them.

"Damn you!" Adam grated harshly. "Where've you got her?"

Mosley answered the question with one of his own. "What could I possibly gain from Miss Tucker's disappearance?"

"You know damn well!" Adam retorted. "You're afraid she will be able to use her visions to help us find her cousin."

Asa Mosley looked startled, then a grin spread across his face. "Her visions? God, man! Do you realize what you're saying? Do you really believe in that stuff?"

Adam seethed with mounting rage. His fists clenched and unclenched again, and if he hadn't been held so tightly between the two men, he would have struck the smile from Mosley's face. The man was a snake. Everyone knew it. But there was nothing they could do about it unless they could prove it. At least, that's what Mosley seemed to think.

"Let Adam go!" Jake ordered.

"Certainly," Mosley said. He looked at Adam's captors. "You can release him."

Mosley's men released Adam, but immediately closed around their employer, as though they believed he was still in danger from Adam. But they needn't have. Adam was in control again. He spared them only a brief look, then met Mosley's eyes again.

"If you harm one hair on Danny's head I'll make you pay for it," he said. "Remember that, Mosley. You hurt her and I'll come after you."

"Come on, Adam," Jake said, shoving past the men.

Realizing he would learn nothing from Mosley at this time, Adam followed Jake. But he wouldn't give up. Victoria Mosley could be the key to finding Danny. Perhaps he'd do better to concentrate on finding her.

Danny's lashes fluttered; she opened her eyes and studied her surroundings. The walls were white and the room was filled with beds. She frowned. She was almost certain she'd never been here before. Was she in a hospital?

Suddenly, her memory returned.

The rats! She had been in a tunnel full of rats . . . a man had been chasing her . . . but not in the tunnel.

The cave! Lucky! Pictures filled her mind. Running through the forest, the house on the hill, Angel! She had found the place where Mosley had hidden Angellee and her babe!

Danny struggled out of the bed, fell to her knees and lost consciousness.

Danny had been missing for two days now and Adam's anguish was a huge aching knot inside his chest. Despair weighed heavy on him; he'd had no luck getting to Victoria Mosley. Her servants said she'd left town for an unknown destination. He was searching the town again when he passed by a large building that he hadn't noticed before. Curious, he asked an elderly woman passing by the nature of the building.

"Why, it be the hospital, sir," came the answer.

"The hospital?" Adam's heart picked up speed. "But . . . do you mean there's more than one hospital here?"

The woman shook her head. "No, sir. This uns the only one that's around here. T'other one is on t'other side of town."

"But it is a hospital?" Adam persisted.

"Just said it was," the woman muttered, sidestepping around him as though she suspected she was in danger. But she had no need to worry. Adam had already left her, intent on searching the building for Danny.

A complaining female voice woke Danny.

"This stuff can't be called food. It ain't even fit for slopping pigs."

Danny turned her head and saw a woman in white standing beside the bed next to her own. "My, aren't we getting finicky these days?" the woman said. "That's a sure sign that you're getting well."

The patient laughed, her good humor seeming to be completely restored. "I am, ain't I, nurse?" Her voice was eager. "Do you think the doctor will let me go home soon?"

"We'll just have to wait and see," the nurse replied. "But I wouldn't be the least surprised. We certainly won't keep you a day longer than we have to. Beds are something we're always short of around here."

"And it's prob'ly a good thing for me too," the

woman said. "Do I have to take some more of that awful-tasting medicine?"

"We'll see," the nurse replied, already turning away from the patient's bed.

Danny stopped her before she could leave. "Nurse," she called, feeling surprised at how weak her voice sounded.

The nurse stopped beside Danny's bed. "So you're finally awake," she said. "That's good. Now we can get some information about you." She picked up Danny's wrist and felt her pulse. "We had no idea who to contact about your illness. Your folks must be getting mighty worried about you. What is your name, dear?"

"My name is Danielle Tucker, and I've been staying at the—" Suddenly, Danny stopped, feeling the color leave her face. Her wandering gaze had fallen on a man who had just walked through the door.

It was Lucky! *God!* Asa Mosley's henchman had found her! And she was too weak to protect herself.

"What's the matter?" the nurse asked sharply, dropping Danny's wrist and bending low, peering into Danny's face. Her body blocked Danny's view of Lucky, but it also blocked her from his view as well.

"I-I-" Danny craned her head, peering around the nurse at the man who was stopping at the foot of each bed to look at each patient in turn. What could she do? Could the nurse protect her from Lucky's wrath? She didn't think so.

The nurse seemed to sense her distress. "Do you need to use the convenience room?" she asked.

The convenience room? Danny grabbed at the

excuse. "Yes," she said quickly, sliding out of the bed, being careful to keep the nurse's large frame between Lucky and herself as she and the nurse moved toward a door set into the far wall. Luck was with Danny, because the man was so busy checking the other beds, he didn't notice the activity at the other end of the room. When the door to the necessary room had closed behind her, Danny heaved a sigh of relief. She stayed in the room, trembling, fighting her fear until the nurse became alarmed and came in after her.

"Are you all right, dear?" she asked.

"Is anyone out there?" Danny asked. "Is a man out there?"

"No." The nurse was obviously puzzled, but Danny didn't enlighten her.

She breathed a sigh of relief. At least she was safe for the moment. But only for the moment. Although her legs were trembling, she forced herself to enter the ward again. A red haze formed behind her eyes and she fought against the dizziness. She couldn't pass out now. Lucky might be back. She had to get out of here! Must return to the Logan mansion where she had some protection. If Lucky found her here, she would have no defense against him.

None at all.

Chapter Twenty-Seven

Adam entered the women's ward and scanned the room. It was empty of furnishings, except for the narrow cots that lined both sides of the wall. Adam's gaze touched on the man who went from bed to bed, obviously searching for someone. All the beds were occupied except one. And a nurse stood beside it, changing the linens that covered the mattress. Had someone died? Or had they only been released?

Ignoring the other man, Adam began his own search. And, although his hopes had been high when he entered the ward, each bed he passed sent his spirits plunging lower.

The other man had apparently satisfied himself the woman he searched for was not in the ward, because he stopped the nurse who had just entered the room.

"Is there another ward for women?" he asked.

"No," the nurse replied. "This one is all there is."

"What about that bed over there? The empty one," the man asked.

The nurse didn't even look up. "If the bed's empty, the patient either died or went home."

The man scowled and left the ward. Adam was on the verge of following him when he saw a nurse enter from a door at the opposite end of the room. She had one arm around a girl while she waved a bottle of something beneath her nose.

Smelling salts? Adam realized he'd guessed right when the girl's head jerked away from the bottle as though she'd been struck.

Suddenly, Adam stopped and froze, his eyes narrowing on the slight figure.

It couldn't be Danny, he told himself. The girl was too small . . . too frail. His mind was just grasping at straws, making him see what he wanted to see.

He swallowed hard, turned to leave, then stopped again. Spinning on his heel, Adam covered the distance between himself and the frail figure the nurse was still supporting.

"Take it easy," the woman said. "Just a few more steps and we'll be back to the bed. The doctor said we could give you another dose of Sulphonal. It should help you to sleep."

"No, please!" the girl protested, pushing against the nurse weakly. "Don't make me take anymore of that stuff. Don't make me—" Her voice broke off as her knees buckled and she crumpled to the floor.

Immediately, the nurse knelt beside the fallen girl and weaved the bottle of smelling salts beneath her nose.

"Take it away," the girl protested, coughing and shoving at the bottle.

"Danny," Adam said, kneeling beside her. "Oh,

Danny! Where have you been?" Without waiting for a reply, he scooped her into his arms and clutched her against his chest.

A wild rush of joy swept through him. She was alive. Danny was alive!

"Adam?" she questioned, blinking up at him with dazed eyes. "Is it really you? Don't let them do it, Adam. Don't let them give me anymore of that stuff."

"Put her down on the bed," the nurse said, eyeing Adam warily. "Do you know who she is?"

"Yes," he said gruffly, casting a brief look at the nurse hovering nearby. "I've been searching for her for the last three days. Her name is Danielle Tucker."

"So she told me. But only moments ago."

"What happened to her?" Adam asked, studying the yellowish purple marks on her forehead. "How did she come by these bruises?"

"I have no idea," the nurse said. She pointed to the bed. "You can put her down there." She pulled back the covers. "A miner brought her in a couple of days ago. He said he found her wandering through the mine where he worked."

"A mine?" Adam questioned. "How did she come to be in a mine? Did the miner who brought her here know why she was there?"

"No," the nurse replied with a frown. "He had no idea." She patted the bed, as though she suspected Adam hadn't understood her orders clearly enough. "Put her down here."

But Adam refused to relinquish his precious bundle, afraid that he would somehow lose her again if he turned her loose for even one moment.

The nurse looked sternly at him. "You'll have to

put her down," she said sharply. "She can't go any-where until the doctor releases her, and he will want to talk to you first."

Adam shook his head. Reaching down with one hand, he pulled a blanket off the bed and wrapped it around Danny. "Call me a hansom cab," he said. "I'm taking her home with me."

"You cannot do that," the woman insisted. "Not without the doctor's approval. He must discharge her first. And I doubt that he will do that unless you prove you have a right to take her away." Her disapproving gaze swept over him. "I'm not so certain that you do."

"Don't be stupid!" Adam said. "Any fool could see that Danny recognized me!"

"That doesn't mean she belongs to you." The sound of approaching footsteps caught her attention and the nurse turned her attention to the man who'd just entered the room. "Doctor," she called. "This man insists on taking my patient out of the hospital."

"You can't do that," the doctor said. "She needs medical care. Put her down on the bed."

"She'll get all the medical care she needs," Adam said, "but it would be dangerous to leave her here. I'll send for the doctor to attend her as soon as I get her home."

"I won't be responsible if you take an unconscious girl out of my hospital," the doctor said. "You have no idea of the harm you could cause by taking her home now."

Adam uttered a sigh. "Look," he said. "I know you mean well. But I can't leave her here. We're staying with Jake Logan, your Attorney General, and if you need answers, then go to him. He'll back me up completely."

At the mention of Jake's name, the doctor subsided. He ordered the nurse to call Adam a cab, and even sent for another blanket to wrap around Danny. When the cab arrived, Adam gave his destination to the driver. Clutching his precious bundle in his arms, he stepped into the carriage.

The ride to the gate seemed incredibly long. "Wait here," he told the driver. "I'll send someone out to pay you."

When Adam walked into the house with Danny held tight against his chest, Jake started forward. "Danny?" he asked.

"Yes. She needs a doctor. And the driver outside needs paying."

Jake issued orders, instructing Mrs. Gruber to pay the driver and send him for the family physician.

Adam sat beside Danny's bed, refusing to leave her side. The doctor, when he came, proved a big disappointment.

"Where's Doctor O'Grady?" Jake asked.

"Down with the fever," the doctor answered. "My name's George Alexander. O'Grady called me in when he first got sick. Been taking care of his patients for three days now. He'll soon be back on his feet." He bent over Danny and began his examination. When he was finished, he looked up at Adam. "She's suffering from exposure," he said. "And possibly concussion. See the bruise on her forehead? Looks like she suffered a blow of some kind, and she's running a high fever too. How long has she been out?"

"She was awake an hour ago," Adam said. "But the nurse said she'd been out for several days. When I saw her, the nurse was waving a bottle of smelling salts under her nose."

The doctor frowned. "Fool woman. Worse thing she could have done. She needs leaving alone until she comes out of it naturally. Otherwise, no telling what could happen. Might be thick in the head."

"Thick in the head?" Adam questioned. "Exactly what does that mean?"

"Daft, man!" the doctor said. "Too much smelling salts could make her go crazy. Wouldn't be surprised if it hadn't already done some damage. Hear how she keeps talking about the angels? Guess she thinks she's gonna join them soon."

"Not the angel," Jake said. "She's talking about my wife, Angel. Is there no way to bring Danny around? We think she knows something about my wife's whereabouts."

"I'm afraid there's nothing we can do. Not without endangering her health," the doctor said. "Best to just let her rest. She'll eventually come out of it."

"But when?" Jake asked. "How long must we wait?"

"It's hard to predict," the doctor said. "I'll be back to check on her in the morning. If there's a change for the worse, be sure and let me know."

After the doctor had left, the men kept watch beside Danny's bed. Jake paced restlessly. "She knows something about Angel. I know she does."

"Take it easy, Jake," Adam said. "As soon as she's able, she'll tell us what she can."

It was dark when Danny woke. Her lashes fluttered

and she lifted lids that seemed incredibly heavy. Then she became aware that, not only was her head pounding, but she hurt all over.

Stifling a groan, she flexed her arms and legs. Every muscle in her body ached. Her puzzled eyes traveled around the room. What had happened to her?

Pushing herself to a sitting position, she slid her legs off the bed. Immediately, she was overcome by a wave of nausea. She lay back and swallowed hard. After waiting a few moments, she tried again, struggling upright and walking shakily across the room to the washstand.

The mirror gave back an appalling reflection to Danny. The pallor of her cheeks only magnified the large purple and yellow bruise on her forehead; her sunken eyes belied the hours she had slept. With her hand visibly trembling, she poured water into the washbasin and splashed it on her face.

Suddenly, weakness assailed her. The room spun wildly around her and her limbs threatened to give way beneath her. She clutched at the washstand for support.

At that moment the door opened. With an exclamation, Adam bounded across the room and, seeming to realize the difficulty she was having, scooped her into his arms and carried her back to the bed.

She took one look at his grim face and closed her eyes to shut it out again. His hands were gentle as he lowered her into the soft cocoon of the feather mattress and tucked the quilt firmly beneath her chin.

"You must stay in bed," he said in an incredibly

gentle tone. Her eyes opened wide. Yes! The grim look was still there, but his eyes were extremely kind.

"What's wrong with me? Why do I feel so weak?" Danny asked, and her voice sounded strange even to her own ears.

"You suffered from concussion," Adam answered. "We don't know what happened. Apparently you received some kind of blow to the head."

"A blow? When? How?"

"That's what we've been waiting to find out."

"I can't remember," she said.

"What do you remember, Danny?" he asked gently.

"I don't know," she said, feeling completely puzzled by his question.

Becoming aware of another presence, she turned to find Jake had entered the room. His eyes were dark and glittering. "So you're finally awake."

"Have I been asleep long?"

"Three days," he said harshly. "Three days of hell for the rest of us." He came closer. "I can't wait any longer," he gritted.

"Give her a few minutes," Adam said sternly. "She's still disoriented."

Danny looked from one man to the other. Why were they glaring at each other that way?

"I can't wait," Jake said. "I have to know now."

"Have to know what?"

"When you were still at the hospital, you kept going on about having to tell about Angel. What did you have to tell us, Danny? Do you know where she is?"

The question jerked her memory back. And her

eyes widened. "Angel! Yes, Jake. Oh . . . I don't know. I think she's in that house on the hill!"

"What house?"

Danny explained about following the old woman to the house on the hill. Told how Asa Mosley's man had found her. How she'd escaped through the tunnels. "I think I banged my head against the rocks just before I found the passageway."

"Where is the house?" Jake asked. "How can I find it?"

She began her halting explanations and Jake shot question after question at her. When she had finished, he said, "I know where the house is, but it doesn't make sense. Mosley doesn't own it."

"Then why did his wife send the old woman there?"

"I don't know, but I'm going to find out."

Without another word, he left her alone with Adam.

Three days had passed since Danny regained her senses. Although Jake had gone to the house on the hill, he had found it empty. If Angel had actually been there, then Mosley had taken advantage of the delay and moved her and the baby to some distant place.

Although Danny continually blamed herself for not having returned faster, she was the only one who did. Adam explained this to her one night in the garden when she was feeling especially low.

"You've no reason to blame yourself," he said, walking beside her.

"Who else is there to blame?" she asked sorrowfully. "If I'd been able to get outta that cave sooner, and if I hadn't come down sick so's I couldn't make no sense, then Jake coulda found them before Mosley had 'em moved."

"You did all you could," he said gruffly. "You followed that woman and found the hiding place. You couldn't know one of Mosley's men would find you." A frown crossed his face. "Dammit! We've got to find a way to stop Mosley."

She shuddered. "He's ruthless. He don't seem to care how many folks get hurt."

"I'm sure he doesn't. But I'm glad you are aware of the danger he presents. Maybe that knowledge will keep you from wandering away from the house until we find a way to stop him."

"When is Asa Mosley's trial coming up?" Danny asked.

"His lawyer asked for a postponement, but I don't think the judge is going for it." Adam studied her intently. "Something's got to be done about Mosley . . . and fast. We've got to find a way to get your cousin back before the trial starts, or I wouldn't give two bits for her chances."

Tears filled Danny's eyes. "What will I tell Pa if something happens to her, Adam. He feels bad enough about Angel and her family now. That's one reason he turned to corn liquor. Guilt is plaguing him something fierce."

Adam's expression darkened and something like pain flickered in his eyes. "Danny," he said, taking her hand in his. "I've been meaning to talk to you about your father. Something happened—" His voice cracked and he broke off.

"What were you going to say?" she encouraged.

He sighed and raked a hand through his dark, unruly hair. "Would you consider staying in the city, Danny? Jake told me he would like you to stay here and make your home here with them."

She shook her head. "I couldn't do that." Danny knew she wouldn't fit in here. Not with her lack of education. She'd seen the way some of the women had looked down their noses at her. Not that she cared what they thought, but Jake might.

"Why not, Danny?" he asked.

She remained silent. She didn't want him to know the reason. If he hadn't noticed how her awkward ways made her stand out in society, then she certainly didn't want to bring it to his attention. Besides, there were other reasons . . . she could tell him those. "I don't like the city life," she said. "I don't like to wake up to carriage wheels instead of birds singing." She looked up at the sky. "An' I want to see the moon hangin' up there, not a chimney belching out flames and smoke. That stuff can't be very good for a body's lungs. It can't be healthy and I don't want to spend my life tryin' to breathe it."

"Your cousin survives quite well on it."

"It's a fact my cousin must purely love Jake. There can't be no other reason she's satisfied here." She turned to him. "Could you live here? Tell me the truth, Adam. Could you?"

He hesitated for a long moment. Finally he spoke. "I suppose it would depend on the circumstances. I don't believe in love, but I've heard it's a powerful emotion for those who do believe. Maybe if you stayed here, you could find yourself someone to love." His voice was curiously gruff.

311

She swallowed hard. She had already found someone to love, but it was obvious he didn't love her. "Maybe if you let yourself, you might find love," she said, turning to look up at him.

His expression hardened. "When I was younger a woman told me she loved me." He lifted a hand and ran his finger across the scar. "She left me this as a reminder of her love."

"What happened?" she asked.

He shrugged. "Nothing worth talking about." He turned away from her. "It's late. You'd better go on to bed now." He moved toward the gate.

"Where are you going?" she asked.

"Just into town for awhile. Perhaps I can get a lead on where Victoria Mosley went. I'm almost certain if we can find her that she could tell us where your cousin and her baby are being held."

Danny felt Adam was right. Victoria did know something about Angel's whereabouts, but Danny had begun to wonder if they would ever see Angel alive again.

Maybe she'd been right all along, Danny silently told herself. Maybe Angellee was really dead. Maybe she'd been dead all these months while Jake was searching for her. And if she was, that meant it wasn't Angellee Danny had been seeing. If she was dead, then it was only her spirit that Danny saw, only a haunt's voice she'd been hearing.

God! Don't let it be true!

Chapter Twenty-Eight

The next day, around mid-morning, a visitor arrived.

Danny was in her room when Bridget knocked on her door. "Mr. Roderic has come calling," Bridget called. "Do you feel up to seeing him, Miss?"

"Yes," Danny replied. "Tell him I'll be right down." Picking up a hairbrush, Danny pulled it through her shining curls. In the mirror, she saw Bridget's reflection. Something was obviously wrong with the girl. "What's the matter, Bridget?"

As though Danny's words had released the finger that plugged the dike, tears began to spill down Bridget's cheeks. "Oh, Miss. Somethin' awful's happened at home. The Brewster doll factory where my papa works is being closed down."

She began to sob in earnest and Danny pushed her down on the bed. "They ain't no good in cryin' over it," she said. "It ain't like it was the end of the world."

"It might as well be," Bridget said, sniffing, and pulling a handkerchief from her apron pocket. After blowing her nose, she began to talk and the words came pouring out. It seemed the Brewster doll factory where Bridget's father worked was losing money. And, according to Bridget, all because the owner wouldn't listen to the good advice of Bridget's father who had been employed there for nearly forty years. Danny listened sympathetically, wishing there was something she could do to help the girl.

When Bridget had got control of herself, Danny left her and descended the stairs. She found Roderic waiting for her in the parlor.

"You are all right?" he asked anxiously, taking her hand and bowing low over it.

"I'm well enough," she said. "But I feel like a fool causing so much worry to everybody. I didn't mean to go off and leave you thataway, but I didn't have time to go and tell you what was happening." She studied him intently. "Did they tell you what's been happening around here?"

"I have been told nothing except that I was a fool for letting you out of my sight," he said gently. "And Adam Hollister was right. It was very foolish of me."

"Adam had no call to go blamin' you for something I done," she said.

"He had every right. It was up to me to protect you and I let you down appallingly."

Danny felt embarrassed that he was insisting on shouldering the blame for her disappearance. Suddenly, remembering her manners, she said, "Set yourself down over there." She pointed at the settee. "Bridget is gonna bring us some tea and cakes."

He smiled wryly. "I would like nothing better than to stay and visit with you," he said. "But it would be just my luck for your protector . . ." He gave a dramatic shudder. ". . . Adam Hollister, to walk in on us. Somehow, I don't think I have endeared myself to him."

Her eyes sparkled. "You might be right about that. But I got a better idea. If you got the time, we could walk through the park. It ain't very far away and we could set on a bench and talk."

"The idea is very appealing," he said. "But are you well enough to take such a walk?"

"Fit as a fiddle," she said. "Wasn't nothing much wrong with me. Just had me a little knock on the head, but it's all healed up now. The doctor had a fancy name for it. Concussed, he said."

His lips twitched with amusement. "Then if you are no longer . . . concussed . . . perhaps we can take that walk?"

When Bridget walked in with the silver tray, they were on the verge of walking out. The girl's eyes widened. "Oh, Miss. You're not leaving the house?"

"I'm not?" Danny smiled at her. "Somehow, I thought that was just what I was doing."

"But, Miss. Mister Hollister won't like it. He said you was to stay here."

"I ain't aimin' to be long, Bridget. Don't worry none about me."

"If he asks me where you went, what will I tell him?"

Danny knew the *he* that Bridget referred to could be no other than Adam Hollister. "Just tell him I went down to the park with Roderic."

Bridget was still standing there, the picture of dismay, when Danny closed the door behind her.

315

Although they were experiencing a warming trend, there were only a few people in the park. Roderic found a park bench for them and they spent a pleasant hour in conversation. She learned that Roderic was an only child and undecided about what he wanted for his future.

"My father calls me a wastrel. Perhaps I am," he said with a frown. "But he has no reason to accuse me when he is the same. That is often the way of it when a man is born to wealth."

"Do you like being a wastrel?"

Although he grinned wryly, she could see he was troubled. "No. I don't particularly like being a wastrel. The gaming houses and endless parties bore me. I want to have a purpose in life. I want to do something that I can be proud of. I want to leave my mark on the world, want to know that I was able to make things better for someone, want my name to live on, even after I'm gone."

"Then do something about it," she said.

"You make it sound so simple, Danielle. But it is not."

"Why?"

"Well . . ." He looked at her, appearing confused. "How does one break a mold?" he asked. "By the time a man reaches my age he has set a pattern. Mine happens to be appearing regularly at the gaming houses and attending the balls that are given almost nightly here in the city. It becomes a tradition. If I did not . . ." His voice trailed away as he thought about the consequences of such an act.

Her lips twitched. "Exactly what would happen if you didn't show up at those fancy shindigs?"

"I guess they would soon forget about me," he said.

"So they ain't really all that important," she said. "Now why don't you forget all that. You already said you got money. Why don't you do something with it?"

"What would you have me do?" he asked. "I have already traveled the world over. No place appealed to me like Pittsburgh."

"Then make a place for yourself here," she said. "You got money. Do something with it."

"Are you suggesting I start a business, Danielle? I have never considered myself a business man."

"It don't have to be a business," she said. "But the way I see it, you got an obligation. They's plenty of people out there that don't have nothing. It's up to people like you to help them."

"You think I should give them money?"

"No. That wouldn't help 'em for long. I think you need to be in a position to give them jobs so they can support themselves."

He nodded thoughtfully. "You are right, Danielle. I must think about this more. There has to be something that I can do . . . perhaps a place of business. . . ."

Suddenly, Danny had a brilliant idea. "I know," she said. "I heard about this doll factory. It's about to close its doors and there's gonna be a lot of folks losing their jobs when it does. You could buy it and keep it open. That way all them folks' jobs will be safe."

"A doll factory?" His brows drew together in a frown. "I don't think that's exactly what I had in mind," he said.

"Why not? You said you was wantin' to help folks, didn't you? Well, they's about twenty five folks is going to lose their jobs when that place closes its doors. And Bridget's pa is one of 'em."

"But, Danielle," he protested. "It would do no good to buy a factory that would only lose money. In the end the money would be all gone and the place would still shut down. That would only prolong the jobs, not secure them."

"The factory wouldn't fail," Danny argued. "Bridget said it was failing because the owner wouldn't listen to the people who know how to make the dolls cheaper and still turn out quality dolls."

"Is there a market for such things?"

"Is there a market?" She looked at him contemptuously. "If you had little ones, then you would know that almost every household in America with children has at least one Brewster doll in it."

His lips curled and he looked across the park. "Is that right? A dollmaker. Hmmmmm." He stroked his chin and actually seemed to be considering her proposition. "Wouldn't my father be upset?"

"Probably. But you gonna let him tell you what to do for the rest of your life?"

"No. I'd have to move out. Buy myself a house." He turned back to her. "You said there are employees who know how to make the factory pay?"

She nodded vigorously, hiding her elation. "Bridget's pa is one of 'em. He's worked there for nigh on to forty years. He knows how to make the dolls and market them at a profit, but the owner's a stubborn man and won't listen to advice. If you was to buy the place and let her pa help you run it, then you'd be doing a world of good. People would come to know your name as the man who put a Brewster doll in every household in America."

"I thought there was already a Brewster doll in every household in America."

"Well, nearly," she conceded. "But you'd put one in every home."

"The idea appeals to me, except for one point," he said.

"What's that?"

"I would rather put a Fortunato doll in every household."

She laughed at him. "Sounds good to me. You gonna do it then?"

"I must check into it thoroughly before I decide," he said. "I will go see Brewster. But first, I would like to speak to Bridget's father. It would seem he knows more than the man who owns the factory."

Danny was delighted. They made their way back to the house where they found Adam on the point of leaving.

"Where the hell have you been?" he questioned angrily.

Roderic spoke up quickly, placing himself in front of her as though he suspected she was in danger. "We have been to the—"

"I wasn't speaking to you!" Adam snarled, turning a look of contempt on the other man. Then, "What the hell do you mean by coming here and carrying Danny off after what you did to her before?"

"He didn't do nothing to me!" Danny protested indignantly. "You ain't got no call to talk to him like that. He didn't do nothing."

"That's exactly what happened last time you went out with him," Adam said sarcastically. "He didn't do anything. And it resulted in your disappearance!"

"That ain't fair!" Danny snapped. "He didn't know I was leaving."

"That's right. He didn't know. And he should have."

"You leave him alone," Danny said.

"Only if he leaves you alone," Adam replied grimly.

"I think I had better leave," Roderic said.

"Don't go," she said. "You ain't seen Bridget yet."

"I will see her later," he said, backing away from them, keeping a wary eye on Adam.

Danny rounded on Adam. "Look what you gone and done," she said. "I had everything fixed and you went and messed it up."

"I don't know what you had fixed, Danny," he said. "But you shouldn't have left here with him."

Taking her arm he pulled her inside. "Next time you want to go out, ask me and I'll take you."

"I ain't gonna run to you whenever I want to leave here," she said.

"You little fool. I'm trying to protect you. Mosley wouldn't stop at having you abducted. Haven't you realized that yet? You barely escaped his henchman in the forest. You may not be so lucky next time."

"They ain't no use in even trying to talk to you," she said angrily.

He grabbed her arm with fingers of steel. "You're not leaving this room without promising me you won't run off like that again."

Hurt stabbed at her and unwanted tears stung her eyes. Danny lowered her lashes, unwilling for him to see her weakness. "All right! I promise!" she snapped, wrenching her arm free.

"Danny." His voice had softened. He reached out a hand to cup her chin, but she jerked away from him. "Danny, I don't mean to be harsh, but you must understand what could happen—"

Whatever he'd been about to say was lost to her, for Danny was no longer there. She had already taken flight.

Chapter Twenty-Nine

It was almost midnight, and although Danny had retired more than two hours ago, she found herself unable to sleep.

Damn you! Adam, she silently swore. *It's all your fault. Why'd you go an' treat Roderic thataway?*

The question had been buzzing around in her head like a swarm of angry bees for the past hour now. His anger had been all out of proportion. And it was totally uncalled for.

"If I didn't know you better, I might think you was jealous," she muttered.

Danny found that an interesting thought and turned the possibility over in her mind for awhile. Then, realizing how foolish she was being, she rejected it.

Heaving a deep sigh, Danny tossed restlessly in the bed, turning over on her back, then shifting to her left side, then back again, as she tried to find a more comfortable position.

But it didn't help. How could she expect to sleep,

she wondered, when her thoughts wouldn't let her rest. If only she could return to the peace of her beloved mountains.

But she couldn't. Not until they found her cousin, or at least, until she learned the fate of Angel and her babe.

Where could they be? God! Where could they be?

Her gaze went to the window. She had left it open a mere crack in order to have fresh air, but her nose was freezing. The temperature must have dropped drastically after night settled in.

Realizing she'd better close the window, Danny flung back the covers, slid to the floor and padded barefoot across the room. She shoved the window down, then stopped to gaze down at the moon-washed lawn.

Was somebody out there?

She narrowed her eyes on the dark shadow that detached itself from the shrubs, then blended with the other shadows.

Was her imagination working overtime, or was someone moving around outside?

With her curiosity piqued, Danny slipped her feet into a pair of pink woolen house slippers. After donning a wrapper, she left her room, closing the door quietly behind her, mindful of the slippers.

Like a thief in the night, she crept down the stairs, past the closed door of the study where a narrow strip of light shone through.

The murmur of male voices, muffled by the thick oaken door, told Danny that Adam and Jake were still up. Were they finding sleep as elusive as she was?

Danny reached out for the doorknob . . . and

paused as sudden realization dawned. She couldn't go in there. Adam would be mad as an old wet hen if she appeared wearing her nightclothes. Even by the dim light in the hall, Danny could see the thin cotton material was much too revealing.

She backed away from the door. She would just peek out the window, and if there was anything out there that shouldn't be, then she'd alert Adam.

Danny was halfway across the parlor when a sound on the porch froze her to the spot. It was a thin wail . . . a cry that bore a striking resemblance to the one she'd heard so many times before.

Why should it come from outside?

It took only one glance for Danny to see the door was bolted.

With her heart thudding heavily in her chest, Danny hurried to the window and peered out into the darkness. Her gaze fell on a yellowish-orange blob as the cry sounded again.

Scaredy cat! she silently chided herself. It was only the tabby cat. Somehow it had gotten left outside and it was missing the warmth it knew could be found in the kitchen.

Smiling at her fears, Danny unlatched the door. "Come on, Kitty," she called softly, mindful of disturbing the men who were in the study.

The cat, usually so friendly, seemed suddenly terrified of her. It ignored her soft whispers of encouragement and stayed where it was, hunched down against the floor, head lifted, eyes glaring at the door that Danny had pushed wide open.

"Come on now," Danny coaxed, her eyes fixed on the cat. "You poor little thing. What are you afraid of anyway? You know I won't hurt you! Come to me. I'm gonna fix you a nice warm bowl of milk."

Although she shivered in the cold night air, Danny continued her careful approach toward the frightened cat. The air was frigid. The temperature was below freezing and the cat would suffer if she left it out overnight.

The cat spit and snarled, covering the sound of movement behind Danny. She didn't know anyone else was there, until she felt a suffocating darkness thrown over her, almost smothering in intensity.

Although Danny struggled and screamed out, she knew her cries were muffled by the rough cloth that was binding her so securely.

Almost immediately, her feet left the floor, she was lifted and slung across something solid . . . someone's shoulder? She was carried away from the house like a sack of potatoes.

God! what was happening? She was almost certain a tow sack covered her, for the cloth was rough and smelled of corn shucks and she found breathing hard. She gasped for breath, felt something hard striking her head and fought against the encroaching darkness. A red haze swirled around her, threatening to consume her. Then, suddenly, Danny went limp and consciousness left her.

The coach bearing Danny wound its way through the mountains into a valley where the air was cold, damp and penetrating. The coachman held himself rigid, crouched over the backs of the horses, his eyes fixed firmly on the icy road ahead. He slowed the horses as he took a final corner on the icy road before it reached the stream. At this point the road doubled, curving back as it came to the stream leaping and glistening at the bottom of the valley. The water ran swiftly; the rocks it bounced over gleamed with a patina of ice; the sound it made as it fled the valley was quick, rushing, and it came up suddenly as the road entered its course. The sudden roaring caused the already unsettled driver's attention to lapse. He failed to rein the horses as the coach turned the bend. Velocity spun the vehicle on the icy roadway and it crashed into a stand of willows growing on the bank.

Everything happened quickly.

One moment the coach was traveling steadily toward the unseen stream, the next it had swung wide and the iron-rimmed wheels were sliding on the treacherous roadway, driving sideways in the direction of the stream bed, spraying powder ice as they cut into the surface.

The horses, feeling the weight behind them shift, lost their gait and scrambled sideways, taken by the body of the coach. Their legs tangled. Their heads were raised in fear and pain.

Above them, the coachman gripped the reins; he stood on the footboard and dragged backward to stay the horses, attempting to straighten the drive of the coach.

But it was too late.

Nothing would stop the sideways motion of the coach now except the willows growing beside the riverbank.

With a huge and overpowering crash the coach plunged into the stand of trees, heeling toward them as it went, skidding violently into their bulk with a sound of splintering wood.

The driver was flung clean. He fell past the willows onto the edge of the riverbank where he lay dazed and unmoving, his boots dangling in the freezing water.

The horses reared and plunged, tearing at their harnesses, tugging at the coach bulked against the trees, but they failed to move it. Their action broke more of the body work, adding to the sound of splintering, but did not free the vehicle. After a short while they quieted and stood in their tangle of leather waiting to be led.

Inside the carriage, Danny groaned and struggled upright. Working her head against the side of the coach, she managed to push the sack from her head and stared around her. Her captor lay unmoving. She didn't know whether he was dead or alive. She didn't take the time to find out. She was intent on getting out of the overturned coach when she heard him groan.

Immediately, she shoved the door open and put a leg out of the carriage and worked her body through the blocked doorway. Just as she thought she was clear, a hand wrapped around her foot and she was held fast.

"Let me go!" she screeched, kicking out at her captor.

He uttered a string of curses and tightened his fingers around her ankle. Another kick caught him on the nose and she was free of him.

But not of the carriage. She found her clothing caught on the broken door. Her efforts to free herself gave the man enough time to recoup his senses and as she felt the material of her dress pull free, she felt his fingers grip her again.

"Let me go!" she snarled, kicking out at him again.

But he had learned his lesson and was quick to dodge the blow. Danny's skittering gaze found a broken board and she reached for it. Her fingers barely brushed it. She stretched farther in her efforts to reach it . . . managed to grasp the end and brought it up with a swift blow aimed at her captor's head.

It struck him a glancing blow, but it was all she needed to be on her way.

Her feet flew over the forest floor as she raced away from the coach, intent on putting as much distance as she could between herself and the man who was so determined to capture her again.

She could hear him threshing through the brush behind her, swearing and stumbling in his haste to recapture her. He finally uttered threats of what he would do when he found her. And she had not the slightest doubts that he meant every word he uttered.

Her heart beat fast as she leapt over fallen logs, circling away from the man who pursued her. The man who seemed to be making an excessive amount of noise while he did it.

She had no idea of his intentions until she was brought up short by a wall of flesh, and a hard grip clamped both her arms against her body.

Jerking her head up, Danny stared in horror at the coachman. God! She should have known what they were about. She'd never had a chance, even at the start. They had laid a trap for her, and she had obligingly fell in.

As though to prove her point, the man who had

pursued her caught up to them.

"Bitch!" he grated, slapping her across the face with enough force to make her head snap back and her ears ring. "That's for making me chase after you like that."

A red haze blurred Danny's vision and she blinked her eyes, trying to chase it away. She mustn't lose consciousness. She couldn't let them win so easily.

"Dammit, you shouldn't'a hit her so hard," Danny's captor said. "I think she's gonna pass out on us."

His words planted the idea in Danny's head. With a moan, she allowed her body to go limp. When his hold loosened, she twisted free and swung around, intending to take flight.

But fate intervened.

Danny's foot slipped on a patch of ice and she felt herself falling. She wasn't prepared for the blow when it came . . . wasn't prepared for the blackness that seemed to have been waiting for such an unlikely event to occur. She wanted to cry out, to rail against fate for betraying her. But when she tried, the words would not come. Her thoughts wouldn't focus . . . and slowly, reluctantly, she yielded to the inevitable and welcomed the enfolding darkness

Chapter Thirty

In the library, Adam watched Jake pace restlessly, knowing exactly how the other man was feeling. Hadn't he felt the same way when Danny was missing?

But Jake's ordeal hadn't lasted only a few days. It had been going on now for months. It was a wonder Jake was still sane.

Adam tried to find words to reassure Jake, but knew it would be impossible. Mere words couldn't help Jake. But Adam knew he must at least try.

"We'll find them, Jake," he said. "Mosley will make a mistake and we'll be right on him. There's no way he can hide them forever."

"It's already been forever," Jake said morosely. "God! These last few months have been an eternity. If only I hadn't agreed to let Angel go visit Heather." He made a fist and slammed it into his palm. "Dammit! Why the hell didn't I make her wait until I could go with her?"

Since Adam had no answer, he remained silent.

Jake began to pace the floor restlessly. He stopped beside the fireplace, braced himself against the mantle and stared into the flames. The shadows cast by the firelight accented the angular planes of his face, making Adam realize Jake was losing weight rapidly.

Realizing the other man needed to be alone with his thoughts, Adam downed the rest of his brandy and set the glass on a nearby table. "It's getting late," he said, arching tired neck muscles. "I guess I'll go on up to bed." He looked over at Jake who had bent to put another log on the fire. "You should try to get some rest."

"You go on up," Jake said, sitting back on his haunches and watching the dancing flames. "I'll be up later. I can't seem to fall asleep anymore and I don't feel like lying in the room I used to share with Angel and staring up at the ceiling." He laughed harshly. "As you can see, I'm wallowing in self-pity tonight. Fit company for neither man nor beast."

"No one has more right."

Jake sighed and rose to his feet. "Good night, Adam."

"Good night," Adam replied.

Casting another sympathetic look at the man still lost in his memories, Adam crossed the room, opened the library door . . . and froze.

The air in the foyer was frigid. It was so cold that Adam's breath was actually visible in the air.

What was going on? His gaze flew to the front door and widened. The door stood open.

"What the hell?" he exclaimed, wondering how it came about. The door was made of oak, too heavy to have opened of its own accord.

"What's wrong?" Jake asked sharply. His boots rapped against the hardwood floor as his long strides carried him toward Adam. "What's the front door doing open?"

"Just what I was wondering," Adam said, hurrying toward it. He shoved the door closed with a quick thud and threw the bolt home. "Whoever used it last must not have shut the door properly."

Jake's dark brows pulled together. "That seems odd. I can't see Mrs. Gruber being so careless. She has been with my family since before I was born. And, to my knowledge, not once in all those years has she failed to lock all the doors and windows before retiring."

Suddenly the door to the kitchen opened. Adam turned to see the housekeeper. She had either been in bed, or preparing for it, because a faded flannel wrapper covered the nightgown she wore. And a mop cap barely concealed the thin strips of white rags she used to curl her hair over night.

"I wondered what all the noise was about, Mister Jake," she said. "Didn't know you was still up, but I should have guessed you was. It's little enough sleep you be getting these days what with worrying over the missus and all." Suddenly, she shivered and wrapped her arms around her upper torso. "Why is it so cold in here?" she asked. "Did the furnace go out?"

"I didn't check it," Jake said. "But I don't think so."

"Then why is it so cold in here?" she asked again.

"The door was standing wide open. Apparently you forgot to bolt it."

Her eyes widened and she stared at him. "Me? Forget to bolt the door? Why I never! In all the time I been with this household, nor any other before I come here, I never once forgot to bolt the front door. You ought to know it's the last thing I do before I go to bed."

Jake smiled grimly. "That's what I was just telling Adam. But the door was standing wide open, Mrs. Gruber. You can feel how cold it is in here."

"That I do," she agreed. "But if that front door was open, then it didn't get that way by itself. Someone must have unbolted it and gone outside."

Adam met Jake's eyes. The woman sounded so sincere. But who would go outside this time of night. Was it possible she was only trying to cover up her mistake?

Suddenly, Adam felt an overwhelming need to check on Danny. To assure himself that she was all right. With that end in mind, he sprinted up the staircase to her room. Outside, he hesitated for a moment. Perhaps he was being foolish in his fears. He didn't want to wake her, but . . .

Grasping the door knob, he pushed the door open and . . . stared at the empty bed.

"Danny?" His heart beat with trepidation as he probed the shadows with his gaze.

But it was useless! Danny was not there!

"Dammit!" Spinning on his heels, he descended the steps two at a time, passed the two people who stood as though transfixed at the foot of the stairs, threw the bolt and yanked open the front door. "Danny!" he shouted, but the wind was the only thing he heard.

"She's gone?" Jake asked from beside him.

"Yes!" Adam snapped, bending to study the porch. There was a light coat of snow on the boards and several bootprints that were scuffed. "When did it start snowing again, Jake?"

"I don't know," Jake said. "I hadn't even noticed it had." He turned back to the housekeeper. "Get us some coats. We must look for her."

Although they searched the grounds around the mansion, there was no sign of Danny. A quick check of the snow in the drive told them a carriage had been there since the snow had started. And that was after everyone but the men had retired for the night.

"She's been abducted," Jake said. "Mosley sent someone for her. But it doesn't make sense. Why would he want Danny when he's already moved Angellee elsewhere?"

"I think I know," Adam said slowly. "He's afraid of her visions. Afraid they will help us find your wife."

"But he doesn't know about them. How could he?"

"Because I was foolish enough to tell him when we met that day in your office building. Don't you remember?" Adam's hands clenched into fists, his nails dug into his palms. "God! why didn't I keep my mouth shut. How could I have told him such a thing?"

"That's not important now," Jake said. "What you don't seem to realize is they've left tracks this time. All we've got to do is follow the carriage tracks and they will lead us to where he's hidden them." His voice was elated and Adam guessed it was because Jake felt Danny's abduction was Mosley's undoing,

334

that it would be the means of bringing Angellee and her baby home.

The first thing Danny became aware of was the shafts of pain targeted behind and above her left eye. She opened her eyes, groaned and quickly closed them again.

God! Her temple throbbed, she felt nauseous, and her mouth seemed to be filled with cotton wool. As though that weren't enough, something hard was digging into her back.

Danny shifted positions and searched the bed with her left hand. Her fingers connected with several hard, round objects and she frowned. If she wasn't mistaken, she was sleeping in a bed filled with pebbles.

Lifting one of them up, she opened her eyes and squinted at it.

It *was* a pebble. What was it doing in her bed?

Suddenly her eyes widened in horror. The carriage! She had been abducted by a man in a carriage. And he had struck her while she was trying to escape.

Miserably, she surveyed her surroundings. She was lying on a bed in a dingy room that was bare of any other furnishings. There was only one window and it was boarded up, but still, a few stray beams of sunlight crept through the cracks between the planks.

Using her elbows, she pushed herself to a sitting position against the big iron bedstead.

Then panic set in.

Beginning in the pit of her stomach, it welled into

her throat, threatening to choke her, and she clenched her teeth to stop it from escaping in a scream.

Desperately, she tried to keep it under control. Whatever mess she'd landed herself in, at least she was still alive and had her wits about her.

For the moment anyway, she reminded herself.

Danny didn't know her captor's intentions, but she wasn't going to wait calmly for him to return. Sliding off the bed, she padded barefoot across to the door and gripped the doorknob.

The door refused to yield. She had been locked in. That fact didn't surprise her much.

Danny crossed to the window and peered through the cracks. She was undoubtedly on the second floor, because the ground was at least fifteen feet below. She stared outside across the snow covered yard that was overgrown with weeds to the piney forest that lay beyond.

"Where am I?" she muttered. "Where have they brought me?"

She returned to the bed and sat down.

Suddenly she froze. Footsteps sounded outside the door. She heard metal grate against metal, then a click as a key turned in the lock. A surge of hope went through her as the door swung slowly open, allowing bright sunshine to flow into the room.

A huge shape filled the doorway and hope died in Danny. It was Lucky, Asa Mosley's henchman.

"Awake, are you?" he growled as he stepped into the room and approached the bed. He seemed even more formidable than he had before.

A shudder of apprehension shivered through her.

Although he had no weapon in sight, that didn't encourage her in the slightest.

"What do you want from me?" Despite her efforts at control, her voice wobbled slightly, sounding weak and uncertain. She clenched her teeth to keep them from chattering as another wave of panic washed over her, leaving her deathly cold.

"What do you think?" he asked, his eyes dark and glittering. The brighter light from the hall was shining behind him, making him appear even more menacing. "You made me look a fool, getting away from me like that. Mosley wasn't too happy with me." He grabbed a handful of her hair and pulled it sharply, causing tears of pain to fill her eyes. "How'd you do it? How'd you get away like that?"

Danny pressed her mouth into a thin line and glared up at him. She wasn't about to let him see her fear. "It wasn't hard fooling the likes of you," she said contemptuously.

"You talk mighty big for somebody that's my prisoner," he said, sneering down at her. "I think before long you'll be singing a different tune." He yanked her hair again, and a cry of pain escaped her before she could stop it. "Before long you'll be begging for my—"

"Lucky!" a sharp male voice interrupted. "What'n hell do you think you're doing here?"

Lucky's body blocked the new arrival from Danny's view, but she gave a silent prayer that the man would prove sympathetic to her plight. Tears of pain stung her eyes and she blinked rapidly, hoping to dry the moisture before Lucky saw the sign of her weakness. She didn't want to give him that pleasure.

"This ain't nothin' to do with you, Donnahey," Lucky said. "This is between me and the little lady." His hand tightened in Danny's hair and, before she could stop it, a groan escaped her lips.

Instantly, Donnahey bounded into Danny's line of vision. His size was comparable to Lucky's bulk and he looked just as formidable. Danny looked pleadingly at him and he responded instantly.

"Let her go, Lucky. Right now."

Perhaps it was the threat in his voice that loosened Lucky's grip, or it may have been that Lucky was just tired of the game. Whatever the reason, Danny was grateful for it. Her scalp continued to sting as her knees buckled and she slid to the floor.

"You ain't seen the last of me," Lucky growled, a chill hanging on the edge of his words. His eyes promised retribution as he glowered down at Danny. "I got me a score to settle with you, and you can bet your life that I'll be back. Take my word for it. When Asa Mosley's through with you, I'll be coming back." Turning on his heel, he stomped from the room.

Danny, feeling incredibly weak and vulnerable, turned her attention to the man who had stopped Lucky. She made a visible effort to pull herself together, swallowing convulsively around the lump of fear that closed her throat.

"I don't know how to thank you," she said. "I don't think I could have—"

"You don't have no reason to thank me," he interrupted. "I was just following Mosley's orders. He said you was to be left alone." His eyes swept over her body, still clad in her flimsy nightclothes. "But Lucky might just as well forget about you," he added. "I brung you here and when Mosley don't need you no more, than I'm the one that's gonna have you."

God! He's just as bad as Lucky! she silently told herself, closing her eyes against the pain of her throbbing temples.

"Go away," she whispered. "Just go away and leave me alone."

"I aim to," he said. "But first, cook sent me to find out if you want something to eat."

Danny's stomach growled at the mention of food, and although she would have liked to have thrown the offer of food back in his face, she realized she would be the only one to suffer if she did. "Yes," she said, trying to infuse some measure of gratitude in her voice. "Guess I could eat something." She added a silent prayer that whoever brought her food would have a little more sympathy for her plight. Perhaps, the unknown person might even be persuaded to help her.

The sun was breaking over the horizon, painting the sky with long ribbons of red and gold, when Adam saw the overturned coach.

His heart thundered wildly as he slid off his mount, scrambled down the embankment and peered inside.

He swallowed the despair that nearly choked him when he realized the coach was empty.

"Is she there?" Jake called.

"The coach is empty," Adam said, his gaze scouring the interior, searching for some clue of where the passengers had gone. He sucked in a sharp breath when he saw the dark stain on the seat.

Was it blood?

He leaned closer, and his nostrils flared at the coppery smell. God! It *was* blood! Someone had obviously been injured when the coach slid into the gully.

"Not Danny," he muttered through tight lips. "God! Don't let it be Danny!"

Realizing he was wasting time, Adam knelt on the snow-covered ground and studied the area around the carriage. There were several sets of tracks. By the size of them, they belonged to men. But, underlying one boot print, he found part of another track. And if his eyes weren't deceiving him, the person who had made it had been wearing houseslippers.

The track was deeper than the bootmarks, which led him to believe that the person who had made it was either extremely heavy, or had jumped into the snow.

He felt certain the print belonged to Danny. Could she possibly have escaped her captors?

Adam's heart fluttered wildly beneath his ribs, as though it were a bird intent on escaping the confines of its cage. But, although he searched the area thoroughly, he found no more clues.

Other than the one partial footprint, there was no sign that Danny had ever been there.

Chapter Thirty-One

Although Danny waited impatiently for her breakfast, it wasn't hunger that caused her anxiety. It was because she hoped to find someone sympathetic to her plight.

But the hope was short-lived. The man who brought her morning meal seemed in an incredible hurry to leave again.

When Danny heard his footsteps in the passageway, she stationed herself near the door. Pasting a wide smile on her face, she waited, listening to the key grating in the lock.

Then the door opened.

Danny had a glimpse of a small, wiry man before he shoved a laden plate at her, then fled from the room as though the hounds of hell were at his heels.

"Wait!" Danny called, clutching the plate in one hand and reaching for the closing door with the other. But the door refused to yield. And a grating sound told her she had been locked in again.

Frustrated, Danny kicked at the door with her slippered foot. Her toes connected with the heavy wood and she swore softly as pain arched through her foot.

Grimacing, she rubbed the injured foot and glared at the plate she was holding. She considered throwing it against the wall, but the gesture would have been useless, serving no purpose except to deprive herself of badly needed nourishment.

She didn't realize how badly it was needed until after she had seated herself on the bed and bit into a rasher of bacon. Moments later she had cleaned her plate of bacon, egg, and biscuit. She laid the fork—the only hardware she had been supplied with—across the plate.

Intending to rid herself of the plate, she stood up and the fork shifted, then fell against the hard wood of the floor with a loud clatter.

Idly, Danny bent over and retrieved it. Her fingers brushed against the sharp tines as she placed it on the plate, and she stilled, her gaze narrowing on the shiny metal of the fork.

Was the idea she was entertaining possible? Could she use the fork to open the door?

It might work. And Danny knew she had nothing to lose by trying.

Hurrying across the room, she wedged the fork in the crack between the door and the facing. But the door was heavy, made of solid wood, and resisted her efforts to pry it open. All she had to show for her efforts were a few gouges in the wood.

Wiping the cold sweat from her brow, Danny bent one tine back and attempted to pick the lock.

Again, her efforts proved useless.

But Danny didn't give up. She couldn't afford to. Somehow, in some fashion, she sensed that Angellee was somewhere in the house. And the knowledge— the absolute certainty that she was right—kept Danny from admitting defeat.

Danny crossed the room to the window. If she could pull the boards off, then perhaps she could escape through it.

Wedging the fork beneath the edge of a board, she pried at the wood. *God! It was working. The nails were pulling loose!*

Half an hour later, Danny worked her fingers beneath the window and pushed it up.

Wind exploded into the room, and snowflakes swirled around Danny, melting against the hard wood floor as she leaned over the sill and looked down.

The ground seemed incredibly far away. Since Danny shrank from the possibility of breaking her bones, jumping from the window was impossible. Her gaze scanned the side of the building, found the narrow ledge located only a floor below, then followed the ledge to the drainpipe located at the far end of the house.

Excitement flowed through her. Would it be possible to balance herself on the ledge long enough to reach the drainpipe?

Suddenly, she heard the sound of voices approaching from beneath her. *Someone was coming.*

Pulling her head back inside, Danny leaned against the wall, shivering with cold. She realized she couldn't go out the window in broad daylight. Even if she could reach the ledge, she would be seen before she had a chance to climb down.

God! There had to be another way out.

Her thoughts whirled furiously, devising and discarding one plan after another. Time passed. Minutes ticked by, then hours, but no one came near her. As night cloaked the land in a blanket of darkness, Danny's gaze returned to the window. It was the only way out. Pulling the blanket off the bed, she removed the sheet, then tore it into wide strips. Then, she began to braid them into a long rope. When she had finished, she tied one end to the iron bedstead and tested it for strength.

Feeling positive the makeshift rope would hold her weight, Danny tied the blanket around her shoulders and lowered herself across the windowsill.

The cold wind stung her face; her heart pounded and Danny realized she was absolutely terrified. The thickly falling snow combined with the darkness of night made it difficult to see the ground, but it would also make it hard for her to be seen from below.

But had she been a fool to attempt this? she silently wondered. *Should she go back inside while she could?*

Even as the thought occurred to her, Danny was lowering herself toward the ledge below. Her foot struck something solid, then slipped off.

God! She was going to fall!

Danny's throat constricted and it was difficult to catch her breath. She hung there, suspended, swaying back and forth as her improvised rope twisted and turned in the icy wind. Her stomach churned and she looked up, feeling almost certain the makeshift rope was already fraying against the window sill. Soon, the strands of fabric that made up her temporary rope would part and she would fall to her death.

But not if she could hold on to the ledge!

Danny's feet searched frantically for purchase, found the ledge and she slid her flimsily-clad toes tight against the side of the house, pressing her face hard against the rocks that formed the wall.

She remained frozen, barely aware of the cold, trying to summon strength into her trembling body.

Adam! Help me!

But even as she silently cried out to him, Danny knew Adam couldn't help. There was no one to help her. She was on her own.

Gathering her courage around her, she began to work her way toward the drainpipe. She was halfway there when she realized the dim light ahead of her was coming from one of the windows.

Was the room occupied? If it was, could she pass the window without being seen? Danny knew she had no option except to try.

She continued to move forward cautiously. At the edge of the window she waited for a long moment, listening, but the only sound she heard was the beating of her heart and the howling wind.

Realizing she couldn't stay where she was, Danny peeped around the casement. At first she thought the room was empty. Then she realized whoever occupied it was in the bed, almost hidden by the quilt. As she watched, the figure tossed restlessly and Danny had an overpowering vision of a huge black mass. An evil darkness that was so strong . . . so crushing . . . that Danny almost lost her grip and fainted.

345

Her breath came harshly as she flinched back against the wall, trying to keep her balance, wondering what on earth she had encountered in that room. She'd experienced the vision once before. The evil mass had surrounded Asa Mosley?

Could he be asleep on the bed?

Danny looked into the window again, studying the covered form intently. It wasn't Mosley who lay abed. The sleeper had the shape of a woman.

Realizing she was wasting time, Danny continued her way across the ledge. She was nearly past the window when the figure turned over in the bed.

Danny's eyes widened with realization as she saw the long, red hair spread out against the sheet.

My God! *It was Angellee!* Danny had found her cousin.

And she couldn't leave now! Now without taking Angellee with her.

Grasping the edge of the window with a trembling hand, Danny tried to lift it. But it was impossible to raise the window and keep her precarious balance on the ledge.

Danny tapped gently against the glass. Angellee turned over on the bed. She tapped again. *Angel,* she silently cried. *Wake up!*

Angellee's movements stilled; her head lifted slowly as though she knew someone had called to her. Danny tapped the glass again.

Angellee's gaze fastened on Danny and her eyes widened. Fumbling with the covers, Angellee pushed them aside and slid to the floor.

Danny frowned as she watched her cousin. Angellee's movements appeared slow and uncoordinated.

346

What was wrong with her? Was she ill?

When Angellee reached the window, she leaned against it for a moment as though weakened by her efforts. Impatient, shivering with cold, Danny tapped on the window again. "Hurry," she said aloud, realizing as she did so there was no way her cousin could hear her voice.

But Angellee understood and reached for the window. She struggled with it as though it weighed a ton. It seemed an eternity before the window was lifted enough for Danny to get her hand beneath it to help. A moment later she threw her leg over the casement and slid inside.

"I-I thought I w-was going to f-freeze out there," she chattered, leaning forward to embrace her cousin.

"Danny. I am so glad to see you," Angellee sobbed, clutching Danny's shoulders while tears slid down her cheeks.

In all her years, Danny had never seen Angellee cry.

"I was afraid you were dead," Danny said, feeling almost overwhelmed with emotion.

Angellee sank down on the bed as though her legs would no longer hold her. "Is Jake with you?" she asked, brushing a trembling hand across her face. "He will have to be careful getting us out. The baby must be found first. I don't know where they have her. Far enough away that I cannot hear her crying." Her eyes brimmed over again and more tears rained down her cheeks. "I am so afraid for her, Danny. She's such a wee bit of a girl. They won't let me keep her for fear that I will escape them. That's why they didn't even bother to lock the window. They knew I wouldn't go off and leave my babe."

"From the looks of you, I'd say you couldn't leave if you did have her. Have you been sick?"

"I don't think so," Angellee said. "But I'm so weak all the time. And so sleepy. It's hard to think clear any more and I even find it hard to stay awake to feed my little girl."

"Maybe they're puttin' somethin' in your food. Somethin' to make you sleep, so's you won't be no bother to 'em," Danny suggested. Even as she said the words, she knew that must be what was happening. That would account for Angellee being unable to contact her at times, and for the weakness Danny had felt in the presence that came to her in her visions.

Angellee's eyes widened. "I never thought about that, Danny. That has to be what they are doing." She gripped Danny's arm. "We must hurry and get out of here! Where is Jake waiting for us?"

"Jake ain't here," Danny said. "It's just me, Angel."

"But . . . I don't understand. Why did you come here alone?" Her gaze traveled over Danny's blanket-wrapped form. "Danny? Why are you dressed that way?"

Danny explained what had happened and Angellee's eyes widened. "Oh, God! Danny! The baby and I are no better off than we were before. Even worse now, because you are in danger too!"

"If they was of a mind to kill us, then they wouldn't of kept you alive all this time."

"Asa Mosley kept me alive so he could have a hold on Jake," Angel said. "And he's keeping the babe alive to keep me under control. He's an evil man, Danny." She put her head in her hands and sobbed.

"We're all doomed to die. You and me and my little babe."

"Stop it, Angellee!" Danny ordered curtly. "I ain't never seen you give up for nobody. And right now I'm plumb ashamed of you. Are you just gonna lay down and let Asa Mosley kill you and your babe?"

"No!" Angellee said sharply, jerking her head up. "I'll do no such thing. They won't kill my babe. I'll fight them with every last breath in my body. But I just don't know how."

"We'll think of something," Danny said. "Just don't give up."

Suddenly, they heard boots in the hallway. Jerking around, Danny stared at the door. A key grated in the lock. *God!* Danny's thoughts whirled furiously. *Had her captors discovered her missing already? Were they even now searching the house for her?*

Chapter Thirty-Two

Adam crouched on one knee behind a snow-laden bush while he watched the house. He had been hiding there for almost an hour, his eyes fixed unwaveringly on the lighted window, while Jake circled around the house, searching for the guards that had surely been posted.

Dammit! He silently cursed the delay. *Danny needed him.* Adam had never felt more certain of anything in his life. The need to find her was almost overpowering, but it had taken them until dusk to locate the house. Jake said the place had been unoccupied for so many years, that he'd forgotten it existed.

God! Would Jake never get back? What was taking him so long? Suddenly, a sharp crack nearby alerted Adam to another presence and he jerked to his feet, his head swiveling around.

"There's guards posted, all right," Jake said. "I counted two. There may be more."

"Armed?" Adam asked.

"They carried sidearms, nothing more. I could have taken one of them out easy enough, but I was afraid it would alarm the other one. I didn't want to take any chances." Jake's face was grim. "Adam, I want Angellee out of there. And my baby too . . . if it's alive. Whatever happens here, one of us has got to see that done."

"It will be done," Adam told him. "But the deal includes Danny too."

"Of course," Jake said. "That goes without saying. But I was almost sure Danny could take care of herself if we get in a bind. I'm not so certain about Angellee anymore. She's been with them so long. I don't know what kind of condition we'll find—" His voice broke off as though he was unable to continue that thought.

"Don't worry, Jake," Adam said. "This thing is about over. You'll be together again. We've just got to figure out the best way to accomplish it, the safest way for the girls."

Adam realized they would be putting the women in danger if they were seen trying to enter the house. Obviously the best way would be to take out the guards first.

Jake agreed with Adam. "Both guards were on the back side of the house a few minutes ago," Jake said. "But they were on the move. Let's take them out first, then we can enter by the front door."

Drawing their weapons, they made their way from tree to tree until they saw the first guard, leaning against the building, smoking a cigarette.

"You take him," Jake whispered. "I'll go after the other one."

Nodding, Adam crept toward the guard, keeping to the bushes, hoping to put the man out of commission without any noise. He was so intent on the man that he didn't notice the brush beneath his feet until he stepped on it.

Crack! Adam froze at the sound, and his eyes shifted to the ice-covered brush at his feet.

"Joe!" The gruff voice warned Adam that he had been heard and he froze. "Is that you, Joe?"

In that moment of time that Adam had looked away, the guard had moved. And, although Adam probed the dense shadows ahead, he saw no movement.

Snap!

Adam's head jerked around. Although Carl's voice came from his right, the sound, as though a limb had broken, came from the brush on his left.

Had the other guard escaped Jake? Or had someone else come up on him?

Reaching for the branch of a tree hanging just above his head, Adam quickly swung himself into the concealing foliage of the oak tree.

Only moments had passed when a man of medium build crept softly beneath the tree. Adam hung from the branch until the man was directly below him, then he dropped.

The weight of his body forced the other man against the ground with a heavy thud. As soon as they hit the ground, Adam drew back his fist and struck out at his opponent. If the blow had landed, it would have rendered the other man unconscious. But it didn't. The man jerked his head back, then, rolled quickly aside.

Adam had already leapt after him when he heard the shout, that told him he'd been heard by someone else. A shot sounded, and Adam felt the bullet whiz by his nose. Adam heard several shots in succession and hot lead traced a path across his cheek. A moment later a bullet connected with his shoulder. The force of the bullet drove Adam backwards; he struck the trunk of the oak tree, felt the bark digging into his back, then the burning agony of another bullet plowing its way through the flesh of his upper torso, realized it was too near his heart. He realized he would more than likely not survive the wound . . . realized it would mean he would never see Danny again . . . *never* . . . *never* . . . *never*.

Danny made a dive for cover, barely concealing herself behind the bed before the door was flung open. Then, she heard a man's voice. "You better feed this baby. She ain't lookin' so good."

"Oh, God!" Angellee moaned. "Give her to me, please."

Danny held her breath as footsteps approached the bed; then Angellee spoke again. "Please . . . leave her with me for awhile?"

"I ain't so sure about that." His voice was hesitant. "Nobody said nothin' about leavin' her here with you."

"How else can I feed her?" Angellee demanded. "The milk won't come when I'm nervous. Surely you know that. And you must know that Asa Mosley will blame you if my baby dies. He knows I can't leave as long as she's alive."

"Guess it won't hurt none to leave her for awhile," he said grudgingly. "But you'd best hurry her along. I got my instructions. And I gotta follow 'em."

Danny heard footsteps receding, then the door closed, but she remained where she was until the sound of the key in the lock told her it was safe to leave her hiding place.

Realizing time was of the essence, Danny took the babe from her cousin, wrapped it in a blanket and hurried to the window. Without a word, she flung a leg over the sill and climbed through. Danny used her body to shield the baby from the cold as she made her way across the ledge.

It seemed an eternity before she reached the chimney. Then, with the moon lighting her way, Danny climbed up the sloping roof with the baby in her arms. When Danny realized she was alone on the rooftop, she looked down at the ledge to find Angellee still there. "What's wrong?" Danny called.

"I don't think I can make it," Angellee replied. "I don't have the strength to climb up there."

"Yes you can," Danny said. "Don't even think that way."

Angellee's legs were spread wide to improve her balance as she clung to the chimney with one hand.

Danny caught her bottom lip between her teeth, breathing harshly with the effort she was expending to hold the baby and cling to the roof top. "You'll be home soon, Angel. Just keep that in mind. We're going to get down from here, and you'll soon be back with Jake."

But even as Danny reassured her cousin, she knew she was giving her false hope. The chance they were taking was slim, and the journey to the rooftop had taken so long—because of Angellee's weakened condition—that their absence was sure to be discovered before long.

Crack! Danny jerked around. Was someone shooting at them? Angellee apparently had the same notion.

"Danny!" she cried, "somebody's shooting at us! Look!" She pointed the way. "There's somebody coming up on the roof!"

Danny's gaze narrowed on the dark figure at the bottom of the roof. Ducking her head down, she motioned her cousin to get behind the chimney. When they were both hidden from view, Danny slid the knotted sheets that held the blanket-wrapped baby from her shoulder and shoved it at Angellee.

"Stay here behind the chimney!" Danny said.

"What are you going to do?" Angellee asked, clutching her precious bundle against her bosom, trying to shield the baby from the cold.

"I'm going to try to lead him away from you," Danny replied.

Angellee closed her eyes tightly, then opened them again. "Whatever happens," she whispered. "Whether we get out of this or not, you have my eternal gratitude for trying to help us."

"Give me the sheet," Danny said.

"What are you going to do?" Angellee repeated, sliding the knotted sheet off the baby. She pulled the blanket aside long enough to look at the infant, then covered the babe's head again.

"Is the babe all right?"

"I don't know," Angellee said. "She looks so cold,

Danny. I've got to get her back inside again. She is such a frail little thing. I should never have attempted this."

"We'll have her safe soon enough," Danny said. "Now stay behind the chimney with her while I go to the other end of the house. You'll be out of the wind, and near the oak tree. The man—whoever he is— won't know you're here. He'll be too busy chasin' after me. And I'm goin' to use the sheet to slide down the side of the house."

"Is it long enough?"

"I don't know," Danny said grimly. "But I reckon I'm fixin' to find out. And whilst I'm doin' it, you'll have enough time to hide amidst the branches of the oak tree."

Without another word, Danny left her cousin. Bending low, she scrabbled across the roof, making her way to the other end of the house, intent on leading the man searching for them away from her cousin and the baby.

Tying the sheet around the drainpipe, she braced herself against the wind, placing her hands just so on the sheet. She could use her left hand for a guide and the right hand for braking.

Then, Danny tightened her grip, leaned backward, and slid from the roof.

The shout came as Adam was sinking into unconsciousness. His lids seemed incredibly heavy, but he forced them open. His gaze fastened on the figure dangling from the roof, and he sucked in a sharp breath. God! He was almost certain it was Danny!

Suddenly, as though appearing from out of nowhere, Jake was beside him.

"Are you all right?" he asked, kneeling beside Adam.

"Never mind me!" Adam said grimly. "Look up there." His finger pointed out the dangling figure.

"My, God! Who is it? It looks like a woman. Doesn't she know what she's attempting is impossible?"

"It's Danny!" Adam answered Jake's first question.

"Are you sure?"

Adam heard the relief in Jake's voice and it made him angry. What right did Jake have to be relieved that Danny was in danger? "It's her, all right! And we've got to get her down from there."

But Jake was already assessing the situation. "There's no way from that angle," he said. "She's stuck up there on the ledge. I think she's hanging on to the end of whatever she's using for a rope."

Adam was struggling to his feet. His body seemed incredibly heavy, at least twice as heavy as his usual body weight. But the sight of Danny on the ledge gave him the strength he needed.

"The tree," he told Jake. "We'll have to climb the tree and go over the roof to her. That's the only way we'll reach her." He looked at Jake for a long moment. "I don't think I could make it to the first limb, Jake. You'll have to do it."

Jake nodded. "Look out for yourself," he said, and hurried toward the side of the house where the oak tree grew.

Adam moved on rubbery legs toward the tree,

357

hoping to be of some help there. He heard Jake's exclamation of surprise, then incredible relief, "God! Angel!"

Adam saw a woman sliding down from the tree into Jake's arms, knew it must be his wife. But Jake must not be dissuaded from his original purpose, Adam reminded himself. No matter that his wife was safe, there was Danny to worry about now. But he needn't have worried.

Angellee's voice was anxious when she spoke. "You must help Danny, Jake!" she said urgently. "She led them away from us and I'm afraid she will die."

"Not if I can help it," Jake said. He spared one brief look at Angellee's blanket wrapped bundle, touched it gently. "Is the baby all right?"

"Yes. But we must hurry and get her away from here. She must be kept warm. Please hurry, Jake."

Hurry! The word echoed in Adam's head, as his thoughts whirled furiously, and dizziness assailed him. He knew he could not hold on to consciousness much longer, but he must try. At least until he knew Danny was safe.

When a red haze began to form behind his eyes, he knew he was fading fast . . . knew he wouldn't live to see Danny again. . . .

Then, his knees buckled and he fell as a blanket of darkness closed in around him.

Danny shivered with cold. The ledge was icy, and her feet kept slipping. The full moon gave off enough light so Danny could barely make out the figures below her. She had seen Adam fall and turned her eyes away, unable to think about what had happened to him. If she did, it would prove her undoing. Instead, she turned her gaze toward the oak tree, saw a man standing below it, saw Angellee, carrying the baby, slide into the man's arms.

Tears welled into Danny's eyes. If she'd accomplished nothing else, at least she had freed her cousin. But at what cost, her heart cried. Was Adam lying dead on the ground?

Danny forced her mind to concentrate on the task ahead of her. Her hands were frozen, her fingers numb. She closed her eyelids against the cold. How long could she hold on with her frozen fingers? Why was she even making the effort? Why didn't she just give up? It was obvious she would never make it down from here alive.

But did she really care? Adam had been shot. He could even be dead. And without him, her life wouldn't be worth living.

Adam, her heart cried. *Oh, God! Adam.*

Becoming aware of the frozen tears on her cheeks, Danny lowered her face to her sleeve and wiped them away.

"I gotcha now!" The voice came from the roof above and jerked Danny's head up.

She had never seen the man before, but he had to be one of Mosley's henchmen. He certainly hadn't come to help her.

"Give me your hand," he said, kneeling and reaching down for her.

When she remained unmoving, he said, "You ain't going nowhere else. And if you stay there you're gonna freeze to death."

He was right, of course. Although she was tempted to resist, the will to live still burned somewhere deep inside. Danny lifted her hand, stretching her arm to the fullest. He clasped it in his and tried to lift her, but she was obviously too heavy for him.

"Brace your feet against the wall and climb," he ordered.

Realizing the cold had slowed her thought processes, she obeyed him. Her right foot found a niche, then her left found another up higher and he began to pull her slowly upwards.

Danny threw a quick glance down. Was that Angel leaning over Adam's prostrate form. *Why didn't she run?* Danny asked herself. Why didn't Angellee use the time Danny had given her to run away? To hide herself?

Grunting with exertion, Mosley's man drew her closer to the roof top where he lay. But something was happening. Danny's fingers were slipping away from his . . .

Was she going to fall to her death?

Chapter Thirty-Three

Adam was cold. He moved and groaned as pain stabbed through him. Beads of sweat popped out on his forehead and he opened his eyes and stared up at the full moon.

"Just lie still." The woman's voice came from somewhere to his left.

"Danny?" he croaked, turning toward the voice.

"No." Adam couldn't make out her features. Was it because of the pale light, or because there was something wrong with his vision? "My name is Angellee. I am Danny's cousin."

Angellee? Yes, he remembered now. She was Jake's wife. His gaze dropped to the bundle in her arms. "The baby?" She nodded her head. "Where's Danny? Isn't she with you?"

"Jake is trying to get to her," Angellee replied. Her head tilted, she looked up toward the roof of the house . . . and froze. "Don't, Jake!" The words were filled with horror. "It's too dangerous!"

Following her gaze, Adam saw a man inching his

way across a narrow ledge. Above Jake, and to his right, a tableau unfolded. A man lay on his stomach, clutching a figure that dangled from the roof.

And Adam remembered! The figure hanging so precariously from the roof was Danny!

Despite the icy wind that buffeted her, sweat beaded Danny's forehead as she fought to retain her grip on the man who literally held her life in his hand.

But it seemed fate was against her.

Whether it was her weight, or the cold, gusty wind, Danny didn't know. She only knew that she was unable to hold on, was slowly slipping away from the man positioned above her.

And Danny didn't want to die! She needed more time to prepare, time that she obviously wouldn't be allowed. "Adam," she whispered, squeezing her eyes shut tight. She didn't want to see death when it claimed her. As it surely would, because suddenly she was falling . . . plunging downward in the snow and ice and wind to where certain death waited.

"Ooooff!" The sound whooshed out of her as, almost miraculously, she was brought to an abrupt halt . . . pulled back against the cold wall of the building by a wall of steel.

Her eyes opened wide and she found herself staring at a man's chest. "A-Adam?" she choked. But even as she did, she knew she was wrong. It wasn't Adam who had saved her. It couldn't be. Adam had been shot.

She looked up and her eyes met those of Jake Logan.

"Hold still," he said gruffly. "We're not out of the

362

woods yet. We have to make it back to the drainpipe."
He looked into her white face. "You can do it, can't you?"

Danny opened her mouth to speak and her teeth began to chatter. She didn't know if it was from the cold or a reaction to her fear. "I w-will," she muttered. "I'll m-make it there."

Suddenly, she remembered the man on the roof. She tilted her head, her gaze moving upwards. Fear closed her throat as she saw the figure, silhouetted against the moon. He was positioned on one knee, his pistol drawn and ready.

"L-look out, Jake!" she stammered. "He's going to—"

A shot rang out and she waited for the bullet, waited for the pain to come. Instead, the man above them staggered, seemed to lose his balance and plunged downward. Her disbelieving gaze followed his body, watched it land with a heady thud against the ground.

Danny didn't know what had happened, but she knew he must be dead. He couldn't be otherwise with his neck twisted in such a position.

She turned back to Jake. "W-what happened?"

"Over there," he said, pointing down and away from them. "It was either Adam or Angel who shot him. Come on, let's get down there."

He didn't have to tell her twice. Together, they inched their way toward the dubious safety of the drainpipe.

Danny's heart beat with dread as she knelt beside

Adam, who still held the pistol he'd used to shoot the man on the roof. He was covered with blood, and very obviously badly injured. When Danny tried to take the gun, his fingers tightened around it.

"Give it to me, Adam," she said. "There's nobody left to shoot." And there wasn't. The woman and the cook was all that was left, and they huddled together near Angellee, a trembling pair who awaited their fate.

Slowly, Adam's grip on the weapon relaxed. Although his eyes were open, he seemed barely conscious. Danny's fingers trembled as she pulled at his shirt, bright with blood, clinging wetly to him. The buttons popped in her haste to open it.

Ripping a strip of fabric from her clothing, Danny made a tourniquet and tied it around Adam's upper arm, then she folded a square of the fabric and pressed it against the wound and his shoulder. His eyes were closed now and his breathing was shallow.

"God! Let him live," she muttered. "Please, let him live."

Suddenly, she was conscious of Jake bending over them. "I hitched the horses to the buggy I found in the barn," he said. "I put blankets in it to keep him and the baby warm, but we'd better hurry and get them to a doctor."

"What about them?" she nodded at the cook and the woman. "Are they comin' too?"

He shook his head. "Angellee said no. They were only hirelings, not really responsible for what happened. Perhaps they will learn a lesson from all this."

The cook helped Jake lift Adam into the carriage where Angellee waited with her baby. After Danny had made sure Adam was covered with blankets, she climbed up beside Jake.

"Heeeahhh!" he shouted, cracking the whip above the horses.

The horses strained at the harness. The carriage lurched, then rolled forward. Danny spared one last look at the man covered with blankets against the cold, howling wind, then she faced forward, realizing there was nothing else she could do for Adam, except to pray.

A long black veil concealed Danny's face as she entered the small church packed with mourners. Her eyes found the casket and froze there. *It can't be true,* her heart cried. *It's all a mistake! Adam can't be dead!*

The air, scented by the flowers that surrounded the casket, felt almost too heavy to breathe. Or perhaps it was the lump in her throat and the ache in her heart that was the problem. Her fingers tightened around the bouquet of wildflowers clutched in her right hand as she forced herself to walk toward the bier. As the ache in her heart intensified, Danny stumbled forward on legs that seemed to be made of rubber.

She couldn't let Adam be buried without one last look at him. *God!* she silently cried. *How will I go on without him?*

A sob caught in Danny's throat and she felt the tears raining down her cheeks. *Somebody made a mistake,* her heart cried. *It ain't really Adam layin' there.* But even though she denied his presence, she knew she was wrong. Because now she could see the corpse . . . could see the scarred face of the man she had loved so dearly.

God! How could she bear it? How could she lose him when she hadn't ever told him she loved him? Pain sliced through her like a knife, twisting and turning with each step that brought her closer to the man she had loved and lost.

"Adam," she cried hoarsely, leaning over him, touching his cold, cold flesh with loving hands. "Don't leave me, Adam. Please don't leave me!"

Cupping his face in her palms, she placed her lips against his.

"Don't, Danny," Angellee said, tugging at Danny's arm. "Adam's gone. You must accept it."

"I want to be with him!" Danny cried, throwing her arms around Adam's cold body. "Don't leave me Adam! Don't leave me!"

"Don't do this Danny," Angellee said. "He's gone. There's nothing you can do about it. He's gone, Danny . . . gone, Danny . . . Danny . . ."

Angellee tugged at Danny's elbow, turned her around and began shaking her . . .

"Wake up, Danny," she cried. "Wake up!"

Danny's heart raced frantically as her eyes popped open and she stared up at Angellee's concerned face.

"Are you all right?" Angellee asked.

"I-I—" Danny broke off, her frantic gaze winging to the bed where Adam was lying, pale and still. "Is-is he still alive?" she whispered hoarsely.

Her cousin nodded sympathetically. "His condition hasn't changed in the last few hours." She smoothed back Danny's hair and studied her intently. "You had a bad dream, didn't you?"

"It seemed so real," Danny choked.

"That's the way of dreams," Angellee said.

"But it wasn't an omen," Danny said fiercely, glaring at her cousin. "Don't you dare go thinkin' it was an omen."

"No, of course it wasn't an omen," Angellee agreed. "Would it help if you talked about it?"

"No!" She couldn't talk about it. That would give it substance and she wouldn't do that . . . couldn't do that.

"You need to get some rest, Danny. Let me take over here for awhile."

"No. Something might happen if I leave."

"Something will happen if you stay," Angellee said severely. "But it will happen to you. It's been three days now."

Danny knew how long it had been. It had been three days of hell . . . three days of constant worry . . . the agony of waiting, of wondering if Adam would make it through another day.

When Adam began to mumble indistinctly, Danny leaned over the bed and wiped the sweat from his brow. Although the doctor had told them three days ago that Adam had a good chance at recovery, he seemed no better. He had been out of his head, talking wildly, alternating between chills and fever.

He tossed restlessly, knocking her hand aside, and pulling at the bandage that circled his chest.

Danny shoved his hand away and leaned closer to him. "Stop it, Adam. Don't touch your bandages. You're gonna break them wounds open an' make 'em bleed again."

His eyelids flickered, but remained closed. "Danny!" he mumbled. "Danny . . ."

"I'm here, Adam," she said, blotting his forehead. "Right here beside you. You're gonna get well, Adam. But you gotta fight harder."

When she tried to straighten his bandage, he knocked her hand aside. "Hurts," he mumbled. "Hurts like hell."

"I know," she said. "But you gotta leave it alone." She smoothed back his hair, leaned over and kissed his forehead. "Go back to sleep, Adam. Go back to sleep now."

His movements stilled as though her words had calmed him.

"I know how you must be feeling," Angellee said softly, and Danny realized she had forgotten her cousin was there. "I felt the same way when Jake was wounded and there was no one but me to look after him." She laid her hand lightly on Danny's shoulder and laughed huskily. "At least you didn't have to dig the bullets out yourself."

"Did you have to do that?" Danny asked, anxious to keep her cousin talking. It was better than the silence, better than the constant watching and . . . waiting in vain for Adam to show some sign of recovery.

"Yes," Angellee said. "I thought for sure Jake was going to die. But he was strong. And so is Adam."

"Buck told me how you rescued Jake from the Comanches."

Angellee's mouth twitched in memory. "I did. But not because I wanted to. I was trying my best to sleep when the vision woke me. I tried to ignore it, but it wouldn't let me. I kept seeing Jake, spread-eagled between two trees. And I knew he'd be dead by morning if I didn't do something about it."

"We haven't talked about the visions, Angel," Danny said. "How did you know about me? How did you know I had the gift too?"

"I sensed it, Danny. I wasn't really sure, though. But after Mosley's men took me and several months had passed . . . I realized you were my only hope."

"So you sent your mind seekin' out mine," Danny finished for her. "How did you do it?"

"I'm not sure," Angellee said. "I've never been sure how it works—or if it will. But I was desperate enough to try."

"I was afraid of you," Danny said. "When you come to me, I was afeared." She sighed. "Maybe if I'da listened to you, then Adam wouldn't be layin' there like that, all shot up, maybe d-dyin'." Her voice broke on the last word and she shuddered. "I never killed nobody before. But I reckon it wouldn't be so hard to do if you're fighting for your own life or somebody close to you." Her hands clenched into fists. "If it would help Adam, then I'd go out right now and kill Asa Mosley. He's the man responsible for what happened out there."

Angellee nodded. "I know. But killing him will do no good. The law will take care of Asa Mosley. He will pay for what happened."

"If Adam dies, he's gonna pay all right," Danny said grimly. "But I ain't so sure the law is the one that'll settle with him."

"Don't think that way," Angellee said. "I know how you feel, but—"

"You changed," Danny said, stopping her cousin's words. "A few years back you didn't talk this away.

369

You'da been the first one to go after Mosley for what he done to you and the babe."

Angellee nodded her head. "And if something had happened to the baby, then I'm not so sure I could take my own advice," she said. "Old habits die hard. Mountain folk are used to settling their own scores."

"Danny!" Adam's voice intruded. "Gotta find Danny. She's—"

"I'm here, Adam," Danny said, leaning over him again. "You don't have to go and find me. I'm already here with you."

She was barely aware of Angellee's hand on her shoulder, of her whispering voice, "If you won't let me stay with him, then I'll go now. But if you change your mind, just let me know."

Danny shook her head. "I ain't gonna change my mind," she said abruptly, blotting Adam's forehead again. "Ain't no need for nobody else to stay with him. I'll be here until he starts getting well."

Danny was barely aware of the closing door as her cousin left the room.

Adam stood at the window of his bedroom, gazing down over the wide lawn. How could the weather have undergone such a drastic change in the last few weeks? he wondered. The snow was only a memory, and the flowers were blooming again.

He sighed, turned away and began to pace restlessly. Why hadn't Danny been to see him? Although he'd been up and around for several days now, he'd been too weak to venture from his room.

Jake had told him they'd nearly lost him several

times before his fever finally broke. But that raised the question again. If he had been that close to death, then why hadn't Danny been to see him?

According to Bridget, Danny had sat with him when he was near death, but since he had regained consciousness, she had been conspicuously absent.

You'd think she would show a little concern, he silently told himself.

He stopped beside the window again, just as a carriage pulled up beside the gate. His gaze narrowed on the woman who stepped down. Wasn't that Danny? And Roderic Fortunato? Anger surged through him and his mouth tightened into a thin line. What the hell was Danny doing with Fortunato?

Intent on finding out, Adam left the room and made his way to the head of the stairs.

Chapter Thirty-Four

Danny watched the carriage leave with Roderic, then turned toward the house. Her gaze went to the bedroom window where Adam was confined. How much longer would she have to wait before she saw him again, she wondered. It seemed like forever since she'd last seen him, but the doctor had seemed to think she was hindering Adam's progress by remaining with him. Now she just had to be satisfied with daily reports.

When Danny entered the house, she found Bridget waiting for her.

"I thought you'd never get back," the girl said, sliding Danny's coat from her shoulders. "How did it go? Do you think he's going to do it?"

Danny knew Bridget was referring to the sale of the doll factory. That seemed to be most important to the girl's peace of mind. But of course it would be. "I'm almost certain of it," Danny replied.

"Oh, Miss," Bridget exclaimed. "It will be so wonderful if he does." She spun around. "You don't know how happy this makes me!"

"Now don't go countin' the chickens afore the eggs is hatched," Danny warned. "Roddy still might not do it."

"Oh, he'll do it, Miss," Bridget said, her eyes glittering with excitement. "He'd have to look a long time before he found anything better. And he knows it. I can see it in his eyes. Yes, he'll do it right enough."

Danny nodded and smiled smugly. "I think you might be right. I couldn'ta found nobody better neither." Danny was certain of that. Roderic would listen to the men with experience. And that would probably mean Bridget's family would fare well in the future. "He's got all the money a body could ever need. Shouldn't be no worry about makin' it work."

"He has that," Bridget agreed. "I've heard folks talking around town. There's plenty of speculating on how big the Fortunato fortune is. And that's a fact."

"Good," Danny said. "Because it's likely gonna take plenty of money to make it work."

"How long do you think before he decides?"

"A week. Maybe two."

Bridget sighed loudly. "How can he wait that long."

Danny laughed. "Guess we don't have much choice," she said.

Suddenly she heard a sound and looked up. A soft gasp escaped her lips and her heart leapt with gladness. Adam stood at the head of the stairs. But why was he staring at her so peculiar-like? Before she could greet him, he turned on his heel and went back into his room.

Adam could hardly believe what he had heard. Danny was actually considering marrying Roderic Fortunato. How could that have happened? When had it happened? Just since he had been laid up, or had she been planning it all along?

Dammit! She didn't love Fortunato. Adam was almost certain of it. Not the way she had talked about his money.

Was that it? Was the money what she wanted? It was hard to believe it of her. He would never have thought Danny could be swayed by wealth.

A harsh laugh escaped him, and he began to pace back and forth. It was a good thing she didn't know about his own money. She might actually have gone after him instead. He stopped abruptly, his expression darkening. Hadn't she done just that?

God! He had been here long enough. It was past time for him to leave.

Danny's mood was buoyant and she joined the others in the parlor. She attributed her happiness to the fact that Adam would be dining with them. She had taken extra pains with her appearance, donning a dress of sky blue velvet and allowing Bridget to arrange her curls high on her head.

"Here's Danny," Angellee said, turning her head to watch her cousin enter the room. "And from the looks of it, she's ready for a celebration."

Danny blushed. She hadn't intended to be so

obvious. Her skirts swished softly around her ankles as she crossed the room to Adam. Since it was the first time they had been together since his fever had broken, she felt incredibly shy with him.

"How do you feel?" she asked.

"Well enough."

Although his voice was polite, it held an undertone of coldness. She met his eyes and confusion swept over her. She knew by the set of his jaw, by the glitter in his eyes, that he was angry about something. But what?

"Danny?" Jake's voice intruded on her thoughts. "Would you like something to drink?"

"Yes, thank you," she replied, turning away from Adam. "A sherry would be nice." She went to join Angellee. "How is the baby doing?"

Angellee's green eyes sparkled. "She's doing absolutely wonderful. She's already gained two pounds since we came home and she's gaining strength every day. Would you believe she actually smiled at me tonight?"

"I don't know," Danny said. "Granny Bess always said babies don't smile when they're that young."

"I know what Granny Bess said," Angellee retorted, "But little Danielle does smile. She's incredibly bright for her age." She turned to her husband for confirmation. "Isn't she Jake?"

"Of course she is," he replied, crossing the room and seating himself on the arm of Angellee's chair.

"You called her Danielle?" Danny asked.

"Martha Danielle," Angelee replied. "We decided to name her after you. Didn't we, Jake?" She looked up at her husband with so much love in her eyes that it caused an ache in Danny's heart just to watch them.

"There was never any question as to the baby's name," Jake said huskily. "If Danny hadn't found you when she did, I could easily have lost you both." He looked at Danny. "If our baby has half your courage, Danny, she'll be able to move mountains."

"Here's to Danny," Angellee said, lifting her glass in a toast.

"Drink with us to Danny," Jake said, turning to Adam.

"Of course," Adam said, his voice carefully colored in neutral shades. "Danny has accomplished miracles in Pittsburgh. In more ways than one."

Danny felt a flush warming her cheeks. What a curious thing for Adam to say. They had finished the evening meal before she found out what he meant by it.

The night was warm, and, needing to escape from Adam's overwhelming presence, Danny sought refuge in the garden. Although the night was cool, it wasn't uncomfortable on her heated flesh. The velvety darkness closed around her as she strolled through the garden. She tried to empty her mind of thoughts of Adam, of his peculiar behavior, but they persisted.

Why was he so angry with her, she wondered.

She was admiring the view of the furnaces when she heard the door open and close behind her. Turning, her gaze found Adam, the man she'd come out here to avoid.

He came toward her with long, purposeful strides. "I thought maybe you were out here," he said.

"You were looking for me?"

Instead of answering, he said, "I understand congratulations are in order."

"Congratulations?" She studied his face. "I don't know what you mean."

His eyes raked her scornfully. "Don't pretend to be innocent, Danny. I heard you talking to Bridget earlier."

"To Bridget?" she parroted. "When?"

"When you left Fortunato."

Suddenly, comprehension dawned, and her lips curled into a smile. "You heard me talking to Bridget about Roddy?"

"Of course. And I know what you're about."

She laughed. "It's not all my doin'," she said. "He was easy to talk around because he wanted it too."

"Then it's already decided. You told Bridget it wasn't."

"That was just because Roddy wanted to tell Bridget about it himself."

"Maybe you shouldn't have been in such a hurry." His lips curled contemptuously. "If you had played your cards right, you could have done better for yourself. I did a little checking on the Fortunato holdings. Although they are considerable, I'm worth a hell of a lot more than they are."

"What're you sayin'?" she asked. Did he want to buy the doll factory? Was that the reason for his anger? But how could she know he wanted it?

"I'm saying you could've married me instead of him!" Adam said.

Her breath caught. "Marry?" She stared at him, feeling totally confused with their conversation.

"Are you saying you want to get hitched up to me?"

"I'm saying it might have been possible if you'd played your cards right. But you didn't, Danny. And now it's too late, because I know what you're about now."

Danny felt as though she had been slapped in the face. This was no marriage proposal. It was an accusation. But of what was he accusing her? "Quit beating around the bush and spit out what you mean!" she snapped.

"You know damn well what I mean! You're the one who's marrying Roderic Fortunato for his money."

She was stunned by his words. "I am not!"

She heard his quick intake of breath. "Are you pretending that you care about him? That the money doesn't matter? Don't forget that I heard you talking to Bridget."

"I ain't saying I wasn't talking to Bridget. But I ain't got no notion to marry up with Roderic Fortunato for his money."

His body was tense, his hands clenched as though he would like to strangle her. "Are you pretending that you love him?"

"No such thing!" Fury almost choked her. "I ain't marrying him at all. I don't know what you thought you heard, but me and Bridget wasn't talking about nothing like that. We was talking about the doll factory that Roddy is goin' to buy. Bridget's pa works there, an' it was fixin' to be closed down. If it's any of your business," she added in a voice that would have melted icicles. "Which it ain't."

"Danny." His voice had softened and he reached

for her, but she stepped back quickly, avoiding his hands. "I'm sorry, I seem to have mixed things all up." He reached for her again.

"Keep your hands offen me," she snapped knocking his hands away from her. "I ain't wantin' you to touch me no more!" She clenched her jaw to kill the sob in her throat. "How could you believe I'd do such a thing. How could—" Danny broke off in midsentence as the door opened, allowing a stream of light into the garden.

"Danny!" Angellee called. "Are you out here?"

"Yes," Danny answered. "But I'm coming in now."

"Danny," Adam said quickly. "Wait a minute. Give me a chance to explain."

"Like the one you give to me?" she whispered fiercely. "Just keep away from me, Adam."

She hurried to join her cousin before Angellee noticed she wasn't alone. There was a hard knot in Danny's chest that she did her best to ignore, but she couldn't ignore the stinging at the back of her eyes. She refused to break down in front of Adam. There was no way she would allow him to see how much he had wounded her by his suspicions.

"Were you talking to someone out there?" Angellee asked.

"No," Danny lied. She didn't feel like explaining to her cousin. The sooner she put Adam out of her mind, the better off she would be.

Danny spent a restless night and by morning had made up her mind to leave. After she was dressed, she sought out her cousin in the nursery to tell her.

Angellee protested. "No, Danny. You can't leave

us. We want you to make your home here with us."

"Pa'll be needin' me," Danny said.

"Danny . . . there's something you don't know about Uncle Silas . . ." Angellee's voice trailed of, as though she didn't know how to continue.

"What about Pa?" Danny said.

"Jake told me Uncle Silas had passed on."

"Passed on where?" Danny asked.

Angellee put a hand on her cousin's shoulder. "He's gone, Danny. Your pa has died."

Danny's heart gave a leap and she felt the blood leave her face. "How could you know that?"

"Adam told us."

Uncertainty held Danny in its grip. Angellee was wrong. Pa couldn't be dead. "How could Adam know?" she whispered.

"He knows, Danny. He got a telegram."

Danny shook her head in denial. "I didn't get no telegram. It's all a lie. Pa can't be dead." Her eyes swam with tears.

"Adam said it happened the day you left."

A red haze swam around Danny and she swayed. "Was it 'cause Pa found out I was gone?" she whispered.

"No!" Angellee said sharply. "Don't think that way, Danny. Jake's been in touch with the sheriff back in Possum Hollow. The sheriff said Uncle Silas never made it back home that day. He didn't even know you were gone." Her eyes held pity. "I am so sorry," she said softly.

Danny's knees felt like rubber, and she fought to keep them from buckling beneath her. Was her father's death her fault? Could she have kept him alive if she'd stayed there? Maybe she hadn't watched him close enough. It was more'n likely the corn liquor that caused his death. She should have found some way to stop his drinking. She voiced her thoughts to Angellee.

"Now you stop that right now," Angellee said. "You know better than that. Uncle Silas was a grown man. You're not responsible in any way for what happened. You couldn't have stopped his dying even if you'd been there."

Realizing Angellee was probably right, Danny tried to let go of her guilty feelings. But it was hard. "I gotta go back," she said. "They'll be things needin' to be took care of."

"Nothing that can't wait, Danny," Angellee said gently. "Don't go just yet. Stay awhile longer. You might even find that you like Pittsburgh. You could live here with us. There's plenty of room in this house."

"Pittsburgh ain't for me," Danny said. "I want to see the mountains again." Her face saddened. "Even if Pa is gone, that's my home. I don't belong nowhere else."

But Angellee refused to accept that. "Think about it," she said. "Don't make up your mind so quickly. You'd have a good life here with us. And you would be with kin." Suddenly the baby let out a wail and Angellee picked her up. "Is Mommy's little love hungry?" she cooed, cuddling the baby against her breast.

Danny realized her cousin's attention had turned from her the moment the baby gave her first cry. But that was only as it should be. She let herself out of the room and went down the hall to her own.

Never before—even when she was lost in the cavern—had she felt so completely alone. It made no difference that Angellee wanted her to stay in Pittsburgh. Danny knew she could never be happy in the city.

Adam! she silently cried.

Then, realizing she was looking to Adam for help . . . Adam, the man who had made her love him and then had rejected her . . . a terrible bitterness assailed her, a bitterness that quickly turned to anguish.

As grief, raw and primitive, overwhelmed her, Danny threw herself across the bed and allowed the tears she had been holding back to fall.

After she had cried herself out, she splashed water on her face, hoping to hide her tears. But it was useless. The face reflected in the mirror looked ravaged and her expression was one of mute wretchedness.

Suddenly, she heard a knock at the door. "Danny?"

Adam's voice sounded muffled, coming through the heavy wood, but even so, it was easily recognized. Although she didn't want him to know she'd been crying, she knew she couldn't just ignore him.

"Just a minute," she called, running a brush through her tousled curls.

Then, hoping she'd made herself a little more presentable, she opened the door.

Adam studied her ravaged face, then silently entered the room and closed the door behind him. "Angellee told me you know about your father," he said quietly.

"No thanks to you," she said accusingly. "Why

didn't you tell me about Pa?"

"Danny. I'm sorry," he said, gathering her close against him. "I thought it would be easier coming from your cousin."

"It ain't easier," she said, laying her head on his chest, accepting the comfort of his arms around her. If only she could stay there forever. "Dead is dead," she mumbled. "You shoulda told me about it as soon as you knowed." She pulled back and met his gaze. "When *did* you find out?"

"Back at the Circle J Ranch." Shoving his hands in his pockets, he turned away as though he couldn't face her misery. Crossing to the window, he stared outside. When he spoke again, his voice was low, barely distinguishable. "I didn't want your father to worry needlessly about you, so the day I went alone to Mineral Wells—while you were out with Michael—I sent a telegram to Possum Hollow." He swung back to face her. "I was still there when the sheriff of Possum Hollow sent a reply."

Pain settled through Danny. "Was that the day you brung me the present?" she asked in a choked voice. "Was that the day you brung me this dress I'm wearin' now?"

His eyes slid down to the blue mohair dress, then back to meet hers. "Yes." He nodded abruptly. "That was the day."

His words tasted like gall in her mouth. "I shoulda knowed they was some reason for that present," she said in a voice that could have frozen icicles. The pain in her heart became a sick and fiery gnawing. Danny remembered how she had rejoiced at receiving the dress. But suddenly she wanted to rip it off . . . the feel of the material against her skin sickened her and she knew she would never feel the same about the dress again. *Never!* Not since Adam had used the gift to assuage his guilt.

He sighed heavily. "I know what you're feeling, Danny. And I know this is hard for you."

Her hands curled into fists. "You don't know a damn thing about me, outlander! Not a damn thing!"

"Danny." The word was a sigh.

Adam pulled her back into his embrace, and Danny swallowed convulsively, fighting against the need to give in to it, to just lay her head against his chest and allow him to comfort her.

But she couldn't, wouldn't. No matter how desperately she needed him! Because to accept his comfort now would only prolong her agony.

Pressing her palms against his chest, Danny shoved hard. Immediately, his arms fell to his side.

Tears stung Danny's eyes as she glared up at him. "I don't need you," she lied. "I don't need nobody!"

Adam's eyes darkened with something like pain. "Danny," he said huskily, gripping her shoulders with fingers of steel. "Don't do this to yourself. Stay here with your cousin and her family. There's nothing for you back in the mountains."

Her despair gave way to anger. "I don't need you fixing my life up for me!" she said. "You done meddled enough in it."

The color left his face, then a flush crept up his neck, staining his cheeks with color. "You don't mean that," he said harshly. "If I hadn't meddled in your life . . . If I hadn't brought you here, Asa

Mosley would still have Angellee and little Danielle. Staying in the mountains wouldn't have made any difference to your father's death, but it made all the difference in the world to your cousin and her baby. Without your intervention, they would probably both be dead."

Danny made no reply, because she realized Adam was right. Instead, she turned away from him. "Get out of here!" she ordered. "I don't want to see you no more." Even as she said the words, she knew they weren't true.

"Certainly," he said stiffly. "If that's what you really want."

Danny heard his boots against the hardwood floor, heard the door squeak open, then close again.

With tears flowing down her cheeks, she turned around.

"Adam," she choked. "Adam! I didn't mean it."

But she might as well have remained silent, because there was no one to hear her.

Adam had taken her at her word, and now she was alone in the room.

Chapter Thirty-Five

A heaviness centered in Adam's chest as he left the house and wandered aimlessly down the street. His shoulders hunched forward, his hands shoved deep in his pocket. He couldn't forget the look on Danny's face as she had accused him. Although he had wanted to comfort her, she had flinched from his touch as though he were some loathsome creature.

God knew he had never meant to hurt her. It was the last thing he wanted. But the fact was, he had hurt her. And the knowledge was tearing him apart inside.

Realizing he was passing the park, he changed his direction, taking the path that led through the flower beds, hoping the profusion of color would soothe his inner turmoil. But he found little comfort there. How could he, knowing that Danny hated him? And she had every right to feel that way. He had accused her of something so vile, had finally succeeded in alienating her completely.

As though that weren't enough, he would always

have to live with the knowledge that she would be alone on Tucker's Ridge when she went back.

Dammit! He struck his fist into his palm and the resulting sound made a woman passerby start. Gazing fearfully at him, she scuttled away as though she were afraid he was a mad man just on the verge of attacking her.

Hearing the sound of laughter, Adam turned his steps toward the children's playground. He paused for a moment to watch a group of boys playing ball, then moved on to where several youngsters were swinging. He allowed the laughter and excitement to wash over him, but it made no difference to his misery. That was too deeply embedded for it to be lifted so easily.

"It's time to leave," he muttered. "Past time for me to go back home." He forced his thoughts away from Pittsburgh, away from Danny, turning them instead to his family home, to the last time he'd been there. The homeplace had seemed so empty with his parents gone, both dead and buried. But perhaps this time he could put aside his guilt, put aside the feeling that he'd betrayed them by not being there when they needed him.

He knew he must at least try, because running away had certainly solved nothing.

With the decision made, he left the park. His mind was already busy composing the telegram he would send to his foreman in Montana.

Danny, still wearing the blue mohair dress, was at the foot of the stairs when she heard the knock on the door. Thinking perhaps it was Roderic, Danny called out. "No need to bother gettin' it, Bridget. I'm already at the door."

But when she opened the door, instead of Roderic, she found herself facing a dark-haired woman, wearing an emerald green day dress. Although the woman looked vaguely familiar, Danny couldn't place her.

"Tell Adam Hollister that Carlotta is here to see him," the woman said, her dark eyes taking in every detail of Danny's appearance.

Danny's gaze narrowed on the woman. It would be an unlikely coincidence if Adam knew two Carlottas in Pittsburgh. That meant this was the woman Adam had been kissing at Mosley's shindig. That fact alone made Danny take an instant dislike to her. "Adam ain't here," she said.

"When do you expect him back?" The woman asked, trying her best to stare down her skinny nose at Danny. An impossible task, since there was very little difference in their height.

"I learnt a long time ago not to expect nothin' from Adam," Danny said. "They's less chance of bein' disappointed thataway."

"You have no business speaking of your betters in such a manner," Carlotta snapped. "Exactly who do you think you are anyway?"

Danny laughed. "My name's Danielle Tucker," she said. "If'n you was really askin' for my name."

"The only reason I would want to know your name would be to report you to Mrs. Gruber for being so rude to a houseguest," Carlotta said. "Now get out of my way and let me pass."

"You ain't comin' into the house." Danny attempted to shut the door on the woman, but Carlotta

388

effectively stopped her by sticking her foot in the door. "If you ain't of a mind to get your foot squashed, then you better get it outta the doorway," Danny said.

"Where is Angellee?" Carlotta asked. "I want to see her this instant."

"Thought you was wantin' to see Adam."

"You told me he wasn't here."

"He ain't."

"Then I want to see Angellee."

"You can just keep wantin' then," Danny said. "She's busy with the baby and I ain't about to call her away for the likes of you." Danny knew she was being rude, but she didn't care.

"Danny?" Angellee's voice called from the stairs. "Who's at the door? Did you invite them in?"

Carlotta threw Danny a scathing look, shoved past her and marched up to Angellee. "Your employee has been rude to me, Angellee," she snapped. "I demand that you dismiss her immediately."

"Are you talking about Danny, Carlotta?" Angellee asked. Something about her voice told Danny that her cousin wasn't particularly fond of the other woman either.

"If you're calling that person—" She pointed at Danny, "—Danny. Then, yes, I do mean her."

Angellee laughed. "You have it all wrong, Carlotta. Danny isn't my employee. She's my cousin."

"How unfortunate for you," Carlotta said sarcastically. "But that explains everything."

Danny's lips tightened and she curbed the impulse to tear into the woman. After all, she realized belatedly, it was Angellee's house. And it was up to

Angellee to say if she didn't want Carlotta in it.

"I came to see Adam," Carlotta told Angellee, "and this *person*, this relative of yours, has refused to give me a straight answer."

"I'm sorry, Carlotta," Angellee said, not sounding the least bit sorry. "But Adam is not here at the moment."

"That is fairly obvious," Carlotta said. "If he were here, then he would most certainly object to the way I'm being treated. What I am trying to ascertain now, though, is exactly when is he expected to return."

"I'm afraid I don't know," Angellee said. "Danny was the last to see him." She turned twinkling eyes on Danny. "When will Adam be back, Danny?"

Danny's lips twitched but she managed to curb her laughter. "He didn't say." Carlotta looked as though she were about to have a fit. "You could leave a message if you wanted to," Danny told her.

"Will you see that he gets it?"

"No," Danny replied. "But you could leave it anyways."

"You're going to be sorry for allowing her to treat me in such a manner, Angellee," Carlotta said. "The ladies of Pittsburgh have only just begun to accept you into their circle. After they hear what happened today, they'll reconsider and you'll be left out in the cold again."

Still muttering threats, Carlotta turned and stalked out the door.

Danny looked up at Angellee. "She can't really do that, can she? She can't really make all them ladies upset with you?"

"I wouldn't care if they were," Angellee said

stoutly. "But you needn't worry about me, Danny. Carlotta is well-known around the city. So are her many affairs. The only reason she's invited anywhere is because she's married to one of the wealthiest men around here."

"She's married?"

"She certainly is." Angellee studied Danny's face for a moment. "Why were you so rude to her? Not that I minded, but I am curious. It's just not like you to be that way. Was it because of her attitude?"

Danny ducked her head. "That wasn't the whole of it. She was kissin' Adam at Mosley's shindig awhile back. I never knew she was a married woman. An' I don't think Adam did neither."

"Adam is too smart to be fooled by her," Angellee said. "Now put her out of your mind and come with me. I want to tell you about my idea for the baby's nursery."

Danny learned of Adam's intended departure at dinner that night.

"There's no reason for me to stay any longer," he said. "With Danny and Angellee both testifying at Mosley's trial, he's sure to be convicted."

"There won't be a trial," Jake said, helping himself to the biscuits.

"No trial?" Adam barked. "Why not?"

"Asa Mosley left town."

"When did this happen?"

"We're not really sure. Today, a representative for the Monongahela Amalgamated Mining Company came to my office. He's the one that told me Mosley was no longer in charge of the company. Seems they decided they'd be better off to appoint someone else." His lips lifted into a slight smile. "And the company is willing to make recompense to William Rafferty for his injuries."

"What kind of price do you put on a man's legs?" Angellee asked angrily. "William is paralyzed from the waist down. He'll be in that wheelchair for the rest of his life."

"The company can't give him back his legs, love," Jake told her, reaching over to take her hand. "But they can make life easier for him. And they've promised to comply with any safety regulations we set down. Curtis Glover, the company representative, said they are determined to make safer working conditions for the miners."

"How are they going to do that?" Angellee asked. "There's no way they can make those mines completely safe for the workers. There'll always be cave-ins."

"The miners know that when they sign on with a mining company," Jake said. "They realize they are taking chances with their lives."

"Dammit, Jake!" Angellee exploded. "Don't let the Amalgamated talk their way out of this! You've got to shut them down. Every mine in Pittsburgh should be closed."

"Angel, you know that's impossible. We must have coal."

"At the cost of human lives?"

"There is no easy solution, my love. But I have Glover's word that the Amalgamated will do whatever they can." He patted her hand. "I know you worry about the miners, but there's nothing more you can do for them. Now try and put it out of your mind while we finish our meal." He turned to Adam. "I wish you would forget about leaving now, Adam. We've hardly had a chance to get to know each other. All our time and efforts were, of necessity, spent on finding Angellee and little Danielle."

"And rightly so," Adam said. "I appreciate the invitation to stay, but it's past time I went home. I've already been away too long."

"When do you plan to leave?"

"Tomorrow. I've already checked at the station. There's a westbound train leaving at ten in the morning."

"If you feel you must go, then I won't press you to stay. But we're going to miss having you around."

Danny's fingers gripped her fork so tightly that her knuckles showed white. Just like that—Adam was going to leave. Without a backward glance he would walk away from her.

Damn him!

Flinging her fork across the room, she leapt to her feet and stared furiously at him. She was aware of the shocked look on his face as she faced him with blazing eyes.

"You ain't going nowhere without me, out-lander," Danny snapped. "It was you that brung me here, now I'll thankee kindly to take me home!"

"Don't be foolish, Danny," he said. "There's nothing for you back there."

"Don't call me names," she said coldly. "I ain't tossed my wits to the wind yet. I still got enough sense to know I don't belong here. The life of society folk

393

ain't for me. They's always puttin' on the dog."

"Putting on the dog?" Jake's voice was puzzled. "That's an expression I haven't heard yet."

She frowned, searching for an explanation and Jake waved toward her chair. "Would you please sit back down, Danny? If you don't, then I'll be forced to stand as well."

"Why?"

Adam answered the question. "Because it's not gentlemanly to remain seated while a lady—and I use the term loosely—is standing."

"What do you mean by that?" Danny snapped, seating herself again. "Are you sayin' I ain't no lady?"

"You were going to tell me what putting on the dog means," Jake interjected hastily.

After sending another baleful glare towards Adam, Danny turned her attention to Jake. "Means puttin' on fine airs like you just nearly done." At his obvious confusion, she explained further. "Them fine manners you got . . . not settin' yourself down less'n a lady sets herself first," she explained. "Such doin's gets mighty wearin' on a body's nerves after a spell. 'Specially when she ain't sure how to act to keep folks from laughing at her."

"I suppose it could be wearing," Jake said thoughtfully, his eyes resting on her face. Suddenly, he pinned Angellee with his gaze. "Did you find it so, sweetheart?"

She grinned impishly. "At first I did. But no longer. But you have to realize the tutor you hired for me did wonders for me."

"I know. And he could do the same for Danny," he

said, his gaze moving back to her. "I hope you will reconsider your decision to leave, Danny. I know you would be much more comfortable if you understood the people around you."

"I ain't got no hankerin' to learn about 'em," Danny said grimly. "I'm awantin' to go back home. And it's Adam's bounden duty to take me there."

"Danny, please—"

Jake was interrupted by his wife. "Leave her alone," Angellee said, her gaze flickering between Danny and Adam as though she sensed the tension between them. "She's right, Jake. Danny wouldn't be happy here."

"If you're going to be so mule-headed and insist on going back, then I guess there's nothing left for me to do except take you," Adam growled.

The next day, at the train station, they made their goodbyes to Jake and Angellee. Jake kissed Danny warmly. "Don't be a stranger here," he said. "We want your namesake to know how wonderful her cousin is." He turned to Adam and took his hand. "I don't know how I'll ever be able to repay you for what you've done. Without you and Danny . . . well, you must know I'm deeply grateful for your help."

"Don't mention it," Adam said.

"All aboa-oa-oard!" the conductor cried. "All aboa-oa-oard!"

"We gotta go now," Danny said, turning to embrace her cousin. "I ain't never gonna forget you, Angel. Be happy."

"And you," Angellee said, wiping at the moisture in her eyes. Flicking a quick glance at Adam, she leaned closer to Danny and whispered, "I want to be at your wedding if the two of you decide to get married. Don't let him get away."

Danny sucked in a sharp breath and her eyes widened. "That ain't likely," she muttered. Was she that transparent? she wondered, bending down to pick up her valise.

But Adam had the same idea and their heads collided. "Sorry," he said gruffly, picking up her bag.

He stood aside while Jake helped Danny up the steps, then boarded himself. They had barely seated themselves when the train whistle sounded. The train lurched, then chugged out of the station.

Chapter Thirty-Six

Clickety-clack, clickety-clack, clickety-clack sounded the wheels against the rails as they picked up speed. *He's takin' you back, he's takin' you back, he's takin' you back.*

But then he'll leave you, an inner voice cried.

She threw a furtive look at Adam who was seated beside her, but he seemed unaware of her presence. Did she matter so little to him?

Pain stabbed through her at the thought of never seeing him again. Lowering her lashes, Danny turned toward the window, intent on hiding the tears that suddenly blurred her vision. She would give up everything . . . even her beloved mountains . . . if she could stay with him. But she couldn't. Not when he had no feelings for her.

Deep misery filled her. Danny let her gaze wander beyond the window. Only then did she notice the storm clouds gathering overhead.

Adam shifted beside her, then rose to his feet. "I'll be back after awhile," he said.

Before she could reply, he was striding down the aisle, leaving her alone with her aching heart. She tried to block the thoughts from her mind, tried to concentrate instead on the scenery flowing past the window, but it was impossible. Her mind kept going over every minute of their time together, as though bent on examining every minute detail before storing it away in an old trunk.

Thunder sounded in the distance, and the trees swayed beneath the wind. Then, rain lashed down, almost obscuring her vision of the countryside. The storm continued to pound them as the hours passed.

Adam remained conspicuously absent until it was time for them to go to the dining car. They ate in silence, then he disappeared again, remaining that way until just before the train pulled into Terre Haute, Indiana, where they changed trains. And so the journey went. Through Illinois and into Missouri, until finally the train pulled into the station at St. Louis, where they disembarked.

"I'll see about getting us some horses in the morning," Adam said gruffly. "There's no hurry about it. We'll have to wait until the rain lets up before we can leave."

She nodded silently and followed along behind him to the hotel where they'd stayed before.

"Glad to have you and your missus back, Hollister," the desk clerk said, pushing the register toward Adam. "Do you want the same room as before?"

"We'd like two rooms," Adam replied.

Taking the keys the clerk held toward him, Adam led the way upstairs. "Do you want something to eat?" he asked, placing her valise inside her room.

"No," Danny said, swallowing around the lump in her throat. "I had plenty on the train." She knew he'd only offered out of politeness.

"Then I'll bid you goodnight."

Wait! Don't go, Adam! The silent words were never spoken aloud. Instead, she watched him turn away and enter the room located across the hall from her. Danny closed the door and threw the bolt, locking herself in with her misery.

But, try as she would, Danny found herself unable to rest. She tossed and turned, in the lumpy bed, her thoughts a whirling vortex that refused to let her sleep. No matter how hard she tried, she couldn't stop thinking about Adam.

Although she'd been angry with him for not telling her about her father's death, she had forgiven him long ago.

Don't let him get away. Angellee's words came back to her, echoing over and over again. *Don't let him get away . . .*

What else was she supposed to do? He didn't want her. *Damn him! He didn't want her!*

If you'd played your cards right, you could've had me instead! Adam's barely-remembered words slammed into her mind.

What did he mean by them?

Her heart began a slow, heavy thud as she stared up at the shadowy ceiling, working his words over in her mind. *If you'd played your cards right, you could've had me instead.* He'd said the words when he'd thought she was going to marry Roderic. *If you'd played your cards right, you could have had me instead.* Danny's heat picked up speed. Was it possible he'd meant he wanted to marry her?

Don't let him get away. Don't let him get away.

Dammit! How could she stop him from getting away?

If you'd played your cards. . . .

Jerking upright, Danny stared through the shadows at the door. Adam was across the hall. Only a few steps away. If she didn't ask him, she'd never know what he'd meant. And if there was even the slightest possibility that he wanted her . . .

Danny slid from the bed, donned her clothing, and padded barefoot across the room. Opening the door, she crossed the hall to Adam's room. Her hand was raised to knock, when he opened the door.

"Danny," he said in a startled voice. "I was just coming to see you."

"I wanta know what you meant when you said I coulda had you?" she demanded, placing a hand on his chest and shoving him back inside the room.

His expression was bemused as he studied her face. "Don't you know?"

"Do you think I'd be askin' if I already knowed?" she asked. "Why'd you say it?"

His hands gripped her shoulders. "Because I was jealous!" he growled, pulling her roughly against him. "I was so damn jealous I could have killed Roderic Fortunato with my bare hands."

"You were jealous?" She studied him with widened eyes. "Why?"

He sucked in a sharp breath. "Are you trying to make me sweat blood, Danny?"

"You ain't makin' sense, outlander. I don't want

400

no blood from you. I want an answer to my question."

"Danny," he groaned. "How can you even stand the sight of me? It's my fault you weren't there to see your father laid to rest."

"Ain't no sense in dwelling on that."

"I don't suppose you'll ever forgive me," he said quietly, smoothing his hand over her hair.

"I forgave you a long time ago, outlander," she said, tracing the edge of the long scar with the tip of her finger. "Didn't you know that?"

He shook his head. "No, Danny." His voice sounded choked. "I didn't know."

She waited a moment longer, but when he remained silent, she asked her question again. "What did you mean?"

For a moment, his expression was confused, then suddenly it cleared. "When I said you could've had me?"

She nodded her head.

"I meant just that. You can have me anytime you want me. Anytime, anywhere. It makes no difference. I'm so damn besotted with you that it's all I can do to keep my hands off you." He tightened his grip on her. "Dammit, Danny. I love you. Don't you know that? Don't you know the thought of leaving you has been tearing me apart? I've loved you since the first day we met. But I tried so hard to deny that love."

"Why?" she asked. Her tears ran freely now, as the words she had been waiting so long to hear filled her with unspeakable joy. "Why'd you want to deny it?"

"Because I'm no good for you," he said. "I'm no

damn good for anybody." He put her away from him. "Do you want to know something about me, Danny? When my folks died I couldn't even go to their funeral."

Danny wiped her eyes with the back of her hand and stared at him. She could see he was in pain. "Why?" she asked.

"Because I was in jail," he said. He began to pace the floor. "I was behind bars when my parents were laid to rest." He gave a short burst of laughter. "How is that for a loving son?"

She stared at him. "But if you were in jail you couldn't help it. You can't go blamin' yourself for not bein' there."

"There's nobody else to blame," he said, and when he turned to her, his eyes were cold. "It was my fault, Danny. I was in jail for killing a man." He turned away from her again, crossed to the window and stared down into the street. "I called a crooked gambler's bluff and he went for his gun. I beat him to the draw."

"But that was self-defense," she protested. "How could they throw you in jail?"

"The circuit judge covered a lot of territory. Despite the witnesses that saw the shooting, the town sheriff went by the book. He tossed me in jail to wait for the judge's decision. It was a month before the judge rode into town. My parents had been in the ground for two weeks by then."

"And you been beatin' yourself over the head with it ever since." She put her hands on her hips and said, "I reckon you bring it out right often and whip yourself kinda regular-like, don't you, outlander? Well, if you're expectin' me to feel sorry for you, then you got another think comin'. What happened ain't none of your doin'. But if you'd rather enjoy your misery than face life with me—"

He stopped and spun around, staring at her as though he couldn't believe what he was hearing. "A life with you?" he asked softly, his eyes glittering with emotion. "Danny. Are you proposing to me?"

She felt a flush staining her cheekbones and ducked her head. "I reckon I might be."

He lifted her chin and she melted under his gaze. "Then I accept," he muttered, crushing her against him.

"Are you fixin' to kiss me, outlander?" she asked, looping her arms around his neck and twining her fingers through his dark hair. "Are you fixin' to make love to me?" Standing on tiptoe, she traced his collarbone with her tongue. "Cause that's what I'm hankerin' for you to do. It's what I been wantin' for a long time now."

Suddenly, he was kissing her deeply and thoroughly. Her lips were pliant and warm beneath his. His kiss deepened, and his fingers found the buttons on her gown. But Danny found she couldn't wait, because his trembling hands were much too slow.

Breathing harshly, she worked at the buttons on his shirt, snapping one off in her haste. His skin was warm beneath her palm and she kissed the bared flesh of his chest, finding it salty to the taste.

She felt the cool air against her naked flesh as he tossed her garments aside and carried her to the bed. She waited impatiently for him to join her, watching as he divested himself of his trousers.

She could see the pulse beating madly at his throat as he joined her on the bed. *He wanted her!* She knew it now, and the knowledge sang in her blood. Winding her arms around his neck, she lifted her mouth to his and reveled in his possession. Then his tongue filled her mouth, searching out the tender, secret places.

Time ceased to exist as he rose above her and she felt a magic that bordered on ecstasy. For a moment he was poised above her, then, as though sensing her need, he entered her, filling her with his strength. Her body arched wildly against his as he pressed rough kisses on her face and neck. His lower body moved rapidly, plunging harder and deeper, stroking the burning fire of passion, and the flames swept higher and higher until they threatened to consume her body.

Danny withheld nothing from him, bringing her body up to meet his again and again. Animal sounds of pleasure broke from her throat as she met him thrust for thrust, arching her body over and over again against him as her senses clamored for relief. She heard a curious keening sound coming from deep within, building in volume as she climbed higher and higher toward some distant peak.

Suddenly, she was there, exploding into a million fragments as she reached completion, and she stared up into Adam's eyes, realizing in wonder, that he'd felt it too. Her heart pounded loudly, sounding like a herd of stampeding horses as spasms shook her body. Then, she collapsed, too stunned by what had happened to move.

Adam rolled aside and took her in his arms. He

pressed soft kisses across her face and then lay quietly beside her until her breathing slowed. She could hardly believe what had happened to them. But it was obvious that Adam felt pleasure at having caused it.

"I didn't know it could be like that," she whispered.

"Neither did I," he admitted.

"Have you had many women?"

"We won't talk about the past, Danny," he said roughly. "Nothing matters now but the future. *Our* future," he amended.

"We'll have it together?"

"I'd have it no other way," he said, raising himself on his elbows and studying her intently. "Life without you doesn't even bear thinking about. I need you, Danny. God, how I need you. Do you think you could forget what a swine I've been to you since the first day we met?"

"Quit sayin' things like that," she said. "You're talking about the man that I'm gonna marry." She looked anxiously at him. "How long will it be before we can get hitched?"

A smile lifted the corners of his mouth. "Are you in a hurry, my love?"

"Dang right, I am," she replied. "I aim to wed with you soon as we can find somebody to do it. And you better not be foolin' me with promises of love and such. Because once the preacher man says the words over us, you're gonna be well and truly bound."

"That suits me just fine," he said, his mouth descending to claim hers again. "Well and truly bound is what I want. Till the end of time."

Chapter Thirty-Seven

When Danny woke, sunlight streamed through a gap in the window curtains, highlighting the scar on Adam's face. She traced the puckered edges lightly with her fingertips and he flinched away from her touch.

"Why do you always do that?" she asked softly. "Does it hurt when I touch it?"

"No. But it's a reminder that it's there."

"Ain't nothing to be ashamed of," she said. "You never did tell me how you got it."

He became still. "It's not a pretty story."

"I never was much for pretty stories," she said. "Fairytales ain't my style."

"Believe me, it's no fairytale," he said bitterly. "Just a foolish one."

"Tell me anyway," she insisted. "Why does it bother you so much?"

"I'd much rather make love to you," he said, bending to kiss her rounded bosom.

But she wouldn't allow herself to be swayed. By

now she knew him well enough to know he was trying to sidetrack her with kisses. "I don't like secrets betwixt us," she said. "Why don't you want to tell me?"

"Because the telling would show you how foolish I was."

"Whatever you are, you ain't no fool," she said, tracing the edges of the scar again. "Tell me what happened."

He sighed, pushed her aside and reached for a cigarette. After it was lit, he put his forearm behind his head and said. "I was really only a boy when it happened. Just turned seventeen. But I was cocky as hell, thought I knew everything worth knowing. We lived in a small town in Montana where my father was a banker. He could afford a good education for me and insisted, against my wishes, that I receive it. I was sent to a university and for the first time I was really on my own."

"Is that where you met Judd?"

"Yes. Judd and Nicholas. Our classmates called us the three musketeers. We were almost inseparable. I made it through the first three years just fine. It was the last year we were at the university that I met Carlotta. Gay, laughing Carlotta."

"The woman at Mosley's ball. The one you was kissin' in Mosley's flower garden." Danny saw no reason to tell him of Carlotta's visit to the Logan mansion. Not yet, anyway.

"The one who was kissing me," he corrected. "I had never met anyone like Carlotta and was immediately infatuated with her. She was a vivid butterfly among moths. I thought I was in love with her and thought she loved me too, but I was a fool." He became silent, thoughtful, drawing on his cigarette.

Danny left him alone for a moment, then she prompted. "She did that to you?"

"She might as well have taken the knife and sliced my face herself," he said bitterly. "The wound would not have hurt me nearly as bad."

"Tell me what happened."

"I was going to marry her."

His words sliced into her, cutting deeply, and she swallowed around the pain. "What happened?"

"Shortly before graduation, I left the campus early. I went to Carlotta's house, expecting to find her alone."

"But you didn't."

"No. The butler let me in and told me to wait in the parlor. The bell rang again and before he could tell her of my presence, he stepped outside to talk to a coachman. But I was impatient to see my future bride. Since I knew where her room was, I went upstairs to surprise her." His hands clenched together, the cigarette snapped in half. "I was the one to be surprised. I found Nicholas in bed with her."

"Nicholas? Your friend?"

"Yes. He was surprised to see me, but I didn't stay for explanations. I found out later I should have. Carlotta lied to him. She'd been keeping us both on the string, telling both of us she would marry us." He sighed deeply. "Nicky believed her lies. She told him that I'd been forcing my attentions on her. I suppose she knew she'd lost me and hurried to patch the fence between them . . . to make certain she had one of us."

"What happened?"

"There was a fight. I was wounded. He was killed."

"What a horrible woman. Sounds a lot like Victoria Mosley."

"Why do you say that?" he asked. "Victoria isn't a bad woman. She only did what she was made to do. Mosley is to blame for it."

"You liked her," she accused.

"I felt sorry for her," he corrected, taking Danny in his arms. "I would feel sorry for any woman who had to put up with Mosley. But I was nearly as bad. I had hoped to use Victoria to find the location of your cousin."

"Didn't look that way to me," Danny muttered. "Looked to me like you was taken in by her looks."

"She couldn't hold a candle to you."

"You're just saying that," she said, "but I reckon the words sound mighty nice anyways."

"I mean every word of it," he said. "You're beautiful, Danny. The most beautiful woman I have ever met. And what's more, you don't even know it." He kissed her nose. Then her eyes. Then his lips closed over her mouth, completely taking her breath away with his kiss.

The arousing movements of his hands across her hips and back started setting off explosive charges inside her until she was clinging weakly to him, molding herself closer against the granite strength of his body. Danny felt the insidious, primitive desire growing and growing inside her until a low moan of passion escaped from her throat.

The blood raced through her veins as his lean fingers cupped the underside of her breasts and softly stroked them.

God! She was on fire for him. Would it always be like this? she wondered, clutching his shoulders tighter, her fingers digging into him as she tried to immerse herself in his flesh.

She wanted him, needed him so badly.

"Adam," she moaned. "Don't make me wait. Take me now."

As though he had been waiting for her words, he moved over her. She gasped at the entry, then gave in to the waves of desire flowing over her, succumbed like a drowning person in an undertow to the waves of desire stirring her senses until she was catapulted on high, soaring with Adam into the netherworld they had found together.

When it was over and they lay sated, their bodies limp with exhaustion and satisfaction, she told him the secret that she'd been holding inside for several weeks now.

His body went rigid, and there was a long, pregnant silence.

"How long have you known?"

"Three weeks."

"You would have let me leave without telling me?"

"I wouldn't want you just for the child's sake. I wanted you to stay because you loved me."

"But you had a responsibility to the child," he said fiercely. "Our son will need a father."

"I woulda raised him myself before I'd'a made you stay when you wanted to go," she said. "My babe is gonna have a ma who wants him. An' if he has a pa, then it'll be a pa that ain't with us cause he has to be. He'll have him a pa that loves us, or no pa at all."

"I love you and I'll love our baby," he promised, hugging her to him. "I'll love the both of you so much you'll get tired of it."

"Never," she said, knowing the love she felt was showing in her eyes. "I wouldn't never get tired of your love."

"We'll go home," he said. "Back to the ranch in Montana. That's the place where our son will grow-up strong. I'll teach him to ride a horse and rope a calf, and . . ."

Danny lay in his arms, completely content as she listened to Adam making plans for their future. Heaven had blessed her. She finally had her man, and soon she would have their child. Her lips curled in a smile and she rolled over, placing a finger across his lips to stop the flow of words.

"When we gonna find the preacher man to hitch us together?"

"The wedding," he said. "Yes, the wedding. I guess we could find a preacher in St. Louis. In fact, I'm sure we could, but . . ." His eyes met hers and he sighed. "We couldn't do that, Danny."

"You ain't fixin' to back out?" she asked anxiously.

"No, little one. Not ever. But your cousin will want to attend our wedding."

"I know. But she couldn't leave Pittsburgh right now," Danny said. "Not with the babe so small."

He sighed. "You're right. There's nothing to do but go back."

She nodded slowly. "It's a mighty long way back, but if you got the money, we oughta do it. She's my only kin and she oughta be there to see us hitched together."

Exactly one week later, as the sun was painting the westward sky with red and gold, Adam, dressed in a formal black suit, waited impatiently in the decorated parlor while Angellee finished arranging Danny's hair. Waiting quietly with the bridal veil, was Rebecca Shaw.

Danny could hardly believe her reflection. Her honey-colored hair was arranged fashionably on top of her head, and her blue eyes glittered with excitement.

But it's true, she silently told herself. *It's really you in that fancy wedding gown.*

"There," Angellee said, securing a last curl with a hair pin. "That oughtta hold until the preacher gets done sayin' the words over you."

Rebecca laughed lightly. "Your tutor would have conniptions if he heard you say that, Angel."

"Heard me say what?" Angellee asked.

"That bit about the preacher saying words over her."

Angellee grinned. "It wasn't very refined, was it? Never mind. Jake doesn't. He's always saying 'you can take the girl out of the hills, but you can't take the hills out of the girl.'" Her grin widened. "I guess I'm living proof of it."

"Well, I for one like the hills in the girl," Rebecca said. "Both girls," she added, with twinkling eyes.

"Now let's get this veil on one girl's head and trot downstairs before they come up here and drag her down there. You'll have to come away from the mirror, Danny. This veil is five yards long."

Obediently, Danny rose to her feet. She bent slightly so Rebecca could attach the long, Irish lace veil to her honey-gold curls.

"There," Rebecca said, arranging the veil so it fell gracefully down Danny's back. "Now look at yourself in the mirror."

Danny turned back to the mirror and stared at the girl reflected there. "Is that me?" she whispered.

"It's you," Angellee said, standing back to view her cousin with moist eyes. "You look like a fairytale princess, Danny."

A fairytale princess.

Angellee had hit the nail on the head. A fairytale princess was exactly what she did resemble, dressed as she was in Rebecca's wedding gown. It was a fragile creation made of ivory silk satin, cut in a long princess style with thousands of hand-sewn seed pearls adorning the bodice and long, flowing sleeves.

Danny's breath expelled in a hissing sigh. She hadn't known she was holding it until she heard the sound. She turned to Rebecca. "It's a funny time to be askin', but are you sure you don't mind me wearin' your wedding gown?"

Rebecca's eyes softened, became moist. "Of course I don't mind," she said. "In fact, I am glad that you are wearing it. It brings back memories of my own wedding to Lone Wolf."

"Lone Wolf?"

"You didn't know, did you?" Rebecca asked.

"Here I thought I was the talk of the town." Seeming to recognize Danny's confusion, she went on. "Grant's mother was an Apache Indian. The Apaches call him Lone Wolf." She smiled in remembrance. "We had two weddings. One performed by his tribe, and another performed in Pittsburgh. In the second one I wore the wedding gown you are wearing. It belonged to my mother."

Danny fingered the silky fabric. "It must be kinda old then, but you sure can't tell it. I'm gonna have to be mighty careful not to tear it."

"I'm not the least bit worried about it, Danny," Rebecca said.

From the parlor came strains of the wedding march. "They're waiting for us," Angellee reminded.

Taking a deep breath to quell the butterflies in her stomach, Danny followed the other two women from the room.

Jake stepped from an alcove in the hall and placed his hand on Danny's arm. "No last minute change of heart?" he whispered.

Danny shook her head, watching as Angellee began the descent to the strains of the wedding march. A few steps behind her was Rebecca, waiting her turn.

"Here we go," Jake said, pulling her forward.

The wedding march began to play over as they walked slowly down the stairs. Bridget and Mrs. Gruber had worked together intertwining clusters of honeysuckle, red roses and fern on the wooden railings of the staircase. Danny could see them standing below now, craning their necks to watch her descend.

Her foot caught on the hem of her gown and she stopped quickly, sucking in a sharp breath. She couldn't tear the gown. She had promised Rebecca she'd take care of it. She nudged the hem outward with her toes and her steps became slow and careful. She wasn't about to tear the wedding gown when Rebecca had been nice enough to let her wear it.

Adam stood beside the minister, watching Danny's descent, his heart thumping in his chest. He could hardly believe that she would soon be his wife. God! She had taken so long upstairs that he had begun to think she had changed her mind about marrying him.

Even now, she seemed reluctant. Her footsteps were slow, uneven, as she came down the steps on Jake's arm. And not once had she looked at him.

She couldn't change her mind. He wouldn't allow it. He was positive she loved him, or nearly. If she didn't, then he could make it happen. If he was given half a chance.

He stood tensely, his fists clenched by his sides, hardly daring to breathe as he waited for her to come to him.

Suddenly his breath hissed out. Danny had stopped halfway down the stairs. God! He should have known this would happen. She *had* changed her mind about marrying him.

Sweat beaded his forehead. *Dammit!* He wouldn't allow it! He had waited too long for this day. Whatever the consequences, he *would* make her his wife.

His mouth tightened into a thin line and he moved quickly, dashing up the stairs and jerking her arm from Jake's grip.

"Don't!" she cried, trying to free herself. "Be careful."

Adam paid no attention to her words, intent on dragging her down the stairs with him, back to the altar. "Get on with it," he told the minister shortly.

A flush stained his neck as he stared hard at the preacher, ignoring the surprised looks of the others. He heard a nervous titter, followed by scattered laughter and the mutter of voices, but his gaze never wavered from the man before him.

The preacher fumbled with his bible, dropped it and bent to retrieve it. Opening it up, he began, "Dearly beloved, we are gathered here . . ."

The words washed over Adam and he felt the tenseness flow out of him. What was he doing? he wondered. He couldn't force Danny to marry him. He turned to her, met her eyes, and wonder overcame him at the love he saw shining there.

"You're in an all mighty hurry all of a sudden, outlander," she whispered. "It'll be over soon enough."

The preacher's grip tightened on his bible and he spoke hurriedly. "Do you, Danielle Tucker, take—"

"You betcha bottom dollar I do," she said. "And so does he. Now finish sayin' the words. This man of mine is gettin' mighty impatient."

The preacher gulped and said, "By the power vested in me I pronounce you man and wife." Pulling a handkerchief from his back pocket, he wiped the sweat from his face. "You can kiss the bride," he added.

But there was no need. Adam was already doing just that, and making a very thorough job of it too.